GEORGES
or THE ISLE OF FRANCE

BY
ALEXANDRE DUMAS

NEWLY TRANSLATED BY
ALFRED ALLINSON

British Library Cataloguing-in-Publication Data
A catalogue record for this book is available from
the British Library

Alexandre Dumas

Alexandre Dumas was born in Villers-Cotterêts, France in 1802. His parents were poor, but their heritage and good reputation – Alexandre's father had been a general in Napoleon's army – provided Alexandre with opportunities for good employment. In 1822, Dumas moved to Paris to work for future king Louis Philippe I in the Palais Royal. It was here that he began to write for magazines and the theatre.

In 1829 and 1830 respectively, Dumas produced the plays *Henry III and His Court* and *Christine,* both of which met with critical acclaim and financial success. As a result, he was able to commit himself full-time to writing. Despite the turbulent economic times which followed the Revolution of 1830, Dumas turned out to have something of an entrepreneurial streak, and did well for himself in this decade. He founded a production studio that turned out hundreds of stories under his creative direction, and began to produce serialised novels for newspapers which were widely read by the French public. It was over the next two decades, as a now famous and much loved author of romantic and adventuring sagas, that Dumas produced his best-known works – the D'Artagnan romances, including *The Three Musketeers,* in 1844, and *The Count of Monte Cristo,* in 1846.

Dumas made a lot of money from his writing, but

he was almost constantly penniless as a result of his extravagant lifestyle and love of women. In 1851 he fled his creditors to Belgium, and then Russia, and then Italy, not returning to Paris until 1864. Dumas died in Puys, France, in 1870, at the age of 68. He is now enshrined in the Panthéon of Paris alongside fellow authors Victor Hugo and Emile Zola. Since his death, his fiction has been translated into almost a hundred languages, and has formed the basis for more than 200 motion pictures.

THE NOVELS OF
ALEXANDRE DUMAS

Messrs. Methuen are publishing a new edition in more convenient form of their famous translations of these great novels. The first volumes are :—

INTRODUCTION

THE scene of the pretty and graceful story which goes by the name of its hero, the romantic half-caste, Georges Munier, is laid in the Mauritius, or as it was called by the French previously to the English occupation, The Isle of France. The leading interest depends on the rivalry between *white* and *black*, the ineradicable prejudice of the former against the latter, and the gallant but unavailing struggle of the hero, a rich mulatto planter's son educated in Europe, to break through the barrier. With this main thread is interwoven the account of a slave revolt, and a pleasing love story, how Georges woos and wins the beautiful creole, Sara de Malmédie, to say nothing of a dashing description of the encounter of the rival squadrons of France and England, and the eventual conquest of the island by the British.

The sea-fight in question is *not* historical, nor are all its details entirely convincing to a sailor's mind, but it makes an exciting episode nevertheless. " Lord Williams Murrey " and " le capitaine Villougby " will be searched for in vain in the Biographical Dictionaries. At any rate, Dumas, when dealing with the sea and ships (did he not own a yacht of his own, and did he not sail her himself ?), is *nothing if not* technical ; and the great fight off Port Louis afforded some fine hard nuts for the translator to crack !

The amiable Eugène de Mirecourt—Jacquot of the " mercantilisme littéraire " accusations—says " Georges " was written by one Félicien Mallefille ; but then Jacquot and Quérard and their like were always ready to affiliate any child of Dumas' pen on anybody—except of course the rightful parent, Alexandre Dumas. According to these gentry " Monte Cristo " itself was one half by Fiorentino, one half by Maquet ! " It was such a simple thing to believe I was the author that they never so much as thought of it," was the great man's laughing comment.

In connection with this same M. Mallefille a good story is told, which we must apologize for borrowing from Mr. A. E. Davidson's admirable " Life and Works of Dumas " : " Speaking of Mallefille—one of his collaborators, and not one of the most remarkable—the master observed, as if pondering a problem, ' There is just something he lacks,— I can't define what it is,—to make him a man of talent.'

" ' Perhaps he lacks the talent,' suggested some one.

" ' *Tiens !* ' said Dumas, ' well, perhaps you are right. I never thought of that.' "

The truth in the case of " Georges " seems to be that Mallefille, or somebody else familiar with the Mauritius, supplied raw material and local colour ; Dumas did the rest. Anyhow there can be no doubt of this, that the hero, Georges Munier, who suffers humiliation and discouragement because of his " dash of the tar brush," but faces every obstacle and insult with irrepressible energy and spirit, is a fancy portrait of Dumas himself, Dumas " the inspired mulatto."

The book appeared in 1843,—just before, that is, the " annus mirabilis " that saw the birth of " Monte Cristo " and " The Three Musketeers."

R. S. G.

CONTENTS

7

GEORGES

CHAPTER I

THE ISLE OF FRANCE

HAS it never been your fate, on one of those long, cold, gloomy winter evenings when, alone with your own thoughts, you stood listening to the wind as it howled down the corridors and the rain as it beat at the windows, your brow resting against the mantelpiece and your eyes gazing, without seeing them, at the logs crackling on the hearth ; has it never been your fate under such circumstances to be seized with a sick disgust of our dismal climate, this wet, muddy Paris of ours, and to dream fondly of some enchanted oasis, all carpeted with greenery and refreshed with cooling waters, where, no matter what the season, you might gently sink asleep beneath the shade of palms and jameroses, soothed by the babbling of a crystal spring and happy in the sensation of physical well-being and a delicious languor ?

Well, this Paradise you dreamed of exists, this Eden you coveted awaits you. The streamlet that should lull you to soft slumber does actually plunge from its rocky height to rebound in spray, the palm that should guard your siesta does really spread its slender leaves to flutter in the sea-breeze like the plume on a giant's helm, the jameroses, laden with many-coloured fruitage, do veritably offer you their scented shade. Up then, and come with me !

Come to Brest, that warlike sister of commercial Marseilles, that armed sentinel watching over the ocean; and there, from among the hundred vessels sheltering in its harbour, choose one of those brigs with narrow beam, well-cut sails, and long tapering masts, such as Walter Scott's rival, the poetic chronicler of the sea, assigns to his pirates bold. We are in September, the month most propitious for long voyages. Get you aboard the ship to which we have entrusted our common fortune ; let us leave the summer behind us and sail to meet the spring. Adieu, Brest! Hail, Nantes and Bayonne ! Adieu, France ! See on our right that giant rising to a height of ten thousand feet, whose granite summit is lost in the clouds, above which it seems to hang suspended, and whose rocky foundations you can distinguish through the clear water descending into the depths. It is the peak of Teneriffe, the ancient Nivaria, the rendezvous of the sea-eagles you see wheeling round their eyries and looking scarce as big as pigeons. Pass on, this is not our journey's end ; this is but the flower-garden of Spain, and I have promised you the Paradise of the World. Do you see on our left that bare and barren rock scorched incessantly by the tropic sun ? It is the rock where the modern Prometheus was chained for six long years ; the pedestal whereon England herself has reared the statue of her own shame ; the counterpart of the pyre of Jeanne d'Arc and of the scaffold of Mary Stuart ; the political Golgotha, for eighteen years the pious rendezvous of all vessels ; but this is not where I am taking you. Pass on, we have no longer any business there ; the regicide St. Helena is widowed of the relics of her martyr.

We are at the Cape of Storms. Do you see that mountain emerging from the haze ? It is the same giant Adamastor which appeared to the author of the "Lusiad." We are passing the extremity of the earth ; yonder jutting promontory is the prow of the world. See how the ocean breaks against it, furious but powerless ; that good ship fears not its tempests, for its sails are set for the harbour of eternity, it has God Himself for pilot. Pass on, for beyond those verdant mountains we shall find barren tracks and sun-scorched deserts. Pass on, I have promised you clear water and sweet shade, fruits ever ripening and everlasting flowers.

Hail to the Indian Ocean ! where the west wind urges us along ; hail to the scene of the "Thousand and One Nights" ; we are approaching the end of our voyage. Here is the melancholy Bourbon, devoured by an eternal volcano. Give a glance at its flames, and a smile for its odours ; sail a few knots farther and let us pass between the *Ile Plate* and the *Coin-de-Mire* ; let us double *Canonneers' Head* and stop at the flag-staff.

Let us drop anchor, the roadstead is good ; our, brig, wearied with her tedious voyage, craves rest. Besides, we have arrived, for this is the fortunate land which Nature seems to have hidden at the ends of the earth, as a jealous mother conceals from profane eyes the virginal beauty of her daughter ; for this is the land of promise, the pearl of the Indian Ocean, the Isle of France.

Now, chaste daughter of the seas, twin sister of Bourbon, favoured rival of Ceylon, let me lift a corner of thy veil to show thee to the stranger-friend, the fraternal traveller, who accompanies me ; let me unloose thy girdle, fair captive ! for we are two pilgrims from France, and perhaps one day France will be able to redeem thee, rich daughter of the Indies, for the price of some petty kingdom of Europe. And you who have followed us with your eyes and thoughts, let me now speak to you of this wondrous land, with its ever-fruitful fields, with its double harvests, with its year made up of springs and summers following and replacing each other without intermission, linking flowers to fruits, and fruits to flowers. Let me tell of the romantic isle which bathes her feet in the sea and hides her head in the clouds ; a second Venus, born, like her sister, of the foam of the waves, ascending from her watery cradle to her celestial empire, crowned with sparkling days and starry nights, eternal ornaments which she has received from the hand of the Creator Himself, and of which England has not yet had power to strip her.

Come then, and if aerial flights alarm you no more than voyages by sea, grasp, like a new Cleophas, a lappet of my cloak, and I will transport you with me to the inverted cone of the Pieterbot, the highest mountain in the island, next to the Peak of the Black River. Once arrived there, we shall look in all directions, successively to right and left, in front, behind, above us and below.

Above us, you see, is a sky always clear, studded with stars—an azure carpet on which God raises at each of His steps a golden dust, whereof each atom is a world.

Beneath us is the island, stretched at our feet like a map

a hundred and forty-five leagues in circumference, with its sixty rivers that look from here like silver threads designed to chain the sea around its shores, and its thirty mountains all plumed with cocoas, *takamakas*, and palm-trees. Amid all these rivers see the waterfalls of the *Réduit* and *La Fontaine*, which, out of the bosom of the woods they spring from, let loose their hurtling cataracts at headlong speed, to meet the sea which waits them, and, whether in calm or tempest, is aye ready to answer their eternal challenge, now with silent contempt, now with reverberating rage—a duel of Titans, each striving which shall make the greater noise and havoc in the world—then near this wild scene of foolish rivalry, see the great, calm " Black River," rolling down quietly its fertilising waters, imposing its respected name on all within its neighbourhood, showing thus the triumph of wisdom over force, and of calm over fury. Among all these mountains, see the gloomy *Brabant*, standing over the northern point of the Island as a gigantic sentinel to defend it against surprises of the enemy, and to break the fury of the ocean. See the peak of the *Trois-Mamelles*, at the base of which flow the rivers of the *Tamarin* and the *Rempart*, as though the Indian Isis had wished to justify her name in everything—see, lastly, the *Pouce*, next after the Pieterbot, where we are standing, the most majestic peak in the Island ; it seems to raise a finger to the sky to show to master and to slave alike that there is a Tribunal above which will render justice to us all.

In front of us is Port Louis, formerly Port Napoléon, the capital of the Island, with its crowded wooden houses, its two streams which, after every storm, become torrents, its *Ile des Tonneliers* defending the approaches, and its hybrid population, which seems to be a sample of all the nations of the earth, from the lazy Creole who is carried in a palanquin if he wants to cross the street, and who finds conversation so fatiguing that he has trained his slaves to obey his gestures, down to the negro hounded by the whip to his work in the morning and from it in the evening. Between these two extremes of the social ladder see the Lascars, distinguished by their red and green turbans, from which two colours they never vary, with bold, bronzed

features, a cross between the Malay and the Malabar types.
See the Yoloff negro, of the tall and handsome Senegambian
race, with complexion black as jet, eyes bright as car-
buncles, teeth white as pearls ; the Chinaman, short, flat-
chested and broad-shouldered, with his bare skull and drooping moustaches, his jargon which nobody understands, but
with whom, notwithstanding, everybody deals; for the
Chinaman sells everything, runs all trades, follows all pro-
fessions, is the Jew of the colony : then the Malays, copper-
coloured, small, vindictive, cunning, always forgetful of a
kindness, never of an injury ; selling, like the Bohemians,
things that one wants quite cheap : the Mozambiques,
gentle, honest and stupid, and valued only for their strength :
the Madagascans, thin, cunning, of an olive tint, flat-nosed
and thick-lipped, distinguished from the negroes of the Senegal by the reddish reflection of their skin : the Namaquais,
slim, skilful and proud, trained from their infancy in hunting the tiger and the elephant, and astonished at being
transported to a country where there are no wild animals
to fight : lastly, in the midst of all this, the English officer,
garrisoned in the island or stationed at the harbour, with
his round scarlet waistcoat, his cap-shaped head-gear, his
white trousers, looking down from the height of his grandeur
upon creoles and mulattos, masters and slaves, colonists and
natives, talking only of London, boasting only of England,
valuing only himself. Behind us, Grand Port, formerly
Port Impérial, first established by the Dutch, but afterwards
abandoned by them, because it lies to windward of the
island and the same breeze which brings vessels in, prevents
them from going out. So, after having fallen into ruins, it
is to-day but a town whose houses barely rise above ground,
a creek where a schooner comes to take shelter from the
pirate's clutches, forest-covered mountains in which the
slave seeks refuge from his master's tyranny. Next, bringing our eyes back to the landscape lying almost beneath our
feet, we shall distinguish, behind the mountains by the
harbour, Moka, perfumed with aloes, pomegranates, and
currants ; Moka, always so fresh that it seems to fold up
the treasures of its attire in the evening to display them in
the morning, which decks itself every day as the other

districts do only on festivals ; Moka, the garden of this island which we have termed the garden of the world.

Let us resume our first position ; let us face Madagascar and direct our eyes to our left : at our feet, beyond the *Réduit*, are the Williams plains, next to Moka the most delightful quarter of the island, bounded, towards the plains of St. Pierre by the *Corps-de-Garde* mountain, shaped like the hind-quarters of a horse ; then, beyond the *Trois-Mamelles* and the great woods, the quarter of *la Savane*, with its sweetly-named rivers, "Lemon-Trees," " Negresses' Bath," and the " Arcade," with its harbour so well defended by the natural escarpment of its sides that it is impossible to land there otherwise than in friendly fashion ; with its pastures rivalling those of the plains of St. Pierre, with its soil still virgin as that of an American prairie, lastly, in the depths of the woods, the great pond where are found murænas so gigantic that they are more like serpents than eels, and which have been seen to carry off and devour alive stags pursued by hunters and runaway negroes who had been so imprudent as to bathe there.

Next let us turn to the right : here is the quarter of the *Rempart*, dominated by the Mount of Discovery, on the summit of which rise ships' masts, which look from here as thin and small as willow branches ; here is *Cap Malheureux*, the bay of the *Tombeaux*, the church of the *Pamplemousses*. In this quarter rose the two neighbouring huts of Madame de la Tour and Marguérite ; on the *Cap Malheureux* the *Saint-Géran* went to pieces ; in the bay of the *Tombeaux* was found the body of a girl holding a portrait clasped in her hand ; in the church of the *Pamplemousses*, two months later, side by side with this girl, a young man of about the same age was buried. You have already guessed the names of these two lovers whom the same tombstone covers ; they were Paul and Virginia, those two halcyons of the tropics, whose death the sea, as it moans on the reefs that surround the coast, seems evermore to bewail, as a tigress evermore laments her whelps rent to pieces by herself in a transport of fury or a moment of jealousy.

And now, whether you traverse the island from the pass of Descorne in the south-west, or from Mahebourg to the

Little Malabar, whether you follow the coast or plunge into the interior, whether you descend the rivers or climb the mountains, whether the sun's blazing disc kindle the plains with flaming rays, or the crescent of the moon silver the mountains with melancholy light, should your feet be weary, or your head grow heavy, or your eyes close; should you feel your senses, intoxicated by the perfumed exhalations of the China rose, the Spanish or the red jasmine, dissolving gently as if under the influence of opium, you can yield, my companion, without fear or reluctance to the deep and penetrating voluptuousness of tropic slumber. Lie down, then, on the lush grass, sleep quietly and awake without fear, for this light noise which makes the foliage rustle at its approach, those two dark sparkling eyes which are fixed on you, are not the poisoned rustling of the Jamaican boqueira, nor the eyes of the Bengal tiger. Sleep softly, and awake without fear; the isle has never echoed the shrill hiss of a reptile, nor the nocturnal howl of a beast of prey. No, it is a young negress who parts two bamboo branches to push her pretty head through and look with curiosity at the newly-arrived European. Make a sign, without even stirring from your place, and she will pick you the savoury banana, the scented mango or the tamarind-husk; speak a word, and she will answer you in her guttural and mournful tone, " Mo sellave, mo faire ça que vous vié " (" Me slave-girl, me do what you will "). Only too happy should a kind look or a word of satisfaction reward her services, she will then offer to act as your guide to her master's dwelling. Follow her; it matters not whither she leads you; and, when you perceive a pretty house with an avenue of trees, engirdled by flowers, you will have arrived; it will be the home of the planter, tyrant or patriarch, according as he is good or bad; but, be he the one or the other, that is not your concern and affects you but little. Enter boldly; go and sit down at the family table; say, " I am your guest "; and then will be placed before you the richest china plate, loaded with the finest bananas, the silver goblet with its bottom of glass, in which will foam the best beer of the island; you will shoot to your heart's content in his savannahs, and

fish in the river with his lines, and each time you come
yourself or introduce a friend to him, the fatted calf will
be killed ; for here the arrival of a guest is made a festival,
as the return of the Prodigal Son was a joy to his father's
household.

So the English, with their eternal jealousy of France,
long fixed their eyes on her beloved daughter, hovering
round her incessantly, now trying to seduce her with gold,
now to intimidate her by threats ; but to all these proposals
the beautiful Creole replied with supreme disdain, so that
it soon became apparent that her lovers, unable to win her
by their wiles, were fain to carry her off by force, and that
she must be kept in sight like a Spanish *monja*. For some
time she had nothing worse to fear than a series of unim-
portant and ineffectual attempts ; but at last England,
unable to resist her charms, threw herself headlong upon
her, and when one fine morning the Isle of France learned
that her sister Bourbon had just been carried off, she
besought her protectors to keep a yet stricter guard over
her than in time past, and knives began to be sharpened
in deadly earnest and bullets to be cast, as the enemy
was momentarily expected.

On the 23rd of August, 1810, a terrific cannonade, reverberating through all the island, announced that the enemy
had actually arrived.

CHAPTER II
LIONS AND LEOPARDS

IT was five in the evening towards the end of one of
those magnificent summer days unknown in our Europe.
Half the population of the Isle of France, arranged in a
semicircle on the mountains which dominate Grand Port,
were breathlessly watching the contest going on at their
feet, as in olden days the Romans leaned over the gallery
of the amphitheatre at a contest of gladiators or a combat
of martyrs. Only, on this occasion, the arena was a large
harbour environed by rocks on which the combatants had
run themselves aground to prevent all possibility of retreat,
and, freed from the distracting anxiety of evolutions, be

able to tear each other to pieces at their ease : neither again were there any vestal virgins with upturned thumbs to put an end to this terrible sea-fight : it was, as was fully understood, a strife of extermination, a combat to the death ; accordingly the ten thousand spectators present at it maintained an anxious silence, while the very sea, so often stormy in those regions, was still, so as not to lose one roar of those three hundred mouths of fire.

This is what had happened. On the morning of the 20th Captain Duperré, coming from Madagascar in .the *Bellone*, accompanied by the *Minerve*, *Victor*, *Ceylan* and the *Windham*, had sighted the Mountains of the Wind in the Isle of France.

As three previous fights in which he had been without exception victorious had caused severe damage to his fleet, he had determined to enter the great harbour and refit there—a course which was the more easy because, as is well known, the Island at this time was entirely in our power, and the tri-coloured flag floating over the fort of the Ile de la Passe, and from a three-master anchored below it, gave the worthy sailor the assurance of being welcomed by friends. Consequently Captain Duperré gave orders to double the Ile de la Passe, situated about two leagues in front of Mahebourg, and, to carry out this manœuvre, ordered the corvette *Victor* to go ahead, followed by the *Minerve*, *Ceylan* and *Bellone*, the *Windham* concluding the line. The squadron then advanced, each ship in front of the next one, the narrow entrance not allowing of two ships passing alongside each other.

When the *Victor* was within cannon-range of the three-master lying broadside beneath the fort, the latter signalled that the English were cruising within sight of the Island. Captain Duperré replied that he was quite aware of it, and that the flotilla which he had observed was composed of the *Enchantress*, *Nereïd*, *Sirius* and *Iphigenia*, commanded by Commodore Lambert ; but that as, on his own side, Captain Hamelin was stationed to windward of the Island with the *Entreprenant*, *La Manche* and *Astrée*, he was sufficiently strong to accept battl should the enemy present himself.

A few moments later, Captain Bouvet, who was second in the line, thought he observed some hostile indications in the vessel that had just signalled ; besides he had in vain examined all her details with that piercing glance that so rarely deceives the sailor, but could not recognize her as belonging to the French navy. He communicated his observations to Captain Duperré, who told him in answer to take precautions, and that he would do the like. As for the *Victor* it was impossible to give her information ; she was too far ahead, and any signal made to her would have been seen from the fort and the suspected vessel.

The *Victor* then continued to advance without misgivings, impelled by a gentle south-east breeze, with all her crew on deck, while the two ships that follow her anxiously watch the movements of the three-master and the fort. Both, however, still keep up an appearance of friendship ; indeed the two vessels when opposite each other exchange a few words. The *Victor* continues her course ; she has already passed the fort, when suddenly a line of smoke appears on the sides of the ship that lies broadside towards her and on the rampart of the fort. Forty-four guns thunder at once, raking the French corvette, cutting her rigging and sails, decimating her crew, carrying away her foretop-sail yard, while at the same instant the French colours disappear from the fort and the three-master and give place to the English flag. We have been duped by trickery, and have fallen into the trap laid for us.

But instead of going back, which might still be possible by abandoning the corvette which has acted the part of a scout and now, having recovered from her surprise, is replying to the fire of the three-master with her two stern-guns, Captain Duperré signals the *Windham*, which makes for sea again, and orders the *Minerve* and *Ceylan* to force the channel. He himself will support them while the *Windham* goes to warn the rest of the French fleet of the situation in which the four vessels are.

Then the ships continue to advance, no longer with the unguardedness of the *Victor*, but with lighted lintstocks, each man at his post, and in that profound silence which always precedes a great crisis. Presently the *Minerve* gets alongside the hostile three-master, but this time it is she who strikes first. Twenty-four mouths burst into flame together ; the broadside pierces her hull through and through ; part of the bulwarks of the English vessel is cut away ; stifled shrieks are heard. Then in her turn she thunders with her whole battery and sends back to the *Minerve* as deadly messengers as she has just received from her, while the artillery of the fort bursts out upon her as well, but without doing her any other injury than killing a man or two and cutting some of her rigging.

Next comes the *Ceylan*, a pretty brigantine with twenty-two guns, taken, like the *Victor*, *Minerve*, and *Windham*, a few days previously from the English, and which, like the *Victor* and *Minerve*, was now about to fight for France, her new mistress. She advances lightly and gracefully, as a sea-bird skims the waves ; then, when opposite the fort and the three-master, all three break out into flames together, firing so simultaneously that the volleys form one sound, and so close to each other that their smoke is intermingled.

There remained Duperré, in the *Bellone*. He was even at this period one of the bravest and most skilful officers in our navy. He advanced, hugging the Ile de la Passe more closely than any of the other vessels had done ; then, at close quarters, broadside to broadside, the two ships burst into flame, at pistol-range. The channel was forced ; the four ships were within the harbour ; they rally at the cliff of the Aigrettes and cast anchor between the *Ile aux Singes* and the *Pointe de la Colonie*. Duperré having at once put himself in communication with the town, learns that Bourbon is taken, but that, in spite of his attempts on the Isle of France, the enemy has only been able to seize the Ile de la Passe. A messenger is at once dispatched in all haste to General Decaen, Governor of the Island, to inform him the four French vessels, *Victor*, *Minerve*, *Ceylan* and *Bellone*, are at Grand Port. At noon on the 21st Decaen receives this advice, transmits it to Captain Hamelin, who orders the ships under his command to get under way, hurries reinforcements of men across country to Captain Duperré, informs him that he will do what he can to come to his aid, inasmuch as everything leads him to the conclusion that he is threatened by superior numbers.

As a fact, in endeavouring to anchor in the Rivière Noire at four a.m. on the 21st, the *Windham* had been captured by the English frigate *Sirius*. Captain Pym, Commander of the latter, had then learned that four French ships under Duperré's orders had entered Grand Port, where they were confined by the wind ; he had at once informed the captains of the *Enchantress* and *Iphigenia* of this, and the three frigates had sailed immediately. The *Sirius* went back towards Grand Port, running before the wind, the two other frigates turning to windward to reach the same point.

These were the movements which Captain Hamelin had seen, and which by their agreement with the news he had just heard cause him to think that Captain Duperré is about to be attacked. He hastens therefore to get under way, but in spite of all diligence he is only ready on the morning of the 22nd. The three English frigates are three hours in advance of him, and the difficulty he must experience in reaching Grand Port is still further increased by the wind, which is set in the south-east and freshening momentarily.

On the evening of the 21st General Decaen mounts his horse and arrives at Mahebourg at five in the morning, followed by the chief planters and those of their negroes on whom they think they can rely. Masters and slaves are armed with guns, and have each fifty rounds, in case the English should attempt to land. A meeting takes place between him and Duperré. At noon the English frigate *Sirius*, which has sailed to leeward of the Island, and consequently experienced less difficulty in her passage than the other two frigates, appears at the entrance of the channel, meets the three-master moored with her broadside to the fort, now recognized as the frigate *Nereïd*, Captain Willoughby. As though reckoning to attack the French division by themselves, both advance upon us, taking the same course as we had done ; but, keeping too close to the shoal water, the *Sirius* runs aground and her crew spend the rest of the day in getting her off.

During the night the reinforcement of sailors sent by Captain Hamelin arrives, and is distributed among the four French ships, making up a total of nearly fourteen hundred men with a hundred and forty-two guns; but as immediately after this distribution Duperré has run his division aground, so that each vessel presents its broadside, only the half of the guns will take part in the sanguinary feast that is preparing.

At two o'clock the frigates *Enchantress* and *Iphigenia* appeared in their turn at the entrance of the channel, met the *Sirius* and *Nereïd* and advanced all four to encounter us. Two ran themselves aground, the other two lay moored at anchor, presenting a total of seventeen hundred men and two hundred guns. It was a solemn and terrible moment when the ten thousand spectators who thronged the mountains saw the hostile frigates advance with furled sails, impelled only by the slow force of the wind through their rigging, and, with the confidence imparted by superiority of numbers, range themselves at half-gunshot from the French division, presenting in their turn their broadsides, grounding as we had grounded, abandoning retreat beforehand, as we had abandoned it.

A battle of extermination, then, was about to commence; lions and leopards had met, and were about to rend each other with brazen teeth and roars of fire.

It was our sailors who, with less patience than the French guards had shown at Fontenoy, gave the signal for slaughter. A long train of smoke rushed from the sides of the four vessels at whose peak flew the tri-colour; then at the same moment bellowed forth the roar of seventy guns, and the iron hurricane fell upon the English squadron.

The latter answered promptly, and then began, with no other manœuvre than that of clearing from the decks the splinters of timber and expiring bodies, with no interval but that of loading the guns, one of those struggles to the death such as, since Aboukir and Trafalgar, naval annals had not witnessed. At first it might be thought the advantage lay with the enemy; for the first English volleys had cut the springs on the hawsers of the *Minerve* and the *Ceylan*, so that, owing to this accident, the fire of these two ships was to a large extent masked. But, under the captain's orders, the *Bellone* met every event, replying to the four ships at once; having arms, powder and shot for all; incessantly belching forth fire like a volcano in eruption, and that for two hours, that is to say, while the *Ceylan* and *Minerve* were repairing their injuries. This done, as though impatient of their inaction, they began again to roar and bite in their turn, forcing the enemy, who had turned from them for a moment to crush the *Bellone*, to pay attention to them once more, and restoring the unity of the fight along the whole line. It then seemed to Duperré that the *Nereïd*, already damaged by three broadsides which the squadron had fired at her when forcing the channel, was slackening her fire, and the order was at once given to direct all the firing at her and to give her no rest. For a whole hour they overwhelmed her with shot and grape, thinking at each moment that she would strike her flag, but, as she did not do so, the hail of iron continued, mowing down the masts, sweeping her deck, piercing her hull, until her last gun died away like an expiring sigh, and she remained a demolished hulk in the stillness and silence of death.

At this moment, and while Duperré was giving an order to his lieutenant Roussin, a grape-shot struck his head and knocked him over against the guns. Realizing that he was dangerously, perhaps mortally, wounded, he calls Captain Bouvet, hands over to him the command of the *Bellone*, orders him to sink the four ships rather than surrender them, and, after giving these final orders, extends his hand to him and swoons away. Nobody perceives this incident; Duperré has not left the *Bellone*, since Bouvet takes his place.

At ten o'clock it is so dark that the men can no longer take aim and have to fire at random. At eleven the firing ceases; but as the spectators understand that it is only a truce, they remain at their post. As a fact, at one o'clock the moon rises, and by its pale light the strife begins afresh.

During this short respite the *Nereïd* has received some reinforcements; five or six of her guns have been refitted; the frigate that was thought dead was only in a swoon and recovers her senses, giving signs of life by attacking us afresh.

Then Bouvet sends Lieutenant Roussin on board the *Victor*, whose captain is wounded, with orders to float the ship again and go and overwhelm the *Nereïd* at close quarters with his whole artillery. This time his firing will not cease until the frigate be really dead.

Roussin carries out his order to the letter; the *Victor* sets her top-sails and jib, moves off and, without firing a single shot, anchors three or four fathoms from the *Nereïd's* stern; from there she opens fire, to which the *Nereïd* can only reply with her stern guns, raking her from poop to prow at each discharge. At dawn the frigate is silent once more. This time she is really dead, yet, notwithstanding, the English flag still floats at her peak. She is dead, but she has not surrendered. At this moment, shouts of " Long live the Emperor ! " resound from the *Nereïd*—the seventeen prisoners whom she took in the Ile de la Passe and had placed in the hold, burst from their place of confinement, and escape up the hatchways with a tri-coloured flag in their hands. The standard of Great Britain is lowered, the tri-colour floats in its place. Roussin gives the order to board, but at the moment when he is about to fasten the grappling-irons, the enemy directs his fire on the *Nereïd*, which escapes him. To continue the struggle is useless; the *Nereïd* is nothing but a hulk, on which he will lay hands as soon as the other ships are subdued. The victor leaves the frigate floating like the carcass of a dead whale, takes on board the seventeen prisoners and resumes her place of battle, announcing to the English, by firing her whole broadside, that she had returned to her position.

All the French ships were now ordered to direct their fire on the *Enchantress*, Bouvet wishing to demolish the hostile frigates one after the other. Towards three p.m. then the *Enchantress* became the target for all their shots ; at five, she answered our fire spasmodically, and breathed like a combatant mortally wounded; at six o'clock it could be seen from the land that her crew were making all preparations for abandoning her. Shouts first, then signals, warn the French division of this; the firing is redoubled ; the two other hostile frigates dispatch their boats to her ; she herself lowers her cutters into the sea ; the remnant of unwounded or slightly-wounded men get into them, but in the space which they have to cross to reach the *Sirius* two boats are sunk by cannon shot, and the sea is strewn wth men making for the neighbouring frigates by swimming.

A moment later a thin smoke issues from the portholes of the *Enchantress* ; then it becomes gradually thicker ; next, at the hatchways wounded men are seen dragging themselves along, raising their mutilated arms, appealing for help ; for already smoke is followed by flames which dart their fiery tongues through every porthole. Then they burst outside, creep along the netting, climb to the masts, envelop the yards, and in the midst of these flames are heard cries of rage and pain ; then all at once the vessel splits, as the crater of a volcano is rent asunder. A fearful explosion is heard ; the *Enchantress* is blown to bits. The eye follows the burning fragments which mount to the sky, descend again and are extinguished with a loud hissing sound in the waves. Of that fine frigate, which the day before thought herself queen of the ocean, nothing remains, not even débris, not even the wounded, not even the dead. A wide space between the *Nereïd* and the *Iphigenia* alone indicates the place where she was.

Then, as though weary of the strife, dismayed at the spectacle, English and French fell silent, and the rest of the night was consecrated to repose.

But at dawn the fight begins again. The French division has chosen the *Sirius* this time as its victim, and the fourfold fire of *Victor, Minerve, Bellone.* and *Ceylan* are about to crush her. Shot and grape are concentrated upon her At the end of two hours she has not a mast left, her bulwarks are cut down, the water enters her hull through twenty wounds ; had she not been aground she must have sunk. Her crew then abandons her, the captain being the last to leave. But, as with the *Enchantress*, the fire has remained there ; a train conducts it to the magazine ; and at eleven in the forenoon a fearful explosion is heard, and the *Sirius* disappears annihilated.

Then the *Iphigenia*, which has fought at anchor, realizes that no more fighting is possible. She remains alone against four ; for, as we have said, the *Nereïd* is nothing now but a sheer hulk ; she makes sail, and, profiting by the fact that she has escaped almost safe and sound from all this destruction, tries to sheer off, in order to place herself under the protection of the fort.

Bouvet at once orders the *Minerve* and *Bellone* to refit and get afloat again. Duperré, on the blood-stained bed where he is laid, has learned all that has happened : he does not want a single frigate to escape destruction, nor a single Englishman to go and announce their defeat in England. We have to avenge Trafalgar and Aboukir. Pursue the *Iphigenia* !

And the two noble frigates, battered as they are, rouse and recover themselves, make sail and away in pursuit, ordering the *Victor* to man the *Nereïd*. As for the *Ceylan* she is herself so damaged that she cannot quit her place until the caulker has stopped her thousand gaping wounds.

Then loud shouts of triumph rise from the land ; the whole population, which has kept silence, recovers breath and voice to encourage the *Minerve* and *Bellone* in their pursuit. But the *Iphigenia*, less damaged than her two foes, gains on them visibly, passes the Ile des Aigrettes, will reach the fort of la Passe, will gain the open sea and escape. Already the shot from the *Minerve* and *Bellone* fail to reach her, dropping in her wake, when suddenly three ships appear at the entrance of the channel, flying the tricolour ; it is Captain Hamelin, who had sailed from Port Louis with the *Entreprenant, La Manche* and *Astrée*. The *Iphigenia* and the fort are caught between two fires ; they will surrender at discretion, not an Englishman will escape. During this time the *Victor* has for the second time drawn close to the *Nereïd* ; and, fearing a surprise, boards her cautiously. But the silence she maintains is truly that of death. Her deck is strewn with corpses ; the Lieutenant, who was the first to set foot on her, is up to his ankles in blood.

A wounded man raises himself and relates that six times the order was given to strike the flag, but six times the French discharges carried away the men told off to carry out this order. Then the Captain retired to his cabin and was seen no more.

Roussin goes towards the cabin and finds Captain Willoughby seated at a table, on which are still a jug of grog and three glasses. He has an arm and a thigh carried away. In front of him his first Lieutenant Thomson, killed by a grape-shot, which struck him in the chest ; at his feet lies his nephew, William Murray, likewise wounded in the side by a grape-shot.

Then Willoughby with his remaining hand makes a movement to give up his sword ; but Lieutenant Roussin, in his turn extending his arm, salutes the dying Englishman, saying : "Captain, when a man uses a sword as you have done, he surrenders it to God alone ! "

And he at once orders every possible attention to be lavished upon Captain Willoughby. But all aid was useless ; the brave defender of the *Nereïd* died on the morrow.

Lieutenant Roussin was more fortunate as regards the nephew than he had been with the uncle. Lord Murray, though wounded deeply and dangerously, was not mortally hurt. Accordingly we shall see him reappear in the course of this history.

CHAPTER III
THREE CHILDREN

AS may well be imagined, the English, though they had lost four vessels, had not abandoned their designs on the Isle of France ; on the contrary, they had now both a fresh conquest to make and an old defeat to avenge. Accordingly, hardly three months after the events which we have just laid before the reader, a second struggle no less desperate, but destined to result very differently, had taken place at Port Louis itself, that is to say, at a spot in exactly the opposite direction to that where the former took place.

This time it was not a question of four ships or eighteen hundred men. Twelve frigates, eight corvettes and fifty transports had landed twenty or twenty-five thousand men

on the coast, and the invading army was advancing on
Port Louis, then called Port Napoléon. This was the
capital of the island, and at the moment of being attacked
by so large a force presented a spectacle difficult to describe.
Everywhere the multitude, hurrying in from different
quarters of the island and crowded together in the streets,
showed signs of the greatest excitement; as nobody knew the
real danger, every one invented some imaginary peril, and
those which obtained most credence were the most exaggerated and unheard-of ones. From time to time some aide-
de-camp of the General in command would appear suddenly,
bringing an order and tossing to the crowd a proclamation
intended to stimulate the hatred which the Nationalists bore
towards the English and to excite their patriotism. On its
being read out, hats were raised on the points of bayonets ;
shouts of " Long live the Emperor ! " resounded ; oaths to
conquer or die were exchanged ; a shiver of enthusiasm
ran through the crowd, which passed from a state of noisy
idleness to one of furious activity, and rushed headlong
from all quarters, demanding to march upon the enemy.

But the real meeting-place was the Place d'Armes, that
is to say, the centre of the town. Thither were continually
arriving, now an ammunition wagon dragged helter-
skelter by two small horses of Timor or Pegu, now a gun
brought in at full gallop by the National Artillery, young
fellows of fifteen to sixteen years of age, for whom the
powder that blackened their faces took the place of
beards. There, too, assembled the Civic Guards in fighting
trim, Volunteers in miscellaneous garments, who had added
bayonets to their sporting guns; negroes clothed in
remnants of uniforms and armed with carbines, sabres
and lances ; all these mingling, colliding, crossing one
another, upsetting one another, contributing each his share
of noise to the insistent rumour which rose above the town,
just as the hum of an innumerable swarm of bees ascends
from a large hive.

Once arrived, however, at the Place, whether rushing in
singly or in groups, these men assumed a more regular appearance and a calmer demeanour. At the Place d'Armes
was stationed, while waiting for the order to march,

against the enemy, half of the garrison of the Island, composed of regular troops and forming a total of fifteen to eighteen hundred men, whose attitude, at once proud and nonchalant, was a silent reproach to the noise and confusion made by those who, less familiar with scenes of this kind, had nevertheless the courage and goodwill to take part in them. Accordingly, while the negroes hurried pell-mell to one end of the great square, a regiment of national Volunteers, restraining themselves at sight of the military discipline of the Regulars, halted in front of the troops, forming in the same order as they, and trying, though without success, to imitate the regularity of their lines.

He who appeared to be the leader of this last body of men, and who, it must be said, gave himself infinite trouble to attain the result we have indicated, was a man from forty to forty-five years of age, wearing a Major's epaulettes, and endowed by nature with one of those insignificant faces to which no emotion can succeed in imparting signs of intelligence or character. For the rest, he was curled, shaved, smartly got up as if for parade ; only, occasionally, he unfastened a clasp of his coat, originally buttoned from top to bottom but which gradually opening, displayed to view an embroidered vest, frilled shirt and white tie with embroidered ends. Near him, a pretty child of twelve, attended by a household negro who stood some yards away, dressed in a suit of dimity, displayed, with that ease which the habit of being well-dressed imparts, his large scalloped collar, his jacket of green camlet with silver buttons, and his grey beaver adorned with a feather. At his side hung with his sabretache the scabbard of a little sword, the blade of which he held in his right hand, trying to copy, as well as he could, the martial bearing of the officer, whom he took care, from time to time to address very loudly as " Father," a title with which the Major seemed no less flattered than by the illustrious rank in the national militia to which the confidence of his fellow-citizens had raised him.

At a short distance from this group which swaggered so gaily might be distinguished another, less brilliant no doubt, but certainly more remarkable. It consisted of a man from forty-five to forty-eight years of age, and two children, one aged fourteen and the other twelve.

The man was tall and thin, of bony frame, a little bent, .not by age, since, as we have said, he was not more than forty-eight at the outside, but by the humility of a subservient position. From his copper tint and slightly woolly hair one could recognize at first glance one of those mulattoes whose fortunes, which are often enormous and the result of their own well-directed industry, avail nothing in the Colonies to excuse their colour. He was dressed with rich simplicity, held in his hand a carbine embossed with gold, armed with a long slender bayonet, and had at his side a cuirassier's sabre which, thanks to his great height, hung along his thigh like a sword. His pockets bulged with cartridges, in addition to those contained in his pouch.

The eldest of the two children who accompanied him was, as we have said, a tall lad of fourteen, whose sporting pursuits, more than his negro origin, had deepened his complexion. Thanks to the active life he had led he was as strong as a young man of eighteen, and thus had obtained his father's leave to share in the engagement which was soon to take place. He, on his side, was armed with a double-barrelled gun, the same which he used in his expeditions across the island, and with which, young as he was, he had already gained a reputation for skill which the most celebrated hunters envied him. But, at the present moment, his actual age overcame his apparent age ; for having laid his gun down on the ground, he was rolling over and over with an enormous Madagascar hound, which seemed to have come there in case the English should have brought any of their bulldogs with them.

The young hunter's brother, younger son of the man of tall stature and humble mien, who completed the group we have endeavoured to describe, was a child of about twelve, whose slim and puny build bore no relation to his father's great height or the powerful frame of his brother, who seemed to have united in himself alone the vigour intended for both ; in contrast therefore to Jacques, as the oldest was called, little Georges seemed two years younger than he really was, so far did his short stature, his pale, thin, and melancholy face, shaded by long dark hair, betoken a lack of the physical strength so common in the Colonies. But, to make up for this, you might read in his uneasy, penetrating look such an eager intelligence, and in the precocious knitting of the brows which was already habitual to him, such a manly reflection and such firmness of will, that you were amazed to meet with such insignificance and such vigour united in one and the same individual.

Having no weapons, he kept close by his father and grasped with all the strength of his little hand the barrel of the handsome embossed gun, turning his eager and inquiring eyes from his father to the Major, asking inwardly, no doubt, why his father, who was twice as rich and strong and clever as the other, did not also boast like him some honourable badge or individual mark of rank.

A negro in waistcoat and trousers of blue cloth was waiting, as his comrade was for the child with the scalloped collar, till the time came for the men to march, for the boy would stay behind with him while his father and brother went to fight.

The noise of cannon had been heard since morning, for General Vandermaesen with the other half of the garrison had marched out to meet the enemy, so as to check them in the defiles of the Long Valley and at the crossing of the Pont-Rouge and Lataniers rivers. He had held on with tenacity the whole morning; but, not wishing to risk all his forces at one blow, and fearing besides that the attack which he met might be merely a feint during which the English would advance on Port Louis by some other route, he had taken with him only eight hundred men, leaving the rest of the garrison, as has been said, and the national Volunteers to defend the town. The result was that, after prodigies of courage, his small force, which had to deal with a body of four thousand English and two thousand sepoys, had been obliged to evacuate position after position, taking advantage of every accident of the ground, but soon forced to retire again; so that from the Place d'Armes, where the reserves were, it was possible, though the actual combatants were invisible, to calculate the progress the English were making by the increasing roar of the artillery drawing nearer and nearer every minute. Presently could be distinguished, between the thunders of the big guns, the crackling of musketry. But it must be confessed that this noise, instead of frightening those defenders of Port Louis who, condemned to inaction by their General's orders, were stationed in the Great Square, only stimulated their bravery; so much so that, while the Regulars were content to bite their lips or swear beneath their moustaches, the Volunteers brandished their weapons, grumbling openly, and crying that, if the order to start was delayed any longer, they would break their ranks and go and fight as skirmishers.

At this moment there was a general shout; at the same time an aide-de-camp galloped up and, without even entering the Place, raising his hat to attract attention, shouted from the end of the street:

" To your entrenchments; the enemy is here ! "

Then he went off as fast as he had come.

At once the drum of the Regulars sounded, and the soldiers, forming line with the quickness and precision of long habit, started off at the double.

Whatever rivalry might exist between the Volunteers and the Regulars, the former could not get away with so rapid a dash. Some moments elasped before the ranks were formed; then as, when they were formed, some led off with the right foot, others with the left, there was a moment of confusion necessitating a halt.

At this moment, seeing a vacant place in the middle of the third file of Volunteers, the tall man with the ornamented gun embraced the youngest of his children and, putting him into the arms of the negro in the blue suit, ran with his eldest boy modestly to occupy the place which the false start of the Volunteers had left vacant.

But, at the approach of the two pariahs, their neighbours on the right and left turned aside, forcing the same movement upon the men next to them, so that the tall man and his son found themselves the centre of circles which went moving from them, just as circles of water retire from the spot at which a stone has been thrown in.

The stout man in Major's epaulettes, who had with great

difficulty just got his first file in order, now perceived the disorder into which the third was being thrown ; rising on his toes, he shouted tô those who were executing the singular manœuvre which we have described :

" To your ranks, my men ! to your ranks ! "

But at this repeated order, made in a tone that admitte no reply, a general shout arose :

" No blacks ! no blacks with us ! "

This cry the entire battalion echoed with a universal roar.

Then the officer understood the cause of this disorder, and saw in the centre of a large circle the mulatto who had remained at the " port arms," while his elder son, red with anger, had already fallen back two paces to get away from those who were pushing him back.

On seeing this, the Major passed through the two front ranks which opened to make way for him, and went straight for the insolent fellow who had dared, man of colour as he was, to mix with the whites. When in front of him he looked him up and down with an indignant stare, the man remaining before him upright and motionless as a post :

" Well, Pierre Munier," said he, " can't you hear, or must you be told twice over, that this is not your place and that you are not wanted here ? "

Pierre with his strong right hand might have crushed at a blow the man who spoke thus ; but instead of this, he made no reply, only raised his head with a scared look, and, meeting the looks of his questioner, turned away his own in confusion.

This added fuel to the other's anger, and still further roused the man's insolence.

" Come ! What are you doing there ? " he asked, giving him a push with his open hand.

" Monsieur de Malmédie," answered Munier, " I had hoped that on a day like this difference of colour would disappear in face of the common danger."

" You hoped ! " said the Major, shrugging his shoulders with a loud chuckle. " You hoped ! and what gave you this hope, if you please ? "

" The desire that I have to die, if needs be, to save our Island."

"*Our* Island!" muttered the Major, "*our* Island! Because these fellows have plantations like us, they fancy the Island belongs to them."

"The Island belongs to us no more than to you white entlemen, I am well aware," replied Munier in a timid voice, "but if we stay for such questions at the hour of fighting, it will soon be no longer either yours or ours."

"Enough!" said the Major, stamping his foot to impose silence both by gesture and voice on his interlocutor. "Enough! Are you in command of the National Guard?"

"No, sir, as you very well know," answered Munier; "for when I presented myself, you rejected me."

"Then what do you want?"

"I wanted to follow you as a volunteer."

"Impossible," said the Major.

"Why impossible? Ah! if you would only let me, Monsieur de Malmédie."

"Impossible," repeated the Major, drawing himself up. "These gentlemen who are under my orders will have no mulattoes among them."

"No, no blacks," shouted the National Guards with one voice.

"But may I not fight them, sir?" said Munier, letting his arms fall dejectedly by his sides, and with difficulty keeping back the large tears which trembled on his eyelashes.

"Form a corps of coloured men and put yourself at their head, or join this detachment of blacks which is going to follow us."

"But——" murmured Pierre.

"I order you to quit the battalion; I order it," repeated M. de Malmédie, bridling up.

"Come, father, come, and leave these men who are insulting you," said a small voice trembling with anger. And Pierre felt himself pulled back with such force that he retreated a step.

"Yes, Jacques, yes I will follow you," said he.

"It is not Jacques, father, it is I, Georges."

Munier turned in astonishment.

It was, in fact, the child who had got down from the negro's arms, and come to give his father this lesson in dignity.

2

Munier let his head sink on his breast, and uttered a deep sigh. During this time the ranks of the National Guard had reformed, M. de Malmédie resumed his post at the head of the first file, and the regiment set off at increased speed.

Pierre Munier remained alone between his two children, one of whom was red as fire, the other pale as death. He glanced at the red face of Jacques and Georges' pale one, and as if these symptoms were a double reproach to him, exclaimed : " What would you have, my poor children ?— there is no help for it." Jacques was indifferent and philosophical. The first feeling had been painful to him, no doubt; but reflection had come quickly to his aid and consoled him.

" Bah ! " he replied to his father, snapping his fingers. " What does it matter to us after all if this silly man despises us ? We are richer than he, aren't we, father ? And for myself," he added, casting a side glance at the child with the scalloped collar, " let me find his cub of a Henri at a lucky moment, and I will give him a drubbing which he will remember."

" Good Jacques ! " said Pierre Munier, thanking his eldest son for having in some degree relieved his shame by his careless attitude. Then he turned to his younger son, to see if the latter would take the matter as philosophically as the elder.

But Georges remained motionless : all that his father could discover in his stony countenance was an imperceptible smile which contracted his lips : still, imperceptible as it was, that smile had such a suggestion of contempt and pity that, as we sometimes reply to words that have not been uttered, Pierre answered to this smile :

" But what do you want me to do then ? "

And he waited for the child's answer, disquieted by that vague uneasiness which we never confess to ourselves, but which, however, disturbs us when we await, from an inferior, whom we fear in spite of ourselves, his opinion of something we have done.

Georges made no reply ; but turning his head towards the extremity of the Great Square, said :

" Father, the negroes down there are waiting for a leader."

" Why, you are right, Georges ! " cried Jacques joyously, already consoled for his humiliation by the consciousness of his strength, and reasoning, no doubt, as Cæsar did— It is better to command these than to obey those.

And Munier, yielding to the advice given by his youngest son and the impetus imparted by the other, advanced towards the negroes, who, engaged in discussing whom to choose as their leader, no sooner perceived the man whom all coloured people in the island looked up to as a father than they grouped themselves round him as their natural chief, and begged him to lead them to battle.

Then a strange change took place in the man. That feeling of inferiority, which he could not overcome in presence of the whites, disappeared and gave way to a proper estimation of his own merit ; his bowed frame drew itself up to its full height ; his eyes, which he had kept humbly lowered or wandering vaguely before M. de Malmédie, darted fire ; his voice, trembling a moment earlier, assumed an accent of formidable sternness, and it was with a gesture of noble energy that, throwing back his carbine slung over his shoulder, he drew his sword, and, extending his sinewy arm towards the enemy, cried, " Forward ! "

Then, taking a last look at his youngest child, who had returned to the protection of the negro in the blue suit and, filled with pride and pleasure, was clapping his hands, Pierre disappeared with his black company round the corner of the same street by which the Regulars and National Guards had just disappeared, shouting once again to the negro in the blue jacket : " Télémaque, look after my son ! "

The line of defence consisted of three divisions. On the left the Fanfaron bastion, situated on the edge of the sea and armed with eighteen cannon ; in the centre the entrenchment, properly so-called, lined with twenty-four field guns ; and, on the right, the Dumas battery, protected by six guns only.

The victorious enemy, after having advanced at first in three columns on the three different points, abandoned the two first, the strength of which they perceived, so as to concentrate upon the third, which was not only, as has been said, the weakest, but which further was only defended by the National Artillery. However, contrary to all expectation, at the sight of the compact mass which marched on them with the terrible regularity of British discipline, this martial band of young men, instead of being alarmed, ran to their posts, manœuvring with the speed and the skill of veteran soldiers, with a fire so well maintained and directed that the enemy thought themselves mistaken as to the strength of the battery and the men who served it ; still, they continued to advance, for the deadlier the battery became, the more imperative it was to silence its fire. But then the confounded battery got angry, and like a juggler who makes us forget one astounding trick by performing another still more astounding, it redoubled its volleys, making shot follow grape, and grape common shot, with such rapidity that disorder began to spread in the hostile ranks. At the same time, and as the British had come within musket-shot, the rifle discharge in its turn began to splutter, so that the enemy, seeing their ranks thinned by cannon shot and whole files swept away by musketry fire, astonished by a resistance as vigorous as it was unexpected, wavered and drew back.

By order of the General in command the Regulars and the National Battalion who had combined on the threatened point now moved off, one to the left, the other to the right, and charged with fixed bayonets on the enemy's flanks, while the formidable battery continued to pound him in front. The Regulars carried out their manœuvre with their customary precision, fell upon the British, cut through their ranks and increased the disorder. But, whether carried away by their courage, or that they executed the given order clumsily, the National Guards, commanded by M. de Malmédie, instead of falling upon the left flank and making an attack parallel to that executed by the Regulars, made a wrong movement and encountered the British front. Consequently the battery was obliged to cease firing, and as it was this fire especially that frightened the enemy, who now had only to deal with men inferior in number to themselves, they regained courage and turned on the Nationals, who, to their credit be it said, sustained the shock without giving way a single yard. However, this resistance could not last on the part of these brave fellows placed between an enemy better disciplined than themselves and ten times superior in numbers, and the battery which was forced to be silent to avoid overwhelming them ; at each moment they lost so many men that they began to give way. Soon, by a skilful movement, the British left outflanked the right of the National Battalion now on the point of being surrounded and who, too inexperienced to adopt the formation in square, were looked upon as lost. The British, in fact, continued their progressive movement, and, like a rising tide were about to surround this island of men with their waves, when suddenly shouts of "France ! France !" resounded in the rear of the enemy. This was followed by a fearful discharge, succeeded by a silence more dreadful than the discharge itself.

A strange undulation passed through the enemy's rear and was felt even in their front ranks; red-coats bent under a vigorous bayonet charge like ripe ears beneath the mower's sickle ; it was now their turn to be surrounded, to have to face front, right and left. But the newly-arrived reinforcement gave them no respite, but kept on charging, so that at the end of ten minutes they had opened a path through a bloody gap to the unlucky battalion and extricated it. Then, seeing that they had accomplished their object, the new arrivals fell back, wheeled to the left with a circular movement, and charged the enemy's flank. Malmédie, on his side, imitating instinctively the same manœuvre, had given a similar impulse to his battalion, so that the battery, seeing itself unmasked, lost no time, and bursting forth once more aided the efforts of this triple attack, belching torrents of grape-shot on the enemy. From this point victory decided in favour of the French.

Then Malmédie, feeling himself out of danger, glanced at his liberators, whom he had already partly seen, but hesitated to acknowledge, so much did it go against the grain to owe his safety to such men. It was, indeed, the corps of blacks, so despised by him, that had followed in his wake and joined him at such an opportune moment, and at their head Pierre Munier, who, seeing Malmédie surrounded by the British who thus presented their backs to him, had with his three hundred men caught them in the rear and over-thrown them; it was Munier who, after having planned this movement with the genius of a general, had carried it out with the courage of a soldier, and who at this moment finding himself in a position where he need fear nothing except death, fought in front of all, erect at his full height, his eyes flashing, his nostrils dilated, his forehead bare, his hair floating in the wind, enthusiastic, daring, sublime. In short, it was Munier's voice that was raised from time to time in the midst of the fighting, drowning all the noise of battle to shout " Forward ! "

Then, as to follow him was to advance, and as the disorder in the British ranks increased, the cry was heard " Com-rades, make for the flag ! " He was seen to hurl himself into the midst of a group of British, fall, spring up again, plunge into their ranks, and after an instant reappear with torn clothes and bleeding forehead, but with the flag in his hand.

At this moment the General, fearing that the victors might advance too far in pursuit of the British and fall into a trap, gave the order to fall back. The Regulars obeyed first, bringing in the prisoners, the National Guard carrying away the dead, the black Volunteers in the rear, surround-ing their flag.

The whole Island had rushed to the port, crowding to see the victors, for the inhabitants of Port Louis thought in their ignorance that the entire army of the enemy had been engaged, and hoped that the British, after being repulsed so vigorously, would not return to the charge, so, as each corps passed, they were greeted with fresh hurrahs !; all were proud, all victorious, all beside themselves. An unexpected happiness fills their hearts, an unhoped for success turns their heads ; the inhabitants had expected to make some resistance, but not to gain a victory : so, when they saw victory so completely and entirely theirs, men, women, veterans and children swore with one mouth that they would work at the entrenchments and die, if needs be, for their defence. Excellent promises, no doubt, and made by all with the intention of keeping them, but not worth, by a great deal, an extra regiment, if an extra regiment could have arrived !

But, amid this general ovation, no object attracted so much notice as the British flag and the man who had taken it ; there were endless cries of astonishment round Munier and his trophy, to which the blacks replied by blustering remarks, while their leader, becoming once more the humble mulatto with whom we are acquainted, satisfied the questions put by each with a timid politeness. Standing near the conqueror, and leaning on his double-barrelled gun, which had not been dumb during the engagement and the bayonet of which was stained with blood, Jacques carried his head proudly, while Georges, who had escaped from Télémaque and joined his father at the port, convulsively clasped his powerful hand and vainly tried to check the tears of joy which fell from his eyes in spite of himself. Close by Munier was M. de Malmédie, no less curled and bedecked than when he started, but with his tie torn, his frill in rags and covered with sweat and dirt ; he, too, was surrounded and congratulated by his family ; but the congratulations he received were such as are offered to a man who has escaped a danger, not the praises lavished on a victor. So he appeared rather embarrassed by the chorus of affecting solicitude, and, to put a good face on it, was asking loudly where his son Henri and his negro Bijou were, when he saw them both appear making their way through the crowd, Henri to throw himself into his father's arms, and Bijou to congratulate his master.

At this moment, some one came to tell Munier that a negro who had fought under him and received a mortal wound, having been carried to a house near the port, wished to see him. Pierre looked round in search of Jacques to entrust him with his flag, but Jacques had discovered his friend the dog again, who in his turn had come with the rest to offer his compliments ; he had placed his gun on the ground, and the child getting the better of the man, he and the dog were rolling over and over, some fifty yards off. Georges, seeing his father's difficulty, stretched out his hand, saying :

"Give it me, father ; I will take care of it for you."

Pierre smiled, and believing that none would dare to touch the glorious trophy which belonged to him alone, kissed Georges on the forehead, handed him the flag, which the child with great difficulty held upright by clasping his hands on his breast, and went off to the house where the sufferings of one of his Volunteers claimed his presence.

Georges remained alone; but the child felt instinctively that, though alone, he was not isolated; his father's fame protected him, and his eyes beaming with pride he looked at the crowd that surrounded him; this bright and happy glance then met that of the child with the embroidered collar, and became disdainful. The latter, on his part, eyed Georges with envy, asking himself no doubt why his father too had not taken a flag. This question naturally led him to say to himself, that, failing a flag of his own, he must monopolize another's. For, rudely approaching Georges, who, though he saw his hostile purpose, did not draw back a step, he said:

"Give me that."

"What?" asked Georges.

"That flag," replied Henri.

"This flag is not yours, it's my father's."

"What has that got to do with me? I want it!"

"You shall not have it."

The child with the embroidered collar then put out his hand to snatch the staff of the flag, an action to which Georges only replied by tightening his lips, becoming paler than usual, and drawing back a step. But this act only encouraged Henri, who, like all spoilt children, thought he had but to ask to get; he stepped forward, and this time laid his plans so well that he grasped the stick, shouting loudly with his little angry voice:

"I tell you I want it."

"And I tell you you shan't have it," repeated Georges, pushing him back with one hand, while with the other he continued to press the captured flag against his chest.

"Ah, you nigger, you! how dare you touch me!" cried Henri. "Well, you will see." And, drawing his little sword from the scabbard before Georges had time to defend himself, he struck him with all his strength on the top of the forehead. The blood at once gushed from the wound and trickled down the boy's face.

"Coward!" said Georges coldly.

Exasperated by this insult, Henri was about to repeat the blow, when Jacques reaching his brother at one bound, sent the aggressor flying ten yards by a vigorous blow in the face, and, jumping on the sword which the latter had let fall in the struggle, broke it into three or four pieces, spat on it, and tossed the pieces at him.

It was now the turn of the boy with the embroidered collar to feel the blood run down his face, but *he* had lost his blood not from a sword blow, but from a blow with the fist.

All this had passed so rapidly that neither M. de Malmédie, who, as we have said, was engaged a few yards off in receiving the congratulations of his family, nor Munier, who was coming from the house where the negro had just breathed his last, had time to anticipate it. They were merely spectators of the catastrophe, and ran up both at once; Pierre panting, troubled and trembling; Malmédie red with anger and choking with arrogance. They met in front of Georges.

"Did you see," cried M. de Malmédie, "what happened just now?"

"Alas! yes, M. de Malmédie," answered Pierre, "and, believe me, had I been there this would not have taken place."

"Meanwhile, sir," cried M. de Malmédie, "your son laid his hand on mine. A mulatto's son has dared to touch a white man's son."

"I am distressed at what has just taken place, M. de Malmédie," stammered the poor father, "and humbly offer my apologies."

"Your apologies, sir," replied the angry settler, bridling up as the other humbled himself; "do you think your apologies are sufficient?"

"What more can I do, sir?"

"What can you do?" repeated Malmédie, himself at a loss to name the satisfaction he wished to obtain; "you can have that wretch who struck my son whipped."

"Have me whipped?" said Jacques, picking up his double-barrelled gun and changing from child to man again.

" Well, come and meddle with me yourself, M. de
Malmédie."

" Hush, Jacques ; hush, my son," cried Pierre.

" Excuse me, father," said Jacques, " but I am right, and
I will not be silent. M. Henri struck my brother, who was
doing nothing to him, with his sword ; and I struck M.
Henri with my fist. So M. Henri is wrong, and I am right."

" Struck my son with his sword, my Georges ! Georges,
dear child," cried Munier, going towards his son, " is it true
that you are wounded ? "

" It's nothing, father," said Georges.

" What, nothing ? " cried Pierre Munier ; " why,
your forehead is cut open. Look, sir," he resumed, turning
to M. de Malmédie, " Jacques spoke the truth ; your son
has almost killed mine."

Malmédie turned towards Henri, and, as there was no
means of resisting the evidence, inquired :

" Come, Henri, how did the thing happen ? "

" Papa," said Henri, " it is not my fault ; I wanted the
flag to bring it to you, and that wretch wouldn't give it
me."

" And why wouldn't you give my son the flag, you little
rascal ? " asked M. de Malmédie.

" Because the flag isn't yours, or your son's, or anybody's
but my father's."

" Well ? " asked Malmédie, continuing to question his son.

" Well, when I saw he wouldn't give it me, I tried to
take it. Then this brute came up and struck me in the face
with his fist."

" Then that is what happened ? "

" Yes, father."

" He is lying," said Jacques, " and I only struck him when
I saw my brother's blood flowing ; but for that, I should
never have hit him."

" Silence, you villain ! " cried M. de Malmédie. Then
going up to Georges, he said :

" Give me the flag."

But Georges, instead of obeying this order, stepped back
once more, pressing the flag to his breast with all his might.

" Give me the flag," repeated Malmédie in a threatening

tone which showed that, if his demand were not complied with, he would resort to the utmost extremities.

" But, sir," muttered Pierre, " it was I who took the flag from the British."

" I know it, sir, but it shall not be said that a mulatto has coped with a man like me with impunity. Give me the flag."

" But, sir——"

" I will have it, I order it ; obey your officer."

It entered Pierre's head to answer, " You are not my officer, sir, since you wouldn't have me as your soldier " ; but the words died upon his lips ; his habitual humility got the better of his courage. He sighed ; and though obedience to such an unjust order grieved him, he himself took the flag from Georges, who ceased to offer any resistance, and handed it to the Major, who walked off laden with his stolen trophy.

It was incredible, strange, miserable, to see a man of a nature so rich, vigorous and determined, yield without resistance to that other nature so vulgar, dull, mean, common and poor, yet so it was ; and, what is still more extraordinary, the thing surprised nobody, for it happened every day in the colonies, not in similar, but in parallel circumstances. So, accustomed from infancy to respect the white as men of a superior race, Munier had all his life let himself be crushed by that aristocracy of colour to which he had just yielded once more without even attempting to resist. He resembles those heroes who hold their heads high in the face of grape-shot, and bend the knee to a prejudice. The lion attacks man, the terrestrial image of God, and flees in alarm when he hears the cock crow.

As for Georges, who had not shed a tear when he saw his blood trickling down, he burst into sobs on finding his hands empty in presence of his father, who looked at him sadly without even trying to comfort him.

Jacques, for his part, bit his fists with rage, and vowed to be avenged one day on Henri, M. de Malmédie and all the whites.

Scarcely ten minutes after the scene which we have just related, a messenger covered with dust rushed up announcing that the British, to the number of ten thousand, were advancing by the Williams plains and the Little River; then, almost immediately, the look-out signalled the arrival of a fresh British squadron which, anchoring in the bay of *Grande-Rivière*, landed five thousand men on the coast. Finally, it was ascertained at the same time that the division repulsed in the morning had rallied on the banks of the *Rivière des Lataniers*, and was ready to march again upon Port Louis, combining its movements with the two other invading corps who were advancing, one by Curtois Bay, the other by the *Réduit*. There was no means of resisting such a force; so, when some despairing voices, appealing to the oath taken in the morning to conquer or die, demanded fight, the Captain-General replied by disbanding the National Guard and the Volunteers, and declaring that, armed with full powers from his Majesty the Emperor Napoléon, he was about to treat with the British for the surrender of the town.

Only madmen could have tried to combat such a step; twenty-five thousand men surrounded less than four thousand; accordingly, on the order of the Captain-General every one went home, so that the town remained occupied only by the Regulars. On the night of the 2nd of December the capitulation was concluded and signed; at five a.m. it was approved and exchanged'; the same day the enemy occupied the lines; on the morrow he took possession of the town and harbour.

Eight hours afterwards the captured French squadron left the harbour under full sail, carrying the whole of the garrison, like a poor family driven from the paternal roof; so long as the last flutter of the last flag could be seen, the crowd remained on the quay; but when the last frigate had disappeared, every one went home in gloom and silence. Two men remained alone and were the last to leave the harbour, the mulatto Pierre Munier and the negro Télémaque.

" M. Munier, we will climb the hill; we shall still be able to see Masters Jacques and Georges."

" Yes, you are right, my good Télémaque," cried Pierre Munier, " and if we do not see *them*, we shall at least see the ship that carries them."

And Pierre Munier, dashing off with the rapidity of a young man, in an instant had climbed the hill of the Discovery, from the height of which he could follow with his eyes, until it grew dark, not his *sons*, for the distance, as he had foreseen, was too great for him to distinguish them any longer, but the frigate *Bellone* on board which they had embarked.

In fact, Pierre Munier had resolved, cost him what it might, to sever himself from his children, and was sending them to France under the protection of the worthy General Decaen. Jacques and Georges started then for Paris with recommendations to two or three of the richest merchants in the capital, with whom Pierre Munier had for a long time had business relations. The pretext for their departure was to get their education. The real cause of their absence was the very evident hatred shown towards both of them by M. de Malmédie since the day of the flag incident, a hatred on account of which their poor father trembled, especially considering their known disposition, lest they should become the victims.

As for Henri, his mother was too fond of him to part from him. Besides, what did he want to learn? unless it was that every coloured man was born to respect and obey him.

Well, as we have seen, that was a thing Henri had already learned by heart.

CHAPTER IV
FOURTEEN YEARS LATER

THE day when a European vessel is signalled off the port is a general holiday in the Isle of France; for, long severed from the mother country, the majority of the inhabitants impatiently await news of their country, their families, and those beyond the seas; each hopes for something, and keeps his eyes fixed, directly she comes in sight, upon the maritime messenger which brings him the letter or the portrait of a friend, male or female, or it may be that friend himself or herself, in person. For this vessel, the object of so many desires and the source of so many hopes, is the over-sea chain joining Europe to Africa, the flying-bridge thrown from one world to the other. Accordingly, no news spreads so rapidly through the whole Island as that which issues from the peak of the Discovery, " A vessel in sight ! "

We say the peak of the Discovery, because in almost all cases the vessel, obliged to keep away to catch the east wind, passes in front of Grand Port, coasts along the land at the distance of two or three leagues, doubles the point of Quatre-Cocos, steers between the Ile Plate and the Coin-de-Mire, and some hours after, having cleared this passage, appears at the entrance of Port Louis, whose inhabitants, warned the previous day by the signals which have traversed the Island to announce its approach, await it in crowds that throng the quay.

After what has been said of the eagerness with which every one in the Isle of France awaits news from Europe, you will doubtless not be astonished at the crowd which one fine morning in the end of February, 1824, about eleven in the morning, assembled at every point from which they could see the entry into the harbour of Port Louis of the *Leicester*, a fine frigate of thirty-six guns, which had been signalled the day before at two in the afternoon.

We ask the reader's permission to introduce to him, or rather to renew his acquaintance, with two of the persons whom she carried on her deck.

The one was a man with fair hair, light complexion, blue eyes, regular features, and calm expression, a little above middle height, whom you would have set down as no more than thirty or thirty-two, but who was really more than forty. At first sight you saw nothing specially striking about him, though it must also be confessed his general appearance was very agreeable. If, after the first glance, you had any reason to continue the inspection, you remarked that he had small and beautifully shaped hands and feet, which in all countries, but especially in England, is a sign of good family. His voice was clear and distinct, but without modulation, and so to speak, unmusical. His sky-blue eyes, which might in ordinary circumstances be charged with want of expression, wandered with a clear glance which seemed to fasten on nothing in particular and to examine nothing deeply. From time to time, however, he blinked his eyes like one tired of the sunshine, accompanying this movement with a slight parting of the lips which exposed a double row of small, well-set teeth, white as pearls. This trick seemed to deprive his face of what little expression it possessed ; but, on looking at him carefully, you noticed, on the contrary, that it was at such moments that his quick and profound glance, darting a ray of fire between his contracted eyelids, probed the thought of his questioner to the very depths of his soul. Those who saw him for the first time seldom failed to take him for a man of no parts ; he knew that this was, in general, the superficial judgment which men formed of him, and almost always, whether designedly or through indifference, he was content to leave them in that opinion, quite sure of undeceiving them when it might suit his humour or when the proper moment should arrive. For this deceptive exterior concealed a singularly profound mind, just as sometimes two inches of snow will mask a precipice of a thousand feet ; so, with the consciousness of an almost universal superiority, he waited patiently till it was given the opportunity to triumph. Then, when he met with an opinion opposed to his own, and in the person giving vent to that opinion, a foeman worthy of his steel, he caught up the conversation which he had allowed to stray into a hundred capricious by-ways, gradually became animated and opened out, growing, as it were, to his full height ; for his harsh voice and blazing eyes ably supported his lively, incisive, and highly coloured speech, at once enticing and serious, dazzling and practical. If on the contrary this opportunity did not occur, he was quite satisfied, and continued to be looked upon by those who surrounded him as a commonplace person. Not that he lacked self-esteem ; on the contrary, he pushed his pride in certain matters to excess. But it was a plan of conduct imposed on himself, from which he never swerved. Every time that an erroneous proposition, a false idea, a badly supported conceit, in short, anything ridiculous, was stated in his presence, the extreme acuteness of his mind brought instantly to his tongue a smart sarcasm or to his lips a scornful smile. But he at once checked this sort of outward irony, and, when he could not entirely suppress the outburst of contempt, he concealed beneath one of those blinkings of the eyes which were habitual to him, the bantering expression which had escaped him in spite of himself, knowing well that the way to see and hear everything was to appear blind and deaf. Perhaps he would have wished, like Pope Sixtus V, to appear paralysed as well; but, as this would have entailed a too lengthy and tiring dissimulation, he had abandoned the idea.

The other was a dark young man of sallow complexion, with long black hair; his eyes, which were large, beautifully formed and velvety, had, behind the apparent softness which was due only to the continual preoccupation of his thoughts, a firmness of character which struck one from the first. If he became excited, which was but seldom, for his whole frame seemed to obey not the physical instincts but a moral force, then his eyes lighted up with an inward flame, the fire of which seemed to lie in the depths of his soul. Though the lines of his face seemed clear, they wanted regularity to a certain extent; his harmonious forehead, though vigorous and square in mould, was furrowed by a slight scar, almost imperceptible in the state of calmness which was habitual to him, but which betrayed itself by a white line when his face became red. A moustache, as dark as his hair and as regular as his eyebrows, shaded, while concealing its size, a mouth with strong lips and furnished with splendid teeth. The general aspect of his countenance was serious; by the wrinkles in his forehead, the almost perpetual frowning of the eyebrows, and the severity of all his features, might be recognized a deep reflection and an unshaken resolve. Accordingly, in contrast with his companion, whose features lacked character, and who, though forty years old, appeared scarcely thirty or thirty-two, he, who was hardly twenty-five, appeared nearly thirty. As to the rest of his person, he was of moderate height, but well-built; his limbs were all perhaps a trifle slender, but one felt that, when animated by any excitement, violent tension of nerve would supply them with strength. By way of compensation, one understood that nature had endowed him with activity and dexterity beyond what she had denied him in the way of clumsy vigour. For the rest, dressed almost always with an elegant simplicity, he wore at this moment trousers, waistcoat and frock-coat whose cut showed that they came from the hands of one of the best Parisian tailors, and in the buttonhole of his frock-coat he wore, knotted with elegant carelessness, the united ribbons of the Legion of Honour and of Charles III.

These two men had met on board the *Leicester*, which had taken aboard the one at Portsmouth, the other at Cadiz. At the first glance they had recognized the fact that they had already seen each other in the saloons of London and Paris, where one sees everybody ; they had greeted each other, therefore, as old acquaintances, but at first without speaking. For having never been introduced, both had been restrained by that aristocratic reserve of fashionable people who hesitate, even in special circumstances of life, to break through the general proprieties. However, the loneliness of the deck, the limited space within which they walked every day, the natural attraction two men of the world instinctively feel for one another, had soon brought them together. At first they had exchanged some trifling remarks, then their conversation had assumed a more serious character. After some days, each of the two had recognized his companion as a man out of the common, and congratulated himself at such a meeting on a three months' voyage ; then, after further waiting, they had become united by that friendship of circumstances which, without roots in the past, forms a distraction in the present, without creating any complication for the future. Then, during those long evenings under the equator, and fine tropical nights, they had had time to study each other, and both had recognized that in art, science and politics, they had, whether by inquiry or by experience, learnt all that it is given to man to know. Both had then remained constantly face to face like wrestlers of equal strength, and in this long voyage the first of these two men had gained but one single advantage

over the second, and that was when in a squall which struck
the frigate after doubling the Cape of Good Hope, and in
which the captain of the *Leicester*, injured by the fall of a
top-gallant-mast, had been carried swooning into his cabin,
the fair-haired passenger had seized the speaking-trumpet,
and, springing on the quarter-deck, had, in the absence
of the second in command, whom severe illness kept
prisoner in his berth, with the firmness of a man accustomed
to command and the knowledge of an accomplished sailor,
at once issued a series of orders which saved the vessel
from succumbing to the force of the hurricane. Then,
when the squall was over, his face, shining for a moment
with that sublime pride which mounts to the brow of
every human creature when struggling against his Creator,
had resumed its ordinary expression; his voice, the
stentorian tones of which had made themselves heard
above the roll of the thunder and the howling of the storm,
had sunk to its normal pitch. Lastly, with a gesture as
simple as the preceding ones had been romantic and exalted,
he had handed the second officer back the speaking-trumpet,
that sceptre of a master mariner which is, in the hands
of him who wields it, the token of absolute and undisputed
authority.

During all this time, his companion, on whose calm face,
let us hasten to say, it would have been impossible to detect
the least trace of emotion, had followed him with his eyes
with the envious expression of a man obliged to recognize
himself as inferior to him whose equal he had hitherto
thought himself. Then, when the danger being over, they
found themselves side by side again, he had contented
himself with saying :

" You have commanded a ship then, my Lord ? "

" Yes," the man to whom this title of honour had been
applied answered simply ; " I have even reached the rank
of Commodore, but six years ago I went into the diplomatic
service ; and at the moment of danger I recollected my old
profession ; that is all."

Then there had been no further talk between the two
men on the subject ; only it was clear that the younger
of the two was inwardly humiliated by this superiority which

his companion had in such unexpected fashion gained over
him, and which he would certainly have known nothing of
but for the incident which had in a way forced it into the
light of day. The question which we have reported and
the answer it evoked show, moreover, that during the three
months they had just spent together, neither of these men
had asked any question as to their respective social positions ; they had recognized each other as brothers in intelligence, and that had been enough for them. They knew
that the Isle of France was for both the object of their
journey, and they had asked nothing more. Both appeared
equally impatient to arrive, for both had given orders to
be told the moment the Island came in view. The order
was needless in the case of one of them, for the young man
with dark hair was on deck, leaning against the taffrail of
the poop, when the look-out man gave the cry, always so
spirit-stirring, even to sailors, of " Land ho ! "

At this cry, his companion appeared at the top of the
companion, and, advancing towards the young man with
a step more rapid than usual, came and leant beside him.

" Well, my Lord," said the latter, " we have arrived, so
at least they assure us ; for I confess to my shame that
I have scanned the horizon without observing anything
but a sort of haze which may quite as well be a mist floating
on the sea as an island that has its roots at the bottom
of the ocean."

" Yes, I dare say," said the elder man, " for it is only
with difficulty that even the sailor's eye can distinguish
with certainty, especially at such a distance, water from
sky, and land from clouds ; but I," he added, blinking his
eyes, " old sea dog that I am, perceive all the outlines of our
Island, I might even say all its details."

" Well, my Lord, that is a fresh superiority I recognize
in your Lordship over myself ; but I assure you it requires
that to assure me of such a thing, so as not to reject it
as incredible."

" Then take my glass," said the sailor, " while I with
the naked eye will describe the coast to you ; will you
believe me then ? "

" My Lord," said the doubter, " I consider you in everything a man so superior to others that I believe what you tell me, you may rest assured, without your needing to add any proof to your words. If I take the glass which you offer me, it is rather to satisfy a longing of my heart than a desire of my curiosity."

" Come, come," said the fair-haired man, laughing ; " I see that the land air is taking its effect, you are becoming a flatterer."

" I a flatterer, my Lord ? " said the young man, shaking his head. " Oh ! your Lordship is mistaken. The *Leicester*, I assure you, might make a voyage farther than from pole to pole and sail round the world more than once before you would see me so changed. No, my Lord, I do not flatter you, I only thank you for the gracious kindness you have shown me throughout this interminable voyage, I will venture almost to say the friendship which your Lordship has evidenced towards an unknown person like me."

" My dear comrade," answered the Englishman, holding out his hand to the young man, " I hope that for you as for me there are no people in the world ' unknown ' except vulgarians, fools, and rogues ; but I hope also that for the one as for the other of us every superior man is a relation whom we recognize as belonging to our family, wherever we meet him. That granted, a truce to compliments, my young friend ; take this glass and look ; for we are drawing near so rapidly that there will soon be no merit in accomplishing the little lesson in geography which I have undertaken to give you."

The young man took the spy-glass and put it to his eye.

" Can you make it out ? " asked the Englishman.

" Perfectly," said the young man.

" Do you see on our extreme right, like a cone rising out of the sea, the solitary *Ile Ronde* ? "

" Wonderfully clearly."

" Do you see closer to us the *Ile Plate*, below which is passing at this moment a brig, which from her shape has to me all the look of a man-of-war ? This evening we shall be where she is, and shall pass where she is passing."

The young man put down the glass and tried to see with the naked eye the objects which his companion made out so easily, and which he himself saw with difficulty by the aid of the telescope he held in his hand. Then he said with a smile of astonishment:

" It is marvellous ! "

And he put up the glass to his eye again.

" Do you see the *Coin-de-Mire*," continued his companion, " which, from here, is almost undistinguishable from *Cap Malheureux*, of sad and poetic memory ?   Do you see the *Piton de Bambou*, behind which rises the mountain of *La Faïence* ? Do you see the hill of Grand Port; and there, do you see on its left the *Morne des Créoles* ? "

" Yes, yes, I see it all and recognize it, for all the peaks and summits are familiar to me from childhood, and I have kept them in my memory religiously ; but," continued the young man, pushing together with the palm of his hand the three tubes of the spy-glass, " this is not the first time that you have seen this coast, and there is more of memory than of actual sight in the description you have just given me."

" True," said the Englishman, smiling, " and I see that there is no means of practising trickery on you. Yes, I have already seen this coast.

" Yes, I speak to some extent from memory, though the recollections which it has left me are probably less tender than those which it recalls to you. Yes, I came here at a time when, in all probability, we were enemies, my dear companion, for it was fourteen years ago."

" That is just the time when I left the Isle of France," replied the dark-haired young man.

" Were you still there at the time of the sea fight that took place at Grand Port, and to which I ought not to allude, from a feeling of national pride, considering what a fine beating we got there ? "

" Oh ! speak of it, my Lord, speak of it," interrupted the young man ; " you have so often taken your revenge, you English, that there is almost pride in your confessing to a defeat."

" Well, that was the time I visited the Island ; for I was serving then in the navy."

" As Midshipman, no doubt ? "

" As Lieutenant of the frigate, sir."

" But at that time, allow me to say, my Lord, you were a child."

" What age do you put me at, sir ? "

" Why, I should think we are nearly of the same age, and you are scarcely thirty."

" I am just forty," replied the Englishman, smiling; " I was quite right in saying just now that you were in a flattering vein."

The young man was astonished, and looked at his companion with more attention than he had hitherto paid him, and noticed, by the slight wrinkles at the corners of his eyes and mouth, that he might actually be the age he declared himself, and which he was so far from appearing to be. Then, leaving his investigation to return to the question which had been put to him, he went on :

" Yes, yes, I remember that battle and also another which took place at the opposite end of the island—Do you know Port Louis, my Lord ? "

" No, sir, I only know this side of the coast. I was dangerously wounded at the battle of Grand Port, and carried as prisoner to Europe. Since that time I have not revisited the Indian seas, where I shall now probably make an indefinite stay."

Then, as though the last words that they had exchanged had just aroused in the two men a source of inward memories, each moved away mechanically and disappeared to meditate in silence, one at the bows, the other at the stern.

It was the day after this conversation that, having rounded the *Ile d'Ambre* and passed at the predicted hour at the foot of the *Ile Plate*, the frigate *Leicester*, as we pointed out at the beginning of this chapter, made her entrance into the harbour of Port Louis, in the midst of the customary crowd which welcomed the arrival of every European vessel.

Of course, the fair-haired Englishman was no other than Lord Murray, member of the Upper House, who after being in turn sailor and ambassador, had just been nominated Governor of the Isle of France by His Britannic Majesty.

We invite the reader, then, to recognize in him the young lieutenant of whom he got a glimpse on board the *Nereïd*, lying at the feet of his uncle, Captain Willoughby, wounded in the side by a discharge of grape, and of whom we announced not only the recovery, but also the approaching reappearance as one of the chief characters of our story.

At the moment of separating from his companion, Lord Murray turned to him and said :

" By the by, sir, in three days I am giving a banquet to the authorities of the Island ; I hope that you will do me the honour of being one of my guests."

" With the greatest pleasure, my Lord," answered the young man ; " but, before I accept, it is right that I should tell your Lordship who I am."

" Your name will be announced when you come in, sir," replied Lord Murray, " and then I shall know who you are ; meanwhile, I know what you are worth, and that is all I want."

Then, giving his travelling companion a shake of the hand and a smile, the new Governor passed down with the Captain to the barge of honour, which shoved off from the ship's side, and impelled by the arms of ten stout oarsmen, soon landed at the fountain of the *Chien-de-Plomb.*

As the Governor landed, a Guard of Honour presented arms, the drums beat a salute, the guns of the forts and the frigate roared simultaneously, and those of the other ships answered them like an echo ; immediately universal shouts of " Long live Lord Murray ! " joyously welcomed the new Governor, who, after graciously saluting those who gave him this honourable reception, went off to his palace, surrounded by the chief authorities of the Island. And yet, these men who thus fêted the representative of His Britannic Majesty and applauded his arrival, were the same men who had formerly lamented the departure of the French. But fourteen years, it is true, had elapsed since that time ; the older generation had partly disappeared, and the new generation only cherished the recollection of the past in ostentation, and as one cherishes an old family pedigree. Fourteen years had elapsed, as we have already said, and that is more than are required in order to forget the death of one's best friend, to violate an oath sworn ; more than are required, in short, for killing, burying, or changing the name of a great man or a great nation.

CHAPTER V
THE PRODIGAL SON

ALL eyes had followed Lord Murray to Government House ; but, when the door of the palace had closed on him and those who surrounded him, all eyes were directed to the ship.

At this moment the young man with dark hair disembarked in his turn, and the curiosity of which the Governor had just been the object, was transferred to him. As a matter of fact, they had seen Lord Murray talking graciously to him and shaking his hand ; so that the assembled crowd decided, with its usual sagacity, that this stranger was some young nobleman belonging to the aristocracy of France or England. This probability had changed to an absolute certainty at the sight of the double ribbon which adorned his buttonhole, one of which ribbons, it must be · confessed, was a little less widely distributed at that period than it is to-day. For the rest, the inhabitants of Port Louis had time to examine the new arrival ; for, after casting his eyes around him as though he had expected to find some of his friends or relations on the pier, he had waited on the quay while the Governor's horses were being disembarked ; then, when this operation was over, a servant of a tawny complexion, dressed in the costume of the African Moors, with whom the stranger had exchanged some words in an unknown tongue, saddled two horses in Arabian fashion, and leading both of them by their bridles, for their legs, stiffened by long confinement, could not yet be trusted, followed his master who had already started on foot towards the street, looking all round him as though he had expected a friendly face to appear suddenly amid all these, to him, unmeaning countenances.

Among the groups awaiting the strangers at the spot characteristically known as *La Pointe-aux-Blagueurs* or " Idlers' Corner," was one in the midst of which stood a man of from fifty to fifty-four, with hair that was turning grey, common features, rasping voice, and pointed whiskers which joined the corner of his mouth on either side, together with a handsome young fellow of twenty-five or six. The elder was dressed in a frock-coat of maroon merino, nankeen trousers and a waistcoat of white piqué. The younger man, whose features were a little more marked than those of his neighbour, but still bore such a resemblance to them that it was clear these two individuals were connected by the closest ties of relationship, wore a grey hat, a silk handkerchief knotted carelessly about his neck, and white waistcoat and trousers.

" My word, there's a nice-looking young fellow," said the stout man, looking at the stranger who was passing close to him at the moment, " and if he is going to remain in the Island, I advise the husbands and mothers to look after their wives and daughters."

" That's a fine horse," said the young man, putting an eyeglass in his eye, " of the very purest Arab blood, if I am not mistaken ; an Arab of the Arabs."

"Do you know this gentleman, Henri?" asked the stout man.

" No, father, but if he wants to sell his horse, I know who will give him a thousand dollars for it."

" And that is Henri de Malmédie, is it not, my son ? and, if you like the horse, you will do well to indulge your fancy for it ; you can afford it, you are rich."

No doubt the stranger heard Henri's offer and the approval given it by his father, for his lip curled contemptuously as he gave father and son alternately a haughty glance that was not without menace ; then, better informed, no doubt, as regards them than they were about him, he passed on murmuring, " Those people again ! there's no escaping them ! "

" What does that dandy want with us ? " asked M. de Malmédie of those who surrounded him."

" I don't know, father," answered Henri ; " but the first time we meet him, if he looks at us in the same fashion, I promise you I'll ask him."

" Why, Henri," said M. de Malmédie with an air of pity for the stranger's ignorance, " the poor young fellow does not know who we are."

" Well, then, I will teach him," murmured Henri.

During this interval the stranger, whose look of contempt had aroused this threatening dialogue, had continued his

way to the Rampart without showing any uneasiness at
the impression which his passing had produced, and without
condescending to turn round to see its effect. When he
had gone about a third of the way along the *Jardin de la
Compagnie*, his attention was attracted by a group of persons
standing on a small bridge which connected the garden
with the courtyard of a fine-looking house. In the centre
of this group was a charming girl of fifteen or sixteen, and
the stranger, who was no doubt a man of artistic tastes
and therefore a lover of beauty in all forms, stopped in
order to get a better look at her. Although she was at her
very door-step, the girl, who no doubt belonged to one of
the wealthiest families in the Island, was accompanied by
a European governess, evidently an Englishwoman, from
her long fair hair and the clearness of her skin, while an old
grey-haired negro in a suit of white dimity held himself
in readiness, with eyes fixed on his young mistress, and foot
uplifted, so to speak, to carry out her slightest orders.

Perhaps, too, as everything is heightened by contrast,
her beauty, which we have described as wonderful, was
increased still further by the ugliness of the person who stood
dumb and motionless in front of her, and with whom she
was endeavouring to enter into business negotiations in
respect of one of those charming fans of carved ivory,
transparent and fragile as lace-work.

The man who was talking to her was bony in frame, of
a yellow complexion, with eyes raised at the corners, and a
broad-brimmed straw hat on his head, from which hung,
like a sample of the hair with which the skull that it shaded
was presumably covered, a long plait which came down to
the middle of his back; he was dressed in blue cotton
drawers, reaching to his knees, and a blouse of the same
material coming half-way down his thighs. At his feet
was a bamboo cane, six feet in length, supporting at each
of its extremities a basket, the weight of which made this
long cane bend like a bow when its middle rested on the
dealer's shoulders. These baskets were filled with the
numerous little knick-knacks which alike in the colonies
as in France, in the open-air bazaars of the tropics as in
the elegant shops of Alphonse Giroux and Susse, turn the

heads of girls and sometimes even of their mothers. Well, as we have said, the beautiful Creole, in the midst of all these wonders spread out on a mat stretched at her feet, had stopped for a moment at a fan representing houses, pagodas, and impossible palaces, dogs, lions, and fantastic birds ; in short, a thousand figures of men, animals and buildings that had no existence save in the very lively imagination of the inhabitant of Canton and Pekin. She was asking then purely and simply the price of this fan. But there lay the difficulty. The Chinaman, who had landed only a few days before, didn't know a single word of French, English, or Italian, and this ignorance was clearly responsible for his failure to reply to the question which had been put to him in these three languages successively. This ignorance was already so well known in the colony that the inhabitant of the banks of the Yellow River was alluded to at Port Louis merely by the name of Miko-Miko, the only two words which he uttered while going along the streets of the town, carrying his long bamboo loaded with baskets, first on one shoulder, then on the other, and which in all probability meant " Buy, buy." The relationship hitherto established between Miko-Miko and his customers was purely and simply that of gestures and signs. As the beautiful girl had never had occasion to make a profound study of the language of the Abbé de l'Epée, she found it absolutely impossible to understand Miko-Miko or to make herself understood by him.

It was at this moment that the stranger approached her. " Excuse me, Mademoiselle," he began, " but, seeing you are in a difficulty, I presume to offer you my services : can I be of use to you in any way, and will you condescend to employ me as interpreter ? "

" Oh, Monsieur," replied the governess, while the young girl's cheeks were covered with a layer of the finest pink, " I am grateful a thousand times for your offer, for Mademoiselle Sara and myself have in the last ten minutes exhausted our philological knowledge without succeeding in making this man understand us. We have spoken to him by turns in French, English and Italian, and he has answered to none of those languages."

"Perhaps Monsieur is acquainted with some language that this man can speak, Henrietta dear," said the young girl; "and I want this fan so much that, if Monsieur succeeds in finding out the price, he will have done me a real service."

"But you see it is impossible," answered Henrietta; "the man talks no language."

"At least he talks that of the country where he was born," said the stranger.

"Yes, but he is a Chinaman; and who can speak Chinese?"

The stranger smiled, and, turning to the dealer, spoke some words in a foreign tongue.

We should try in vain to describe the astonishment that came over the features of poor Miko-Miko, when the accents of his mother tongue sounded in his ears like the echo of distant music. He dropped the fan which he held, and, staring open-mouthed at the man who had just addressed him, seized his hand and kissed it several times; then, as the stranger repeated the question that he had already put to him, he at last decided to answer. But it was with an expression in his look and a tone of voice that formed one of the strangest contrasts imaginable; for with the most affected and sentimental air possible he told him quite simply the price of the fan.

"It is twenty pounds sterling, Mademoiselle," said the stranger, turning to the girl, "about ninety dollars."

"A thousand thanks, sir," answered Sara, blushing once more. Then, turning to her governess, "Is it not really most fortunate, dear Henrietta," she went on in English, "that Monsieur speaks this man's language?"

"And also most surprising," said Henrietta.

"And yet it is very simple, ladies," answered the stranger in the same language. "My mother died before I was three months old, and I was given as nurse a woman from the Island of Formosa, who was in the service of our house. So her language was the first that I prattled, and, though I have not often had occasion to speak it, I have, as you have seen, retained some words, for which I shall congratulate myself all my life, since, thanks to those words, I have been able to render you a slight service."

Then, slipping into the Chinaman's hand a Spanish doubloon, and, signing to his servant to follow him, the young man went off, saluting Mademoiselle Sara and her friend Henrietta with perfect grace.

The stranger took the road to Moka ; but he had hardly gone a mile on the road leading to Pailles and reached the foot of Discovery Hill, when he suddenly stopped, and his eyes fastened on a bench placed half-way up the ascent, on which was seated an old man perfectly motionless, his hands resting on his knees and his eyes fixed on the sea. For a moment the stranger surveyed this man with a doubtful air ; then, as if this hesitation had given way to an absolute conviction, he murmured :

" It is he, I am certain ; great heavens ! how changed he is ! " Then, after looking at the old man with an air of remarkable interest, the young man took a path by which he might approach him without being seen, a plan which he carried out successfully, after stopping twice or thrice on the way and placing his hand on his breast, as if to give a strong emotion time to calm down.

As for the old man, he did not stir at the approach of the stranger, so that it might have been thought that he had not even heard the sound of his step ; but this would have been a mistake, for scarcely had the young man sat down upon the same bench than he turned his head towards him and, saluting him in a timid manner, got up and began to walk away.

" Oh ! don't disturb yourself for me, sir," said the young man.

The old man at once sat down, no longer in the middle of the seat but at its extremity.

Then a moment's silence ensued between the old man who continued to gaze at the sea, and the stranger who looked at the old man.

At last, after five minutes of silent and deep contemplation, the stranger spoke :

" Sir," said he to his neighbour, " doubtless you were not down at the harbour just now when the *Leicester* came to anchor there—about an hour and a half ago ? "

" Pardon me, I was not there, sir," answered the old

man in a tone of mingled humility and astonishment.

" Then," resumed the young man, " you took no interest in the arrival of this vessel from Europe ? "

" Why so, sir ? " said the old man with increasing astonishment.

" Because in that case, instead of stopping here, you would have gone like everybody else down to the harbour."

" You are wrong, sir, you are wrong," replied the old man sadly, shaking his white head ; " on the contrary I take, I am certain of it, a greater interest than any one in this sight. Every time a ship has arrived, no matter from what country, I have come for fourteen years to see if it does not bring me a letter from my children, or even my children themselves. And, as it would tire me too much to remain standing, I seat myself here in the morning at the same spot from which I saw them depart ; and I remain here the whole day until, when every one has gone away, I have given up all hope."

" But why do you not go down yourself to the harbour ? " asked the stranger.

" So I did during the first years," replied the old man ; " but then I learned my fate too quickly ; and, as each fresh disappointment became too painful, I ended by staying here and sending my negro Télémaque in my place. In this way hope lasts longer. If he comes back quickly, I think he brings me word of their arrival ; if he is slow in returning, I think he is waiting for a letter. He comes back most times with empty hands. Then I get up and go back alone as I came ; I enter my deserted house and pass the night in tears, saying to myself, no doubt it will be the next time."

" Poor father ! " murmured the stranger.

" You pity me, sir ? " asked the old man with astonishment.

" Certainly, I pity you," answered the young one.

" You do not know then who I am ? "

" You are a man, and you suffer."

" But I am a mulatto," answered the old man in a low and profoundly humble tone.

A deep blush passed over the young man's forehead.

" And I, too, sir, am a mulatto," he answered.

" You ? " cried the old man.

" Yes," answered the stranger.

" You a mulatto ? " and the old man looked with astonishment at the red and blue ribbon knotted in the stranger's frock-coat. " You a mulatto ? Oh ! then I am not surprised at your pity. I had taken you for a white; but, since you are a man of colour like myself, it becomes another thing at once ; you are a friend, a brother."

" Yes, a friend, a brother," said the stranger, extending both his hands to the old man.

Then he murmured under his breath, looking at him with an indescribable expression of tenderness, " and even more than that, perhaps."

" Then I can tell you everything," the old man went on. " Ah ! I feel that to speak of my sorrow will do me good. Picture to yourself, sir, that I have, or rather had, for God only knows if both are still alive—picture to yourself that I had two children, two sons, both of whom I loved with a father's love, one especially."

The stranger gave a start and came closer to the old man.

" Oh ! if you had known them both," he continued, " you would have understood that. It is not that Georges —his name was Georges—was the most handsome : on the contrary, his brother Jacques was a finer lad than he ; but he had in his poor little body a mind so intelligent, so keen, so resolute, that, had I put him to the College at Port Louis with the other boys, I am quite certain that, although he was only twelve, he would soon have left all the other scholars behind."

The old man's eyes shone for an instant with pride and enthusiasm, but this change passed with the swiftness of lightning, and his look had already resumed its vague, timid, dull expression when he added :

" But I could not put him to school here. The College was founded for whites, and we are only mulattoes."

The young man's countenance brightened in turn, and a flame, as it were of contempt and fierce anger, passed over his face.

The old man continued without even noticing the feeling displayed by the stranger.

"That is why I sent them both to France in the hope that education would settle the roving propensities of the elder, and subdue the too self-willed character of the younger. But it seems that God did not approve my resolve; for, in a visit that he made to Brest, Jacques embarked on a privateer, and I have only heard from him three times since, and each time from a different quarter of the world; while Georges in growing up has allowed the germ of self-will which alarmed me in him to develop. He has written to me more often, sometimes from England, sometimes from Egypt, sometimes from Spain, for he too has travelled a great deal, and, though his letters are very good, I assure you I have not ventured to show them to any one."

"Then neither of them has ever mentioned to you the date of his return?"

"Never; and who knows even if I shall ever see them again; for though, on my part, the moment when I saw them once more would be the happiest of my life, I have never spoken to them of returning. If they stay away, it is because they are happier there than they would be here; if they do not feel a desire to see their old father again, it is because they have found people in Europe whom they love better than him. So let them have their wish, especially if that wish can lead them to happiness. Still, though I regret them both, it is Georges I miss especially, and it is he who causes me the most grief by never alluding to his return."

"If he does not speak of his return, sir," replied the stranger in a tone from which he vainly tried to repress the emotion, "it is perhaps because he is reserving for himself the pleasure of surprising you, and that he wishes you to conclude in happiness a day begun in expectation."

"God grant it!" said the old man, lifting his eyes and hands to heaven.

"Perhaps it is," continued the young man in tones of increased emotion, "that he wishes to creep up to you without being recognized by you, and so to enjoy your presence, your love, and your blessing."

"Ah! it would be impossible for me not to recognize him."

" And yet," cried the young man, unable to resist any longer the feeling which agitated him, " you have not recognized me, father ! "

" You ! you ! " exclaimed the old man, devouring the stranger with an eager glance, while he trembled in all his limbs, his mouth half open and smiling doubtfully. Then, shaking his head :

" No, no," said he, " it is not Georges ; there is some resemblance between you and him ; but he is not tall, not handsome like you ; he is but a child, and you are a man."

" It is I, father ; it is I ; you must recognize me," cried Georges ; " remember that fourteen years have passed since I have seen you ; remember that I am now twenty-six, and if you doubt, here, look at this scar on my forehead, the mark of the blow which M. de Malmédie gave me the day when you so gloriously captured an English flag. Oh ! father, open your arms, and, when you have embraced me and pressed me to your heart, you will no longer doubt that I am your son."

And with these words the stranger threw himself on the neck of the old man, who, looking now at the sky, now at his child, could not believe in so much happiness, and only made up his mind to embrace the handsome young man when the latter had repeated for the twentieth time that he was really Georges.

At this moment Télémaque appeared at the bottom of the hill of *La Découverte*, his arms hanging down, his eyes mournful and his head drooping, grieved that he was returning once more to his master without bringing him any news of either of his children.

CHAPTER VI

A TRANSFORMATION

AND now our readers must allow us to leave father and son to the enjoyment of reunion, and consent to go back with us over the past, and trace the physical and moral transformation which had taken place during the space of fourteen years in the hero of our tale, of whom

3

we have given them a glimpse as a child and whom we have just shown them as a man.

We had at first intended to put before our readers' eyes purely and simply the history which Georges gave his father of the events of these fourteen years ; but we reflected that, this story being entirely one of inmost thoughts and private feelings, the veracity of a man of Georges' character, especially when that man speaks about himself, might with good reason be distrusted. We have determined, therefore, to relate the facts, with every detail of which we are acquainted personally, and in our own way, promising beforehand, since our own self-esteem is not concerned in the matter, to conceal no feeling, whether good or bad, no thought, whether creditable or disgraceful.

Let us start then from the same point from which Georges himself had started.

Pierre Munier, whose character we have tried to describe, had, from the time that he first entered on active life, that is to say, from the time that he changed from boyhood to manhood, adopted a system of conduct towards the whites from which he had never swerved ; feeling neither the strength nor the wish to combat as a duellist an overwhelming prejudice, he had formed the resolve of disarming his enemies by an unalterable submission and an inexhaustible humility, his whole life was occupied in apologizing for his birth. Far from soliciting, in spite of his wealth and intelligence, any public office or political employment, he had constantly tried to efface himself by losing himself in the crowd ; the same motive which had withdrawn him from public life guided him in his private capacity. By nature generous and magnificent, he regulated his house with an almost monastic simplicity. There was abundance everywhere, but a total absence of luxury, though he had nearly two hundred slaves, which constitutes in the Colonies a fortune of nearly two hundred thousand pounds per annum. He went about always on horseback until forced by age, or rather by the troubles which had broken him down before his time, to exchange this modest custom for a more aristocratic one, he bought a palanquin quite as unpretending as that of the poorest inhabitant of the Island. Always careful to avoid the slightest quarrel, always polite, agreeable, obliging to everybody, even to those whom, at the bottom of his heart, he disliked, he would rather have lost ten acres of land than commence or even sustain a lawsuit which might have gained him twenty acres. If any inhabitant wanted plants of coffee, manioc or sugar-cane, he was sure of getting them from Pierre Munier, who even thanked him for giving him the preference. Well, all this good behaviour, which proceeded from the instincts of his excellent heart, but which might have appeared to be the result of his timid disposition, had doubtless gained for him the goodwill of his neighbours, yet merely a passive friendliness which, never having included the idea of doing him good, was limited purely and simply to doing him no harm. Still, there were some among them who, unable to pardon Pierre Munier his immense fortune, his numerous slaves and spotless reputation, tried constantly to crush him beneath the prejudice of colour. M. de Malmédie and his son were of that number.

Georges, born in the same condition as his father, but whose weakness of constitution had debarred him from physical exercise, had directed all his mental faculties to reflection, and precocious beyond his age, as weakly children generally are, had observed instinctively his father's conduct, the motives of which he had penetrated while still young ; and the manly pride which surged in the child's breast had caused him to hate the whites who despised him, as well as the mulattoes who allowed themselves to be despised. Accordingly, he firmly resolved to follow a line of conduct precisely the opposite of that which his father had observed, and, when he had grown big and strong, to advance vigorously and boldly to confront these ridiculous sentimental prejudices, and, if they did not give way before him, to seize them by the body as Hercules did Antæus, and crush them in his arms. Did not the youthful Hannibal, at his father's instigation, vow eternal hatred against a nation ? Well, the youthful Georges, in spite of his father, swore war to the death against a prejudice.

Georges quitted the Colony after the scene that we have related, arrived in France with his brother, and entered

the Collège Napoléon. Hardly was he seated on the benches
of the lowest class before he grasped the difference of
ranks and wished to reach the top : for him, superiority
was a necessity of his organization ; he learnt quickly and
well. A first success strengthened his desire by giving him
the measure of his capabilities. His desire became stronger
and his successes greater. True this mental work, and this
development of his thoughts, left his body in its primitive
state of feebleness, the moral absorbed the physical, the
steel wore away the scabbard ; but God had given a support
to the tender plant. Georges enjoyed peace under the
protection of Jacques, who was the strongest and idlest
fellow in his class, as Georges was the hardest worker and
the weakest. ·

Unfortunately, this state of things did not last long. Two
years after their arrival, when Jacques and Georges had
gone to spend their holidays at Brest with a business
correspondent of their father's to whom they had been
recommended, Jacques, who had always had a decided
liking for the sea, profited by the opportunity which offered
and, weary of his prison, as he termed the College, embarked
on a privateer, which he described to his father, in a letter
he wrote him, as a Government vessel. On his return to
school Georges felt his brother's absence cruelly. Without
protection against the jealousy which his scholastic triumph
had aroused, and which, from the moment that it could be
gratified, turned into absolute hatred, he was insulted by
some, beaten by others, ill-treated by all ; each had his
favourite torture for him. It was a rough experience
which Georges endured bravely.

Only, he reflected more deeply than ever on his position
and realized that moral superiority was nothing without
physical superiority ; that the one was required to make
the other respected, and that only the union of these two
qualities made a man complete. From this time he changed
his manner of life completely ; from being the timid
retiring, inactive creature that he had been, he became
playful, noisy and rowdy. He still worked pretty hard
but only sufficiently so to maintain the intellectual pre
eminence he had gained in the preceding years. At the

start he was clumsy and they made fun of him. Georges took their mockery in bad part, and that of set purpose. He had not by nature the courage of hot temper, but that of brooding anger ; that is to say, his first impulse, instead of throwing him into danger, was to make him retire in order to avoid it. He needed reflection to make him act bravely, and, though this bravery is the most real, since it is moral bravery, he was afraid of it as though it were an act of cowardice. He fought then on every quarrel—or rather he was beaten ; but, though beaten once, he started afresh every day until he proved victorious, not because he was the stronger, but because he was the better disciplined. For in the thick of the most stubborn fight he preserved an admirable coolness, and, thanks to this coolness, profited by the least mistake on the part of his antagonist. This gained him respect, and his schoolfellows began to think twice before insulting him ; for, however weak an enemy may be, you hesitate to enter into a contest with him when you know he is determined. Besides, the prodigious ardour with which he embraced this new kind of life bore its fruit ; Georges gradually gained strength, and, encouraged by his first attempts, never opened a book during the next holidays, but began to learn to swim and ride, continually inflicting fatigue upon himself—fatigue which more than once threw him into a fever, but to which in the end he grew accustomed. Next to exercises of skill he added feats of strength ; for whole days he dug like a labourer, and carried loads like a workman, then, in the evening, instead of lying warm and comfortable in his bed, he wrapped himself in his cloak, threw himself on a bearskin mat, and so slept all night. For an instant nature hesitated in amazement, not knowing if she should give in or win the day. Georges felt that he was risking his life, but what did his life matter unless it brought him the strength and skill that would give him superiority over others ? Nature proved victorious ; physical weakness, vanquished by energy of will, disappeared like a faithless servant dismissed by an implacable master. In short, three months of this system so set up the weakly lad that on his return his comrades scarcely recognized him. Then it was he who sought out

quarrels with others, and who thrashed in his turn those
who had so often thrashed him. Then it was he who was
feared, and who, being feared, was respected. Besides,
in proportion as his bodily strength developed, the beauty
of his countenance increased in harmony with it. Georges
had always possessed fine eyes and perfect teeth ; he
allowed his long black hair to grow, and by dint of care
reduced its natural coarseness, making it supple by constant
use of the scissors. His unhealthy pallor was replaced by a
fine morbidezza, suggestive of melancholy and distinction ;
in short he made a study of becoming handsome as a man,
just as he had made a study of becoming strong and skilful
as a boy.

So, when Georges, after having completed his course of
philosophy, left College, he was a graceful young fellow,
five feet four in height, and, as we have said, though a
trifle slim, very well proportioned. He knew almost everything that a young man of the world ought to know. But
he realized that it was not enough to possess in all respects
the power of the average man ; he determined to surpass
him in all respects.

Besides, the course of training which he had determined
to undergo became easy to him, now that he was set free
from the routine of school work and henceforth master of
his own time. He laid down rules for the employment of
his day, from which he resolved never to deviate ; he rode
every morning at six ; at eight, he practised pistol-shooting ;
from ten to twelve, fencing ; from twelve to two, attended
University lectures ; sketched, from three to five, sometimes in one studio, sometimes in another ; his evenings
he spent at the theatre or in society, where all doors were
open to him, less on account of his wealth than of his charming manners.

Georges accordingly became intimate with all the best
known artists, literary men, and leaders of society in Paris ;
connoisseur alike in art, science, and fashion, he was soon
cited as one of the most intelligent minds, as one of the
most logical thinkers, as well as one of the most charming
squires-of-dames in the capital. Georges had almost
attained his ambition.

There remained, however, a final experiment for him to make. Certain of his mastery over others, he did not yet know if he was master of himself. Now, Georges was not the man to remain in doubt on any point whatever ; he resolved to be enlightened on the question of self-mastery. Georges had often dreaded becoming a gambler.

One day he went to Frascati's with his pockets full of gold, having said to himself, " I will play three times, each time for three hours, and during those three hours I will risk ten thousand francs ; when the three hours are up, I will leave off, whether I have won or lost."

The first day Georges lost his ten thousand francs in an hour and a half. He spent the rest of his three hours, however, in watching the others, and though he had bank-notes in his pocket-book for the twenty thousand francs which he had decided to risk in the two remaining attempts, he did not put upon the table a louis more than he had in the first instance intended to.

On the second day, he started by winning twenty-five thousand francs ; then, as he had meant to play for three hours, he went on, and lost all his winnings, besides two thousand francs of his original capital. At that moment, noticing that his three hours had expired, he left off with the same punctuality as the day before.

On the third day, he began by losing ; but, with his last bank-note, luck changed and declared in his favour ; he had three-quarters of an hour left, during which he played with one of those curious runs of luck which frequenters of the saloons perpetuate by tradition. During these three-quarters of an hour Georges seemed to have made a compact with the devil, by whose aid an invisible sprite whispered to him beforehand the colour which would turn up and the winning card. The pile of gold and notes in front of him mounted up to the astonishment of the onlookers. Georges left off calculating, and threw his money on the table, saying to the banker, " Put it where you please." The banker staked it at random, and still Georges won. Two professional gamblers, who had followed his luck and won enormous sums, thought the moment had arrived to take the opposite line, and accordingly laid against him ; but

fortune remained faithful to Georges. They lost all they
had won, as well as all the money they had about them ;
then, as they were known as safe customers, the banker
lent them fifty thousand francs, which they also lost.

Georges watched his heap of gold and notes increasing
without betraying by his features the slightest trace of
excitement, merely glancing now and then at the clock
which would sound the hour for him to cease playing. At
last the time arrived. Georges left off at once, handed his
winnings to his servant, and with the same calmness, the
same sang-froid, with which he had played, whether winning
or losing, went out, an object of envy to all who had witnessed the scene that had just taken place, and who fully
expected to see him come back next day.

But contrary to everybody's expectation, Georges did
not appear again. Nay more ; he shovelled the gold and
notes into a drawer of his desk, determining not to open
the drawer for a week. When the day arrived, Georges
opened the drawer and counted his winnings; they amounted
to two hundred and thirty thousand francs.

Georges was well satisfied with himself ; he had overcome a passion.

Georges had the strong sensual passions of men who live
in tropical countries.

One evening after an orgy, some of his friends took him
to the house of a courtesan celebrated for her beauty and
capricious likes and dislikes. On this particular evening
this modern Laïs was seized with a virtuous fit. The evening was spent in edifying conversation ; the lady of the
house might have passed for a candidate for the *Prix
Montyon*. The eyes, however, of the fair preacher might
have been seen occasionally fixed on Georges with an
expression of eager desire which belied the coldness of her
words. Georges, on his side, thought her even more attrac-
tive than she had been described to him, and for three days
the recollection of this seductive Astarté haunted the young
man's maiden fancy. On the fourth day Georges took the
road to the house where she lived, and, with his heart beating loudly, pulled the bell so violently that the rope nearly
broke in his hand. Then, hearing the footsteps of the maid

approaching, he bade his heart stop beating and his face look unconcerned, and in tones in which not the slightest trace of emotion was apparent, asked the servant to conduct him to her mistress. The latter, hearing his voice, sprang to him with joy; for Georges' image, the sight of which had made a deep impression on her the moment she saw it, had never left her mind since. She hoped, then, that love, or at any rate lust, was bringing back this handsome young fellow, who had so captivated her fancy.

She was mistaken; Georges had determined to put himself to a further trial; he had come there to make a will of iron give battle to his ardent feelings. For two hours he remained with the woman, alleging a wager as the excuse for his want of passion, wrestling against the torrent of his desires and the caresses of the siren; then, after two hours he went away, having come off victorious in this second trial, as he had done in the first.

Georges was well satisfied with himself; he had subdued his feelings.

We have said that Georges did not possess the physical courage which rushes into the midst of danger, but only the brooding courage that waits until it cannot avoid it. Georges feared that he was not really brave, and had often trembled at the notion that, if danger threatened, he might not be sure of himself and might, in fact, behave perhaps like a coward. This idea troubled him greatly; so he resolved to seize the first opportunity that offered to pit his mind against danger. The opportunity presented itself in a curious manner.

One day Georges was at Lepage's with a friend of his, and, while waiting till there was a vacant place, watched the performance of a frequenter of the establishment, who, like himself, was acknowledged to be one of the best pistol-shots in Paris.

The man who was practising at this moment was performing nearly all the incredible tricks of skill attributed by tradition to Saint-George and which are the despair of the neophyte; that is to say, he hit the bull's eye every time, repeated his shots so that the second mark exactly covered the first, sliced a bullet on the edge of a knife, and performed many other similar feats without a single failure. It should be said that the presence of Georges acted as a further incentive to his efforts, for the attendant when handing him his pistol had whispered to him that Georges was quite as skilful a shot as himself, the result being that he surpassed himself at each turn, but without winning from his rival the praise he undoubtedly deserved, for, in answer to the applause from the gallery, Georges merely observed :

" Oh ! he shoots well, of course, but firing at a target is a very different thing from firing at a man."

This depreciation of his skill as a duellist surprised and mortified the marksman. So, when Georges had for the third time uttered this qualified form of praise, the other turned and remarked in a tone that was half bantering, half threatening :

" It seems to me, sir, that this is the second or third time you have insinuated a doubt as to my courage ; will you be good enough to give me the clear and precise meaning of your words ? "

" My words need no explanation," answered Georges, " and seem to me to speak for themselves quite sufficiently."

" Then, sir, will you be good enough to repeat them once more, that I may estimate their import and the intention that prompted them.'

" I said," replied Georges, with the most perfect calmness, " when I saw you hit the mark every time, that, if you were aiming at a man's breast instead of at a target, you would not be so sure either of your hand or your eye."

" And why, may I ask ? "

" Because it seems to me that in shooting at a fellow-creature there must always be a degree of excitement that is bound to disturb the aim."

" You have fought many duels, sir ? "

" Not one," replied Georges.

" Ah ! then I am not surprised at your supposing it possible to feel alarm in such circumstances," replied the stranger with a slightly ironical smile.

" Excuse me, sir," answered Georges ; " but I think you misunderstood me ; I imagine that one would tremble with something else besides fear at the moment of killing one's man."

" I never tremble, sir," answered the other.

" Possibly," answered Georges in the same calm manner,
the säinm none the less convinced that at twenty paces, at
your bull's eyes . that is to say, at which you make all
" Well, what ? " said tut

" At twenty paces you would miss ,
Georges.
" ~~nlied
" And I am convinced of the contrary, sir."

" Allow me to doubt your statement."

" You give me the lie then ? "

" No, I maintain a fact."

" A fact which I imagine you would shrink from putting
to the proof," replied the champion shot in a sneering tone.

" Why should I ? " answered Georges, looking him hard
in the face.

" But you would prefer the experiment made on some
one else than yourself, I take it ? "

" On somebody else, or on myself, it does not matter
which."

" You would be something rash, I warn you, in risking
such a proof."

" No, for I have given my opinion, and consequently
am convinced that I should run a very slight risk."

" So, sir, you tell me for the second time that at twenty
paces I should miss my man ? "

" You are wrong, sir, it is the fifth time, if I remember
right."

" Sir, this is too much ; you evidently want to insult me."

" You are quite at liberty to think that if you like."

" Very well, sir. Your hour ? "

" This very moment, if you choose."

" Where ? "

" We are only five hundred yards from the Bois de
Boulogne."

" What weapons ? "

" What weapons ? Why, the pistol of course ; it is not
a question of fighting a duel, but of making an experiment."

" I am at your service, sir."

" And I at yours."

The young men, each accompanied by a friend, got into
two cabs. On arriving at the spot the two seconds so.
to settle the matter, but found a diffig;' while Georges
Georges' antagonist demanded uue, unless he should be
declared that no ~suive only in that event would he be
wounded-ung; and a quarter of an hour was wasted by
uue seconds in fruitless negotiations. Then they wanted
to place the combatants thirty yards apart, but Georges
objected that it was not a genuine experiment unless they
stood at the ordinary distance for shooting at the target,
namely, twenty-five yards. Accordingly they measured
out this distance. Then they wished to toss up to decide
who should fire first, but Georges declared that he considered
this preliminary useless, as, under the circumstances, the
right of priority naturally lay with his opponent; while
his opponent made it a point of honour that an advantage
which, between two men of so much skill, would give every
chance to the one who fired first, should be decided by lot.
Georges, however, stuck to his point, and his opponent
had to give way.

The attendant from the shooting-gallery had followed
the combatants. He loaded the pistols with the same
quantities of powder and shot that had been used in the
previous target-practice; in fact, they were the same pistols,
for Georges had insisted on this point as a *sine qua non*.

The opponents stood at twenty-five paces and each
received from his second a pistol ready loaded. Then the
seconds walked away, leaving the combatants free to fire
at each other in the order agreed upon.

Georges took none of the precautions usual in such
circumstances; not attempting to guard any part of his
body with his pistol, he let his arm hang down his thigh
and presented the whole of his breast entirely unprotected.

His opponent was puzzled at such behaviour. He had
often been in a similar situation, but had never seen such
coolness, and the firm conviction Georges had expressed
now began to produce its effect; this skilful shot, who had
never yet failed, had misgivings about himself. Twice he
levelled his pistol at Georges and twice he lowered it. This

was contrary to all the rules of duelling, but Georges contented himself each time with the remark:

"Take your time, sir; take your time."

At the third attempt he felt ashamed and fired. It was a moment of terrible suspense for the seconds; but directly after the report Georges turned first to right and then to left, and, bowing to the seconds to show that he was not wounded, remarked to his opponent:

"Well, sir, you see that I was right, and that it is more uncertain work shooting at a man than shooting at a target."

"That is so, sir; I was wrong," answered Georges' opponent. "It is your turn to fire."

"Mine?" said Georges, picking up his hat, which he had placed on the ground, and handing his pistol to the attendant, "why should I shoot at you?"

"But, sir, you are entitled to do so, and I insist upon it; besides, I should like to see how you shoot, yourself."

"Excuse me," said Georges with his imperturbable calmness, "let us understand one another, please. I did not say that I should hit you; I said you would not hit me, and you have not done so; that is all."

And in spite of all entreaties from his opponent that he would fire in return, Georges got into his cab again, repeating to his friend:

"Well, didn't I say that it made a difference whether you shoot at a wooden figure or a human being?"

Georges was well satisfied with himself, for he was now sure about his courage.

These three adventures got talked about and established our hero firmly in Society. Two or three coquettes made it a point of honour to captivate this modern Cato; and, as he had no motive for resisting them, he soon became a man of fashion. But just when they thought him most firmly secured, the time that he had fixed for his travels arrived, and one fine morning Georges took leave of his mistresses, and, sending a princely present to each of them, started for London.

In London Georges was received everywhere. He kept horses, dogs and cocks, and went in for racing and cock-fighting, took all the wagers offered, and lost and won large amounts with quite aristocratic unconcern. In short, after a year he left London with the reputation of a thorough gentleman, as he had left Paris with that of a charming ladies' man. It was during this stay in the capital of Great Britain that he came across Lord Murray, but, as we have said, without making further acquaintance with him.

It was the period when travelling in the East became fashionable. Georges visited Greece, Turkey, Asia Minor, Syria and Egypt in succession. He was presented to Mehemet-Ali at the moment when Ibrahim Pacha was starting on his Saïd expedition, accompanied the Viceroy's son, fought under his eyes, and was presented by him with a sword of honour and two Arab horses, selected from the finest of his stud.

Georges returned to France through Italy. Preparation was being made for the Spanish expedition ; Georges rushed to Paris and asked permission to serve as a volunteer. This being granted, he joined the ranks of the first battalion that started, and was constantly to the front.

Unfortunately, contrary to all expectation, the Spaniards offered no resistance, and the campaign, which was thought at first likely to prove a stiff affair, turned out to be merely a military promenade. At the Trocadero, however, the aspect of affairs changed, and it was seen that it would be necessary to sweep away by force this last bulwark of revolution in the Peninsula.

The regiment which Georges had joined was not told off for the assault, so Georges exchanged and joined the Grena- diers. When the breach was effected and the signal for scaling given, Georges dashed in at the head of the attacking column and was the third to enter the fortress. His name was quoted in dispatches, and he received from the hands of the Duc d'Angoulême the cross of the Legion of Honour, and from Ferdinand VII the cross of Charles III. Georges had only aimed at one distinction ; he had obtained two. The gallant fellow was at the height of delight.

He thought the moment was at last arrived for his return to the Isle of France. He had accomplished all that he had dreamed of, and passed every goal he had desired to reach ; there was nothing more for him to do in

Europe. His strife with civilization was over, while his strife with barbarism was about to begin. His was a mind full of a pride that would not be consoled by squandering in the pleasures of Europe the strength painfully acquired for a combat nearer home ; all that he had gone through for the last ten years was in order to surpass his fellow-countrymen, white as well as black, and be able to crush by his sole influence the dislike which no coloured man had as yet dared to combat. Little cared he for Europe and its hundred and fifty millions of inhabitants, for France with her thirty-three millions ; little for parliament or ministry, republic or kingdom. What he preferred above all the rest of the world and what took up all his thoughts was his own little corner of the earth, a mere dot upon the map, like a grain of sand at the bottom of the sea. But then, on this little spot of earth, he had a great achievement to perform, a great problem to solve. He cherished but one recollection, of having undergone humiliation ; he had but one hope, of getting the upper hand.

Meanwhile the *Leicester* put into port at Cadiz. She was on her way to the Isle of France, where she was to be stationed. Georges asked for a passage on board this fine vessel, which he obtained through the recommendation of the French and Spanish authorities. In reality, he owed the favour to the fact that Lord Murray had discovered the person requiring the passage was a native of the Isle of France, and was not at all sorry to have some one who would give him beforehand, during a voyage of four thousand leagues, those numerous bits of information on politics and customs which it is so important for a Governor to have acquired before entering upon his new sphere.

We have seen how Georges and Lord Murray had gradually formed acquaintance and arrived at a certain degree of intimacy on landing at Port Louis. We have seen, too, how Georges, dutiful son as he was and devoted to his father, had been obliged on his arrival to submit to a lengthy proof before being recognized. The old man's joy was all the greater for his having reckoned so little on his son's return. Moreover, the man who had come home was so different from the man who was expected, that all the way back to Moka the father could never cease looking at his son, stopping occasionally as if lost in thought. Each time he did this, the old man pressed his son to his heart with such effusion that Georges, spite of the self-control on which he prided himself, felt the tears come into his eyes.

After three hours' walking they came to the plantation; Télémaque, at a quarter of an hour's distance from the house, had gone on in advance, so that on their arrival Georges and his father found all the negroes awaiting them with a joy that was mingled with fear, for this young man whom they had only seen as a child was come to them as a fresh master, and they wondered what sort of a master he would prove.

His return indeed had a most important bearing on the future happiness or misery of all these poor people. The auguries were favourable. Georges began by giving them that day and the next as a holiday, and, as the day following that again was a Sunday, this holiday meant a good three days' rest. Then Georges, eager to judge for himself what importance his landed estate would give him in the island, scarcely allowed himself time to dine, and then, followed by his father, visited the whole estate. Fortunate speculations, no less than diligent and well-directed labour, had made it one of the finest properties in the Colony. In the centre of the estate was the house, a plain but roomy building, shaded by a triple row of trees that surrounded it, bananas, mangoes, and tamarinds; it opened in the front on a long avenue of trees leading to the road, and at the back on fragrant orchards where the double-flowering pomegranates softly swaying in the wind kissed in turn a cluster of oranges or a bunch of yellow bananas, rising and sinking continually like a bee hovering between two flowers, or a soul hesitating between two desires. Lastly, all around it, as far as the eye could reach, stretched great fields of cane or maize which, as though overweighted with the rich store of food they bore, seemed to implore the hand of the reaper.

Last of all you came to what is called, in every plantation, the Negroes' Cantonment. In the middle of this rose a large building, used in winter as a barn, in summer as a dancing-hall, whence now proceeded loud shouts of delight, mingled with the sound of the tambourine, the drum and the Madagascar harp. The blacks, eagerly availing themselves of their holiday, had at once put themselves *en fête* ; for their primitive nature knows no gradations ; they pass straight from toil to pleasure, and rest from their fatigue by dancing. Georges and his father opened the door and appeared suddenly among them.

Instantly the dance was interrupted ; each pressed to his neighbour's side, all trying to fall into their places, like soldiers surprised by their Colonel. Then, after a moment of agitated silence, they greeted their masters with a triple shout, which for once was a perfectly frank expression of their feelings. Well clothed and well fed, and seldom punished since they seldom failed in their duty, they worshipped Pierre Munier, the only mulatto, perhaps, in the Colony who, while subservient towards the whites, did not treat the blacks with cruelty. As for Georges, whose return, as we have said, had inspired these poor fellows with grave fears, as though he had guessed the effect produced by his presence, he now raised his hand as a sign that he wished to speak. The deepest silence at once ensued, and the Negroes listened with eagerness to the following words which fell from his mouth with a slowness and solemnity befitting a promise and an undertaking :

" My friends, I am touched by the welcome you have given me, and even more by the happiness beaming on your faces. My father makes you happy, I know, and I thank him for it ; for it is my duty, as it is his, to make happy those who will obey me, I hope, as dutifully as they obey him. There are three hundred of you here, and you have only ninety huts ; my father wishes you to build sixty more, one for every two of you ; each hut will have a small garden, where every one will be allowed to plant tobacco, yams and sweet potatoes, and to keep a pig and fowls. Those who want to turn these things into money will go and sell them on Sundays at Port Louis, and dispose of the produce of the sale as they please. If any theft is committed, there will be a severe punishment for him who has robbed his neighbour ; if any one is unjustly flogged by the overseer, let him prove that his punishment is not deserved, and justice will be done him. The case of run-aways I do not anticipate, for you are and will be too happy, I hope, ever to think of leaving us."

Fresh cries of joy greeted this short speech, which will no doubt seem trifling and frivolous to the sixty millions of Europeans who have the good fortune to live under a constitutional system, but which, out there, was received with the more enthusiasm since it was the very first charter of the kind which had ever been granted in the Colony.

CHAPTER VII
THE DINNER DRUM

DURING the evening of the next day, which was, as we have said, a Saturday, an assembly of Negroes, less merry than the one we have just left, was gathered under a large shed, and seated round a huge fire of dried branches, was quietly spending the dinner-drum or *berloque,* as it is termed in the Colonies. That is to say, each individual, according to his needs or his disposition, was engaged either in some manual work intended to be sold next day, or in cooking rice, manioc, or bananas. Some were smoking in wooden pipes tobacco not only of native growth but even gathered from their own gardens ; others were talking together in subdued tones. In the middle of all the groups the women and children, whose business it was to keep up the fires, went to and fro continually. But, notwithstanding all this bustle and movement and the fact that the evening would be followed by a day of rest, a feeling of sadness and uneasiness seemed to oppress these unfortunate people. This was caused by the tyranny of the Manager, who was himself a mulatto. The shed was situated in the lower part of the Williams Plains, at the foot of the *Trois-Mamelles* mountain, round which lay the property of our old acquaintance M. de Malmédie.

Not that M. de Malmédie was a bad master in the French acceptation of the term. No, M. de Malmédie was an easy-going man, incapable of spite or revenge, but infected in the highest degree with his own civil and political importance, filled with pride as he reflected on the purity of the blood that ran in his veins, and sharing, with an innate faith which had been handed down from father to son, in the prejudice which still at that period in the Isle of France pursued men of colour. As for the slaves, they were no worse off on his estate than they were elsewhere; they were unhappy everywhere, for the Negroes, in the eyes of M. de Malmédie, as of others, were not regarded as human beings, but as machines for yielding certain produce. Now, when a machine fails to do the work which it is expected to do, it is set going again by mechanical means, and so M. de Malmédie simply applied to the Negroes the theory which he would have applied in the case of machines. When the Negroes ceased to work, either from idleness or fatigue, the overseer started them again with the whip; the machine resumed its movement, and, at the week's end, the total output reached its proper amount.

As for Henri de Malmédie, he was the replica of his father, only twenty years younger, and with an extra dose of pride.

The moral and material condition then of the slaves in the district of the Williams Plains differed widely from that of the labourers in the Moka district.

Accordingly, at the dinner-drums, called, as we have said, berloques, gaiety came quite spontaneously to the slaves of Pierre Munier, while, on the other hand, in the case of those of M. de Malmédie it had to be stimulated by a song, or a story, or something to be seen. There are always to be found, in the tropics as well as in our own land, beneath the negro's shed as well as in the soldier's camp, one or two of those comic people who undertake the business —a more tiring one than might be supposed—of amusing society, and whom society in its gratitude repays in many different ways; it being understood that if society forgets, as sometimes happens, to pay its debts, the comedian very naturally reminds it of the fact that he is its creditor.

Well, the man who discharged in M. de Malmédie's establishment the functions which Triboulet and l'Angeli formerly fulfilled at the court of François I and Louis XIII was a little fellow whose corpulent body was supported by such slender legs that it seemed at first sight impossible they could bear its weight.

However, the balance upset by the middle of his person was restored at its two extremities, the big trunk carrying a small head with a yellow complexioned face, while the thin legs ended in a pair of enormous feet. As for his arms, they were of extraordinary length, like those of monkeys—animals which, while walking on their hind feet, pick up objects which they find in their path, without stooping.

The result of all this want of proportion in the limbs of this new character whom we have brought upon the scene was a singular mixture of the grotesque and the terrible. To European eyes, the latter would have predominated so as to cause a feeling of intense repulsion; the Negroes, however, who are less susceptible to beauty in the human form than ourselves, looked at him generally from the comic point of view, though occasionally beneath his monkey's skin the tiger in him extended its claws and showed its teeth. His name was Antonio, and he was born at Tingoram; so, to distinguish him from the other Antonios, who would no doubt have felt hurt at being confused with him, he was usually called Antonio the Malay.

The *berloque* then was proceeding somewhat sadly, as we have said, when Antonio who, without being seen, had glided behind one of the posts supporting the shed, raised his yellow head and uttered a little hiss like that made by the hooded snake, one of the most terrible reptiles in the Malay peninsula. This noise, if uttered in the plains of Tenasserim, the marshes of Java, or the sands of Quiloa, would have frozen the hearer with terror; but in the Isle of France where, with the exception of the sharks that swim in shoals round its shores, no deadly creature is ever seen, the noise in question produced no other result than that of making the assembled blacks open their eyes and mouths wide. Then, as though guided by the sound, all heads were turned to the new-comer, and all lips uttered the same cry:

" Antonio the Malay! hurrah for Antonio! "

Two or three of the Negroes, however, started and half

‗‗ , they were Malagasies, Yoloffs, or Zanzibar blacks, who had heard that sound in their childhood and had not forgotten it.

One of them got up altogether, a dark, handsome fellow, whom, apart from his colour, you might have taken as belonging to the finest Caucasian race. But no sooner had he recognized the cause of the sound that had drawn him from his meditation, than he lay down again, muttering with a contempt that equalled the delight of the other slaves : " Antonio the Malay ! "

Antonio with three bounds of his long limbs found himself in the centre of the circle ; then, jumping over the fire, he came down on the other side, and seated himself cross-legged like a tailor.

" A song, Antonio ! a song ! " they all shouted.

Antonio, unlike those artists who are sure of producing their effect, needed no pressing ; he took from his wallet a jew's harp, and, putting it to his mouth, extracted from it some preparatory sounds by way of prelude. Then, accompanying his words with amusing gestures suitable to the subject, he sang the following :—

I

My home's a little hut,
　I stoop to pass the door ;
My head the ceiling strikes
　When my feet are on the floor.
At night I go to sleep,
　But never need a light ;
There's plenty holes, thank God,
　Through which the moon shines bright.

II

My bed an Island mat,
　My pillow is a log ;
My cellar an old gourd,
　Wherein I keep my grog.
On Saturday my wife
　My fav'rite supper hashes,
And in my small hut cooks
　Bananas on the ashes.

III

My coffer is not shut,
　Because it has no locks,

For who would look for pelf
   Inside a bamboo box.
I empty it on Sunday
   My 'baccy for to buy,
And all week smoke my carob pipe,
   Until my stock runs dry.

To have an idea of the effect produced by Antonio's song, in spite of the poverty of the rhyme and the simplicity of the ideas, one must have lived among these primitive people, with whom everything whatsoever is matter for sentiment. At the end of the first and second verses there was laughter and applause. At the end of the third there were shouts and hurrahs. Only the young Negro, who had manifested his contempt for Antonio, shrugged his shoulders with a grimace of disgust.

As for Antonio, instead of enjoying his triumph as one might have expected, and swelling with pride at the vehemence of the applause, he leaned his elbows on his knees, letting his head sink upon his hands, and seemed to give himself up to deep thought.

Now, as Antonio was the life and soul of the company, with his silence gloom once more settled upon the assembly. They begged him accordingly to tell them a story or sing another song. But Antonio turned a deaf ear to them, and the most urgent entreaties obtained no other answer but the same incomprehensible and obstinate silence.

At last one of those nearest to him, tapping him on the shoulder, asked :

" What's the matter, Malay ? Are you dead ? "

" No," answered Antonio, " I'm all alive."

" What are you doing then ? "

" Thinking."

" What about ? "

" I am thinking," said Antonio, " that the time of the *berloque* is a pleasant one. When the kind God has lighted the sky and the hour of the *berloque* comes, every one works with cheerfulness ; for everybody is working for his own benefit, though there are some idle fellows who waste their time in smoking, like you, Toukal ; or greedy ones who amuse themselves by cooking bananas, like you, Cambeba. But, as I said, there are others who work ; you, for instance,

Castor, are making chairs ; you, Bonhomme, wooden spoons ; you, Nazim, are making—nothing."

" Nazim does as he pleases," answered the young Negro ; " Nazim is the stag of Anjouan, as Laïza is its lion, and what lions and stags do is no concern of serpents."

Antonio bit his lips ; then, after a moment's silence during which the young Negro's voice seemed still to vibrate, he continued :

" I was thinking, then, and telling you that the time of the *berloque* was a pleasant one ; but in order that you, Castor and Bohomme, may not feel tired with your work, and that the smoke of your tobacco may seem nicer to you, Toukal ; and that you, Cambeba, may not go to sleep while your banana is cooking, you want some one to tell you stories or to sing to you."

" That's true," said Castor, " and Antonio knows some right good stories and songs too."

" But," went on the Malay, " when Antonio doesn't sing his songs or tell his stories, what happens ? Why, everybody goes to sleep, because they are all tired out with the week's work. Then the *berloque* is a failure ; you, Castor, don't make your bamboo chairs, or you, Bonhomme, your wooden spoons ; you, Toukal, let your pipe go out, and you, Cambeba, let your banana burn ; isn't it so ? "

" Quite true," replied not only those particularly addressed, but the whole crowd of slaves, with the exception of Nazim, who continued to maintain a contemptuous silence.

" Then you ought to be grateful to the man who tells you good stories to keep you awake, and sings nice songs to make you laugh."

" Thank you, Antonio, thank you," shouted all the voices.

" Is there any one, besides Antonio, who can tell you stories ? "

" Laïza—he knows some fine stories, too."

" Yes, but his stories frighten you."

" That's true," answered the Negroes.

" And, besides Antonio, is there any one who can sing you songs ? "

" Nazim—he too has some fine songs."

" Yes, but they make you weep."

" That's true," continued the Negroes.

" And who gave you a song four days ago ? "

" You, Malay."

" Who told you a story three days ago ? "

" You, Malay."

" Who sang you a song the day before yesterday ? "

" You, Malay."

" Who told you a story yesterday ? "

" You, Malay."

" And who has already sung you a song to-day and will tell you a story to-morrow ? "

" You, Malay, you again."

" Well, then, if it is I who amuse you at your work, and give you more pleasure in smoking, and prevent you from sleeping while your bananas are cooking, it is only right that you should give me, who can make nothing, since I sacrifice myself for your sake, something for my trouble."

The justness of this observation struck everybody ; however, our veracity as historians compels us to confess that only a few voices, coming from the hearts of the most fair-minded of their number, answered in the affirmative.

" So," continued Antonio, " it is fair that Toukal should give me a little tobacco to smoke in my pipe, isn't it, Cambeba ? "

" Quite fair," cried Cambeba, delighted that not himself but some one else was laid under contribution.

And Toukal was compelled to share his tobacco with Antonio.

" Now the other day," continued Antonio, " I lost my spoon, and had no money to buy another, because, instead of working, I was singing you songs and telling you stories ; isn't it fair then that Bonhomme should give me a wooden spoon to eat my soup with ?   Don't you think so, Toukal ? "

" Quite fair," cried Toukal, delighted at not being the only one taxed by Antonio.

And Antonio held out his hand to Bonhomme, who gave him the spoon he had just finished.

" Now," resumed Antonio, " I have tobacco for my pipe, and a spoon to eat my soup with, but I have no money to buy stock—meat. Castor ought therefore to give me that pretty little stool so that I can sell it at market and buy a small piece of beef, oughtn't he, Toukal? oughtn't he, Bonhomme? oughtn't he, Cambeba?"

"Quite right," exclaimed all three.

And Antonio drew, partly with his consent, partly by force, from Castor's hands the stool on which he had just nailed the last piece of bamboo.

"Now," continued Antonio, "I have sung you a song which has already tired me, and am about to tell you a story which will tire me still more. I think I ought to keep up my strength by eating something, don't you, Toukal, and Bonhomme and Castor?"

"Certainly," shouted with one voice the three who had contributed.—A terrible idea came into Cambeba's mind.

"But," said Antonio, disclosing a double row of grinders, large and shining like a wolf's, "I have nothing to put between my little teeth."

Cambeba felt his hair begin to stand up, and mechanically stretched out his hand towards the fire.

"It is fair then," Antonio went on, "that Cambeba should give me a little banana, isn't it, all of you?"

"Yes, yes, quite fair," cried Toukal, Bonhomme and Castor; "hand over the banana, Cambeba."

And all the voices shouted in chorus:

"The banana, Cambeba!"

The unhappy man regarded the assemblage with a frightened look and rushed to the fire to rescue his banana; but Antonio stopped him on the way, and, holding him with one hand with a strength of which nobody would have believed him capable, he seized with the other the rope by which the sacks of maize are hauled up to the loft, passed the hook through Cambeba's belt, signalling at the same time to Toukal to pull the other end of the rope. Toukal grasped the situation with a quickness that did credit to his intelligence, and, at the moment when he least expected it, Cambeba found himself lifted from the ground, and, to the great amusement of the company, began to ascend to the sky, twisting round and round. At about ten feet from the ground the ascent ceased, and Cambeba remained suspended, still holding out his shrivelled hands towards the unlucky banana, about which he had no longer any means of arguing with his enemy.

"Bravo, Antonio, well done!" shouted all the spectators, holding their sides with laughter, while Antonio, now perfectly master of the object in dispute, carefully pushed aside the embers and drew out the smoking banana, cooked to perfection and browned fit to make your mouth water.

"My banana, my banana!" cried Cambeba in a tone of the deepest despair.

"Here it is," said Antonio, holding out his arm towards Cambeba.

"Me too far off to take it."

"Don't you want it?"

"Me can't reach down to it."

"Then," replied Antonio, mimicking the language of the hanging wretch, "me eat him to prevent him being spoilt."

And Antonio began to peel the banana with such comic gravity that the laughter became convulsive.

"Antonio," cried Cambeba; "me beg you give me back my banana; banana, him for my poor wife who is ill and can't eat anything else. Me stole him, me wanted him so badly."

"Stolen goods never profit," answered Antonio philosophically, continuing to peel the banana.

"Ah! poor Narina! she will have nothing to eat, and will be very hungry."

"Come, take pity on the unfortunate man," said the young Negro of Anjouan, who, in the midst of the general merriment, had alone remained grave and sad.

"Not such a fool," said Antonio.

"I wasn't speaking to you," replied Nazim.

"Who were you speaking to then?"

"I am talking to men."

"Well, I speak to you," replied Antonio, "and I say, hold your tongue, Nazim."

"Untie Cambeba," said the young Negro in a dignified tone that would have done honour to a king.

Toukal, who was holding the rope, turned to Antonio, uncertain if he should obey; but, without answering his questioning look, Antonio continued:

" I said, hold your tongue, Nazim, and you have not done so."

" When a cur yaps at me I make no reply and go on my way. You are a cur, Antonio."

" Look out for yourself, Nazim," said Antonio, shaking his head ; " when your brother Laïza is not here, you are not much good. So I fancy you won't repeat what you said just now."

" You are a cur, Antonio," repeated Nazim, getting up.

All the Negroes who were between Nazim and Antonio made themselves scarce, so that the handsome Anjouan and the hideous Malay found themselves face to face, but at ten paces from each other.

" You say that at a good distance," replied Antonio, grinding his teeth with anger.

" And I repeat it at close quarters," cried Nazim.

And with one bound he came within two paces of Antonio ; then, with a contemptuous tone and haughty look, his nostrils dilating, shouted for the third time :

" You are a cur ! "

A white man would have thrown himself upon his enemy and strangled him, if it lay within his power ; Antonio, on the contrary, took a step backwards, folded his long limbs, gathered himself up like a snake, drew his knife from his coat pocket, and opened it.

Nazim saw the movement and guessed his purpose ; but, without deigning to make a gesture of defence, waited, standing erect, dumb and motionless, like the statue of a Nubian deity.

The Malay glanced for an instant at his foe ; then raising himself with the suppleness and agility of a snake :

" Woe to you ! " he cried, " Laïza is not here."

" Laïza is here ! " said a grave voice.

The man who uttered these words had spoken them in his usual tone ; he had not added a gesture, he had not accompanied them by a sign, yet, at the sound of that voice, Antonio stopped dead, and his knife, which was but two inches from Nazim's breast, fell from his hand.

" Laïza ! " cried all the Negroes, turning to the new-comer, and assuming in an instant the same attitude of submission.

The man who had but to speak a single word to produce such a powerful impression upon them all, including even Antonio, was in the prime of life, of ordinary height, but his muscular limbs betokened herculean strength. He stood upright, motionless, his arms crossed, and from his eyes, half closed like those of a lion when brooding, there flashed a bright glance, calm and imperious. To see all these men awaiting thus in respectful silence a word or a glance from the other, one would have deemed it a horde of African savages awaiting a nod of the head from their king as a signal for peace or war. Yet he was but a slave among slaves.

After remaining for some minutes motionless as a sculptured figure, Laïza slowly raised his hand and pointed to-towards Cambeba, who had remained all this time suspended from the end of the rope, surveying dumbly, like the others, the scene that had just passed.

Toukal at once lowered the rope, and Cambeba to his great delight found himself on the ground once more. His first care was to search for the banana which, however, in the confusion that naturally followed the incident we have just described, had disappeared.

While the search was proceeding, Laïza had gone out, but reappeared almost immediately, carrying on his shoulders a wild pig, which he threw down by the fire. "Here, my children," said he; "I thought of you; take it and divide it."

This action, and the generous words accompanying it touched two chords in the hearts of the blacks, greediness and enthusiasm, too closely for them not to produce their effect. They all surrounded the animal and gave vent to their ecstasy in their own fashion.

"What a good supper we shall have this evening," said a Malabar.

"Him black as a Mozambique," said a Malagasy.

"Him fat as a Malagasy," said a Mozambique.

But, as may easily be imagined, this kind of admiration was of too ideal a nature not to be soon replaced by something more practical. Before you could say "knife" the animal was cut in pieces, half of it put aside for the next day, and the other half carved into fairly thin slices that were laid on the coals, and more solid bits that were roasted before the fire.

Then each went back to his place, but with a brighter face, for each was expecting a nice supper. Cambeba alone stood sadly in a corner.

" What are you doing there, Cambeba ? " asked Laïza.

" Me doing nothing, papa Laïza," Cambeba answered sadly. " Papa " is, as everybody knows, a title of honour among the blacks, and all the Negroes on the estate, from the youngest to the oldest, bestowed this title on Laïza.

" Are you still suffering from having been hung up by your belt ? " asked the Negro.

" Oh, no, papa, me not so soft as that."

" Then you are vexed ? "

This time Cambeba only answered by moving his head up and down in an affirmative manner.

" And why are you vexed ? " asked Laïza.

" Antonio, he take my banana which me forced to steal for my wife who is ill, and me have nothing to take her now."

" Well then, give her a bit of this wild pig."

" Her no able to eat meat ; no, her no able, papa Laïza."

" Here ! " said Laïza in a loud voice, " who can give me a banana ? "

A dozen bananas sprang as if by a miracle from beneath the ashes. Laïza took the largest and gave it to Cambeba, who made off without even taking time to say " thank you"; then turning to Bonhomme, whose banana it was :

" You shan't lose by it, Bonhomme," he said ; " you shall have Antonio's share of meat instead of your banana."

" And what am I going to have ? " asked Antonio impudently.

" You shall have the banana which you stole from Cambeba."

" But it's lost," answered the Malay.

" That is not my business."

" Bravo ! " exclaimed the Negroes, " stolen goods bring no profit."

The Malay got up, glanced at the men who but an in-

stant before had applauded his persecutions and who now
applauded his punishment, and left the shed.

" Brother," said Nazim to Laïza, " look after yourself ;
I know him, he will be doing you some bad turn."

" Look after yourself rather, Nazim ; for he would not
venture to attack me."

" Well then, I will guard you, and you shall guard me,"
said Nazim ; " but that is not the question now, and we
have got, you know, something else to speak about."

" Yes, but not here."

" Come out, then."

" Presently : when they are all busy over their meal,
no one will pay any attention to us."

" You are right, brother."

And the two Negroes began to converse in low tones
and upon indifferent topics ; but, when the slices were
grilled, and the pieces of steak roasted, profiting by the
close attention always bestowed on the first part of a meal
that is seasoned by a good appetite, they both slipped out
without the rest of the party noticing their disappearance,
exactly as Laïza had foreseen.

CHAPTER VIII
THE RUNAWAY'S TOILET

IT was nearly ten in the evening ; the moonless night was
fine and starry, as the nights generally are in the tropics
towards the end of summer. In the sky were to be seen
some of those constellations with which we are familiar
from childhood by the name of the Little Bear, Orion's
Belt, and the Pleiades, but in a position so different from
that in which we are accustomed to see them, that a European would hardly have recognized them ; by way of
exchange the Southern Cross, invisible in our northern
hemisphere, blazed in the midst of them. The silence of
night was broken only by the noise which the numerous
woodpeckers, which swarm so plentifully in the neighbourhood of the Black River, made in tapping the bark of the
trees, by the song of the blue fig-eaters and the *fondi-jala*,
those warbling nightingales of Madagascar, and the almost

imperceptible rustle of the dry grass as it bent beneath the feet of the two brothers.

The two Negroes walked in silence, glancing round uneasily from time to time, stopping to listen and then resuming their way. At last, arriving at a more bushy spot, they entered a sort of little bamboo-copse, and, having reached its centre, they halted, still listening and looking around them again. The result of this last examination was doubtless more reassuring than the previous ones, for they exchanged a look that indicated that all was safe, and both sat down at the foot of a wild banana, that spread its broad leaves, like a magnificent fan, among the slender leaves of the roses which surrounded it.

" Well, brother ? " asked Nazim, with that feeling of impatience which Laïza had always checked when the other had wished to question him in the hearing of the other Negroes.

" You are still in the same mind, Nazim ? " said Laïza.

" More than ever, brother. I should die, you see, if I stayed here. I have hardened my heart to work up to now, I, Nazim, a Chief's son, and your brother. But I am weary of this wretched life ; I must go back to Anjouan or die."

Laïza uttered a sigh.

" Anjouan is a long way from here," said he.

" What does it matter ? " answered Nazim.

" It is the stormy time of year."

" The wind will drive us all the faster."

" But if the boat capsizes ? "

" We will swim as long as we have strength ; then, when we can swim no longer, we will take a last look at the sky, where the Great Spirit is waiting for us, and sink to the bottom in each other's arms."

" Alas ! " said Laïza.

" That would be better than being a slave," said Nazim.

" So you want to leave the Isle of France ? "

" I do."

" At the risk of your life ? "

" At the risk of my life."

" It is ten to one you never reach Anjouan."

" There is one chance to ten that I do."

" Very well," said Laïza ; " be it as you wish, my brother. But think over it again."

" I have been thinking over it for two years. When the Chief of the Mongallos captured me in battle, as you yourself had been captured four years previously, and sold me to the Captain of a slave-ship, as you yourself had been sold, I made up my mind that very instant. I was put in chains, I tried to strangle myself with my chains, so they riveted me to a bulkhead in the hold. Then I wanted to beat out my brains against the ship's side, so they spread straw under my head. Then I was for letting myself die of hunger, so they opened my mouth, and, not being able to make me eat, forced me to drink. They were obliged to sell me quickly, they landed me here and got rid of me at half price, and even that was dear ; for I was determined to throw myself from the first cliff that I should climb. All at once, I heard your voice, brother ; all at once, I felt my heart beat against your heart, I felt my lips on your lips, and I felt so happy that I thought I could live. That lasted for a year. Then, brother, forgive me, your friendship was not enough for me. I remembered our island, I remembered my father, and Zirna. Our labour seemed to me first wearisome, then humiliating, then intolerable. Then I said to myself that I wanted to flee, to go back to Anjouan, to see Zirna again, and my father, and our island ; and you were kind to me, as ever, and said ' Rest yourself, Nazim, you who are weak and I, who am strong, will work.' Then you went out every evening for four days, and worked while I rested. Did you not, Laïza ? "

" Yes, Nazim, but listen : you had better wait a bit longer," replied Laïza, raising his forehead. " Slaves to-day, in a month, in three months, in a year, we shall perhaps be masters ! "

" Yes," said Nazim ; " yes, I know your plans ; yes, I know your hope."

" Then, you understand what it would be," resumed Laïza, " to see these whites, so proud and cruel, humiliated and suppliants in their turn ? to make them work twelve hours a day ? to beat them, lash them with whips, and bruise them with sticks ? They are but twelve thousand,

and there are eighty thousand of us. And on the day when we come to settle accounts, they will be lost."

"I will say to you what you said to me, Laïza ; it is ten to one that you do not succeed . . ."

"But I will answer you as you answered me, Nazim ; there is one chance in ten that I do. Let us wait then . . ."

"I cannot, Laïza, I cannot . . . I have seen my mother's spirit ; she told me to return to my country."

"You have seen it ? " said Laïza.

"Yes ; every evening for a fortnight, a *fondi-jala* has come and perched above my head ; it is the same one that sang at Anjouan over her grave. It has crossed the sea with its little wings, and has come here. I recognized its song ; listen, it is here."

And at that very moment a Madagascar nightingale, perched on the highest branch in the mass of trees beneath which Laïza and Nazim were lying, began its melodious song above the heads of the two brothers. Both listened, bending their heads sadly, until the nocturnal songster broke off, and, flying in the direction of the native land of the two slaves, uttered the same strains at a distance of fifty yards ; then, flying off again, still in the same direction, repeated for the last time its song, as a distant echo from their country, of which at this distance they could only just catch the highest notes ; then, once more, it flew away, but this time so far that the two exiles listened in vain ; they could hear its song no more.

"It has gone back to Anjouan," said Nazim ; "and it will return in the same way to call me and show me the way, until I return myself."

"Go then," said Laïza.

"Now ? " asked Nazim.

"Everything is ready. I have chosen the largest tree I could find in one of the most deserted spots near the Black River ; I have hollowed out a canoe in its trunk, and have cut two oars out of its branches. I have sawed it through above and below the canoe, but I have left it standing for fear lest its top should be seen missing among the other tree tops. Now all that is left is to push it over, to drag

4

the canoe to the river and launch it in the stream. Since you will go, Nazim, well, you shall go to-night."

" And you, my brother, are you not coming with me ? " asked Nazim.

" No," said Laïza ; " I remain behind."

Nazim in his turn heaved a deep sigh.

" And what hinders you then," asked Nazim, after a moment's silence, " from returning with me to the land of our forefathers ? "

" I have told you, Nazim, what hinders me ; for more than a year we have been determined to rise in revolt, and our friends have chosen me as their leader. I cannot betray our friends by leaving them."

" It is not that which keeps you back, brother," said Nazim, shaking his head ; " there is something besides."

" And what else do you suppose can keep me back, Nazim ? "

" The Rose of the Black River," answered the young man, looking fixedly at Laïza.

Laïza started ; then, after a moment's silence :

" It is true," he said ; " I love her."

" Poor brother ! " replied Nazim. " And what is your plan ? "

" I have none."

" What is your hope ? "

" To see her to-morrow, as I saw her yesterday, as I saw her to-day."

" But she, does she know of your existence ? "

" I doubt it."

" Has she ever spoken a word to you ? "

" Never."

" Then what of your country ? "

" I have forgotten it."

" Nessali ? "

" I remember her no longer."

" Our father ? "

Laïza let his head sink into his hands. Then, after an instant :

" Listen," he said. " All you can say to make me go is as vain as all that I have said to make you stay. She is everything to me, family and country! I must see her, to live, just as I must have the air that she breathes, to breathe. Let us each follow our own destiny. For you, Nazim, the return to Anjouan; for me, to remain here."

"But what shall I say to my father, when he asks me why Laïza has not returned?"

"You will tell him that Laïza is dead," answered the Negro in a choking voice.

"He will not believe me," said Nazim, shaking his head.

"Why not?"

"He will say to me, 'If my son were dead, I should have seen my son's spirit: the spirit of Laïza has not visited his father: Laïza is not dead.'"

"Well then, you will tell him that I love a white girl," said Laïza, "and he will curse me. But never will I quit the Island where she is!"

"The Great Spirit will inspire me, my brother," answered Nazim, rising; "take me to the canoe."

"Wait," said Laïza.

And the Negro went up to a hollow maple tree, drew from it a piece of glass and a gourd filled with coco-oil.

"What is that?" asked Nazim.

"Listen, my brother," said Laïza: "it is possible that with the help of a good wind and your oars you may, in eight or ten days, reach Madagascar, or even the Continent of Africa; but it is possible that to-morrow, or the day after, a storm may throw you back on this coast. Then your departure will be known, then signals about you will have been sent all over the Island, then you will be obliged to play the runaway, and fly from wood to wood, from rock to rock."

"Brother, I was called the stag of Anjouan, as you were called the lion," said Nazim.

"Yes, but, like the stag, you may fall into a trap. Then it will be needful for you to give them no hold upon you; you will have to slip through their hands. Here is some glass to cut your hair with, and some coco-oil to grease your limbs. Come, brother, let me perform the toilet of the runaway Negro."

Nazim and Laïza made for a thinner part of the wood,

and Laïza began, by the light of the stars, with the help
of his broken piece of glass bottle to cut his brother's hair
as quickly and as thoroughly as the most skilful barber
with the sharpest razor could have done it. When the
operation was finished, Nazim threw off his jacket, while
his brother poured over his shoulders a portion of the
coco-oil contained in the gourd, and the young fellow
spread it with his hands over every portion of his body.
Thus anointed from head to foot, the handsome Anjouan
Negro looked like an antique athlete prepared for the race.

But, in order quite to satisfy Laïza, an experiment was
required. Like Alcides of old, Laïza could grasp a horse
by his hind feet, and the horse would try in vain to escape
from his hands. Laïza, like Milo of Croton, could take a
bull by his horns and throw him over his shoulder or knock
him down at his feet. If Nazim could escape from Laïza,
he could escape from everybody : accordingly, Laïza seized
Nazim by the arm, tightening his fingers with all the strength
of his iron muscles. Nazim pulled his arm away and it
slipped through the fingers of Laïza like an eel in a fisher-
man's hands. Laïza seized Nazim by the middle, pressing
him against his breast as Hercules pressed Antæus ; Nazim
placed his hands on Laïza's shoulders and slipped between
his arms and breast just as a snake slips between the claws
of a lion. Then, and not till then, was the Negro satisfied ;
Nazim could not be captured by a surprise, and, if it came
to a chase, Nazim himself could outlast the stag from which
he took his name.

Then Laïza gave Nazim the gourd three parts filled with
coco-oil, bidding him keep it even more carefully than the
roots of manioc for appeasing his hunger, and the water
to quench his thirst. Nazim passed his strap through the
gourd and fastened it to his girdle.

Then the two brothers examined the sky, and, seeing
from the position of the stars that it must be midnight at
least, took the road by the hill of the *Rivière Noire*, and
soon disappeared into the woods that clothe the base of
the *Trois-Mamelles*. But behind them, at twenty paces
from the mass of bamboos, where the conversation which
we have just related took place, a man who, from his

absolute immobility, might have been taken for one of the tree-trunks among which he lay, slipped like a ghost into the underwood, appeared for an instant on the edge of the forest, and, making a menacing gesture after the two brothers, went off, as soon as they had disappeared, in the direction of Port Louis.

It was the Malay, Antonio, who had promised to be revenged on Laïza and Nazim, and who was going to keep his word.

And now, quick as he may travel with his long legs, we must, if our readers permit, precede him to the capital of the Isle of France.

CHAPTER IX

THE ROSEBUD OF THE *RIVIÈRE NOIRE*

AFTER paying Miko-Miko for the fan, the price of which, to her great astonishment, Georges had found out for her, the girl, of whom we had a momentary glimpse at the door of her house, ordered her Negro to help the Chinaman to pack up his wares, and went in, followed, of course, by her governess. She was quite delighted with her new acquisition, which, nevertheless, was fated to be forgotten the very next day. She now went, with that undulating and unconstrained gait which adds so much charm to Creole women, and lay down on a large sofa, which was evidently intended to be used either as a bed or as a lounge. This piece of furniture was placed at one end of a charming little boudoir, filled to overflowing with many coloured Chinese porcelains and Japanese vases; the hangings which covered the walls were made of that fine printed calico which the inhabitants of the Isle of France get from the Coromandel coast, and which is called patna. The chairs, as is usual in hot countries, were made of cane, and two windows at opposite sides of the room, the one opening on the main court which was full of trees, the other on a large back enclosure, allowed the sea breeze and the scent of flowers to penetrate freely through the bamboo mats which served as shutters.

Hardly had the girl stretched herself on the sofa when a

small green parrot with a grey head, as plump as a sparrow, flew from its perch, and, alighting on her shoulder, amused itself by picking the end of the fan which its mistress, amusing herself in her turn, was opening and shutting mechanically.

We say *mechanically*, for it was manifest the girl was no longer thinking about her fan, charming though it was, and greatly as she had desired to possess it. Her eyes, fixed apparently on some part of the room where there seemed to be no special object to account for her steady gaze, had evidently ceased to take in objects present to her sight, in order to pursue some internal train of thought. Nay more; this internal vision evidently possessed for her all the appearance of reality; for, from time to time, a slight smile passed over her face, and her lips moved, answering in dumb language to some mute remembrance. This preoccupation was too foreign to the girl's usual manner not to be noticed by her governess; so, after having watched in silence for some moments her pupil's play of features, Henrietta asked:

" What is the matter, Sara dear ? "

" Nothing," answered the girl, starting like a person aroused from sleep. " I am playing, as you see, with my parrot and my fan, that's all."

" Yes, I can see you are playing with your parrot and your fan; but I am certain that, at the moment when I disturbed you in your reverie, you were not thinking of either one or the other."

" Oh ! my dear Henrietta, I declare to you . . ."

" You don't usually tell fibs, Sara, and least of all to me," interrupted the governess; " why begin to-day ? "

The girl blushed deeply; then, after a moment's hesitation:

" You are right, dear creature," said she; " I was thinking of something quite different."

" And what were you thinking of ? "

" I was wondering who that young man could be who passed by at such an opportune moment and got us out of our difficulty. I have never seen him before to-day; and no doubt he came with the vessel that brought the

Governor. Is there any harm in thinking about him ? "

" No, my child, there is no harm in thinking about him, but it was an untruth to tell me that you were thinking of something else."

" I was wrong," said the girl, " forgive me." And she turned her charming head to the governess, who stooped towards her and kissed her on the forehead.

Both were silent for a moment, then, as Henrietta, like the strictly conscientious Englishwoman that she was, did not like to allow her pupil's imagination to linger too long on the recollection of a young man, and as Sara on her part, experienced a certain embarrassment in being silent, they both opened their mouths at the same instant. Thus their first words clashed, and each stopping short in order to let the other speak, the result was another interval of silence, broken this time by Sara.

" What were you going to say, my dear Henrietta ? " asked the girl.

" Nay, you were saying something yourself, Sara. What was it ? "

" I was going to say I should like to know if our new Governor is a young man."

" I suppose you would be very glad if he were young ? "

" Of course. If he is young, he will give dinners, and fêtes, and balls, and that will wake up our dull Port Louis a little. Oh ! balls, especially—if he would only give balls ! "

" You are fond, then, of dancing, my child ? "

" Oh ! am I not ? " cried the girl.

Henrietta smiled.

" Is there any harm then in being fond of dancing ? "

" There is harm, Sara, in running to extremes in everything, as you do."

" Can I help it, dear ? " said Sara, in a sweetly coaxing manner, which she could assume on occasions, " I am made that way ; I like or I dislike, and I cannot hide either my liking or my disliking. Haven't you often told me pretence was a wicked sin ? "

" No doubt ; but there is a vast difference between disguising one's feelings and yielding unceasingly to one's desires, I might almost say to one's natural instincts,"

replied the severe Englishwoman, who was sometimes as
much embarrassed by the ready-witted arguments of her
pupil as she was alarmed at other times by the outbursts
of her wild nature.

" Yes, I know you have often told me that, dear. I
know that European women, those of the fashionable world
at least, steer in a wonderful way between frankness and
concealment by means of reticence of speech and immobility
of feature. But, dear, from me you must not expect too
much ; I am not a civilized girl, but a little savage, reared
in the wide forests and on the banks of great rivers. When
I see anything that pleases me, I want it, and if I want it
I must have it. Then, you see, I have been rather spoilt,
by you too, dear Henrietta, among the rest ; which has
made me wilful. When I have asked for things, they have
generally been given to me ; and, when it has happened
that I have been refused, I have taken them, and have
been allowed to."

".And, such being your disposition, how shall you manage
when you are M. Henri's wife ? "

" Oh ! Henri is a good fellow ; we have already agreed,"
said Sara, with the most perfect simplicity, " that I shall
let him do as he pleases, and that I, too, shall do as I please.
Haven't we, Henri ? " continued Sara, turning to the door,
which opened at this moment to admit M. de Malmédie
and his son.

" What is it, Sara dear ? " asked the young man, going
up and kissing her hand.

" Haven't we agreed that, when we are married, you
will never oppose me, and will give me everything I want ? "

" Upon my word ! " said M. de Malmédie, " I hope this
young lady knows how to make her conditions beforehand ! "

" Haven't we agreed," continued Sara, " that if I like
to be always going to balls, you will take me to them and
stay as long as I wish, and not be like those wretched
husbands who go off after the seventh or eighth dance ?
That I may sing as much as I like, and go fishing as much as
I like ; and that if I want a nice hat from Paris, or a nice
English or Arab horse, you will buy them for me ? "

" Oh ! of course," said Henri, smiling, " but, talking of

Arab horses, we saw two fine ones to-day, and I am glad you did not see them, Sara ; for as they are probably not for sale, I could not have given them to you, if you had happened to take a fancy to them."

" I saw them too," said Sara ; " they belong, do they not, to a dark young stranger of twenty-five or twenty-six, with fine hair and splendid eyes ? "

" Confound it, Sara," said Henri ; " you seem to have paid even more attention to the rider than to the horses."

" It is easily explained, Henri ; the gentleman came up and spoke to me, while the horses I saw only at a certain distance, and they did not even neigh ! "

" That young fop spoke to you, Sara ? and why ? "

" In the first place," said Sara, " I noticed no signs of foppishness about him at all, nor did my dear Henrietta, who was with me. Next, you ask why he spoke to me. Oh, good gracious ! nothing more simple. I was returning from church, when I saw waiting for me at the doorstep a Chinaman with his two baskets filled with boxes, fans, pocket-books, and a host of other things. I asked him the price of this fan . . . look how pretty it is, Henri——"

" Well, go on," said M. de Malmédie ; " all this has nothing to do with the stranger's speaking to you."

" I am coming to it directly, uncle," answered Sara. " I asked him the price of the fan, but his answer gave us some trouble, for the worthy man spoke nothing but Chinese. Then Henrietta and I were quite at a loss, and asked those who were standing round us, looking at the beautiful wares displayed by the dealer, if there was no one who could act as our interpreter, when this young man came forward and placed himself at our service, spoke to the Chinaman in his own language, and, coming back to us, said, ' Ninety dollars.' It isn't dear, uncle, is it ? "

" Ahem ! " said M. de Malmédie ; " it is the price we paid for a Negro before the English put a stop to the trade."

" Then this gentleman speaks Chinese ? " asked Henri in astonishment.

" Yes," answered Sara.

" Just fancy, father," cried Henri, bursting into laughter. " he speaks Chinese."

" Well, is there anything to laugh at in that ? " asked Sara.

" Oh, nothing at all," replied Henri, continuing to give way to merriment. " Why, this is a charming accomplishment possessed by the handsome foreigner. He can chat with the tea-chests and folding-screens."

" The fact is that Chinese is a very little-known tongue," answered M. de Malmédie.

" He must be some mandarin," said Henri, continuing to enjoy himself at the expense of the stranger, whose haughty look had rankled in his mind.

"At any rate," answered Sara, "he is an educated mandarin ; for, after speaking Chinese to the dealer, he spoke French to me, and English to my dear Henrietta."

" Hang it ! The fellow speaks every language ! " said M. de Malmédie. " He is just the sort of man I want in my office."

" Unfortunately, uncle," said Sara, " the person of whom you are speaking seems to be in a service that will give him a distaste for all other employments."

" What is that ? "

" In that of the King of France. Didn't you notice that he wears in his buttonhole the ribbon of the Legion of Honour, and another ribbon besides ? "

" Oh ! these ribbons are bestowed nowadays without its being necessary for the recipient to have seen service."

" But still, speaking generally, the man who gets them must be a person of note," replied Sara, vexed without knowing why, and defending the stranger by that instinct, so natural to simple hearts, of defending those who are unjustly attacked.

" Well," said Henri, " he must have been decorated for knowing Chinese, that's all."

" Anyhow, we shall know all this soon," replied M. de Malmédie in a tone that showed that he did not notice the quarrel between the young people ; " for he arrived on board the Governor's ship, and, as people do not come to the Isle of France to leave it next day, we shall no doubt have the advantage of having him with us for some time."

At this moment a servant entered with a letter that bore the Governor's seal, and which had just come from

Lord Murray. It was an invitation for M. de Malmédie, Henri, and Sara, to the dinner which would take place on the following Monday, and to the ball that would follow the dinner.

Sara's uncertainties were at once decided in respect to the Governor. He must be a most delightful man who started by giving invitations for a dinner and a ball, and Sara uttered a cry of joy at the thought of spending a whole night in dancing.

This fell out the more opportunely as the last vessel from France had brought her some lovely trimmings of artificial flowers, which had not given her half the pleasure they ought to have done, since she did not know, when she received them, what opportunity she would get of showing them off.

As for Henri, in spite of the dignity with which he received the news, he was not, at heart, indifferent to it. Henri regarded himself as one of the best-looking young men of the Colony, and, although he was engaged and his marriage with his cousin quite settled upon, he lost no opportunity meanwhile of flirting with other women. Besides, this was not difficult for him, as Sara, whether from indifference or habit, showed not the slightest jealousy in this respect.

As for his father, he was extremely proud when he saw the invitation, which he read three times, and which gave him a still higher idea of his own importance at finding himself, two or three hours after the Governor's arrival, invited to dinner with him, an honour which in all probability was extended only to the most considerable personages in the Island.

The invitation, however, necessitated some change in the family plans. Henri had arranged a grand stag-hunt for the Sunday and Monday following in the district of the *Savane*, which at this period, being still uninhabited, abounded in big game. Moreover, as the hunt was to take place partly over his father's property, he had invited some dozen of his friends to meet on the Sunday morning at a charming country-house which he owned on the banks of the *Rivière Noire*, one of the most picturesque parts of the Island. It was impossible to keep to the days agreed

upon, seeing that one of these days was that selected by
the Governor for his ball, so it became necessary to ante-
date the party by twenty-four hours, not only on account
of the Malmédies, but also for some of their guests who
would no doubt have the honour of being asked to dine
with Lord Murray. So Henri went to his room to write
some dozen letters, telling the sportsmen of the change
made in their original plan, which Bijou was ordered
to deliver at their respective addresses. M. de Malmédie,
in his turn, took leave of Sara, making the excuse of a
business-meeting, but in reality to announce to his neighbours that in three days he would be able to give them
frankly his opinion of their new Governor, inasmuch as he
was dining with him the following Monday.

As for Sara, she declared that, in these unexpected and
serious circumstances, she had so many preparations to
make that she would be unable to start with them on the
Saturday morning, and would be content with joining
them on Saturday evening or Sunday morning.

The rest of that day, then, and all the next, was spent,
as Sara had foreseen, in preparations for the important
evening, and, thanks to the calm and method which Henrietta imported into all the arrangements, Sara was ready
to start on Sunday morning, as she had promised her
uncle. The most important matter, the trying on of the
frock, was finished, and the dressmaker, a trustworthy
woman, undertook that Sara should find it completed next
morning; if anything wanted alteration, there remained
part of the day to do it in.

So Sara started in the most joyous frame of mind possible.
Next to a ball, what she loved best in the world was the
country; there she felt free to be idle or to rush about at
will—a freedom which she, so fond of running to opposite
extremes, never quite found in the town. Besides, when
in the country, Sara ceased to recognize any authority,
even that of her dear Henrietta, the person who, after all,
had the most influence over her. If she was in an idle
mood, she chose a beautiful spot, lay down beneath a
clump of jameroses or shaddocks, and there lived like the
flowers, drinking in the dew, the air, and the sunshine at

every pore, listening to the songs of the blue fig-eaters and *fondi-jala*, amusing herself with watching the monkeys leaping from bough to bough or hanging by their tails, following with her eyes the graceful and rapid movements of the pretty green lizards speckled and striped with red, that are so common in the Isle of France that at every step you disturb three or four of them. There she would remain whole hours, putting herself in communication, so to speak, with all nature, to whose thousand voices she listened, whose thousand aspects she studied, whose thousand harmonies she compared. If, on the other hand, she was in an active mood, then she was no longer a girl, but a gazelle, a bird, or a butterfly ; she jumped the streams in pursuit of dragonflies with heads sparkling like rubies ; she hung over the cliff to gather the broad-leaved lilies, on which the dewdrops quiver like globules of quicksilver ; she sped, like a water-fairy, beneath a waterfall whose damp spray shrouded her as with a gauzy veil, and then her cheeks, in marked contrast to the other Creole girls whose dull tint so seldom takes colour, would be flushed with so vivid a pink, that the Negroes, accustomed in their poetic and flowery language to give a descriptive name to everything, called Sara the Rosebud of the Dark River.

So Sara, as we have said, was very happy, since she had in prospect, one for that very day, the other for the day following, the two things she loved best in the world, to wit, the country and the dance.

CHAPTER X
A PERILOUS BATHE

AT this period the Island was not, as it is to-day, intersected by roads on which you may travel by carriage to the different parts of the Colony, and the only means of transport were horses or the palanquin. Whenever Sara went into the country with Henri or M. de Malmédie, horses were preferred without any discussion, for riding was one of the exercises with which the girl was most familiar. But when she travelled in company with Henrietta 'this method of locomotion had to be abandoned, since Henrietta much preferred the palanquin. So it was in a palanquin carried by four Negroes, followed by a relay of four others, that Sara and her governess travelled side by side, sufficiently close to one another to be able to talk through the drawn curtains, while their bearers, assured beforehand of a *pourboire*, sang at the top of their voices, announcing thus to the passers-by the liberality of their young mistress.

Henrietta and Sara presented the most complete contrast, physical and moral, that can be imagined. The reader is already acquainted with Sara, the capricious girl with dark hair and eyes, complexion as changeful as her mind, with pearly teeth, hands and feet small as a child's, and body supple and undulating as a sylph's. He must now allow us to say a few words about Henrietta.

Henrietta Smith was born in London ; her father was a teacher who, having intended her for the teaching profession, had had her instructed from childhood in Italian and French, which, thanks to this early study, were as familiar to her as her mother tongue. Teaching, as everybody knows, is an employment in which as a rule large fortunes are not made. Jack Smith, then, died a poor man, leaving his daughter Henrietta very highly accomplished, but without a dowry, and in consequence this young lady attained the age of twenty-five without finding a husband.

Just then, one of her friends, an excellent musician, as she herself was a perfect linguist, proposed to Miss Smith to amalgamate their talents and start a school in partnership. The offer was accepted. But, though each of the two partners gave every attention and all the pains and devotion of which they were capable to the education of the pupils who were entrusted to them, the establishment did not prosper, and the two mistresses were obliged to dissolve partnership.

Meanwhile, the father of one of Miss Smith's pupils, a rich London merchant, received from M. de Malmédie, a correspondent of his, a letter asking him for a governess for his niece, offering her advantages sufficient to compensate her for the sacrifice she would make in expatriating herself. The contents of this letter were communicated to Henrietta. The poor girl was without resources ; she was not wedded to a country where she had no other prospect than that of dying of starvation. She looked upon the offer made to her as a blessing from heaven, and embarked on the first vessel sailing for the Isle of France, recommended to M. de Malmédie as a lady worthy of the highest respect. M. de Malmédie consequently received her gladly, and entrusted her with the education of his niece Sara, who was then nine years old.

Miss Henrietta's first question was to ask M. de Malmédie what sort of education he wished his niece to receive. M. de Malmédie answered that that did not in the least matter ; that he had engaged a governess to free him from anxiety on this score, and that it was her business, having been recommended to him as a very intelligent person, to teach Sara what she knew ; adding only, by way of afterthought, that the girl being definitely intended as the future wife of her cousin Henri, it was important that she should not conceive an affection for any one else. This decision of M. de Malmédie's in regard to the union of his son and niece was influenced, not only by the affection which he had for both, but still more by the fact that Sara, who had been left an orphan at the age of three, had inherited nearly a million francs, a sum which would double itself during M. de Malmédie's guardianship.

Sara at first stood in great awe of this governess who had come from overseas, and it must be admitted that, at first sight, the appearance of Miss Smith did not greatly reassure her. She was at that time a tall woman of thirty or thirty-two, to whom school work had imparted that dry, stiff look so often to be seen in ladies engaged in education ; her cold eye, pale complexion and thin lips gave her a wonderfully wooden appearance, the frigidity of which was only partly redeemed by the warmth of her auburn hair. From early morning fully dressed and with hair neatly done up, Sara had never once seen her carelessly attired, and for a long time believed that Miss Henrietta, instead of going to bed at night like ordinary people, was hung up in a wardrobe, as dolls are, and came out in the morning just as she had entered it the evening before. The consequence was that in early days Sara was fairly obedient to her governess, and learned a little English and Italian. As for music, Sara was constituted like a nightingale, and played the piano and guitar almost by instinct, though the instrument she preferred to all others was the Malagasy harp, from which she drew sounds which delighted the most famous virtuosos of Madagascar in the Island.

Sara had made all this progress, however, without losing any of her individuality, or her primitive nature being in any degree modified, while Miss Henrietta, on her side, remained such as God and education had made her ; so that these two beings, so widely different, lived side by side without ever yielding to each other. Still, as both, in their different ways, were endowed with excellent qualities, Henrietta came to form a deep attachment for her pupil, and Sara, in her turn, entertained a lively friendship for her governess, and the token of this mutual affection was that the teacher called Sara " my child," while Sara, thinking the title of " Miss " or " Mademoiselle " too cold for the affection she bore to her governess, invented the more affectionate address of " ma mie Henriette."

But it was especially in regard to physical exercises that Henrietta maintained her feeling of dislike. Her education, exclusively scholastic, had only developed her moral faculties, leaving her bodily faculties in their natural clumsiness, so, however much Sara might try to persuade her, Henrietta had never cared to ride, even on *Berloque*, a quiet Java pony that carried vegetables for the gardener. The narrow roads made her feel so giddy that she had often preferred to make a détour of a mile or two rather than pass close to a precipice. It was not without deep searchings of the heart that she went on board ship, and scarcely had she sat down, and the aforesaid ship begun to move, than the poor governess declared she was overtaken by sea-sickness, which did not leave her for a moment during the whole voyage from Portsmouth to Port Louis, that is to say for more than four months. The result was that Henrietta's life was passed in perpetual apprehension in regard to Sara ; when she saw her riding with the boldness of an Amazon, with her cousin, or bounding with the lightness of a fawn from rock to rock, or gliding with the grace of a water-nymph on the surface of the water, or disappearing for a moment in its depths, her poor heart was wrung with a terror almost maternal. She was like those unfortunate hens who have hatched swans, and who, seeing their adopted progeny plunge into the water, remain on the edge of the bank, unable to understand such boldness, and clucking sadly to call back the rash young ones who are exposing themselves to such awful danger.

So Henrietta, though for the moment carried quite comfortably and safely in a palanquin, was none the less already anticipating the countless agonies which Sara, according to her wont, would make her go through, while the young girl was elated at the thought of these two days of happiness.

The morning, too, was magnificent. It was one of those beautiful days at the beginning of autumn (for the month of May, which is our spring time, is autumn in the Isle of France), when Nature, getting ready to hide herself behind a veil of rain, pays the sweetest adieux to the sunshine. As they advanced, the country grew wilder and wilder ; they crossed, by bridges, the fragility of which made Henrietta tremble, the double source of the river of the Rampart, and the falls of the Tamarin. On reaching the foot of the *Trois-Mamelles* mountain, Sara made inquiries about her uncle and cousin, and heard that they were at that moment hunting with their friends between the big pool and the plain of St. Pierre. Finally, they crossed the little river of the *Boucaut*, rounded the hill of the great *Rivière Noire*, and found themselves facing M. de Malmédie's abode.

Sara began by paying a visit to the inmates of the house, whom she had not seen for a fortnight ; then she went off to say good morning to her aviary, a large enclosure of wire netting that surrounded an entire thicket, in which were confined together Guida turtle-doves, blue and grey fig-eaters, *fondi-jala*, and fly-catchers. From there she went on to her flowers, almost all brought from London ; there were tuberoses, carnations, anemones, ranunculuses, and Indian roses, while in the middle of them the beautiful Cape immortelle reared its head as queen of the flowers.

All these were enclosed by hedges of jasmine and China roses, which latter, like our roses of the four seasons, bloom the whole year round. This was Sara's kingdom; the whole island was her conquest. So long as Sara remained in the grounds belonging to the house, all went well for Henrietta, who enjoyed the gravel paths, the cool shade, and the air redolent with perfumes. But you may guess that this period of tranquillity was very brief. By the time Sara had said a kind word or two to the old mulatto woman who had been in her service and was spending her declining years by the banks of the *Rivière Noire*, by the time she had kissed her favourite dove, and gathered a few flowers to put in her hair, this part of the day's proceedings was over. Then came the turn for the walk, and then began the anguish of the unhappy governess. At first, Henrietta tried to oppose the child's independent spirit and limit her to amusements that involved less roaming about, but she soon recognized that this was an impossibility. Sara had escaped from her hands and made her excursions without her ; so that, at last, her anxiety for her pupil proving greater than her fears for her own safety, she made up her mind to accompany her. It is true she nearly always contented herself with sitting on some point of vantage from which she could follow the girl with her eyes as she climbed up hill or down, but at least she seemed to be checking her by gestures and keeping her in sight. On this occasion, seeing Sara prepared to start, she resigned herself as usual, took a book to read, while Sara ran about, and got ready to accompany her.

But Sara had planned something else than a walk this time ; she had promised herself a bathe in the beautiful, calm, and peaceful bay of the *Rivière Noire*, the water in which was so clear that at a depth of twenty feet you could see the polypes which grew at the bottom, and the different tribes of shell-fish crawling among their branches. But Sara had taken good care, as usual, to give no hint of her intention to Henrietta ; only the old mulatto woman had been told, and she was to wait for Sara with her bathing-dress at the place which she had pointed out.

So Sara and her governess descended, following the

banks of the *Rivière Noire*, which continually grew wider, and at the end of which could be seen the bay shining like a vast mirror. On each side of the stream rose a high bank of woods, the trees of which shot up, like tall pillars, seeking for air and sun, in the midst of a vast dome of leaves so thick that the sky could only here and there be seen ; while their roots, like countless snakes, unable to dig into the rocks which are continually rolling down from the top of the hill, surrounded them with their folds. In proportion as the bed of the river widened, the trees on the two banks bent over, profiting by the space left by the water, and formed an arch like a gigantic tent ; the effect of the whole was sombre, desolate, peaceful and silent, full of romantic sadness and mysterious calm. The only sound to be heard was the harsh cry of the grey-headed parrot; the only living creatures to be seen, as far as the eye could reach, were some of those reddish monkeys called aigrettes, which are the scourge of the plantations, but are so common in the Island that all attempts to exterminate them have failed. Only from time to time, scared by the noise made by Sara and her governess, a green kingfisher with white throat and breast, darted, with a shrill and plaintive cry, from the mangroves which dipped their boughs in the river, crossed the stream swift as an arrow, shining like an emerald, plunged into the mangroves on the opposite bank and disappeared. This tropical vegetation, this profound solitude, these wild harmonies, so much in keeping with each other, rocks, trees and river, all this was nature as Sara loved it ; it was the country as her primitive imagination understood it ; it was a panorama such as neither pen, nor crayon, nor brush could reproduce, but such as her soul reflected it.

Let us hasten to say that Henrietta was not insensible to this magnificent spectacle ; but, as we know, her perpetual fear prevented her thorough enjoyment of it. So having reached the top of a small hill which commanded a fairly wide prospect, she sat down, and after having, though without hope of success, invited Sara to sit beside her, she saw the girl bound away from her side, and, drawing from her pocket the tenth or twelfth volume of *Clarissa*

Harlowe her favourite novel, began to read it for the twentieth time.

The girl proceeded to the bank of the river, springing from rock to rock like a wagtail admiring itself in the water ; then, after satisfying herself with the timid modesty of a nymph of olden days, that there was no one in sight of her, she began to let her garments slip off her one after the other, and put on a white woollen tunic, which, drawn tight round the neck and below the bosom, and coming down to the knees, left her arms and legs bare, and consequently free to move. Standing thus in her fresh costume, the girl resembled Diana the huntress ready to enter her bath.

Sara advanced to the edge of a rock which overhung the bay, at a spot where the water was very deep ; then boldly, and with confidence in her skill and strength, certain of her superiority over an element in which she had been, in some degree, born, like Venus, she plunged in, disappeared beneath the water, and came up again swimming at some yards from the place where she had jumped in. All at once Henrietta heard a call, and, raising her head looked all round her ; then her eyes, directed by a second call, lighted on the fair bather, and she saw her water-nymph in the middle of the bay gliding on the surface of the water. Her first impulse was to recall Sara, but knowing that that would be trouble thrown away, she contented herself with giving her pupil a reproachful gesture, and, getting up, she approached the river bank as closely as the slope of the rock on which she had been sitting allowed.

At this moment her attention was for the moment distracted by signals which Sara was making. While swimming with one hand, Sara pointed with the other to the depths of the wood to indicate that something fresh was taking place beneath those sombre arches of verdure. Henrietta listened, and heard the distant baying of a pack of hounds. After an instant the baying seemed to her to come closer, and she was confirmed in this opinion by fresh signals from Sara ; the sound, in fact, became more and more distinct, and presently could be heard the sound of feet rushing through the depths of the forest. At last,

all of a sudden, at two hundred yards above the spot where
Henrietta was seated, a fine stag was seen to crash through
the branches and burst out of the forest, spring with one
bound over the river, and disappear on the other side.
After an instant, the hounds in their turn appeared, jumped
the river at the spot where the stag had jumped it, and,
hotly pursuing the scent, disappeared into the forest.

Sara had shared this spectacle with all the delight of a
keen lover of the chase. So, when the stag and hounds
had disappeared, she gave a cry of pleasure ; but this cry
was answered by a shout of terror so deep and heart-
rending that Henrietta turned in amazement. The old
mulatto woman, standing on the bank, like a statue of
wonder, was pointing her arms to an enormous shark that
with the aid of the flood-tide, had cleared the barrier reef,
and, scarcely sixty yards from Sara, was swimming on the
surface of the water towards her. The governess had not
even the strength to cry out, but fell upon her knees.

On hearing the woman's shout, Sara had turned and
seen the danger that threatened her. Then, with admirable
presence of mind, she made for the nearest point of the
shore. But this point was at least forty yards off, and, no
matter with what skill and strength she swam, the monster
seemed likely to overtake her before she could reach land.

At this moment another shout was heard, and a Negro,
clasping a long dagger between his teeth, rushed through
the middle of the mangroves that bordered the shore, and,
with one spring, covered nearly half the width of the bay.
Then, instantly beginning to swim with almost superhuman
strength, he tried to intercept the shark, which all this
time, as if sure of its prey, was advancing, without quicken-
ing the movements of its tail, towards the girl, who, turning
her head at each stroke, could see her foe and her defender
coming up together with almost equal swiftness.

It was a moment of awful suspense for the old mulatto
and Henrietta, both of whom, standing on a higher level,
could see the progress of this appalling chase. Both of
them gasping, with outstretched arms and open mouths,
without any means of helping Sara, uttered broken exclama-
tions at each alternative of fear or hope ; but presently

the fear preponderated, for, spite of the swimmer's efforts, the shark gained on her. The Negro was still twenty yards from the monster, which was but a few strokes from Sara. A terrible twist of his tail brought him still closer. The girl, who was pale as death, could hear the wash of the water ten feet behind her. She threw a last glance at the shore which she had now no time to reach. Then she realized how it was useless to struggle any longer for her doomed life; she raised her eyes to heaven, clasped her hands above the water, imploring God Who alone could succour her: And now the shark turned over to seize his prey; and, instead of his green back, his silver belly was seen on the surface of the sea. Henrietta covered her face with her hands so as to shut out the sight of what was about to happen; but, at this supreme moment, a double report from a gun sounded to the governess's right hand; two bullets followed one another with the rapidity of lightning, making the water spout up, and a calm, sonorous voice uttered, in the satisfied tone of a marksman well pleased with himself, the words:

"Well hit."

Henrietta turned and saw, dominating the whole of the dreadful scene, a young man who, grasping his still smoking rifle in one hand and holding on with the other to a cinnamon tree, while his feet were supported by the edge of a rock, watched the convulsions of the shark. The latter, wounded in two places, had at once turned over, as if to seek the invisible enemy who had just struck him. Then, seeing the Negro, who was not more than three or four strokes from him, he abandoned Sara in order to pursue him; but, on his approach, the man dived and disappeared under the water. The shark dived in turn; presently the water was agitated by the lashings of the monster's tail, its surface was tinged with blood, and it became evident that a struggle was taking place beneath the waves.

During this time Henrietta had come down, or rather, let herself slide down from her rock, and had reached the shore so as to hold out her hand to Sara, who, utterly exhausted and still unable to believe she had really and truly escaped such a fearful peril, no sooner touched the land than she fell on her knees. As for Henrietta, no sooner did she see her pupil safe than, her strength failing her in her turn, she collapsed in an almost swooning condition.

When the two women regained their senses, the first thing they noticed was Laïza standing, covered with blood from wounds in his arm and thigh, while the carcass of the shark was floating on the surface of the sea.

Then both women at the same instant and with a spontaneous movement directed their eyes towards the rock on which had appeared the delivering angel. The rock was deserted : the delivering angel had disappeared, though not so quickly but that both had had time to recognize him as the young stranger of Port Louis.

Then Sara turned towards the Negro who had just given her so signal a proof of his devotion. But, after an instant of mute contemplation, the latter had betaken himself again into the wood, and Sara looked around her in vain ; like the stranger, the Negro had vanished.

CHAPTER XI

A SALE OF STOCK

AT the same moment two men rushed up, who had seen, from a point higher up the river, a part of the scene that had just taken place ; they were M. de Malmédie and Henri.

The girl then remembered that she was but half-dressed, and, blushing at the idea of being seen in that state, she called the old mulatto woman, put on a dressing-gown, and, leaning on Henrietta's arm, who was still palpitating with terror, advanced towards her uncle and cousin.

The latter, following the trail of the stag, had reached the bank of the river just as the double report of Georges' gun made itself heard. Their first impression was that one of their companions had fired at the animal ; so they had looked in the direction whence the sound had come, and had seen, as we have said, from a distance and indistinctly, part of the incident which has been related. Behind the Malmédies came the rest of the shooting party.

Sara and Henrietta soon found themselves the centre of a

group of men who questioned them on what had happened, but Henrietta was still too agitated and upset to give any coherent answer, and it was Sara who told the whole story.

There is a vast difference between being an eyewitness of a scene so terrible as the one we have tried to describe, following all its details with looks of horror, and merely hearing the relation of it, whether from the lips of her who had nearly been the victim, or on the actual spot where it has occurred. Still, as the smoke from the reports of the gun had hardly cleared away, and as the carcass of the monster was still afloat there, quivering in convulsions of pain, Sara's story produced a great effect. Each man was gallant enough to regret that he had not happened to be there in the place of the unknown stranger or the Negro. Each man was confident that he would certainly have aimed as correctly as the one, or swum as vigorously as the other. But to all these declarations of skill and protests of devotion, a silent voice replied inwardly in Sara's heart: " None but those two could have done what they did."

At this moment the noise of the hounds showed that the stag was brought to bay. Every one knows what a delight it is for a keen sportsman to be present at the death-halloo of an animal which they have hunted the whole morning. Sara was saved and had nothing to fear. It was useless, therefore, to waste in condolences over an accident which, after all, had had no serious result, the time that might be spent more profitably elsewhere. Two or three of the sportsmen who were farthest from the girl moved away, going off in the direction the noise came from, and four or five others soon followed their example. Henri remarked that it would be bad manners not to go with his invited guests, to whom he ought to do the honours of his estate under all circumstances ; so at the end of ten minutes the only person remaining with Sara and Henrietta was M. de Malmédie.

The three returned to the dwelling-house, where an excellent dinner awaited the sportsmen, who were not long in arriving, with Henri at their head. He courteously brought his cousin one of the stag's hoofs, which he had himself cut off, to offer it to her as a trophy. Sara thanked him for this delicate attention, and Henri, on his side, congratulated her on having regained her beautiful colour so completely that one would have said, to look at her, that nothing at all out of the way had happened ; and Henri's remark was echoed in chorus by the rest of the company. The meal was of the gayest. Henrietta had asked to be excused from it ; the poor woman had received such a shock that she felt a feverish attack coming on. As for Sara, she was, as Henri had said, to all outward appearance, at least, perfectly calm, and did the honours of the dinner with her customary grace. At dessert several toasts were drunk, among which, it is but right to say, some had reference to the event of the morning ; but in these toasts no mention was made of the unknown Negro or the strange hunter. The whole honour of the miracle was credited to the grace of Providence wishing to preserve to M. de Malmédie and Henri a niece and a fiancée so tenderly beloved.

But if during the toasts no word was breathed of Laïza or Georges, whose names, in fact, were known to nobody, each individual, to make up for this omission, spoke at great length of his own prowess, and Sara with charming irony distributed to each the portion of the praise that was due to him for his skill and courage.

As they were rising from table, the Overseer entered, coming to tell M. de Malmédie that a slave who had attempted to escape had been caught and had just been brought back to the slaves' quarters. As this was a matter that happened almost every day M. de Malmédie contented himself with the answer :

" All right ; let him have the usual punishment."

" What is the matter, Uncle ? " asked Sara.

" Nothing, my child," said M. de Malmédie.

And the conversation which had been interrupted, was resumed. Ten minutes later it was announced that the horses were ready. As Lord Murray's dinner and ball were on the next day, everybody was anxious to have the whole of the rest of the day to prepare for this solemnity ; so it had been arranged that they should return to Port Louis immediately after dinner.

Sara went into Henrietta's bedroom ; the poor governess, without being seriously ill, was still so agitated that Sara insisted on her remaining at the *Rivière Noire* ; besides, Sara would be the gainer by Henrietta's prolonged stay, for, instead of returning in the palanquin, she would go on horseback.

As the cavalcade was starting, Sara observed three or four Negroes busy cutting up the shark ; the mulatto woman had told them where they would find its carcass, and they had gone to fish it out, so as to make it into oil.

On approaching the *Trois-Mamelles* the sportsmen saw from a distance the Negroes all assembled. When they reached the spot, they realized that the crowd was caused by the expectation of the punishment of a slave, the custom being, on such occasions, to collect the Negroes on the estate and compel them to witness the correction of any of their companions who had been guilty of misconduct.

The culprit was a youth of seventeen, who stood waiting, bound and gagged, near the ladder on which he would be fastened at the hour fixed for his punishment. This, at the urgent entreaty of another Negro, had been delayed until the cavalcade of riders should pass by, the slave who had importuned this favour having said that he had an important communication to make to M. de Malmédie.

At the moment, indeed, when M. de Malmédie arrived opposite the youth, a Negro who was sitting beside him occupied in stanching a wound which he had received in the head, got up and came close to the road ; but the Overseer barred his further advance.

" What is the matter ? " asked M. de Malmédie.

" Sir," said the Overseer, " it is the negro Nazim, who is about to receive the hundred and fifty lashes to which he has been sentenced."

" And why has he been sentenced to a hundred and fifty lashes ? " asked Sara.

" For running away," answered the Overseer.

" Oh ! " said Henri, " that is the man whose escape you came to tell us of."

" Yes, the same."

" And how did you recapture him ? "

" Oh ! quite easily. I just waited until he was too far

from the shore either to row or to swim back to it ; then I got into a long-boat with eight rowers and started in pursuit ; on rounding the cape at the south-west we saw him at about two miles out to sea. As he had but two arms and a miserable canoe, while we had sixteen and a good pirogue, we very soon came up with him. Then he plunged in and swam, to try and reach the island, diving like a porpoise ; but, to cut the matter short, he was the first to tire, and, finding the business troublesome, I took an oar from the hands of one of the rowers, and, when he came up again to the surface, struck him such a well-aimed blow on the head that I thought, the next time, that he had gone under for good and all. However, we saw him come up again after a moment, but he was unconscious, and did not recover his senses until we reached the Brabant hill, and here we are."

" But," said Sara eagerly, " perhaps the poor man is badly hurt."

" Oh, good gracious ! no, Mademoiselle," replied the Overseer, " a mere scratch. These wretched Negroes are as soft as anything."

" And why have you been so long in administering the punishment he has so richly deserved ? " said M. de Malmédie. " After the orders I gave, it should have been already done."

" And so it would have, sir," replied the Overseer, " if his brother, who is one of our best workers, had not assured me that he had something of importance to tell you, before the orders were carried out. As you were to pass the cantonment, and as it only involved a quarter of an hour's delay, I took upon myself to suspend your orders."

" And you have done quite right, Overseer," said Sara. " And where is he ? "

" Who ? "

" The brother of this wretched man ? "

" Yes, where is he ? " asked M. de Malmédie.

" Here," said Laïza, coming forward.

Sara uttered a cry of surprise ; she had just recognized, in the brother of the condemned slave, the man who had so nobly devoted himself to saving her life that morning. To her astonishment, however, the Negro had not once glanced in her direction, and seemed not to recognize her ; instead of imploring her interference, as he certainly had the right to do, he continued to advance towards M. de Malmédie. It was not possible, however, to be mistaken : the gashes left by the shark's teeth on his arms and thigh were still open and bleeding.

"What do you want ? " said M. de Malmédie.

" To ask a favour of you," answered Laïza in a low tone, so that his brother, who was twenty yards off, guarded by some other Negroes, should not hear.

" What is it ? "

" Nazim is weak, Nazim is young, Nazim is wounded in the head and has lost a great deal of blood ; Nazim is perhaps not strong enough to endure the punishment he deserves ; he may die under the lash, and then you will have lost a Negro who, upon the whole, is worth a good two hundred dollars. . . ."

" Well, what do you want ? "

" I want to propose an exchange ? "

" Of what sort ? "

" That the hundred and fifty lashes which he has earned should be given to me instead. I am strong, and can bear them ; and the punishment will not prevent my doing my work to-morrow as usual, while he, I repeat, is but a child, and it would kill him."

" It cannot be done," answered M. de Malmédie, while Sara, keeping her eyes fixed on the Negro, looked at him with the most profound astonishment.

" And why not ? "

" Because it would be an injustice."

" You are wrong, for it is I who am really to blame."

" You ! "

" Yes, I," said Laïza ; " it is I who stirred Nazim up to run away, I who hollowed out the canoe which he used, and shaved his head with a piece of bottle glass, and gave him coco-oil to rub his skin with. So you see that it is I who should be punished, and not Nazim."

" You are wrong," answered Henri, taking part in the discussion. " You ought both to be punished ; he for running away, you for having helped him to do so."

" Then give me three hundred lashes, and the matter will be settled."

" Overseer," said M. de Malmédie, " give each of these rogues a hundred and fifty lashes, and let that end it."

" One moment, Uncle," said Sara ; " I ask for these two men to be let off."

" And why ? " asked M. de Malmédie in astonishment.

" Because this is the man who threw himself in the water so bravely this morning to save me."

" She recognizes me ! " cried Laïza.

" Because, instead of the punishment he deserves, we must give him a recompense," cried Sara.

" Then," said Laïza, " if you think I have earned a recompense, grant me that Nazim shall be let off."

" Confound it ! " said M. de Malmédie, " how you stick to it ! Was it you who saved my niece ? "

" It was not I," answered the Negro ; " but for the young hunter, she would have been lost."

" But he did what he could to save me, Uncle, and he fought with the shark," cried the girl. " Why, look at his wounds, which are still bleeding."

" I fought with the shark, but in my own defence," replied Laïza. " The shark attacked me, and I had to kill it in order to save myself."

" Well, Uncle, you will not refuse to let them off for my sake ? " Sara persisted.

" Yes, I shall certainly refuse," answered M. de Malmédie ; " for if once an exemption were to be made on such an occasion, these blackamoors would all be running away, hoping that there would be some pretty mouth like yours to intercede for them."

" But, Uncle . . ."

" Ask these gentlemen if the thing is possible," said M. de Malmédie in a confident tone, turning to the young men who accompanied his son.

" It is a fact," they answered, " that such an exemption would be a ruinous precedent."

" You see, Sara."

" But a man who has risked his life for me," said Sara, " ought not to be punished on the very same day ;

for if you owe him a punishment, I owe him a reward."

"Well, we will each pay our debt; when I have had him punished, you shall reward him."

"But, Uncle, how does the fault which these unhappy men have committed affect you, after all? What harm have they done you, having failed to carry out their design?"

"What harm has it done? Why, it takes off part of their value. A Negro who has tried to run away loses a heavy percentage of his price. Here are two fellows who yesterday were worth, one five hundred, the other three hundred dollars—eight hundred dollars in all. Well, if I were to ask six hundred to-day, I should not get them."

"For my part, I wouldn't give six hundred for them now," said one of the sportsmen.

"Well, sir, I will be more liberal than you," said a voice, the tones of which made Sara start, "I will give a thousand."

The girl turned and recognized the stranger of Port Louis, the Saving Angel of the rock, who was standing, dressed in an elegant shooting suit and leaning on his double-barrelled gun. He had heard all that had passed.

"Oh! it is you, sir," said M. de Malmédie, while Henri's face flushed from a cause that he could not explain to himself; "accept, in the first place, my best thanks, for my niece has told me that she owes her life to you; and, had I known where to find you, I should have hastened to see you, not to try to acquit myself of my obligation to you, which would be impossible, but to express my gratitude."

The stranger bowed without replying, and with an air of haughty modesty that did not escape Sara. Accordingly she hastened to add:

"My Uncle is right, sir; such a service cannot be repaid. But be assured that, as long as I live, I shall remember that I owe you my life."

"A couple of charges of powder and two lead bullets do not deserve such thanks, Mademoiselle. So I shall consider myself fortunate if M. de Malmédie's gratitude will go so far as to let me have, at the price I have offered him, these two Negroes, whom I need."

"Henri," said M. de Malmédie *sotto voce*, "were we not told yesterday that there was a slave-ship in sight?"

" Yes, father'! " answered Henri.

" Good," continued M. de Malmédie, speaking this time to himself, " good, we shall be able to replace them."

" I await your answer, sir," said the stranger.

" Why, sir, with the greatest pleasure. The Negroes are yours, you can take them ; but, if I were in your place, and could spare them from work for three or four days, I should have them punished this very day in the way they deserve."

" That is my affair," said the stranger, smiling. " The thousand dollars shall be sent you this evening."

" Excuse me, sir," said Henri, " you are mistaken : my father's intention is not to sell you these two men, but to give them to you. The life of two wretched Negroes cannot be put in comparison with a life so precious as that of my fair cousin. Let us, at least, offer you what we have, and what you appear to desire."

" But, sir," said the stranger, raising his head haughtily, while M. de Malmédie gave his son a most meaning look, "that was not our agreement."

" Well, then," said Sara, " allow me to make an alteration in it, and for the sake of her whose life you have saved take these two Negroes whom we offer you."

" I thank you, Mademoiselle," said the stranger ; " it would be absurd of me to insist further. So I accept ; and it is I who now regard myself as in your debt."

And the stranger bowed and stepped back, as a sign that he did not wish to detain the company from their journey any longer.

The men exchanged bows ; but Sara and Georges exchanged looks.

The cavalcade resumed its journey, and Georges followed it with his eye for some time with that contraction of the brows which was habitual to him when a bitter thought preoccupied him. Then, turning to the Negroes and approaching Nazim, he said to the Overseer :

" Unbind that man ; for he and his brother are now my property."

The Overseer, who had heard the conversation between the stranger and M. de Malmédie, made no difficulty.

Nazim accordingly was unbound and handed over with Laïza to his new master.

"Now, my friends," said the stranger, turning to the Negroes and drawing from his pocket a purse filled with gold, "as I have received a present from your master, it is right that I, in my turn, should make you a small present. Take this purse and divide its contents amongst you."

And he handed the purse to the Negro who was nearest to him, then, turning to the two slaves, who, standing behind him, were awaiting his orders, he said to them :

"As for you two, do what you like now, go where you will, you are free."

Laïza and Nazim both uttered a cry of joy mingled with doubt, for they could not believe this act of generosity on the part of a man to whom they had rendered no service. But Georges repeated his words, upon which Laïza and Nazim fell on their knees and kissed the hand of the man who had set them free with an outburst of gratitude impossible to describe.

As for Georges, he replaced on his head his large straw hat, which up to now he had been holding in his hand, threw his gun over his shoulder, and, as it was beginning to grow late, resumed his road to Moka.

CHAPTER XII

THE BALL

THE dinner and ball, the announcement of which had caused such excitement in Port Louis, were to take place, as we have said, on the next day at Government House.

No one who has not lived in the Colonies, and especially in the Isle of France, has any idea of the luxury prevalent below the twentieth degree of South latitude. In addition to the marvels from Paris which cross the sea for the adornment of the graceful Creoles of Mauritius, they can make choice, at first hand, from among the diamonds of Visapore, the pearls of Ophir, the cashmeres of Siam, and the beautiful muslins of Calcutta. Not a vessel from the land of the "Thousand and One Nights" stops at the Isle of France

without leaving behind a portion of the treasures she is
carrying to Europe, and the dazzling effect presented
by an assembly in the Isle of France causes astonishment
even to one who is accustomed to the elegance of Paris or
the profusion of England.

Accordingly the drawing-room in Government House,
which in the space of three days had been entirely refur-
nished by Lord Murray in the most fashionable and comfortable style, presented, towards four o'clock in the afternoon all the appearance of an apartment in the Rue
du Mont-Blanc or Belgrave Square. The whole aristocracy of the Colony, male and female, were there assembled ;
the men in the simple dress imposed by modern fashion ;
the women sparkling with diamonds, loaded with pearls,
attired all ready for the ball,with nothing to distinguish them
from our European women but that languid grace and charming morbidezza of complexion possessed by none but Creole
women. As each fresh arrival was announced, the person
who entered was greeted with a general smile, for, at Port
Louis, everybody knows everybody else and the only curiosity evinced at the entrance of a lady into the salon is to
discover what new gown she has bought, where that gown
comes from, of what material it is made, and how it is
trimmed. It was especially in regard to the English women
that the curiosity of the Creoles was aroused ; for, in that
perpetual strife of female vanity of which Port Louis is the
scene, the great question with the native ladies is how to
outdo their foreign sisters in magnificence. The murmurs
and whisperings which were heard at each fresh arrival
were therefore louder and more prolonged when the lackey
made the official announcement of some British name, the
harsh sound of which contrasted as strongly with the soft-
sounding native names as the fair pale daughter of the
North differed from the dark maidens of the tropics. As
each fresh guest entered, Lord Murray, with the politeness that characterizes Englishmen in high society,
advanced to meet them. If it was a lady, he offered
his arm to lead her to her seat, paying her some compliment on the way ; if it was a man, he shook hands
with him and said a gracious word in his ear, so that every-

body acknowledged the new Governor to be a charming man.

Presently the Malmédies were announced. Their arrival was expected with as much impatience as curiosity, not only because M. de Malmédie was one of the richest and most important men of the Island, but even more because Sara was one of the wealthiest and most elegant of its heiresses. Every one's eyes accordingly followed Lord Murray as he went to meet her, for the question of how she would be dressed was the one that chiefly filled the minds of all the prettiest women among the guests.

Contrary to the custom of Creole women and to all expectation, Sara was dressed exceedingly simply, in a charming gown of Indian muslin, transparent and light as the gauze which Juvenal terms "woven air," without embroidery, without a single pearl or diamond; its sole adornment was a spray of pink hawthorn. A garland of the same leaves surrounded her head, while a bunch of the flowers was pinned at her waist; not so much as a bracelet set off the lustrous tint of her skin. Only her fine, dark, and silky hair fell in long ringlets over her shoulders, and in her hand she held the fan, that marvel of Chinese workmanship, which she had bought from Miko-Miko.

As we have said, every one knew every one else in the Isle of France; so that, after the arrival of the Malmédies, it was felt that there was no one else to come, since all those who, by their rank and wealth, were in the habit of meeting in society, were assembled. The company therefore naturally ceased to turn their eyes to the door, through which no one else was expected to enter, and, after waiting for ten minutes, began to ask each other what other guest Lord Murray could be expecting, when the door opened once more, and the servant in a loud voice announced " Monsieur Georges Munier."

Had a thunderbolt fallen into the middle of the company whom we have just brought together under the reader's eyes, it would certainly not have caused the effect produced by this simple announcement. On hearing the name, every one turned towards the door, wondering who it could be that was coming in, for, although the name was well known in the Isle of France, the person who bore it had been so long absent that people had almost forgotten his existence. Georges entered.

The young mulatto was dressed with simplicity, but with extremely good taste. His well-fitting black coat, from the buttonhole of which were suspended at the end of a gold chain the two little crosses with which he had been decorated, showed off all the elegance of his figure. His tight-fitting trousers revealed the graceful, lithe shape of limb peculiar to men of colour, and, contrary to the custom of these latter, he wore no jewellery except a thin gold chain like the one in his buttonhole, the only visible end of which disappeared into the pocket of his white piqué waistcoat. In addition, a black cravat tied with that studied negligence only acquired by fashionable habits, and over which a round shirt-collar was turned down, framed his handsome face, the fine morbidezza of which was set off by his dark moustache and hair.

Lord Murray advanced farther to meet Georges than he had done in the case of any one else, and after shaking hands with him, introduced him to three or four ladies and five or six English officers who were in the room as a travelling companion, on whose society he had congratulated himself during the whole of the voyage. Then, turning to the rest of the company he said :

" Gentlemen, I present to you M. Georges Munier. M. Munier is your fellow-countryman, and the return of a man so distinguished as he is, ought almost to be the occasion of a national festivity."

Georges bowed in token of acknowledgment, but, whatever respect might be due to the Governor, especially in his own house, scarcely a single voice found strength to stammer a few words in answer to the introduction just made by Lord Murray.

Lord Murray either did not notice this, or appeared not to, and on the servant announcing that dinner was served, the Governor gave his arm to Sara, and a move was made to the dining-room.

After what we know of Georges' character it will be easily guessed that it was not unintentionally that he had made the company wait for him, now that he was on the point of

entering upon his struggle with that prejudice which he
had determined to combat ; he had wanted, at the first
onset, to see his enemy face to face, and what he wished
for had happened ; the announcement of his name and his
entrance had produced all the effect he could have expected.

But the person most stirred in the whole august assembly
was undoubtedly Sara. Knowing that the young hunter
of the *Rivière Noire* had arrived at Port Louis with Lord
Murray, she had expected beforehand to see him, and
possibly it was with a view to this fresh arrival from Europe
that she had dressed herself with the elegant simplicity so
much appreciated among ourselves, and which, it must be
confessed, is so often replaced in the Colonies by an overdone
smartness. So, on entering the salon, she had looked
everywhere for the young stranger. One glance had
sufficed to tell her that he was not there, but she concluded
that he would arrive presently, and that when he was
announced, as he no doubt would be, she would then learn
for a certainty both his name and who he was.

What Sara had foreseen had happened. Scarcely had
she taken her place in the circle of ladies, and the Messieurs
Malmédie joined the group of men, than M. Georges
Munier was announced.

At this name, so well known in the Island, but not usually
heard mentioned in such circumstances, Sara started
violently and then recovered herself, but yet was overcome
with anxiety. She saw the young stranger of Port Louis
appear, with his calm face, his haughty look, his lip curling
with contempt, and on the third appearance he seemed,
let us hasten to add, even more handsome and romantic in
her eyes than on the two previous occasions. Then she followed, not only with her eyes but with her heart, the introduction of Georges into society made by Lord Murray and
her heart was wounded when the repulsion inspired by the
young mulatto's birth expressed itself by silence on the
part of the guests, and it was with eyes almost blinded by
tears that she responded to the swift and penetrating
glance bestowed upon her by Georges.

Then Lord Murray gave her his arm and she saw nothing
further, for she felt herself turning red and pale almost simul-

taneously beneath Georges' glance, and, feeling convinced
that all eyes were directed towards herself, had immediately
hastened to escape from the general curiosity. But on this
point Sara was mistaken ; nobody had given her a thought,
for, with the exception of M. Malmédie and his son, they
were all in ignorance of the two preceding incidents which
had brought the young man and the girl in contact with
each other, and nobody dreamed that there could be anything in common between Mademoiselle Sara de Malmédie
and M. Georges Munier.

When once seated at table, Sara ventured to look round
the room. She was placed on the right of the Governor,
who had on his left the wife of the Military Commandant
of the Island ; opposite to her was the Commandant himself, seated between two ladies belonging to the most
important families in the Island. Next, to the right and
left of these two ladies, came M. de Malmédie and his son,
and so on ; while Georges, either by accident or by the
graceful forethought of Lord Murray, was placed between
two English ladies.

Sara breathed more freely : she knew that the prejudice
that pursued Georges did not affect the minds of strangers,
and that any one coming from a European country must
have lived a very long time in the Colonies before sharing
in it ; she saw Georges therefore carrying out in the most easy
fashion his rôle of an agreeable guest between the alternate
smiles of Lord Murray's compatriots, who were delighted
to have as their neighbour a man who spoke their language
as well as if he had been himself an Englishman by birth.

While thus directing her glance towards the centre of
the table, Sara noticed that Henri's eyes were fixed upon
her. She understood perfectly what was passing in her
fiancé's mind, and, with a movement which her will could
not control, lowered her own eyes and blushed.

Lord Murray was, in the fullest meaning of the term, a
great nobleman, admirably skilled in playing the part of
host—a part so difficult to learn, unless it is fulfilled instinctively, and unless a man is, so to speak, born to it. Accordingly, when the constraint and uneasiness which usually pre-
vail during the first courses of a formal banquet were

dispelled, he began to address remarks to his guests, speaking to each on the subject calculated to elicit the best replies, reminding the English officers of some noted engagement, and the merchants of some brilliant piece of speculation, in the midst of all this making an observation from time to time to Georges, which showed that with him he could converse on all topics, and that he was addressing a man of universal information, and not a specialist on military affairs or on questions of commerce.

In this way the dinner progressed. Georges, with his quick intelligence, but with perfect modesty, had answered every observation and every question from the Governor in a way that proved to the officers that he, like themselves, had seen service, and to the merchants that he was acquainted with those great commercial concerns which make the whole world one single family, united by the bond of common interests. Moreover, interspersed with his fragmentary conversation, there had sprung to his lips the names of all those who in France or England or Spain occupied a high position in the world of politics, or of society, or of art, each accompanied by one of those remarks which show, in a single flash, that the man who is speaking speaks with a full knowledge of the character, or the genius, or the position of the men whom he has just mentioned.

Although these tit-bits of conversation, if one may so express it, had passed over the heads of the majority of the guests, there were among their number men who were capable of appreciating the superiority with which Georges had touched upon all these topics, so that, although the feeling of repulsion which they had shown towards the young mulatto still remained, their astonishment had increased, and together with the astonishment, envy had entered the hearts of some of them. Henri especially, taken up with the idea that Sara had bestowed more notice on Georges than, considering her position as his fiancée and her dignity as a white woman, she had any business to do, Henri, I say, felt an uncontrollable bitterness rising in his heart. Then, at the mention of the name of Munier, recollections of his boyhood were awakened; he recalled the day when, wishing to snatch the flag from Georges' hands, the latter's brother Jacques had struck him that severe blow in the face with his fist. All these bygone misdeeds of the two brothers stirred menacingly in his breast ; and the thought that Sara had on the previous day been rescued by this man, instead of effacing these accusing murmurs in respect to the past, only fanned his resentment against him the more. As for M. Malmédie, he had been occupied throughout the dinner in a discussion with his neighbour on a new method of refining sugar, which would have the result of increasing by thirty per cent. the value of the produce of his estate. Consequently, apart from his first astonishment at finding in Georges the preserver of his niece, and at meeting Georges in Lord Murray's house, he had paid no further attention to him.

But, as we have said, this was not the case with Henri, who had not lost a word of the questions put by Lord Murray and the answers given by Georges. He had recognized the sound sense and cultivated thought in each of these answers ; he had studied the firm glance which was the exponent of Georges' authoritative will, and realized that here was no longer, as on the day of his departure, a down-trodden boy whom he saw before him, but a powerful opponent who came to challenge him.

Had Georges, on his return to the Isle of France, relapsed humbly into the condition for which, according to the views of white men, Nature had intended him, and suffered himself to be eclipsed by the obscurity of his birth, Henri would in that case have passed over, or at any rate have cherished no malice against him for, the wrong inflicted upon him by Georges fourteen years ago. But the case was far otherwise.

He had come back proudly in broad daylight, as it were, and had, by a service rendered to his family, intermeddled in its life, and now came as his equal in rank and his superior in intelligence to sit at the same table with himself. This was more than Henri could bear, and Henri in his own mind deliberately declared war against him.

So, on leaving the table, and when they had just passed out into the garden, Henri went up to Sara, who, with several other ladies, was seated in an arbour parallel to the one beneath which the gentlemen were taking their coffee.

Sara started, feeling an instinctive certainty that what Henri was about to say concerned Georges.

"Well, fair cousin," said the young man, leaning over the bamboo chair on which the girl was sitting, "what did you think of the dinner?"

"That question, I presume, does not relate to the menu?" answered Sara with a smile.

"No, dear cousin, though, with some of our fellow-guests, who do not live, like yourself, on dew and air and perfumes, that question would not be out of place. No, my question refers to the social aspect, if I may say so."

"Well, it was excellent, I thought. Lord Murray appeared to me to do the honours of his table admirably, and to have made himself, as far as I could see, as agreeable as possible to everybody."

"Yes, certainly; and therefore I am greatly astonished that he should have run the risk of compromising us all as he has done."

"In what way?" asked Sara, who understood perfectly what her cousin was driving at, and who, drawing upon a strength that lay, unknown to herself, at the bottom of her heart, looked her cousin straight in the eyes as she put this question to him.

"Why," answered Henri, somewhat embarrassed not only by her clear gaze, but also by the low murmur of his conscience, "in inviting M. Georges Munier to meet us at the same table."

"And I am no less astonished, Henri, that you should not have left to somebody else the task of making this observation to me, of all people."

"And why am I alone forbidden to make this remark, my dear cousin?"

"Because, but for M. Georges Munier, whose presence here you think so unbecoming, your father and you, that is if a cousin is worth bewailing and a niece deserving of mourning, would now be in mourning and tears."

"Yes, of course," answered Henri, reddening; "I acknowledge all the gratitude we owe to M. Georges for having saved a life so precious as your own, and you saw yesterday how, when he wanted to buy those two Negroes whom my father was going to have punished, I hastened to give them to him."

"And by the present of those two Negroes you think you have discharged your obligation to him? I thank you, cousin, for valuing the life of Sara de Malmédie at the sum of a thousand dollars."

"Good heavens! my dear Sara," said Henri, "how strangely you twist things to-day! Was I thinking for a moment of putting a price upon a life, for which I would sacrifice my own? No, I only intended to point out to you into what a false position, for instance, Lord Murray would put any lady who was invited to dance by M. Georges Munier."

"Then, in your opinion, my dear Henri, that lady should decline?"

"Undoubtedly she should."

"Without reflecting that by declining, she offers a man who has done her no harm, and who has even perhaps rendered her some small service, an insult for which he would necessarily demand satisfaction from her father, her brother, or her husband?"

"I presume that, in such a case, M. Georges would examine himself and have the justice to suppose that a white man would not condescend to measure swords with a Mulatto."

"Pardon me, cousin, for venturing to express an opinion in such a matter," replied Sara; "but either, after the little I have seen of him I have misjudged M. Georges, or I do not think that, if it was a question of avenging his honour, a man who wears two crosses on his breast, as he does, would be stopped by that inward feeling of humility with which you have credited him—quite gratuitously, I think."

"At any rate I hope, my dear Sara," replied Henri, his face red with anger, "that the fear of exposing my father or myself to the wrath of M. Georges will not make you so imprudent as to dance with him, should he have the effrontery to ask you to do so."

"I shall dance with no one, sir," replied Sara coldly, rising and taking the arm of the English lady who had sat next to Georges at table, and who was a friend of hers.

Henri remained for a moment quite dumbfounded by this unexpected firmness, then he joined a group of young Creoles, among whom he doubtless found more sympathy with his aristocratic notions than his cousin had evinced.

During this time Georges, in the centre of another group, was chatting with some English officers and merchants, who did not share, or only to a very slight extent, the prejudice of his compatriots.

An hour passed thus during which all the preparations for the ball were completed, and then the doors were thrown open, giving admission to the rooms from which the furniture had been removed, and which were now ablaze with lights. At the same instant the orchestra struck up, as a signal for the quadrille.

Sara had had a severe internal struggle in condemning herself merely to watch the dancing, for, as we have said, she was passionately fond of balls. But all the bitterness of the sacrifice she was making recoiled upon the man who had demanded it of her ; while, on the contrary, a more deep and tender feeling than any she had yet experienced began to stir in her heart in favour of the man for whose sake she had made the sacrifice, for it is one of the sublime characteristics, of women, whom Nature and Society have combined to make so weak and so winning, to display a strong interest in all who are oppressed, as well as a lofty admiration for such as will not let themselves be oppressed.

So, when Henri, hoping that his cousin would be unable to resist the temptation of the opening strains, came, in spite of her expressed decision, to ask her to dance the first quadrille with him as usual, Sara merely answered:

" You know I am not dancing to-night, cousin."

Henri bit his lips until the blood came, and, by an instinctive movement, sought with his eyes for Georges. The latter had taken up his position and was dancing with the Englishwoman whom he had taken in to dinner. With a feeling that was merely one of sympathy Sara's eyes had followed in the direction of her cousin's. Her heart was wrung with pain, for Georges was dancing with some one else, perhaps was not even thinking of the Sara who had just made a sacrifice for his sake which but yesterday she would have deemed herself incapable of making for any one in the world. The minutes during which this quadrille lasted were perhaps the most unhappy that Sara had ever spent.

When the quadrille was over, Sara, in spite of herself, could not keep her eyes from following Georges. He escorted the Englishwoman to her place and then appeared to look about for some one. It was Lord Murray whom he sought. As soon as he discovered him, he went up and spoke a word or two to him, and then both advanced towards Sara. Sara felt the blood rush to her heart.

" Mademoiselle," said Lord Murray, " here is a fellow-traveller of mine who is perhaps a too scrupulous observer of European customs, and therefore does not venture to ask you to dance before he has had the honour of being intro-duced to you. Allow me then to present to you M. Georges Munier, one of the most distinguished men of my acquaint-ance."

" As you say, my lord," replied Sara, in a voice which, by dint of self-control, she succeeded in rendering almost steady, " this fear on the part of M. Georges is somewhat exaggerated ; for we are already old acquaintances. On the very day of his arrival M. Georges did me a kindness ; while yesterday he did more than that, for he saved my life."

" What ! the young hunter who had the good fortune to be on the spot and shoot that dreadful shark, while you were bathing, was he M. Georges ? "

" The same, my lord," replied Sara, blushing at the mere thought of Georges having seen her in her swimming-dress ; " and I felt so agitated and alarmed yesterday that I had hardly strength to offer M. Georges my thanks. But to-day I renew them all the more gratefully, since it is to his skill and coolness that I owe the pleasure of being present at your delightful entertainment, my lord."

" And we add our thanks to yours," put in Henri, who had joined the little group of which Sara formed the central figure ; " for we too, yesterday, were so disturbed and upset by this accident that we scarcely had the honour of saying a word to M. Georges."

Georges, who had not uttered a word, but whose piercing eyes had penetrated to the depth of Sara's heart, bowed in token of acknowledgment, but without making any other reply to Henri.

"Then I hope," said Lord Murray, "that the request M. Georges wanted to make of you will be successful on its own merits, and I leave my protégé to speak for himself."

"Will Mademoiselle de Malmédie give me the honour of a dance?" said Georges, bowing once more.

"Oh! sir," said Sara, "I am truly sorry, and I hope you will forgive me. I have just refused my cousin, as I do not intend to dance to-night."

Georges smiled with the air of a man who grasps the whole situation, and drew himself up, giving Henri a glance of such utter contempt that Lord Murray perceived, from this glance and the way in which it was answered by Henri, that between these two men existed a deep and inveterate hatred. But he concealed this observation in the depths of his heart, and, as though he had noticed nothing, remarked to Sara:

"No doubt the effects of your alarm yesterday are reacting upon your enjoyment to-day."

"Yes, my lord," answered Sara; "and I even feel so unwell that I will ask my cousin to let M. de Malmédie know that I should like to go away, and that I depend upon him for taking me home."

Henri and Lord Murray both made a movement in order to carry out the girl's wishes. Georges stooped quickly and said in a low tone:

"You have a noble heart, Mademoiselle, and I thank you."

Sara started, and would have answered him, but Lord Murray had already returned, so she only exchanged looks, almost in spite of herself, with Georges.

"You are still resolved to leave us, Mademoiselle?" said the Governor.

"Yes, alas!" answered Sara. "I should be so, so delighted to stay, my lord, but—I really feel ill."

"In that case, I feel that it would be selfish to try to keep you; and, as M. de Malmédie's carriage is probably not within reach, I will give orders for the horses to be put to my own."

And Lord Murray went off at once.

" Sara," said Georges, " when I left Europe to come back here, my one desire was to meet with a heart like yours ; but I did not expect to do so."

" Sir," murmured Sara, swayed in spite of herself by the deep tones of his voice, " I do not know what you mean."

" I mean that, since the day of my arrival, I have cherished a dream, and that, should that dream ever be realized, I shall be the happiest of men."

Then, without waiting for Sara's answer, Georges bowed with respect and, seeing M. de Malmédie and his son approaching, left Sara with her uncle and cousin.

Five minutes later, Lord Murray returned to tell Sara that the carriage was ready, and offered her his arm to cross the salon. As they reached the door, the girl gave a last look of regret at the scene where she had promised herself so much enjoyment, and disappeared. But her look had encountered one from Georges, which seemed as though it would pursue her all the rest of her days.

On coming back from taking Mlle. de Malmédie to the carriage, the Governor, passing through the ante-room, met Georges who, in his turn, was getting ready to leave the ball.

" You going also ? " said Lord Murray.

" Yes, my lord ; you know that for the present I am living at Moka, and that, consequently, I have nearly eight miles to go ; Antrim fortunately can do that in about an hour."

" You have had no private quarrel, have you, with Henri de Malmédie ? " asked the Governor with an expression of interest.

" No, my lord, not yet," replied Georges, smiling ; " but in all probability it will not be long delayed."

" Either I am much mistaken, my young friend," said the Governor, " or the causes of your enmity towards this family date from a long time back ? "

" Yes, my lord, little bullyings between boys which produce first-class hatred between grown-up men ; pin-pricks that develop into sword-thrusts."

" And is there no way of settling all this ? " asked the Governor.

" I hoped so at one time, my lord ; I thought fourteen years of British rule might have killed the prejudice which I came back to combat. I was mistaken ; and nothing remains but that the wrestler should rub his body with oil and step down into the arena."

" Will you not be encountering windmills rather than giants, my dear Don Quixote ? "

" I leave you to judge," said Georges, smiling. " Yesterday I saved Mlle. de Malmédie's life. Do you know how her cousin thanked me for it to-day ? "

" No."

" By forbidding her to dance with me."

" Impossible ? "

" It is as I have had the honour to tell you, my lord."

" And why did he do this ? "

" Because I am a Mulatto."

" And what do you intend to do ? "

" What do I intend ? "

" Forgive my indiscretion ; but you know what an interest I take in you, and besides, we are old friends."

" You ask what I intend to do ? " said Georges with a smile.

" Yes ; I am sure you have thought out some plan on your side."

" I have decided upon one this very evening."

" What is it ? Come, I will tell you if I approve of it."

" It is this, that in three months I will be Mademoiselle de Malmédie's husband."

And, before Lord Murray had time to express either approval or disapproval, Georges took his leave and went out. His Moorish servant was waiting at the door with his two Arab horses.

Georges mounted Antrim and galloped off towards Moka. On entering his house, the young man inquired where his father was, but learned that he had gone out at seven o'clock that evening and had not yet returned.

CHAPTER XIII

THE SLAVER

NEXT morning Pierre Munier came into his son's room.

Since his arrival, Georges had gone over his father's fine

estate several times, and, from his knowledge of industrial matters as carried on in Europe, had made several suggestions by way of improvement, which his father, as a practical man, had grasped immediately. The carrying out of these ideas, however, necessitated the employment of additional labour ; while the abolition of public slave-dealing had so greatly increased the value of slaves that there was no way of procuring in the Island, except at an enormous expense, the fifty or sixty Negroes whom the father and son wanted to add to the establishment. Accordingly, Pierre had heard with joy the evening before, in the absence of Georges, the news that there was a slave-ship in sight, and had gone down to the coast that very night, in accordance with the custom then adopted by the Colonists and the traders in ' " black ivory," to answer the signals made by the slave-ship by other signals which indicated an intention to trade with her. These had been duly exchanged and Pierre Munier came to tell Georges the good news. It was accordingly arranged that the father and son should repair at nine in the evening to the *Pointe-des-Caves*, below the *Petit-Malabar*. Having made this arrangement, Pierre went out to inspect, according to his custom, the work on the estate, while Georges, also according to his custom, took his gun and made for the woods, in order to give himself up to his dreams.

What Georges had told Murray the previous evening was no empty boast, but, on the contrary, a resolve firmly determined. The whole life and training of the young Mulatto had, as we have seen, been directed towards the object of imparting to his will the force and persistency of genius. Having reached such a superiority in every department, as, aided by his wealth, would have assured to him in France or in England, in London or in Paris, a career of distinction, Georges, eager for combat, had desired to return to the Isle of France. It was there that the prejudice existed which his courage believed itself destined to combat, and his pride believed itself able to overcome. He returned then with the advantage of being unknown by sight, of being able to study his enemy while the latter was in ignorance of the war which Georges had declared against him

in his inmost heart, ready as he was to spring upon him at
the moment when he least expected it, and to enter upon a
struggle in which either the man must perish, or the whole
system he was vowed to combat. On setting foot upon
the quay, and seeing once more on his return the same
men that he had left at his departure, Georges had realized
a fact of which he had often been doubtful when in Europe,
namely, that everything remained *in statu quo* in the Isle of
France, although fourteen years had elapsed, although the
Island which had been French was now English, and instead
of being called the Isle of France was now called Mauritius.
Then, and from that moment, he had put himself on his
guard, had prepared for the moral duel which he had come
in search of, just as another prepares for a physical duel,
if we may so express it ; and had waited, sword in hand, till
the first opportunity of striking a blow at his adversary
should present itself.

But just as Cæsar Borgia, who had by his genius foreseen
everything necessary for the conquest of Italy after the
death of his father, except the fact that he would then be a
dying man himself, Georges found himself engaged in a
manner that he had been unable to foresee, and found
himself struck at the very moment that he wished to
strike. On the day of his arrival at Port Louis, chance
had thrown in his path a beautiful girl, whom he could
not forget, do what he would.

Then Providence had brought him there in the nick of
time for saving her life—the life of the very girl of whom
he had been dreaming vaguely ever since he had seen her,
so that this dream had entered more deeply than ever into
his life. Finally, chance had brought them together the
previous evening, and there a single glance, at the same
moment that he knew he loved, had told him that he was
loved in return. Henceforth, the struggle presented a
fresh interest for him, an interest in which his happiness was
doubly bound up, since henceforth this strife was carried
on, not merely for the satisfaction of his pride, but also
for that of his love.

Only, as we have said, Georges, being wounded at the
beginning of the combat, lost the advantage of his coolness ;

though it is true that in the exchange he gained the vehemence of his passion.

But, if the sight of the girl had made the impression we have described upon a man like Georges, satiated with life, and with passions no longer unsullied, the sight of the young man and the circumstances in which he had successively appeared before her were bound to produce a vastly deeper impression upon the budding life and virgin soul of Sara. Brought up, since the time when she lost her parents, in M. de Malmédie's house, destined from that time to double, by her dowry, the fortune of the heir to the estate, she had accustomed herself henceforth to look on Henri as her future husband, and had the more easily submitted to this prospect, since Henri was a handsome and worthy youth, ranking among the wealthiest and most fashionable Colonists, not only of Port Louis, but throughout the whole Island. As for Henri's other young friends, who were her companions in the chase and her partners in the dance, she had known them all too long for it ever to have entered her head to make any preference among them ; to her they were merely the friends of her childhood who would be associated in peaceful friendship with her for the rest of her life, and that was all.

Sara then was in this perfectly tranquil condition of mind when she had noticed Georges for the first time. In the life of all young girls, the appearance of a young man unknown, handsome, of gentlemanly bearing and graceful build, is an event, and still more so, as you may readily believe, in the Isle of France.

The young stranger's face, the tone of his voice, the words he had spoken, had all dwelt in Sara's memory, without her knowing why, like a tune which you have only heard once, but which, nevertheless, you repeat over and over again in your head. No doubt Sara would have forgotten this event after a few days' time, had she met this young man again in ordinary circumstances ; possibly a closer examination, such as is bestowed upon a second meeting, instead of involving the man more deeply in her life, might even have obliterated him from it entirely. But things had turned out differently. God had so willed that Georges and Sara should meet again at a supreme crisis; the episode of the *Rivière Noire* had occurred. To the curiosity which accompanied his first appearance were joined the romance and the gratitude that surrounded the second. In an instant Georges had been transformed in the girl's eyes. The unknown stranger had become an angel of deliverance. All the agony of the death with which Sara had been threatened, Georges had spared her; all the pleasure, and promise of future happiness that life holds out at the age of sixteen, Georges had restored to her at the moment when she was about to lose them. Yet when having scarcely seen him, having scarcely addressed a word to him, she found herself face to face with him and was about to pour out all the gratitude of her heart, she was forbidden to grant this man what she would have granted to the first stranger who asked it, and moreover was ordered to offer him an insult which she would not have offered to the meanest of men. Then the gratitude driven back to her heart had changed to love; a look had told Georges everything; a word from Georges had told Sara everything. Sara had been unable to deny anything, so Georges had the right to believe everything. Then, after the impression made upon her, had come reflection. Sara had been unable to prevent herself from comparing the behaviour of Henri, her future husband, with that of this stranger, with whom she was scarcely acquainted. On the first day, Henri's sneers at the unknown stranger had hurt her feelings. His indifference, as he rushed off to the death-halloo of the stag when his fiancée had only just escaped a mortal peril, had wounded her heart; lastly, the masterful tone in which Henri had spoken to her on the day of the ball had offended her pride. So during that long night which should have been a happy one, but which Henri had turned into a sad and lonely one, Sara had questioned her feelings for the first time, perhaps, and had realized for the first time that she did not love her cousin. From that, to knowing that she loved another, was but a step.

What usually takes place in such cases happened now. Sara, after directing her eyes upon herself, turned them next upon her surroundings; she weighed in the balance of interest her Uncle's conduct towards her ; she remembered that she had a fortune of about a million and a half francs, that is to say, that she was nearly twice as rich as her cousin. She asked herself if her Uncle would have shown the same care and tenderness for her as a poor orphan which he had shown for her as a wealthy heiress, and she saw nothing more in M. de Malmédie's adoption of her than what it was in reality, namely, the calculating policy of a father who prepares a good marriage for his son. All this was no doubt rather severe, but so it is with wounded hearts ; the wound drives gratitude away, and the grief which remains becomes a stern judge.

Georges had foreseen all this, and had counted upon it as an aid in pleading his cause and damaging that of his rival. So, after a good deal of reflection, he determined to attempt nothing further that day, though, in the depth of his heart, he felt very impatient to see Sara again. That is why he now had his gun on his shoulder, hoping to find, in his favourite amusement of shooting, a distraction which would help him to pass the day. But Georges had deceived himself ; his love for Sara was already speaking in his heart more loudly than any other feelings. Accordingly, towards four o'clock, unable any longer to resist his desire—I will not say to see Sara once more, for not being able to visit her, it would only be by chance that he could meet her—but his wish to be somewhere near her, he had Antrim saddled ; then, giving the rein to the fleet child of Arabia, in less than an hour he found himself in the capital of the Island.

Georges came to Port Louis with but a single hope ; but, as we have said, this hope was entirely at the mercy of chance, and chance this time proved inflexible. Georges rode in vain through all the streets in the neighbourhood of M. de Malmédie's house ; he rode in vain twice through the Jardin de la Compagnie, the usual promenade of the inhabitants of Port Louis ; he went in vain three times round the Champ de Mars, where preparations were being made for the forthcoming races—nowhere, even at a distance, did he see any woman whose appearance could have led him to think her to be Sara.

At seven, Georges gave up all hope, and, with a pain

at his heart as though he had met with some misfortune,
or undergone some dreadful hardship, he took once more
the road of the *Grande-Rivière*, but slowly this time and
holding his horse in; for now he was riding away from
Sara, who doubtless had not guessed that Georges had
ridden ten times up and down the *Rue de la Comédie* and
the *Rue du Gouvernement*, that is to say, scarcely a hundred
yards from where she was. He was passing then the cantonment of the free blacks, situated outside the town, still
holding in Antrim, who could not at all understand this
unaccustomed pace, when suddenly a man came out of one
of the huts and threw himself at his horse's stirrup, grasping his knees and kissing his hand. It was Miko-Miko, the
Chinese dealer, the man of the fan.

On the instant Georges perceived vaguely the use which
he could make of this man, whose business permitted him
to gain entrance into every house, and who, through his
ignorance of the language, could inspire no distrust.

Georges dismounted and went into the shop of Miko-
Miko, who at once made him inspect all his treasures.

There was no mistaking the feeling which the poor fellow
had expressed for Georges, and which issued from the
depths of his heart at each word he said. The explanation
was quite simple; with the exception of two or three of
his fellow-countrymen, who were dealers like himself, and,
consequently, if not hostile to him, at least in rivalry with
him, Miko-Miko had not yet found a single person at Port
Louis with whom he could converse in his own language.
Accordingly he asked Georges in what way he could make
a return for the happiness which he owed to him.

The request which Georges had to make was a very
simple one; nothing more than a plan of the interior of
M. de Malmédie's house, so that, should circumstances
require it, he might know how to reach Sara's apartments.

At the first words spoken by Georges, Miko-Miko understood the whole matter; we have said that the Chinese
were the Jews, so to speak, of the Isle of France.

In order, however, to facilitate the negotiations between
Miko-Miko and Sara, and possibly also with a further
intention, Georges wrote upon one of his visiting-cards the

prices of various objects which might tempt the girl's fancy, bidding Miko-Miko let nobody see this card but Sara herself.

Then he gave the dealer another doubloon, telling him to come to Moka next day at about three in the afternoon.

Miko-Miko promised to be at the appointed meeting-place, and undertook to carry in his head as exact a plan of the house as could be traced by a draughtsman.

After this, inasmuch as it was now eight o'clock, and at nine Georges had to meet his father, as we have said, at the *Pointe-aux-Caves*, he remounted his horse and continued his journey along the road of the *Petite-Rivière*, with a lighter heart than before. For those who are in love, a very little thing is needed to change the aspect of the horizon.

It was quite dark when Georges arrived at the meeting-place. His father, true to the habit of punctuality, which he had always observed when dealing with white men, had been there for ten minutes. At half-past nine the moon rose.

This was the moment for which Georges and his father were waiting. They at once directed their gaze between the *Ile Bourbon* and the *Ile de Sable*, and there they saw a light flash three times. This was the customary signal, given by a mirror reflecting the moon's rays, and well understood by the Colonists. On seeing it, Télémaque, who had accompanied his employers, lighted a fire on the shore which he extinguished five minutes later, and then they waited.

Half an hour had not elapsed when they saw faintly appearing on the sea a dark line, like a great fish swimming on the surface of the water ; then this line grew larger and more distinct, assuming the appearance of a pirogue. Soon after, a large boat could be made out, and, by the shimmering rays of the moon on the sea, the movement of oars striking the water could be discerned, though their sound was as yet inaudible. Eventually the boat entered the bay of the *Petite-Rivière*, and landed in the creek just opposite the small fort.

Georges and his father advanced down the beach. A man who had been seen sitting in the stern of the boat had already stepped ashore.

Behind him came some dozen sailors armed with guns and axes. They were the same men who had been rowing, with their guns slung over their shoulders. The man who had landed first gave them a signal, upon which they began to disembark the Negroes, of whom there were thirty lying in the bottom of the boat, while an equal number were to be brought in a second boat.

Then the two Mulattoes and the man who had landed first came together and exchanged a few words, as the result of which Georges and his father were convinced of what they had already guessed, namely, that they were in the presence of the Captain of the slaver himself.

He was a man of about two-and-thirty, tall in stature, and bearing all the signs of physical strength developed to a pitch that instinctively commands respect. He had dark frizzled hair, whiskers that met under the chin, and moustaches that joined the whiskers. His face and hands, tanned by the suns of the tropics, had acquired very much the complexion of the Indians of Timor or Pegu. He was dressed in the jacket and trousers of blue cloth worn by sportsmen in the Isle of France, and, like them, had a broad straw hat and carried a gun over his shoulder. Only, unlike them, he wore in addition, suspended from his belt, a curved sword, shaped like an Arab scimitar, but larger, and with a hilt resembling that of the Scotch claymore. If the Captain of the slaver had been the object of a close examination on the part of the two inhabitants of Moka, they too, in their turn, had had to undergo an examination no less searching. The trader in black flesh glanced from one to the other with equal curiosity, and the more closely he scrutinized them, the more did he appear unable to withdraw his eyes from them. Georges and his father failed apparently to notice the persistence of his gaze, or, at any rate, were not made uneasy by it, for they entered upon the negotiation for which they had come, examining one after another the Negroes who had been brought in the first boat, and who were nearly all natives of the West Coast of Africa, that is to say, of Senegambia and Guinea, —a circumstance which further increases their value, inasmuch as, not having, like the natives of Madagascar, the Mozambiques, or the Kaffirs, any hope of reaching their country again, they hardly ever make an attempt to escape. In spite of this excuse for raising the price, the Captain was very reasonable in his demands, and so, when the second boat-load arrived, the bargain for the first had been already concluded.

The Negroes in the second boat were as good in quality as those of the first. The Captain's stock was first-rate, and showed him to be a thorough connoisseur in his own line of business. This was a piece of real good luck for the Isle of France, to which he had come for the first time to ply his trade, having heretofore shipped slaves more especially for the Antilles.

When all the Negroes had been disembarked and the deal was concluded, Télémaque, himself a native of the Congo, came up to them and delivered a discourse in his mother-tongue, which was theirs also. The aim of this discourse was to boast to them of the mild lot in which their future life was cast, compared with the life led by their countrymen in the employment of the other planters of the Island, and to tell them that they had had the good fortune to come into the hands of MM. Pierre and Georges Munier, who were the kindest employers in the Island. Then the Negroes approached the two Mulattoes, and, falling on their knees, promised, Télémaque acting as their mouthpiece, that they would prove worthy of the happiness which Providence had kept in store for them.

At the name of Pierre and Georges Munier, the Slave-Captain, who had followed the discourse of Télémaque with an attention which showed that he had closely studied the different dialects of Africa, had given a start, and looked even more attentively than before at the two men with whom he had just concluded with such promptness a transaction of nearly a hundred and fifty thousand francs. But Georges and his father appeared to notice the other's reluctance to take his eyes off them no more than they had done before. At last the moment for settling up arrived. Georges asked the Captain how he would like to be paid, in gold or in notes, his father having brought gold in his saddlebags and notes in his pocket-book, so as to be ready for every emergency. The Captain preferred gold. The amount was accordingly counted out on the spot and conveyed into the second boat ; then the sailors embarked again. But, to the great astonishment of Georges and his father, the Captain did not go down with them to the boats, which, at an order given by him, pulled away from the shore.

The Captain followed them with his eyes for some little time ; then, when they were out of sight and hearing, turned to the astonished Mulattoes, and advancing towards them with a hand outstretched to each, exclaimed :

"Good day, father! Good day, brother!" Then, seeing them hesitate, he added :

"Why, do you not recognize your Jacques?" Both uttered a cry of surprise and held out their arms to him. Jacques threw himself into his father's arms, then passed from them to those of his brother ; after which Télémaque, too, had his turn, although, be it said, it was not without trembling that he ventured to touch the hands of the Slave-Captain.

Thus, by a strange coincidence, did chance reunite in the same family the man who had laboured all his life under the prejudice of colour, the man who was making his fortune by trading in it, and the man who was ready to risk his life in order to combat it.

CHAPTER XIV
THE SLAVE TRADE

THE man was really Jacques—Jacques, whom his father had not set eyes on for fourteen, or his brother for twelve, years.

Jacques had left France on board one of those privateers, furnished with letters of marque from the Government, which at this period darted suddenly out of our harbours, like eagles from their eyries, and attacked the English.

It was a rough school of training, and quite as valuable as that of the Imperial Navy, the ships of which, at this time, constantly blockaded in our ports, were as often lying idly at anchor as those of this other branch of marine, swift, light, and independent, were scouring the high seas.

Every day, indeed, there was some fresh fighting; not that our privateers, bold as they were, picked quarrels with men-of-war, but that they were for ever attacking the great, big-bellied merchantmen, bursting with freight from India and China, homeward bound from Calcutta, or Buenos Ayres, or Vera Cruz. Now, either these vessels, harmless as they were to look at, were convoyed by some English frigate, by no means without beak and claws, or they had elected to arm and defend themselves on their own account. In the latter case, it was mere child's play, a two hours' skirmish, and all was over; but, in the first case, the aspect of affairs was much more serious. Shots were exchanged, men were killed, and rigging damaged. Finally it came to boarding the vessel, and, after having been pounded from a distance, she was destroyed at close quarters.

Whilst this was taking place, the merchant-ships sheered off, and, if they did not meet, like the ass in the fable, with any other privateer to lay hands upon them, made some port in England, to the great satisfaction of the India Company, who voted rewards of money to their defenders.

Such was the state of things at this period. Out of the thirty or thirty-one days which make up the month, fighting took place on twenty or twenty-five of them; then, by the way of respite from fighting, came days of tempest. Well, we repeat, in such a school a man learned quickly. At the first, as there was no conscription for the purpose of recruiting, and as this little amateur warfare did not discontinue until in the long run a good number of men had been used up, the crews were hardly ever up to their full strength. True, the sailors being all volunteers, quantity, in this case, was advantageously replaced by quality; so, during the fighting or the storms, nobody had any fixed duties, and each man could put his hand to every-thing. For the rest, there was absolute obedience to the Captain, when he was there, and to the First Officer, in the Captain's absence. Though this was the case through-out, it was particularly so on board the *Calypso*, which was the name of the ship which Jacques had chosen for serving his naval apprenticeship in; in six years she had had only two refractory seamen, one from Normandy, the other a Gascon, the one having disobeyed the authority of the Captain, the other that of his Lieutenant. The Captain had smashed in the first man's skull with an axe, while the Lieutenant had sent a pistol shot through the other's body.; and both had died on the spot. Then, as nothing is so much in the way of working a ship as a dead body, the corpses had been chucked overboard, and there the matter ended. Only these two events, if they left no trace behind them except in the recollection of the crew, had none the less exercised a wholesome influence over their minds. None, after that, ever dreamed of picking a quarrel with Captain Bertrand or Lieutenant Rébard, for such were the names of these two worthies, who henceforth enjoyed the privilege of absolutely despotic authority on board the *Calypso*.

Jacques had always had a decided liking for the sea; when quite a boy he had been constantly on board the ships riding at anchor at Port Louis, climbing into the shrouds and tops, swinging on the yards, sliding down the halliards; and, as it was especially on board vessels with which his father had business transactions that Jacques practised these gymnastic exercises, the Captains treated him with great kindness, satisfying his boyish curiosity, explaining everything to him and allowing him to climb from hold to top-gallants and back again. The result was that, at the age of ten, Jacques was a most efficient cabin-boy, inasmuch as, in default of a vessel, everything in his eyes represented a ship. He climbed trees, of which he made masts, and along bind-weed, which played the part of ropes, and at twelve years of age, knowing the name of every part of the ship, and every detail of the drill which takes place on its deck, he could have entered as a first-class candidate in the first vessel that appeared.

But, as we have already seen, his father had decided otherwise for him, and, instead of sending him to the Ecole d'Angoulême, to which his tastes summoned him, he had sent him to the Collège Napoléon. Here was afforded a fresh confirmation of the proverb, " Man proposes, and God disposes." Jacques, after spending two years in drawing ships in his composition books and launching frigates on the big pond of the Luxembourg, availed himself of the first opportunity that offered of passing from theory to practice ; and having, during a stay at Brest, gone to visit the brig *Calypso*, he told his brother, who had accompanied him, that he might go back to land by himself, but that, for his part, he had decided to become a sailor. Both submitted to this sudden decision, and Georges returned alone, as has been duly related, to the Collège Napoléon. As for Jacques, whose frank face and gallant bearing had at once won over Captain Bertrand, he was raised forthwith to the rank of able seaman, at which his comrades grumbled loudly.

Jacques let them grumble ; he had in his own mind very clear ideas of justice and injustice ; the men with whom he had just been put on an equality were ignorant of his worth, and so it was quite natural that they should be annoyed that a mere novice should have been treated with such favour. But, on the occurrence of the first storm, he cut away a top-gallant-sail which was blocked in the tackle, and which threatened to carry away the mast ; while the first time they boarded a ship, he sprang upon the enemy's deck in front of the Captain, a proceeding which earned him such a tremendous blow from the latter's fist that he remained unconscious for three days, the rule on board the *Calypso* being that the Captain must always set foot on the enemy's deck before any of the crew. However, as this was one of the breaches of discipline for which one brave man readily forgives another, the Captain admitted the validity of the apology made by Jacques, and told him that in future, next after himself and the Lieutenant, he was at liberty, in similar circumstances, to take what order pleased him. At the second boarding Jacques was the third man on deck.

From that time the sailors ceased to grumble at Jacques, and even the old hands came up to him, and were the first to shake hands. So matters went on until the year 1815. We say 1815, because Captain Bertrand, who was of a very sceptical turn of mind, had never chosen to take the fall of Napoleon seriously. Possibly too this feeling was influenced by the fact that, having nothing to do, he had made two voyages to the Isle of Elba, and that, on the occasion of one of these voyages, he had had the honour of being received by the ex-master of the world. What had passed between the Emperor and the buccaneer at this interview no one ever discovered; all that was remarked was that Captain Bertrand returned on board whistling:

> "Ran tan plan tirelire
> How we shall laugh, to be sure!"

which, with Captain Bertrand, denoted an inward feeling of most intense satisfaction. After this, the Captain betook himself to Brest, where, without saying a word to any one, he began to put the *Calypso* in fighting trim, to lay in a stock of powder and shot, and to make up the few men who were wanting in order that his crew should be at its full strength. So that any one must have had a very imperfect acquaintance with Captain Bertrand who did not grasp the fact that he was cockering up behind the scenes some spectacle which would greatly astonish the audience.

As a matter of fact, six weeks after Captain Bertrand's last voyage to Porto-Ferrajo, Napoleon landed at the Gulf of St. Juan. Twenty-four days after his landing at the Gulf of St. Juan, Napoleon entered Paris; and seventy-two hours after Napoleon's entrance into Paris, Captain Bertrand left Brest with all sail set and the tri-colour flying at the peak.

A week had not elapsed when Captain Bertrand entered the harbour again, hauling in tow a magnificent English three-master, laden with the finest spices from India; she had been so utterly astonished at seeing the tri-coloured flag, which was thought to have disappeared off the face of the earth, that it never entered her head to make even the slightest show of resistance.

This prize had made Captain Bertrand's mouth water. So, no sooner had he got rid of his capture at a suitable price and divided the proceeds among the crew, who had lain idle for nearly a year and were getting very weary of this inaction than he went off in search of a second three-master. But, as everybody knows, you do not always find precisely what you are looking for; one fine morning, after a very dark night, the *Calypso* found herself cheek by jowl with a frigate. This frigate was none other than the

Leicester, the same vessel which we have seen at Port Louis, conveying the Governor and Georges.

The *Leicester* had ten guns and sixty men more than the *Calypso* possessed ; nor had she any cargo of cinnamon, sugar, or coffee ; but, instead of these, a magazine perfectly equipped, and an arsenal stuffed full with shot and grape. Scarcely had she discovered, moreover, what country the *Calypso* hailed from than, without giving her the slightest warning, she sent her a sample of her goods, in the shape of a fine thirty-six pounder, which buried itself in her hull.

Quite differently from her sister *Galatea*, who fled in order to be seen, the *Calypso* would have been very glad to fly, without being seen. She had nothing to gain from the *Leicester*, even should she come off victorious, which was in the last degree unlikely. Unfortunately, it was hardly probable that she would escape, since her Captain was this same Lord Murray, who had not yet, at this period, quitted the navy, and who, for all his elegant appearance, to which, later on, his diplomatic labours had given yet a fresh colour, was one of the most intrepid sea-dogs between the Straits of Magellan and Baffin's Bay. Accordingly Captain Bertrand trained his two largest guns astern and sheered off.

The *Calypso* was a veritable ship of prey, designed for speed, narrow and long in the lines. But the poor little Sea-swallow was engaged with the Ocean-eagle ; consequently, in spite of her agility, it was soon evident that the frigate was wearing the schooner down.

This superiority in pace soon became all the more noticeable from the fact that, every five minutes or so, the *Leicester* dispatched leaden messengers to summon the *Calypso* to stop. To which the *Calypso*, still in flight, replied with her stern guns by messengers of the same character. All this time, Jacques was examining with the greatest attention the masting of the brig, and making some most sensible remarks to Lieutenant Rébard on the improvements that might be made in the rigging of vessels intended, like the *Calypso*, either to chase or to be chased. There was above all a radical change to be effected in the top-gallant-masts, and Jacques, with his eyes fixed on this weak spot in the ship, had just finished his demonstration, when not receiving any signs of approval from the Lieutenant, he turned his eyes from the sky to the deck, and realized the cause of the silence of his interlocutor ; Lieutenant Rébard had just been cut in two by a cannon-shot. The situation was becoming serious ; it was plain that, before another half hour was over, the two ships would be alongside each other, and that the *Calypso* would be obliged, to use a technical term, to *judge it out* with a crew a third again as strong as her own. Jacques was communicating, in an aside, this rather disconcerting reflection to the captain of one of the two stern guns, when the fellow, in stooping to aim, apparently took a false step and fell with his nose on the breech of the gun. Seeing that he was slower in getting up again than a man ought to have been in such circumstances, and in so responsible a position, Jacques took him by his coat-collar and restored him to the perpendicular. But this done, he perceived that the poor wretch had swallowed a grape-shot ; only, instead of following the perpendicular, the grape-shot had taken a horizontal line. Hence had come the accident. The poor man had died, as they say, from being unable to digest cast-iron.

Jacques, who, at the moment, had nothing better to do, stooped in his turn towards the gun, rectified the sight by a degree or so, and cried :

" Fire ! "

At the same instant the gun thundered, and Jacques, anxious to see the result of his skill, jumped upon the nettings in order to watch, as far as he could do so, the effect of the projectile which he had just hurled at the enemy.

The effect was instantaneous. The mizen-mast, shattered a little above the main-top, bowed like a tree bent by the wind, then fell with a terrible crash, littering the deck with sails and rigging, and crushing a portion of the starboard bulwarks. A loud shout of triumph resounded on board the *Calypso*. The frigate had stopped in mid-chase, dipping her broken wing in the sea, while the schooner, safe and sound, but for a few ropes cut away, continued her course, freed from the enemy's pursuit.

The Captain's first care, on seeing himself out of danger, was to appoint Jacques Lieutenant in place of Rébard ; this rank had devolved upon him, long since, in case of a vacancy, in the minds of all his comrades. The announcement of his promotion was accordingly welcomed with unanimous acclamations. In the evening a public service was held for the dead. The bodies had been thrown into the sea as they passed from life to death, only that of the second in command having been reserved, in order that the honours due to his rank might be paid him. These honours consisted in being sewn up in a hammock with a thirty-six pounder at each foot. The ceremonial was carried out exactly, and poor Rébard went to rejoin his companions, having preserved the very slender advantage over them of being plunged into the depths of the sea, instead of floating on its surface.

In the evening, Captain Bertrand took advantage of the darkness to alter his course, that is to say, thanks to a slant of wind, he was able to reverse his course, so that he entered Brest, while the *Leicester*, which had hastened to substitute a fresh mast for her broken one, pursued her in the direction of Cape Vert.

This made Captain Murray extremely angry, and he swore that, if ever the *Calypso* came within reach of the *Leicester* again, she should not get off so cheaply the second time as she had done on the first occasion.

As soon as ever his damages were repaired, Captain Bertrand returned to his old game, and, well seconded by Jacques, performed many remarkable exploits. Unfortunately, Waterloo supervened ; after Waterloo, came the second abdication, and, after the second abdication, peace. This time there was no longer room for doubt. The Captain saw the prisoner of Europe pass by on board the *Bellerophon*, and, as he was acquainted with St. Helena from having called there twice, he realized at once that there is no escaping from that island as there is from Elba.

Captain Bertrand's prospects were greatly compromised by that great cataclysm in which so many things were shattered. He was obliged, therefore, to create for himself a fresh trade. He had a fine schooner, a good sea boat, with a crew of a hundred and fifty men ready to follow his fortunes, good or bad ; it occurred to him quite naturally to engage in the slave trade.

This was quite a nice business before the profession was ruined by a heap of philosophical preachments, which nobody at that time had so much as thought of, and there were immense fortunes to be made by those who were the first to embark in it. War, occasionally smothered in Europe, in Africa is perpetual ; there is always some tribe that is thirsty, and, as the inhabitants of that fine country observed, once and for all, that the surest means of procuring liquor was to have plenty of prisoners to dispose of, you needed only at this period to follow the coasts of Senegambia, Congo, Mozambique or Zanzibar with a bottle of trade brandy in each hand, and you were sure of returning to your ship with a Negro under each arm. When prisoners ran short, mothers sold their children for a glass of liquor ; true, these brats were of no great value ; but any lack of quality was made up for by their quantity.

Captain Bertrand carried on this business with credit and profit for five years, that is to say, from 1815 to 1820, and was looking forward to carrying it on for a good many more, when an unforeseen accident put an end to his life. One day as he was ascending the *Rivière des Poissons*, situated on the West Coast of Africa, in company with a Hottentot chief, who was going to hand over to him, for the consideration of two casks of rum, a party of Grands-Namaquois Negroes for which he had just negotiated, and who were booked in advance for Martinique and Guadeloupe, he happened to set foot on the tail of a boqueira that lay basking in the sun. The tail of this species of snake is, as is well known, so sensitive, that Nature has endowed this part of its body with a number of little bells, so that the traveller, warned by the sound, may avoid treading upon it. The snake rose erect as quick as lightning, and bit Captain Bertrand in the hand. The Captain, though well inured to pain, uttered a cry. The Hottentot chief turned round, saw what had happened, and said in a grave tone :

"Man bitten, man die."

" I know it, God help me ! " answered the Captain, " and that is why I called out."

Then, either for his own personal satisfaction, or from motives of philanthropy, and to insure that the snake which had bitten him should not bite any one else, he seized the boqueira with both hands and wrung its neck. Hardly had the brave Captain accomplished this before his strength suddenly forsook him, and he fell dead beside the reptile.

All this had happened with such rapidity that when Jacques, who was about twenty-five yards behind the Captain came up to him, he had already turned as green as a lizard. He tried to speak, but could only stammer a few incoherent words, and expired. Ten minutes later, his body was covered with black and yellow spots, just like a poisonous fungus.

Owing to the marvellously subtle nature of the poison, decomposition set in so rapidly that to carry the Captain's body on board the *Calypso* was not to be thought of. Jacques and the twelve sailors who accompanied him dug a grave in which they laid the body, heaping over it all the stones they could find in the neighbourhood, so as to preserve it, if possible, from the ravages of hyenas and jackals. As for the snake, one of the sailors, remembering that his uncle, who was a chemist at Brest, had requested him, in case he ever came across one of these reptiles, to try and bring it to him, carried it off to be placed later on in a phial at the door of his uncle's shop between a bottle filled with red water and another filled with blue.

There is a commercial adage which says : " Business before everything." In virtue of this adage, it was decided by the Hottentot chief and Jacques that this catastrophe should not stand in the way of carrying out the bargain which had been concluded. Accordingly Jacques went to fetch from the neighbouring kraal the fifty Grands-Nama-quois who had been sold ; after which the Hottentot chief brought away from the brig the promised casks of rum. Having effected this exchange the two dealers separated, each delighted with the other, and with the mutual promise that their commercial relations should be renewed on a future occasion.

The same evening Jacques piped all hands on deck, from the boatswain's mate to the junior cabin-boy, and after touching briefly but eloquently on the numerous good qualities that had distinguished Captain Bertrand, he made two propositions to the crew : first, to dispose of the complete cargo and then of the, ship, which was readily saleable, and, after distributing the proceeds of the whole in the customary proportions, to part good friends, and each to seek his fortune in whatever direction pleased him ; or secondly, to appoint a successor to Captain Bertrand and continue the business under the style of " Calypso and Co.," declaring beforehand that, though he was the Lieutenant, he would submit to be re-elected, and would be the first to recognize the new Captain appointed as the result of the ballot. These words were followed by the very appropriate result that Jacques was elected Captain by acclamation.

Jacques immediately chose as his Lieutenant the boatswain's mate, a worthy Breton hailing from Lorient, who was usually called, in allusion to the remarkable toughness of his skull, M. Tête de Fer.

The same evening the *Calypso*, with shorter memory than the nymph whose name she bore, sailed for the Antilles, already consoled, in appearance at least, not for the departure of King Ulysses, but for the death of Captain Bertrand.

However, if she had lost one master, she had found another, and quite as good a one. The late Captain was one of those old sea-dogs who do everything by rule of thumb rather than by calculation. This was not the case with Jacques, who was always guided by circumstances, and was an all-round man in every branch of seamanship, knowing as well as any Admiral how to give orders in a battle or storm, yet, if occasion required, making a sailor's knot as well as the youngest cabin-boy. Jacques was never idle, and, consequently, never felt dull. Each day witnessed some improvement in the trim or rigging of the schooner. Jacques was as fond of the *Calypso* as a man is of his mistress, and so his thoughts were constantly employed in adding something to her adornment ; now it was a sail, the shape of which he altered, now a yard, of which he simplified the working. And so, like the coquette that she was, she obeyed her new lord as she had never obeyed any other ; roused into animation at the sound of his voice, bending and rearing under his hand, leaping beneath his feet like a horse that feels the spur, she and Jacques appeared so admirably matched, that you could not imagine it possible that henceforth one could live apart from the other.

So, but for the recollection of his father and brother, which occasionally clouded his brow, Jacques was happier than any man on land or sea. He was not one of those grasping Slave-Captains who lose half their profits by trying to gain too much, and in whom cruelty, after passing into a habit, becomes a pleasure. No, he was a decent trader, carrying on his business conscientiously, treating his Kaffirs, his Hottentots, his Senegambians and Mozambiques with almost as much care as if they had been bags of sugar, chests of rice, or bales of cotton. They were well fed, had straw to lie on, and took exercise on deck twice a day. Only the refractory ones were chained, and, speaking generally, he endeavoured, as far as possible, to sell the husbands along with their wives, and the children with their mothers—a kindness hitherto unheard of and which found but few imitators among those who followed the same profession as Jacques. The result was that his Negroes generally reached their destination in capital condition and in good spirits, so that he nearly always sold them at an enhanced price.

It is unnecessary to remark that Jacques never stayed long enough on land to form any serious attachment. As he was swimming in gold and rolling in silver, the fair Creoles of Jamaica, Guadeloupe and Cuba had more than once set their caps at him ; there were even fathers who, not knowing him to be a Mulatto, and taking him for a gentlemanly European Slave-Captain, made him overtures of marriage with their daughters. But Jacques had his own ideas on the subject of love. He knew by heart his mythology and his Bible ; he was acquainted with the legend of Hercules and Omphalé, and the story of Samson and Delilah. Accordingly he had resolved to have no other

wife but the *Calypso*. As for mistresses, there were plenty
of them, thank Heaven : black, red, yellow, or chocolate,
according as he loaded up at the Congo, Florida, Bengal or
Madagascar. Every voyage he took with him a fresh one,
whom he handed over on his arrival to some friend by
whom he was sure that she would be well treated ; having
made it his rule never to stick to the same one for fear lest,
be her colour what it might, she should acquire an influence
over his heart, for, it must be said, what Jacques loved
before all else was his freedom.

Let us add that Jacques had a whole host of other pleasures. He was as sensuous as Creoles generally are. All
the grand effects of Nature impressed him agreeably ; only,
instead of stirring his spirit, they worked upon his senses.
He loved the immensity of space, not because it made him
think of God, but because, the greater the space, the more
freely you breathe ; he loved the stars, not because he
conceived of them as so many worlds circling in space,
but because it was pleasant to see overhead an azure canopy
studded with diamonds ; he loved the lofty forests, not
because their depths were full of mysterious and romantic
voices, but because their dense vault cast a shade through
which the sun's rays could not penetrate.

As for his opinion on the business in which he was engaged,
he looked upon it as a perfectly lawful occupation. He had
seen Negroes bought and sold all his life, and so he honestly
believed that they were made to be bought and sold. As
for the validity of the right claimed by men to traffic in
their fellow-creatures, that in no way concerned him. He
bought and paid ; consequently, the goods were his, and,
from the moment he bought and paid for them, he had the
right to sell them again. Never had he imitated the example
of his fellow-captains, whom he had seen hunting down
Negroes on their own account; he would have looked upon it
as a fearful injustice personally to seize upon a free creature,
whether by force or by stratagem, in order to make a slave
of him. But, the moment that free creature had become
a slave through circumstances for which Jacques was not
responsible, he made no scruples about bargaining for him
with his owner.

You can understand, then, that Jacques' life was a pleasant one, all the more so as, now and then, there came days of fighting, as in the time of Captain Bertrand. The trading in blacks had been abolished by a Congress of Governments, which had probably discovered that it affected injuriously the trade in whites ; so that it sometimes happened that vessels which meddled in what was no business of theirs, peremptorily demanded to know what the *Calypso* was doing on the coast of Senegal or in the Indian seas. Then, if it was one of Captain Jacques' good-humoured days, he began by amusing the too inquisitive vessels by running up flags of all colours ; next, when he was tired of playing charades, he would hoist his own flag, three Negroes' heads sable, two and one on a field gules ; upon which the *Calypso* took to her heels, and the fun began.

In addition to the twenty guns which adorned her portholes, the *Calypso* possessed, with a view to such occasions only, two thirty-six pounders astern, superior in range to those of ordinary ships ; now, as she was a splendid sailer, and obeyed implicitly her master's nod, she hoisted just so much sail as was required to keep the pursuer within range of these two guns. The result was that, while the shots from the enemy fell uselessly in her wake, each of her own shots (and Jacques, as you may suppose, had not forgotten his business as a gunner) raked from bow to stern the vessel that displayed such an interest in Negroes. This went on for as long as Jacques chose to play what he called his game of skittles ; then when he considered the ship to have been sufficiently punished for her indiscretion, he added sundry royals and top-gallant studding sails, with some spankers of his own invention, to the sail already set, dispatched a couple of shots in token of farewell to his partner in the sport, and skimming over the water like some belated bird making for its nest, left her to plug her holes, put her rigging in order, and repair her halliards, disappeared on the horizon.

These pranks, as you will readily understand, made the business of entering harbours somewhat risky ; but the *Calypso* was a jilt who could alter her figure and even her face, as circumstances required. Sometimes she assumed some artless name and a guileless look, calling herself *la belle Jenny* or *la Jeune Olympe*, and appeared with an air of innocence quite pleasant to behold, having, as she said, just freighted tea at Canton, coffee at Mocha, or spices at Ceylon. She displayed samples of her cargo, took orders, and inquired for passengers. Captain Jacques became an honest native of Lower Brittany, with his big jacket, long hair, and broad hat, all the cast-off wardrobe, in fact, of the defunct Bertrand. Sometimes the *Calypso* changed her sex; was called *le Sphynx* or *le Léonidas*; her crew assumed French uniforms, and she entered harbour, flying the white flag, courteously saluting the fort, which returned her salute as courteously. Then the Captain would be, according to his whim, either a seaman, fuming, swearing and cursing, talking of nothing but port and starboard, not knowing what was the use of the land except to put in at from time to time for fresh water or to dry his fish. Or again, he would be some dandy young officer just fresh from College, to whom the Government, to recompense the services of his ancestors, had given an appointment which a dozen officers of long standing were applying for. In this case, Captain Jacques called himself M. de Kergouran or M. de Champ-Fleury; he was short-sighted, looked at you with a blinking eye, and lisped. All this would have been soon recognized as a piece of acting in a French or English harbour, but it enjoyed an enormous success in Cuba, in Martinique, in Guadeloupe or Java.

As to the investment of the money which accrued from his trade, Jacques, who did not understand movements of *agio* or rates of discount, had a very simple plan : in exchange for his gold or bank notes he took from Visapore or Gujerat the finest diamonds he could find in those places, so that he had come to be almost as good a judge of diamonds as he was of Negroes. Next he placed the newly-purchased stones, with those bought previously, in a belt which he always wore. When he ran short of money he rummaged in his belt and extracted, according to his needs, a stone as large as a pea or a diamond the size of a nut, walked into a Jew's shop, had it weighed, and let him have it at the tariff price. Then, like Cleopatra, who

drank the pearls which Anthony gave her, he ate and drank
away his diamond; only, unlike the Queen of Egypt,
Jacques usually made it last for several meals.

Thanks to this method of investing money, Jacques
always carried on his person property to the value of two
or three million francs, which, as he could hold it, literally,
in the hollow of his hand, was easily concealed should
occasion demand. For Jacques did not disguise from
himself that a profession like his had its unlucky side;
that the business which he carried on was not all a bed of
roses, and that after years of good fortune he might meet
with a day of reverse.

But, while awaiting this unlucky day, Jacques led, as
we have said, a very pleasant life, and would not have
exchanged positions with any monarch in the world, seeing
that at this date to be a King was already beginning to
be a very poor amusement. Thus our adventurer would
have been perfectly happy, had not the recollection of his
father and Georges occasionally saddened his thoughts;
so, one fine day, he could hold out no longer, and having
freighted in Senegambia and Congo, and then come on to
complete his cargo on the coasts of Mozambique and
Zanzibar, he determined to go on to the Isle of France,
and inquire if his father had not left it, or if his brother
had not returned to it. Accordingly, on approaching the
coast, he had made the signals usually adopted by slave-
ships and had received a corresponding reply. Chance
had brought it about that these signals were exchanged
between father and son; so that, the same evening, Jacques
found himself not only on his native shore, but also in the
arms of the very persons he had come to seek.

CHAPTER XV
PANDORA'S BOX

IT was, as you will readily believe, a great happiness
for the father and brothers who had not seen each
other for so long a time to find themselves thus once more
together, just when they least expected it. True, Georges
at the first moment, thanks to his European education,

experienced a feeling of regret at finding his brother a merchant of human flesh ; but this first feeling soon disappeared. As for Pierre Munier, who had never left the Island, and who necessarily therefore looked at everything from the Colonial point of view, he took no notice of it at all ; besides, the poor father was entirely absorbed in the unlooked-for delight of seeing his sons again.

Jacques, as was quite natural, returned to sleep at Moka. He and Georges and their father did not separate until well on into the night. During the first delightful chat each revealed to these intimates of his soul all that was in his own heart. Pierre Munier poured forth his joy, his sole topic being his paternal love. Jacques related his life of adventure, his strange amusements, his eccentric happiness. Then came Georges' turn, and Georges related the story of his love.

On hearing this, Pierre Munier trembled in all his limbs. Georges, a Mulatto, and the son of a Mulatto, loved a white girl, and declared, while confessing his love, that this girl should be his wife. Such arrogance was an unheard-of audacity and unprecedented in the Colonies, and would draw down upon the man in whose heart it had been kindled all the sorrows of earth and all the wrath of heaven.

As for Jacques, he quite understood Georges loving a white girl, although, for many reasons, which he detailed with admirable logic, he much preferred black women for his own part. But Jacques was too much of a philosopher not to understand and respect the tastes of others. Besides, he considered that Georges, handsome, wealthy and superior to other men as he was, might aspire to the hand of any white girl whatsoever, were she Aline herself, Queen of Golconda !

In any case, he suggested to Georges a plan that would greatly simplify matters ; namely, that in case of a refusal on the part of M. de Malmédie, he should carry off Sara and deposit her in some corner of the world, wherever Georges chose, to which he might go and join her. Georges thanked his brother for his obliging offer, which, however, he declined, as he had at the moment decided upon another plan.

Next day the three met again almost before daybreak,

so much was there fresh to tell one another that had been
forgotten the previous evening. At about eleven o'clock
Jacques felt a longing to visit all the spots where his childhood had been spent, and proposed to his father and brother
a walk round the estate by way of reviving the memories of
his early days. Pierre Munier agreed to this ; but Georges,
as the reader will remember, was expecting news from the
town. So he was obliged to let the two go off together and
to remain at the house, where he had directed Miko-Miko
to meet him.

At the end of half an hour Georges saw his messenger
appear ; he was carrying his long bamboo rod and his
two baskets, just as though he had been doing business in
the town ; for the prudent trader had thought it possible
that he might meet, on his way, some fancier of Chinese
workmanship. Georges, in spite of the power of self-
control which he had been at such pains to acquire, went
to open the door with beating heart, for this man had seen
Sara and would speak to him about her.

Everything had happened in the most natural manner, as
you may easily suppose. Miko-Miko, making use of his
privilege of gaining admittance everywhere, had gone into
M. de Malmédie's house, and Bijou, who had already seen
his young mistress purchase a fan from the Chinaman,
had taken him straight to Sara's apartments.

On seeing the dealer, Sara started ; for, by a perfectly
natural connection of ideas and circumstances, Miko-Miko
brought back Georges to her mind. Accordingly she welcomed him with eagerness, having but one regret, namely,
at being compelled to converse with him by signs.

Miko-Miko then drew from his pocket Georges' card, on
which he had written, with his own hand, the prices of the
different objects which Miko-Miko had thought likely to take
Sara's fancy, and gave it to the girl with the side on which
its owner's name was engraved uppermost.

Sara blushed involuntarily and turned the card over
quickly. It was clear that Georges, being unable to see her,
employed this means of recalling himself to her memory.
She bought, without any bargaining, all the articles of which
the price had been written in the young man's handwriting,

and, as the dealer did not think of asking to have the card returned, neither did she think of giving it back to him.

On coming out from Sara's apartments, Miko-Miko was stopped by Henri, who in his turn took him to his rooms to inspect his stock. Henri bought nothing at that moment, but gave Miko-Miko to understand that, being on the point of marrying his cousin, he wanted some of the choicest knick-knacks which the dealer could procure for him.

This double visit to the girl and her cousin had given Miko-Miko the opportunity of examining the house in detail. Now, as Miko-Miko, among the bumps that adorned his bare skull, had the bump of locality developed in the highest degree, he had perfectly retained in his memory the arrangements of the buildings constituting M. de Malmédie's house.

The house had three entrances: one which led, as we have said, by a bridge over the stream, into the *Jardin de la Compagnie*; the second, at the back, led, by means of a winding path planted with trees, into the *Rue du Gouvernement*; and, lastly, the third, which was a side entrance, opened into the *Rue de la Comédie*.

Approaching the house by its main entrance, that is to say, by the bridge which crossed the stream and led to the *Jardin de la Compagnie*, you found yourself in a large square court, planted with mango-trees and China lilacs, through whose foliage and flowers you saw, directly opposite, the principal dwelling, which was entered by a door almost in a line with the one leading from the street; standing at this main entrance you had, first of all, the Negroes' quarters to your right, the stables to your left. Farther on, on the right, stood a summer-house, shaded by a magnificent " dragon's-blood," and opposite it, on the left, a second building, also reserved for the slaves. Last of all, you saw on the left the side entrance leading to the *Rue de la Comédie*, and on the right a path leading to a little staircase and winding on until it reached the lane, planted with trees, which formed a terrace opposite the Theatre.

From this, if you have followed clearly the description we have just given, you will see that the summer-house was separated from the main body of the house by the passage.

Now, as this summer-house was Sara's favourite retreat, and as she spent the greater part of her time there, the reader will permit us to add a few words to what we have already said in a preceding chapter.

This summer-house had four fronts, although it was itself visible only on three sides, since the fourth side abutted on to the Negroes' quarters. The other three overlooked, one, the entrance court planted with mango-trees, China lilies, and the dragon's-blood; another, the passage leading to the little staircase; the third overlooked a large wood-yard, almost deserted; while the wood-yard, in its turn, overlooked, on one side, the same stream which flowed past one flank of M. de Malmédie's house, on the other, the lane planted with trees, which was about twelve feet above the level of the wood-yard. Leaning against this lane were two or three buildings the roofs of which, slightly inclined, offered an easy access to anybody who, from any motive, should desire to avoid the public path and slip down unobserved from the lane into the wood-yard.

The summer-house had three windows and a door leading, as we have said, into the court. One of the windows was close to this door, the second looked on to the passage, and the third on to the wood-yard.

During Miko-Miko's narrative Georges smiled thrice, but with very different expressions; first, when his messenger told him that Sara had kept the card; secondly, when he mentioned Henri's marriage with his cousin; lastly, on hearing that it was possible to enter the summer-house by the window facing the wood-yard.

Georges put pencil and paper in front of Miko-Miko, and, while the latter, to make things doubly sure, drew a plan of the house, Georges took up a pen and began to write a letter.

This letter and the plan of the house were completed simultaneously.

Then Georges got up and fetched from his room a wonderful little Buhl cabinet, worthy of having belonged to Madame de Pompadour, placed inside it the letter he had just written, locked the cabinet, and handed both to Miko-Miko, giving him his instructions. Miko-Miko next received another doubloon in payment for the fresh commission he was about to undertake, and then, balancing his bamboo rod on his shoulder once more, took the road to the town at the same pace at which he had come, which would bring him to Sara's abode in somewhere about four hours.

Just as Miko-Miko had disappeared from sight at the end of the avenue of trees leading to the plantation, Jacques and his father entered through a gate behind. Georges, who had been on the point of starting to meet them, was surprised at their quick return; but Jacques had seen in the skies signs that foretold a storm, and though he had absolute confidence in M. Tête de Fer, his Lieutenant, he was much too fond of the *Calypso* to entrust her safety to another in such a crisis. So he came back to bid this brother good-bye; for, from the top of the *Montagne du Pouce*, which he had climbed to see if the *Calypso* still remained at her station, he had seen her tacking about at nearly two miles distance from the shore, and had then made the signal arranged between the Lieutenant and himself, in case circumstances should compel him to return on board. His signal had been observed, and Jacques had no doubt but that in two hours the boat that had brought him ashore would be ready to take him back.

Poor old M. Munier had done all he could to keep his son with him, but Jacques had answered quietly:

" It is impossible, father."

And the firm, though tender, manner in which he said this had convinced the old man that his son had fully made up his mind, so he pressed him no further.

As for Georges, he so thoroughly entered into the motive which took Jacques back on board, that he did not even attempt to dissuade him from his purpose. Only he declared that he and his father would go with him as far as the ridge of the Pieterbot, from the opposite side of which they could see Jacques embark, and, once on the sea, follow him with their eyes as far as the ship.

Jacques accordingly started accompanied by Georges and his father, and the three, taking paths known only to sportsmen, reached the source of the *Rivière des Calebasses*. There Jacques took leave of his father and brother, whom he had seen for so short a time, giving a solemn promise to visit them again before long.

An hour later, the boat had left the shore with Jacques, who, loyal to the love which a sailor feels for his ship, went back to save the *Calypso* or perish with her.

The moment Jacques was on board, the schooner, which had been tacking to and fro off shore till then, headed for the *Ile de Sable*, and sheered off to the northward as quick as possible.

Meanwhile sky and sea had assumed a more and more threatening aspect. The sea roared loudly and was visibly rising, although the tide was still on the ebb; while the sky, as though wishing to rival the ocean, rolled along hurrying masses of clouds that parted suddenly to give passage to squalls of wind varying from east-south-east to south-east and south-south-east. These symptoms, however, to any one but a sailor, betokened only an ordinary tempest. Several times previously during the year the aspect of things had appeared as threatening without being followed by any catastrophe. But on entering the house, Georges and his father were obliged to acknowledge how sagacious the prognostications of Jacques had been. The mercury in the barometer had sunk to below twenty-eight inches.

Pierre Munier at once ordered the overseer to have all the stalks of the manioc cut in order to protect the roots, which, if this precaution is neglected, are nearly always torn up from the ground and carried off by the wind.

Georges, in his turn, ordered Ali to have Antrim saddled by eight o'clock. On hearing this order Pierre Munier started.

" What do you want your horse saddled for ? " he asked in alarm.

" I have to be at the town at ten, father," answered Georges.

" But, my poor lad, it is impossible ! " cried the old man.

" I must, father," said Georges.

And in the tone of these words, as in those of Jacques, the unhappy father recognized such a determination that he dropped his head with a sigh and insisted no further.

Meanwhile Miko-Miko was fulfilling his mission.

No sooner did he reach Port Louis than he made for

M. de Malmédie's house, now doubly open to him owing to the order given by Henri. He presented himself this time with even more confidence, since in passing the harbour he had seen M. de Malmédie and his son occupied in watching the ships riding at anchor, whose skippers, in expectation of the threatening storm, were laying out extra anchors. Accordingly he entered the house without fear of being disturbed by anybody while transacting his business, and Bijou, who had seen Miko-Miko that same morning in conference with his young master as well as with her whom he already regarded as his young mistress, took him straight to Sara, who, as usual, was in the summer-house.

As Georges had anticipated, among all the fresh objects which the dealer offered to the curiosity of the young Creole, the charming Buhl cabinet at once attracted her notice. Sara took it up, turned it round and round, and, having admired the outside, wished to examine it within, and asked for the key to open it, upon which Miko-Miko pretended to search for it everywhere, but without success. Finally he intimated by signs that he had not got it, and had doubtless forgotten it at home, but would go and fetch it; so he went off at once leaving behind the cabinet and promising to return with the key.

Ten minutes later, while the girl, with childish eagerness and curiosity was turning the wonderful cabinet backwards and forwards, Bijou entered and gave her the key, which Miko-Miko had been content to send by the hands of a Negro messenger. Little mattered it to Sara how the key reached her, so long as it did reach her; so she took it from the hands of Bijou, who withdrew quickly to close all the shutters of the house that were threatened by the storm. Sara, left alone, hastened to open the cabinet, which, as we know, contained nothing but a piece of paper, not even sealed, but folded in four.

Georges had anticipated everything, and made every calculation.

Sara must be alone at the moment when she discovered the letter, and the letter must be open so that Sara could not send it back and say that she had not read it.

Accordingly Sara, seeing she was quite alone, hesitated for a moment; guessing, however, from whom the letter came, and carried away by curiosity, by love, in short, by the thousand feelings which surge in a young girl's bosom, she could not resist the desire to see what Georges had written to her, and with much agitation and a great deal of blushing, took the letter, unfolded it, and read as follows:—

"SARA,

"I have no need to tell you I love you, for you know it; the dream of my life has been to find a companion like yourself. Now there are exceptional cases, supreme in one's life, when all the conventionalties of society break down in the presence of an overwhelming necessity.

"Sara, do you love me?

"Weigh carefully what your life with M. de Malmédie will be, weigh carefully what your life will be with me.

"With him, the respect of all men.

"With me, the scorn of all men—except the few able to rise superior to deeply-rooted prejudice.

"Only, I repeat, I love you, more than any man on earth has ever loved you, or ever will. I know that M. de Malmédie is hurrying on the hour when he will become your husband. There is, then, no time to be lost; you are free, Sara; lay your hand on your heart, and decide between M. Henri and myself.

"Your answer I shall hold sacred as a mother's commands. This evening, at ten o'clock, I shall be at the summer-house to receive it.   "GEORGES."

Sara glanced around her in terror. It seemed as though on turning round she would see Georges.

At this moment the door opened and, instead of Georges, Sara saw Henri appear; she hid the letter in her bosom.

Henri generally, as we have seen, chose unfortunate times for his interviews with his cousin, and on this occasion he was no more happily inspired than usual. It was an inopportune moment for appearing before Sara, taken up as she was with her thoughts of another.

"Forgive me, Sara dear," said Henri, "for coming in thus unannounced, but it seems to me, whatever you may think about it, that, situated as we are, and going to be, in a fortnight, man and wife, such freedom is permissible. Besides, I have come to tell you that, if you have any nice flowers outside that you care for particularly, you would do well to bring them indoors."

" Why ? " asked Sara.

" Don't you see there is a storm brewing, and that it would be better for flowers, as well as for people, to be indoors than out to-night ? "

" Oh ! good heavens ! " cried Sara, thinking of Georges, " will there be any danger then ? "

" Not for those of us who have solid houses," said Henri ; " but for the poor wretches who live in huts or who have business in the streets, yes ; and I shouldn't like to be in their place."

" Do you really think so, Henri ? "

" Think so ? by George, I do ! There, do you hear ? "

" What ? "

" The cypresses in the *Jardin de la Compagnie.*"

" Yes, I hear. They are moaning ; it is a sure sign of tempest, is it not ? "

" And look at the sky, how black it is. So, I repeat, Sara, if you have any flowers to bring in, you have no time to lose ; I am going to shut up my dogs in the kennels."

And Henri went out to put his pack under shelter from the storm.

Night, in truth, was coming on with unusual rapidity, for the sky was covered with great, black clouds ; from time to time gusts of wind shook the house, then all became still again, but it was that oppressive stillness that seems the agony of gasping Nature. Sara looked out into the court-yard and saw the mango-trees shivering as though they were endowed with feeling and had a presentiment of the coming struggle between wind, earth and sky, while the China lilacs drooped their flowers sadly towards the ground. At this sight the girl was seized with deadly terror, and clasped her hands together, murmuring :

" O God, protect him ! "

At this instant Sara heard her Uncle's voice calling her, and opened the door.

"Sara," said M. de Malmédie, "Sara, come here, my child, you won't be safe in the summer-house."

"Here I am, Uncle," said the girl, shutting the door and turning the key after her, lest any one should go in in her absence.

But instead of joining Henri and his father, Sara went into her own room. A moment later M. de Malmédie came to see what she was doing there, and found her on her knees before the crucifix at the foot of her bed.

"What are you doing there," said he, "instead of coming to have your tea with us ? "

"Uncle," answered Sara, "I am praying for all wayfarers abroad to-night."

"Oh, indeed!" said M. de Malmédie. "I am sure there won't be a man in the whole island such a fool as to stir out of doors in this weather."

"Heaven grant it, Uncle," said Sara.

And she continued her prayers.

There was, in fact, no longer room for doubt that the event which Jacques, sailor as he was, had foretold at a glance, was to be accomplished ; one of those terrible hurricanes, which are the terror of the Colonies, threatened the Isle of France. Night, as we have said, had come on with alarming swiftness, but the lightning flashes followed each other with such rapidity and brightness that this darkness was replaced by a blue, livid light which gave to all objects the sickly hue of those extinct worlds which Byron represents Cain as visiting under the guidance of Satan. Each of the short intervals during which the almost incessant lightning allowed the darkness to reign was filled with heavy peals of thunder, which, starting from behind the mountains, seemed to roll over their slopes, passed above the town and died away in the depths of the horizon. Then, as we have said, mighty gusts of wind followed the travelling thunder-claps and passed over in their turn, bowing as if they had been willow rods the stoutest trees, which rose up again slowly and fearfully, only to bend and moan and sigh once more beneath some fresh squall, ever fiercer than the preceding one.

It was especially in the centre of the Island, in the district of Moka and the Williams plains, that the hurricane, as if delighting in its liberty, was grandest to behold.   Pierre Munier was therefore doubly terrified at seeing Jacques start off and Georges ready to start as well, but, always feeble in presence of any moral force, the poor father had yielded, and, though shuddering at the roaring of the wind, turning pale at the growling of the thunder, and starting at each fresh lightning flash, did not even attempt to keep Georges back. As for the young man, you would have said that he rose to greater heights of hardihood the nearer he approached the danger.   In contrast to his father, at each threatening peal he raised his head ; at each flash of lightning he smiled ; you would have said that he who had hitherto battled in every human strife, longed, like Don Juan, to battle with his Creator.

So when the hour for his departure had arrived, with that inflexible determination which was the distinctive result of the education—we will not say which he had received, but which he had given himself—Georges approached his father and gave him his hand, and, without seeming to understand the old man's reluctance, went out with as firm a step and as composed a face as though he were leaving the house in quite ordinary circumstances.   At the door he met Ali who, with the passive obedience of Orientals, was holding Antrim ready saddled.   The son of the desert neighed and reared as though he sniffed the hiss of the simoom, or the roar of the khamsin ; but, on hearing his rider's well-known voice, seemed to calm down, and turned his wild eye and foaming nostrils towards him. Georges patted him for a moment on the shoulder, and spoke a few words in Arabic ; then, with the lightness of a perfect horseman, jumped into the saddle without the aid of the stirrup.   At the same moment Ali let go of the bridle, and Antrim dashed off like lightning without Georges even noticing his father, who, to avoid losing sight of his favourite son sooner than he could help it, had partly opened the door, and followed him with his eyes until he disappeared at the end of the avenue leading up to the house.

It was, indeed, wonderful to see the intrepid rider borne

along as rapidly as the hurricane through which he passed, overleaping space, like Faust hurrying to the Brocken on his infernal steed. All around him were disorder and confusion. Nothing was to be heard save the crash of trees, broken by the beating of the storm. Sugarcanes and manioc plants torn from their roots were flying through the air like feathers carried by the wind. Birds, surprised in their sleep and whirled away in a flight which they could not control, wheeled round Georges, uttering shrill cries, while occasionally a terrified stag crossed the road swift as an arrow. Georges was now happy, for he felt his heart swell with pride ; he alone was calm amidst this universal confusion, and, while all around him was bending and breaking, he alone pursued his course towards the goal determined by his will, suffering nothing to turn him from his path, or divert him from his purpose.

He went on thus for about an hour, leaping over trunks of fallen trees, streams that had swollen into torrents, and rocks that had been torn from their roots and rolled down from the mountain-top ; then he perceived the sea, tossing its dark waves, foaming and roaring, as it beat with terrific din against the shore, as though the hand of God could no longer restrain it. Georges reached the foot of the *Montagne des Signaux* ; he turned its base, still carried onwards by his steed's impetuous career, crossed the *Pont Bourgeois*, turned to the right up the *Rue de la Côte-d'Or*, passed behind the walls of the *Quartier* and, crossing the rampart, descended by the *Rue de la Rampe* into the *Jardin de la Compagnie*. Thence making his way through the deserted streets in the midst of fragments of fallen chimneys, tottering walls, and flying tiles, he followed the *Rue de la Comédie*, then turned sharp to the right up the *Rue du Gouvernement*, plunged into the blind alley opposite the Theatre, jumped down from his horse, opened the wicket which separated the alley from the lane planted with trees that overlooked M. de Malmédie's house, closed the gate to behind him, and threw his bridle over Antrim's neck, who, having no outlet, could not run away. Then, letting himself slide down the roofs abutting on the lane, and jumping from them to the ground, he found himself in the wood-yard, into which opened the windows of the summer-house we have already described.

Meanwhile, Sara was in her room, listening to the roaring of the gale, crossing herself at each flash of lightning, praying unceasingly, calling upon the tempest, for she hoped that the tempest might stop Georges. Then starting suddenly as she told herself that when a man such as her lover says that he will do a thing, do it he will, though the whole world should fall upon his head. Then she besought God to calm the wind and quench the lightning; she saw Georges crushed beneath some tree, overwhelmed by some rock, rolling at the bottom of some torrent; and she realized in alarm how strong and swift an influence her rescuer had acquired over her; she felt that all resistance to what so attracted her was useless, that all struggle, in short, was vain against that love, born but the day before, yet already so powerful. She knew her poor heart could but struggle and groan, acknowledging itself vanquished without having so much as tried to show fight.

As the hour advanced, Sara's excitement became more intense. With eyes fixed on the clock, she followed the movement of the hands, and a voice whispered in her heart that, as the hand marked each minute, Georges was coming nearer. The hand pointed in succession to nine o'clock, half-past nine, a quarter to ten, and the storm, far from diminishing, became every moment more appalling. The house shook to its foundations; you would have thought each instant that the wind would tear it from its base. From time to time, amidst the wail of the cypresses and the cries of the Negroes, whose huts, less solid than the houses of the Whites, were demolished by the breath of a hurricane just as a child blows down the house of cards which he has erected, you could hear, in answer to the thunder, the mournful appeal of some building in distress imploring help that no human being could render it.

Among all these various sounds that echoed the destruction that was going on, Sara thought she heard a horse neigh.

Then she got up suddenly; her resolve was taken. The man who through the midst of such dangers, when the bravest were quaking in their houses, came to her across uprooted forests, swollen torrents, yawning gulfs, and all to say " I love you, Sara ! Do you love me ? " this man was truly worthy of her. And if Georges had done this, Georges who had saved her life, then she belonged to Georges as he belonged to her. It was no longer a resolution formed by her free will ; a hand divine bowed her, without her being able to resist it, beneath a preordained destiny ; it was no longer hers to choose her lot, but passively to obey her fate.

Then with that firmness imparted, by a crisis, Sara quitted her room, reached the end of the corridor, descended by the little outer staircase we have mentioned, which seemed to quake beneath her feet, found herself at the corner of the square courtyard, went on, stumbling against fragments at each step, and leaning against the wall of the summer-house so as not to be blown down by the wind, until she reached the door. At the moment she turned the handle, the lightning flashed, showing her the mango-trees all twisted, the lilacs dishevelled, her flowers crushed ; then only did she fully realize the depths of the convulsion in which Nature was struggling, and thought that perhaps she would wait in vain, and that Georges would not come, not because he feared to come, but because he was dead. In face of this idea, everything disappeared, and Sara quickly entered the summer-house.

" Thank you, Sara," said a voice that startled her to the depths of her heart, " thank you ! Oh! I was not mistaken ; you love me, Sara ; bless you a hundred times ! "

And Sara felt a hand that grasped her own, a heart beating against hers, a breath that mingled with her breath. An unknown sensation, rapid, devouring, ran through all her frame ; panting, distracted, bending as a flower bends upon its stalk, she fell upon Georges' shoulder, having exhausted, in the struggle which she had maintained for two hours, all the strength that she possessed, and only able to murmur :

" Georges ! Georges ! have pity on me ! "

Georges understood this appeal from weakness to strength, from the modesty of the girl to the loyalty of her lover. It may be he had come with a different object, but he felt from that moment Sara was his ; that any favour obtained from the maid would be so much ravished from the bride, and, though quivering himself with love, desire, and happiness, contented himself with drawing her closer to the window to see her by the flash of the lightning, and, laying his hand on that of the young Creole, said :

" You are mine, Sara, are you not ? mine for life ? "

" Oh, yes, yes, for life ! " murmured the girl.

" Nothing shall ever part us but death ? "

" Nothing but death."

" You swear it, Sara ? "

" By my mother, Georges ! "

" Good ! " said the young man, trembling both with joy and pride. " From this moment you are my wife, Sara, and woe to him who tries to rob me of you ! "

At these words Georges pressed his lips on those of the girl, and, dreading doubtless lest he should no longer control himself in the presence of such love, and youth, and beauty, dashed into the neighbouring room, the window of which, like that of the summer-house, overlooked the wood-yard, and disappeared.

At this moment there was such a deafening peal of thunder that Sara fell upon her knees. Almost immediately the door of the summer-house opened and M. de Malmédie and Henri entered.

CHAPTER XVI

A MOMENTOUS INTERVIEW

DURING the night the hurricane ceased, but it was not until the next morning that the havoc due to it could be properly estimated.

Many of the ships lying in the harbour had sustained very considerable damage ; several had been dashed against one another and seriously injured.

The majority had been dismasted and swept bare like sheer hulks ; two or three had dragged their anchors and grounded on the Ile des Tonneliers. Lastly, one had sunk in the harbour and perished, crew and cargo, without any one being able to afford her the slightest assistance.

On land, the destruction was no less great. Few of the houses of Port Louis had altogether escaped the terrible cataclysm. Nearly all such as were covered with shingles, slates, tiles, copper or tin, had had their roofs carried away. Only those which were terminated by *argamasses*, that is to say, by terraces in the Indian fashion, had offered a complete resistance. So, next morning the streets were found strewed with fragments, and some of the buildings were only kept upright upon their foundations by the aid of numerous struts.

All the stands erected on the Champ-de-Mars in preparation for the races had been blown down. Two heavy guns belonging to the Battery near the *Grand-Rivière* had been overturned by the wind and were found in the morning lying in an opposite direction to that in which they had been left the evening before.

The interior of the Island presented an aspect no less deplorable. What was left of the harvest, which happily had been almost all got in, had been torn up out of the ground ; in several places whole acres of forest presented the appearance of wheat laid by the hail. Scarcely any tree standing by itself had been able to resist the hurricane, and even the tamarinds, those pre-eminently flexible trees, had been broken off short, a thing hitherto regarded as an impossibility.

The house of M. de Malmédie, one of the highest in Port Louis, had suffered greatly. There had even been a moment when the shocks had been so violent that M. de Malmédie and his son determined to seek refuge in the summer-house, which, being built entirely of stone, with only one storey, and sheltered by the terrace, evidently afforded less hold to the wind. Henri had therefore run to his cousin's room, but, finding it empty, concluded that Sara, like his father and himself, had thought of seeking refuge in the summer-house, where, upon going down, they found her. The reason for her being there was quite natural, and her terror required no excuse. Consequently neither father nor son suspected for a moment the cause which had made Sara leave her room, but assigned it to a feeling of fear, from which they themselves had not been exempt. Towards dawn, as we have said, the tempest lulled. But, though nobody had slept all night, they dared not seek repose as yet, and each individual occupied himself in examining what amount of personal loss would fall upon him. The Governor, on his side, as soon as it was light, visited all the streets in the town, putting the garrison at the disposal of the inhabitants. The result was that, even before night fell, some portion of the traces left by the catastrophe had disappeared.

Everybody was doing his very best to restore to Port Louis the aspect it had worn the day before, inasmuch as the festival of the Yamsé, one of the greatest solemnities in the Isle of France, was approaching. Now as this festival, the name of which is probably unknown in Europe, is intimately connected with the events of this story, we ask the reader's permission to make a few introductory remarks on the subject which are necessary for our purpose.

Everybody knows that the great Mohammedan family is divided into two sects, not merely different, but even hostile : namely, the *Sunnite* and the *Shyite*. The one, to which the Arab and Turkish populations belong, recognize Abu-Bekr, Omar and Osman as the legitimate successors of Mohammed ; the other, consisting of the Persians and Mussulman inhabitants of India, look upon the three Caliphs as usurpers, and assert that Ali, the son-in-law and minister of the Prophet, had the sole right to his political and religious inheritance. In the course of the long wars waged by the pretenders, Hoseïn, Ali's son, was seized near the town of Kerbela, by a band of soldiers sent by Omar in pursuit of him, and the young Prince, together with sixty of his relatives who accompanied him, was massacred after an heroic defence.

It is the anniversary of this ill-fated event which is celebrated every year with a solemn festival by the Mohammedans of India, and is called the Yamsé, from a corruption of the cries of " Va Hoseïn ! ô Hoseïn ! " repeated in chorus by the Persians. They have, moreover, transformed the festival as well as the name, by introducing into it certain customs of their native country and ceremonies belonging to their ancient religion.

Well, it was on the following Monday, being the day

of the. full moon, that the Lascars, who represent the Indian *Shyites* in the Isle of France, were to celebrate the Yamsé according to their custom, and to afford the Colony the spectacle of this strange ceremony, which was looked forward to with even greater curiosity than in preceding years.

In fact an unwonted circumstance was to render the festival on this occasion more magnificent than it had ever been before. The Lascars are divided into two bands, the Lascars of the sea and the Lascars of the land ; those of the sea being distinguished by their green robes, and those of the land by their white robes. Each band ordinarily celebrates the festival in its own way with the greatest amount of display and splendour possible, trying to outshine its rival ; the result is an emulation which resolves itself into disputes, and the disputes degenerate into quarrels. Then the sea Lascars, who are poorer but more courageous than those of the land, often avenge themselves for the financial superiority of their opponents with sticks and sometimes even with swords, and the police are obliged to interfere to prevent fatal results.

But this year, thanks to the active intervention of an unknown merchant who was inspired no doubt by religious zeal, the two parties had abandoned their jealousies, and had united, so as to form but one body. Accordingly, as we have said, the report had been generally spread abroad that the solemnity would be at once more peaceful and more brilliant than in preceding years.

You can readily understand that, in a place where there is so little diversion as in the Isle of France, this festival, always regarded with curiosity, even by those who have witnessed it from childhood, is awaited with impatience. For three months beforehand it is the chief topic of conversation, and people talk of nothing else but the *gouhn*, which is to be the chief ornament of the fête.

The said *gouhn* is a kind of pagoda made of bamboo, consisting generally of three storeys one above the other, each narrower than the one below, and covered with paper of all colours. Each of these storeys is constructed in a separate hut, square like itself, one of its four sides being eventually demolished to admit of the edifice inside being

removed. These three floors are then placed inside a fourth
hut, high enough to allow of their being erected one above
the other. The whole fabric is then joined together with
ropes, and the finishing touch put both to its general appearance and its several details. Moreover, in order to arrive at
a result worthy of the proposed structure, the Lascars often
four months beforehand search the whole Colony through for
the most skilful workmen; Hindoos, Chinese, free blacks
and black slaves, are all put under contribution. Only
instead of paying these last their daily wage, it is handed
over to their masters.

Among all the individual losses which each inhabitant had
to deplore the news was received with general delight that
the house containing the *gouhn*, which had already reached
a state of completion, had escaped all damage, sheltered
as it was behind a spur of the *Montagne du Pouce*. Nothing
then would be wanting this year to the festival, which the
Governor, in celebration of his arrival, had supplemented
by public races, reserving to himself with aristocratic liberality the right of giving the prizes, on condition that owners
should ride their own horses, after the fashion of gentlemen
riders in England.

So, as you see, everything concurred to make the pleasure
to which all were looking forward soon efface the disagree-
able experience which they had just gone through.

Sara, contrary to her wont, absorbed as she was by
thoughts unknown to those about her, appeared to take no
interest in a solemnity which, in previous years, had given
her a much appreciated opportunity of exhibiting her
fascinations.

For the whole aristocracy of the Isle of France was in
the habit of appearing at the races, as well as at the Yamsé,
either in stands expressly erected or in open carriages;
in either case it was an opportunity for the handsome
Creoles of Port Louis to air their showy elegance. Naturally,
therefore, it created surprise that Sara, on whom the announcement of a ball or any spectacle whatsoever generally
produced such an impression, now remained so indifferent
to what was going on. Henrietta herself, who had brought
the girl up, and could read her mind to its depths, as

though it were the clearest crystal, could not make her out at all, and became lost in thought on the subject.

Let us hasten to say that " ma mie Henriette "—whose return to Port Louis we have not had the opportunity, amid such grave incidents, to mention—had been so alarmed during the night of the storm that, although not yet recovered from the effects of the incident that had so agitated her, she had started from the *Rivière Noire* as soon as the gale had ceased, and arrived in the course of the day at Port Louis, where she had now been for two days in the company of her young charge, whose unaccustomed absent-mindedness was beginning, as we said, to cause her serious uneasiness.

The fact is that during the last three days a great change had taken place in the girl's life. From the moment when she saw Georges for the first time, the face and appearance, nay, even the very voice, of the handsome young fellow had dwelt in her heart. Then, with an involuntary sigh, she had thought more than once of her future marriage with Henri, a marriage to which, for the last ten years, she had given her tacit consent, owing to the fact that she had never expected that circumstances could arise which would render it an obligation impossible for her to fulfil. But from the day of the banquet with the Governor, she had felt that to take her cousin as a husband would be to condemn herself to perpetual unhappiness. Finally, there came a time, as we have seen, when not only had this fear become a conviction, but when she had given a solemn promise to Georges that she would never belong to any one but him. Well, you will allow that here was a situation calculated to make a girl of sixteen reflect seriously, and to make her regard as of less importance all those fêtes and amusements which hitherto she had looked upon as the chief events of her life.

Neither had M. de Malmédie and his son been free from anxiety during the last five or six days. Sara's refusal to dance with any one else from the time she declined to dance with Georges, her retirement from the ball when it was just opening, whereas as a rule she was the last to come away, her persistent silence, whenever her cousin or

her uncle broached the question of her coming marriage, all
this seemed to them unnatural. Accordingly they had both
decided that the preparations for the wedding should go
forward without saying anything more about it to Sara,
and that she should only be informed when everything was
in readiness. This course was all the easier, inasmuch as
no definite time had ever been fixed for the marriage,
while Sara, who had just reached the age of sixteen, was
quite old enough to fulfil the purpose which M. de Malmédie
had always entertained with regard to her.

All these individual anxieties constituted a general
preoccupation, which had for three or four days imparted a
coolness and a feeling of constraint to the meetings which
took place between the different persons who lived in M.
de Malmédie's house. These meetings generally occurred
four times a day ; in the morning, at the breakfast hour ; at
two o'clock which was the hour for dinner ; at five, which was
the tea hour ; and at nine, which was the time for supper.

For three days Sara had requested and obtained breakfast in her own room. At this meal embarrassment and
constraint, saved up, as it were, from the previous day,
always prevailed ; but there still remained three daily
meetings which she could not avoid, except by making
illness her excuse. Well, this excuse could not last for
very long, so Sara hardened her heart and came down at the
accustomed hours.

On the third day after the storm, Sara was seated accordingly at five o'clock in the large drawing-room, working
near the window at some embroidery which necessitated her
keeping her eyes lowered. Henrietta was giving to the
tea-making all the attention which English ladies usually
bestow on that important occupation, and M. de Malmédie
and his son were standing before the fire-place talking in low
tones, when suddenly the door opened and Bijou announced
Lord Murray and M. Georges Munier.

This double announcement affected each of those present
differently, as you will readily understand. MM. de Malmédie, thinking they had heard wrongly, made Bijou
repeat the names. Sara blushed and lowered her head over
her work, while Henrietta, who had just opened the tap of

the tea-urn, was so confused that, occupied in looking successively at the MM. de Malmédie, Sara, and Bijou, she let the boiling water overflow, which now began to trickle from the urn over the table and from the table to the ground. Bijou repeated the names he had already pronounced, accompanying them with the most agreeable smile he could assume.

M. de Malmédie and his son looked at one another with increasing astonishment; then M. de Malmédie, feeling that the situation must be put an end to, said :
" Show them in."

Lord Murray and Georges entered, both dressed in dark coats, which denoted a visit of ceremony.

M. de Malmédie took a step or two towards them, while Sara rose blushing, and, after a timid bow, sat down again, or rather fell down again on her chair, and Henrietta, noticing the thoughtless act which her astonishment had caused, hastily turned the tap of the urn.

Bijou, at a sign from his master, brought forward two arm-chairs, but Georges bowed to indicate that they were unnecessary, and that he would stand.

" Sir," said the Governor, addressing M. de Malmédie, "here is M. Georges Munier, who has begged me to accompany him to your house, and support by my presence a request which he has to make of you. As I am sincerely anxious that this request should be granted, I thought I ought not to refuse to take this step which, besides, procures me the honour of seeing you." The Governor bowed, and the two men answered by a similar movement.

" We are under an obligation to M. Georges Munier," said M. de Malmédie at last ; " we shall therefore be delighted to be of service to him in any way."

" If you mean by that, sir," answered Georges, " to allude to the pleasure I have had in saving Mademoiselle from the danger in which she was placed, allow me to declare to you that all the gratitude is due from me to God, who brought me there to do what any one else would have done in my place. Besides," added Georges, with a smile, " you will see presently that my conduct on that occasion was not free from selfishness."

" Excuse me, sir, but I do not understand you," said Henri.

" Make your mind easy, sir," replied Georges, " you will not be long in doubt of my meaning, which I am about to explain clearly."

" We are listening to you, sir."

" Shall I retire, Uncle ? " asked Sara.

" If I dared hope," said Georges, half turning and with a bow, " that a wish expressed by me would influence you, Mademoiselle, I would beg you, on the contrary, to remain."

Sara sat down again. There was a moment's silence ; then M. de Malmédie indicated by a gesture that he was waiting.

" Monsieur," said Georges in a perfectly calm tone, " you know me, you know my family, you know my fortune. I am worth at this moment two million francs. Forgive my entering into these details, but they are unavoidable."

" All the same, sir, I must confess," replied Henri, " that I fail to see how they can interest us."

" Well, it is not as a matter of fact to you that I am speaking, sir," said Georges, preserving the same calmness of voice and demeanour, while Henri showed a visible impatience, " but to your father."

" Allow me to tell you, sir, that I do not see that my father, either, requires such information."

" You will understand it presently, sir," replied Georges coldly.

Then, fixing his eyes upon M. de Malmédie, he continued :

" I have come to ask you for the hand of Mademoiselle Sara."

" For whom ? " asked M. de Malmédie.

" For myself, sir," answered Georges.

" For yourself ! " cried Henri, making a movement which the young Mulatto checked by a stern look.

Sara turned pale.

" For yourself ? " asked M. de Malmédie.

" For myself, sir," replied Georges with a bow.

" But," cried M. de Malmédie, " you know quite well, sir, that my niece is destined for my son ? "

" By whom, sir ? " asked the young Mulatto in his turn.

" By whom, by whom !. . . Why ! by me," said M. de Malmédie.

" I would observe to you, sir," replied Georges, " that Mademoiselle Sara is not your daughter, but only your niece, consequently she owes you only a qualified obedience."

" But, sir, this whole discussion appears to me more than extraordinary."

" Pardon me," said Georges, " it is, on the contrary, perfectly natural. I love Mademoiselle Sara ; I believe that I am destined to make her happy ; I am obeying at once the desire of my heart and the duty imposed by my conscience."

" But my cousin does not love you, sir," cried Henri, allowing his natural impetuosity to carry him away.

" You are mistaken, sir," answered Georges, " and I am authorized by Mademoiselle to tell you that she does love me."

" By her ! by her ! " cried M. de Malmédie. " Impossible ! "

" Why, cousin, do you dare . . . ? " cried Henri, moving towards Sara with a gesture that looked like a threat.

Georges moved forward ; the Governor restrained him.

" I now repeat unflinchingly," said Sara, answering her cousin's gesture by a look of supreme contempt, " what I have already said to M. Georges. The life which he has saved is his, and I will never belong to any other but him."

And, at these words, with a gesture full of grace and dignity, the gesture of a Queen, she extended her hand to Georges, who bent over it and placed a kiss there.

" Ah ! this is too much ! " cried Henri, lifting a cane which he held in his hand.

But Lord Murray checked Henri, as he had already checked Georges.

As for Georges, he contented himself with a contemptuous smile at Henri, and then led Sara to the door, bowing once more. Sara, in her turn, bowed, signed to Henrietta to follow her, and went out with her. Georges came back.

" You have seen what has passed, sir," said he to Sara's Uncle. " You no longer doubt the feelings which Mademoiselle entertains towards me. I venture then to ask you a second time for a positive answer to the request which I have the honour to address to you."

"An answer, sir!" cried M. de Malmédie in his turn; "an answer! Have you the audacity to expect that I shall make you any answer than the one you deserve?"

"I do not dictate to you, sir, what answer you should give me; only, be it what it may, I beg you to give me one."

"I should hope you don't expect anything but a refusal?" cried Henri.

"It is your father I am asking, and not you, sir," answered Georges; "allow your father to answer me, and we will discuss *our* affairs afterwards."

"Well, sir," said M. de Malmédie, "understand that I refuse absolutely."

"Very well, sir," answered Georges; "I expected that answer, but courtesy required that I should make you the application, and I have done so."

And Georges bowed to M. de Malmédie with the same politeness and ease as if nothing had passed between them; then, turning to Henri:

"Now, sir," said he, "as regards us two, if you please. This is the second time, recollect, at an interval of fourteen years, that you have lifted your hand to me—the first time with a sword in it."

He lifted his hair, and pointed with his finger to the scar which furrowed his brow.

"The second time with that cane."

And he pointed to the cane which Henri held.

"Well?" said Henri.

"Well," said Georges, "I demand satisfaction for these two insults. You are a brave man, I know, and I hope that you will answer as a man the appeal which I make to your courage."

"I am glad, sir, you are acquainted with my bravery, though your opinion on that point is indifferent to me," answered Henri with a sneer; "it puts me at my ease in the answer I have to give you."

"And what is that answer, sir?" asked Georges.

"The answer is that your second request is at least as presumptuous as the first. I do not fight with a Mulatto."

Georges turned deadly pale, yet an inscrutable smile strayed across his lips.

"That is your last word?" he said.

"Yes, sir," answered Henri.

"Very good, sir," replied Georges; "now I know what I have to do."

And, saluting M. de Malmédie and his son, he withdrew, followed by the Governor.

"I warned you how it would be, sir," said Lord Murray, as they reached the door.

"And you told me nothing I did not know already, my lord," answered Georges; "but I have returned here to accomplish a destiny, and I must see it out to the end. I have a prejudice to combat: it must crush me, or I must kill it. Meanwhile, my lord, accept my grateful thanks."

Georges bowed, and, grasping the hand which the Governor held out to him, crossed the *Jardin de la Compagnie*. Lord Murray followed him with his eyes as long as he remained in sight; then, when he had disappeared at the corner of the *Rue de la Rampe*, he shook his head, saying to himself sadly:

"There is a man going straight to his own destruction. It is a pity truly; there was something noble in that heart of his."

CHAPTER XVII

THE RACES

THE festival of the Yamsé began on the following Saturday, and the town had decked itself, in honour of the day, with such bravery that it was hard to realize that but six days previously it had all but been destroyed.

At early morning the Sea Lascars and the Land Lascars, now united in a single band, started from the Malabar encampment situated outside the town between the brook *des Pucelles* and the *Fanfaron* brook, and, preceded by barbaric strains of music from tambourines, flutes and jews' harps, took the road to Port Louis, in order to make what is called the *quête*, or collection. The two chiefs walked

7

side by side, dressed according to the party which they represented, one in a green, the other in a white robe, and each carrying a drawn sabre with an orange fixed upon its point. Behind them walked two Mullahs, each holding in both hands a plate filled with sugar and covered with leaves of China roses ; next, after the Mullahs came, in fairly good order, the phalanx of native devotees.

The collection began at the first houses in the town ; for, doubtless in a spirit of equality, the collectors do not despise the smallest huts, the offerings from which, as in the case of the wealthiest houses, are intended to defray a part of the enormous expense which all this poor population has incurred in order to render the ceremony as splendid as possible. Further, it must be stated, the method of begging adopted by the collectors is affected by the pride characteristic of Orientals, and, far from being low and servile, exhibits something noble and touching. After the chiefs, to whom all doors are opened, have saluted the owners of the house by lowering the points of their sabres before them, the Mullah advances and offers to the spectators sugar and rose leaves. Meanwhile other natives, selected by the chiefs, receive in plates the gifts which have been made to them ; then they all withdraw, saying, " Salaam." In this way they seem not so much to receive alms as to invite those who are strangers to their creed to a symbolic communion, by sharing with them in a fraternal way the expenses of their worship and their religious offerings. Usually the collection extends not only, as we have said, to all the houses in the town, but even to the ships in the harbour, to solicit from which is the province of the Sea Lascars. But on this occasion, as regards this last item, the collection was much curtailed, the majority of the vessels having suffered so greatly in the hurricane that their Captains felt more need of help than disposed to give it. However, at the very moment when the collectors had reached the quay, a ship which had been signalled that morning appeared between the Labourdonnaie Redoubt and Fort Blanc, and entered the harbour, flying the Dutch flag, with all sails set, saluting the fort, which returned her salute gun for gun. She must no doubt have been a long way from the Island when the hurricane occurred, for not a rope in her rigging was missing, and she came onward, leaning over so gracefully the hand of some marine goddess might have been pushing her along the surface of the water. From a distance, by the aid of glasses, you could see her whole crew on deck, in the full uniform of King William, as if they had donned festival costume on purpose to be present at the ceremony. So you may guess that, thanks to its joyous and prosperous appearance, this vessel became at once the object aimed at by both chiefs. Consequently, hardly had she cast anchor ere the leader of the Sea Lascars got into a boat, and, accompanied by his plate-bearers and a dozen of his followers, put off towards the vessel, which certainly did not belie, when seen close at hand, the favourable opinion she had inspired at a distance.

Indeed, if ever Dutch spruceness, so famed all the world over, deserved a hearty eulogy, it was at the sight of this gallant ship, which appeared as the floating embodiment of that spruceness; her deck washed, sponged and polished might have contested the prize for elegance with the parquet floor of the most sumptuous drawing-room. Her copper-work shone like gold; the companion-ladders, carved in the most precious Indian wood, seemed rather for ornament than for purposes of ordinary utility. As for her guns, you would have called them guns *de luxe*, intended more for a museum of artillery than for the armoury of a ship.

Captain Van den Broek—for such was the name of the master of this charming vessel—seemed to know what the business was which brought the Lascars on board, for he went to the head of the ladder to receive the chief, and, having spoken a few words to him in his own language, which proved that this was not the first time he had sailed the Indian seas, placed upon the plate held out to him, not a piece of gold, nor a rouleau of silver, but a nice little diamond worth, perhaps, a hundred louis, apologizing for having no other money at the moment, and begging the chief of the Lascars to be satisfied with this offering. This gift so far exceeded the anticipations of the worthy adherent of Ali,

and was so little in harmony with the natural thriftiness of
the compatriots of John de Witt, that the chief of
the Lascars hesitated a moment, not venturing to take
such liberality seriously, and ,it was not until Captain
Van den Broek had assured him three or four times over
that the diamond was really intended for the *Shyite* band,
with whose efforts he declared himself fully in sympathy,
that the Lascar thanked him and presented to him with
his own hands the plate of rose leaves powdered with
sugar. The Captain gracefully took a small pinch, which
he raised to his mouth and pretended to eat, to the great
satisfaction of the Indians, who did not leave the hospitable
ship until after many " Salaams." Then they continued
their collection elsewhere, but without finding that the
story which they told every one of the fine windfall which
had fallen to them from the sky was successful in producing
a similar donation.

The day was spent in this way, each preparing himself
rather for the festival of the morrow than taking part in the
proceedings of this day, which are only, so to speak, the
prologue to the play.

On the morrow the races were to take place. Now the
ordinary races were already a great institution in the Island ;
but the present ones, occurring in the midst of the other
fêtes and, above all, being given by the Governor, were
going to surpass, as you may suppose, anything of the
kind seen before.

The Champ-de-Mars was, as usual, the spot chosen for the
fête, and all the unreserved space had been crowded with
sightseers from early in the morning ; for although the
great race, that of the gentlemen jockeys, was the chief
attraction of the day, it was by no means the only one. It
was to be preceded by other events of a comic nature, which,
for the populace especially, were all the more interesting,
inasmuch as they themselves would take part in them.
These introductory sports were a pig-hunt, a sack race,
and a pony race. The Governor had offered a prize
for each of these, as he had done for the big race. The
winner of the pony race was to receive a splendid double-
barrelled gun by Manton ; of the sack race, a fine umbrella ;

while the winner in the pig-hunt kept the pig itself as a prize.

The prize for the great race was a silver-gilt cup of the finest design and less valuable for its material than for its workmanship.

We have said that from early in the morning the ground open to the public was thronged with spectators, but it was not until about ten o'clock that the fashionable people began to put in an appearance. As in London, Paris, or anywhere, in short, where there are races, stands had been reserved for the upper ten ; but, whether from caprice, or to avoid being jumbled up together, the prettiest women in Port Louis had decided to attend the races in their carriages, and, with the exception of those who had been invited to sit with the Governor, were all drawn up in line opposite the winning-post or at points of vantage nearest to him, leaving the other stands to the townspeople or inferior merchants.

The young men were, for the most part, on horseback, ready to follow the runners in the inner circle ; while the gentlemen who were members of the Isle of France Jockey Club were on the lawn, making bets with all the reckless nonchalance and prodigality characteristic of Creoles.

By half-past ten the whole of Port Louis was assembled in the Champ-de-Mars. Among the prettiest women in the most elegant carriages might be noticed Mademoiselle Conder and Mademoiselle Cypris de Gersigny, at that time one of the loveliest girls, to-day still one of the loveliest women, in the Isle of France, whose magnificent dark hair has become proverbial, even in the salons of Paris ; lastly, there were the six Demoiselles Druhn, so fair, so white, so fresh, so graceful, that the carriage in which they generally drove out all together was called the " Basket of Roses."

The Governor's stand might also have deserved on this particular day the name given on ordinary days to the carriage of the Demoiselles Druhn. Any one who has not travelled in the Colonies, and who has not, in particular, visited the Isle of France, is unable to form an idea of the charm and grace of all these Creole faces with their velvet eyes and jet-black hair, among which were sprinkled, like flowers of the North, some of the pale daughters of England, with their transparent skin, aërial hair, and swan-like necks. In the opinion of the young men, the bouquets in the hands of all these fair onlookers would in all probability have been far more valuable prizes than all the cups by Odiot, all the guns by Manton, and all the umbrellas by Verdier, which the Governor, in his magnificent liberality, could have offered them.

In the front row of Lord Murray's stand was Sara, placed between M. de Malmédie and "ma mie Henriette," while Henri was on the lawn taking all the odds staked against him, though it must be admitted these were not very numerous. For, in addition to his being a splendid rider, with a great reputation on the race-course, he owned at that moment a horse which was considered to be the fastest ever seen in the Island.

At eleven, the garrison band, placed between the two stands, gave the signal for the first race, which was, as we have said, the pig-hunt.

The reader is acquainted with this comic amusement, which is a popular diversion in many French villages. The tail of a pig is smeared with lard and the competitors endeavour one after the other to hold the animal, being allowed to grasp it only by the said tail. The man who succeeds in stopping him is the winner. This race taking place on the public ground, and every one having a right to take a part in it, no entries have been made.

Two Negroes brought in the animal—a fine pig of the largest size, greased beforehand, and all ready to enter the lists. On seeing it there was a general shout, and Negroes, Hindus, Malays, Madagascans and natives, bursting the barrier which had hitherto been respected, rushed at the animal, which, in astonishment at this onslaught, started to run away.

Precautions had however been taken that he should not escape from his pursuers ; the poor animal had his two forelegs tied to the hind ones, much in the way that horses' feet are hobbled to restrict them to a walking pace. The result was that the pig, being unable to go at more than a very moderate trot, was soon overtaken, and the disappointments of the competitors began once more.

As you may well suppose, the chances of winning in such a game do not rest with those who make the first attempts. It is impossible to retain a grasp of the newly-greased tail, and the pig eludes his antagonists without any difficulty ; but, as the first layers of lard are removed in the successive attempts to grasp its tail, the animal comes slowly to perceive that the pretensions of those who hope to stop him are not so ridiculous as he at first thought them. At times even when he is pressed too hard, he turns round upon his most determined foes, who then, according to the degree of courage with which nature has endowed them, either pursue their object or relinquish it. At last comes the moment when the tail, deprived of all adventitious aid, and reduced to its natural substance, only slips with difficulty, and finally betrays its owner, who struggles, grunts, utters unavailing cries, and finds himself by general acclamation adjudicated to the winner.

On this occasion the chase followed its usual course of progress. The unhappy pig freed himself with the greatest ease from his first pursuers, and, though hampered by his bonds, began to escape from the enclosure over the Martyrs' Common. But a dozen of the best and most active runners dashed upon his heels, making successive grabs at the tail of the poor animal with a rapidity that did not allow him a moment's peace, and which must have warned him that, however bravely delayed, the hour of his defeat approached. As a matter of fact, five or six of his antagonists, breathless and panting, now gave up the struggle. But, in proportion as the number of claimants diminished, the chances of those who still stuck to it increased, and they thereupon became doubly active and skilful, being further encouraged by the shouts of the spectators.

In the number of the competitors, and among those who seemed determined to see the matter through, were two of our old acquaintances, namely, Antonio the Malay, and Miko-Miko the Chinaman. Both had pursued the pig from the start, and had not lost sight of him for a moment. More than a hundred times already had the tail slipped through their hands ; but, each time this happened, they felt that they were making way ; and these fruitless attempts,

far from discouraging them, had only added fresh fuel to
their ardour. At last, having tired out all the other competitors, there remained only these two. It was then that
the struggle became really interesting, and that the serious
betting began.

The chase continued for another ten minutes or so ;
so that after having made almost the entire round of the
Champ-de-Mars, the pig had come to what is called in
sporting parlance his last push, and was squealing, grunting,
and wriggling without this heroic defence appearing in
the least degree to disconcert his two enemies, who held on
by turns to his tail with a regularity worthy of the shepherds
of Virgil. At last Antonio stopped the fugitive for a
moment, and was thought to have won. But the animal,
collecting all his strength, shook himself off so vigorously,
that, for the hundredth time, the tail slipped once more
from between the Malay's hands, while Miko-Miko, who was
on the look-out, seized it instantly, and all Antonio's
chances appeared to be transferred to himself. Then
you saw him, in a manner worthy of the hopes which
part of the spectators had reposed in him, holding on
with both hands, stiffening his legs and being dragged
along, tugging with might and main, followed by the
Malay, who was shaking his head, as though he thought the
game was up, but nevertheless held himself in readiness to
take the other's place. He kept close alongside the pig,
letting his long arms hang down and, almost without the
need of stooping, rubbing his hands in the sand, in order to
give them a better grip. Unfortunately, all this commend-
able pertinacity seemed thrown away, as Miko-Miko seemed
on the point of carrying off the prize. After dragging the
Chinaman along for about ten yards, the pig looked like
giving in, and came to a standstill, still straining forward,
but checked by an equal force that dragged him from
behind ; and, as these two equal forces neutralized each
other, both pig and Chinaman remained for a time quite
motionless, each making violent efforts, the one to advance,
the other to hold his ground, and all to the loud plaudits of
the crowd. Things remained in this position for a few
seconds, and to all appearance were likely to continue so

for the required time, when suddenly the two antagonists were seen to part with a violent jerk. The pig rolled over in front, while Miko-Miko rolled over behind at the same moment, only the one sprawled upon his belly, and the other upon his back. Antonio at once rushed in eagerly, encouraged by shouts from all those who were interested in his success and who now felt sure of victory. But his delight was short-lived, and his disappointment a cruel one ; for at the moment of seizing the animal by the part specified in the programme, he looked for that part in vain. The unlucky pig no longer owned a tail ! This appendage had remained in the hands of Miko-Miko, who got up in triumph, holding out his trophy and appealing to the impartial verdict of the public.

The case was a novel one. It was referred to the decision of the Judges, who after a short deliberation, declared, by three votes to two, that inasmuch as Miko-Miko would indubitably have stopped the animal if the latter had not elected to part with his tail, he must be considered the winner.

Miko-Miko's name was accordingly proclaimed, and he was authorized to carry off the prize which belonged to him. To this the Chinaman, to whom the result was intimated by signs, responded by seizing his property by the hind-legs and marching it off in front of him as you would push a wheel-barrow, while Antonio retired grumbling into the crowd, which, with that instinct of justice which characterizes the populace, gave him that honourable reception which it generally bestows in cases of bad fortune.

As generally happens on the conclusion of an event which has engaged all the attention of the spectators, there was now a good deal of bustle and conversation among the crowd ; but these were soon arrested by the announcement that the sack race was about to commence, and everybody resumed his place, having enjoyed the first event too much to run the risk of losing a sight of the second.

The distance to be run by the competitors was from the *Dreaper* post to the Governor's stand, or about a hundred and fifty yards. On the signal being given, the runners, fifty in number, jumped out of a hut that had been put up as a dressing-room, and ranged themselves in a line.

To account for the large number of competitors wh
presented themselves for this race, it must be remembered
that the prize was, as we have said, a magnificent umbrella
and an umbrella has always been in the Colonies, and
especially in the Isle of France, the Negro's chief objec
of ambition. Whence has this idea sprung, amounting as i
does, almost to a monomania with them ?

I, for my part, cannot tell, and men more learned thar
myself have made it the subject of deep but fruitless
research. We simply state a fact, without assigning a
reason ; but certainly the Governor had been well advised
in choosing the article in question as the prize for the sack
race.   .

There are none of our readers who have not, once in
their lives, witnessed a similar race ; each of the competitors
for the prize is tied up in a sack, the mouth of which is
fastened round his neck, his arms and legs being enclosed.
Under such circumstances, it is not a matter of running,
but of jumping ; well this kind of race, which is always
sufficiently comic, becomes still more so in present conditions, for the drollery is increased by the strange heads
surmounting the sacks, which present a curious assortment
of different colours, this race, like the pig-hunt, being confined to Negroes and Hindus.

In the front rank of those who had acquired a reputation
from numerous victories in this kind of race were Télémaque
and Bijou, who, having inherited the feuds of the families
to which they belonged, rarely met without exchanging
abusive remarks, remarks which often, to the credit of
their valour be it said, led to a vigorous exchange of fisti-
cuffs ; but, on this occasion, as their hands were not free,
and their feet were confined, in addition to their being
separated by three or four of their comrades, they contented
themselves with turning up the whites of their eyes at each
other. At the last moment a fifty-first starter sprang out of
the hut and joined the company ; this was Antonio the
Malay, who had been defeated in the first race.

On the signal being given, they looked for all the world
like a herd of kangaroos, jumping in the most grotesque
fashion, bumping, upsetting, rolling over, getting up again,

bumping again and falling again. For the first sixty yards it was impossible to forecast the winner; a dozen competitors were so close together, while the falls were so unexpected, and so altered the face of things, that, like those who run the road to Paradise, the first found themselves last, and the last first. Still, among the most experienced who were always ahead of the others, were to be seen Télémaque, Bijou, and Antonio. At a hundred yards from the start these three drew away, and the race was clearly confined to a struggle between the three.

Antonio with his customary sharpness had promptly recognized, by the furious glances which they exchanged, the hatred which Télémaque and Bijou cherished towards each other, and had reckoned upon this furious rivalry almost as much as upon his own agility. So, as chance had brought it about that he found himself placed between the two and, consequently, separating them, the wily Malay had taken advantage of one of his numerous falls to roll to one side and leave his two opponents close to each other. What he had foreseen now occurred; scarcely did Télémaque and Bijou see the obstacle which had hitherto separated them disappear, than they instantly made for each other with the most terrible grimaces, grinding their teeth like monkeys quarrelling over a nut, and interspersing this threatening pantomime with words of abuse. Happily, confined as they were in their sacks, they could not pass from words to actions; but it was easy to see, by the shaking of the canvas, that their hands were itching to avenge the abuse uttered by their tongues. Accordingly, excited by their mutual hatred, they came close alongside of one another, so that they jostled at each spring, uttering abuse of the most virulent kind and promising each other that, when once they were out of their sacks, they would have an encounter more desperate than all their preceding ones. Meanwhile Antonio was rapidly gaining on them.

On seeing the Malay, who was five or six yards ahead, a momentary truce ensued between the two Negroes; and both endeavoured, by more gigantic leaps than they had yet made, to regain their lost advantage; indeed, both did actually begin to regain it, especially Télémaque, when a fresh fall gave him a fresh opportunity. Antonio tumbled, and, quickly as the Malay got up, Télémaque found himself with the lead.

Matters were becoming all the more serious as they were now but a dozen yards or so off the finish. Accordingly Bijou uttered a veritable roar, and, with a desperate effort, came up with his rival, but Télémaque was not the man to let himself be passed, so he continued to jump with such ever increasing agility that you might have sworn the umbrella was already his. But, as the proverb has it, man proposes and God disposes. Télémaque tripped, staggered for a moment, and then fell, amid the yells of the crowd ; but in falling, still faithful to his hatred, he directed his fall in such a way as to bar the road for Bijou. The latter, whose impetus prevented his getting out of the way, stumbled over Télémaque and rolled in his turn in the dust.

Then, the same idea entered both their heads at the same moment ; namely, that, sooner than allow a rival to triumph, it would be better that a third party should obtain the prize. So, to the great astonishment of the spectators, the occupants of the two sacks, instead of getting up and making for the winning-post, were no sooner on their feet than they rushed at one another, pommelling each other as fiercely as the canvas prison in which they were enclosed permitted ; butting with their heads in Breton fashion, and leaving Antonio to continue in peace, free from all opposition on the part of his rivals, who, rolling one over the other, in default of feet and hands, the use of which was precluded, went for each other with their teeth.

Meanwhile Antonio arrived in triumph at the goal, fairly winning the umbrella, which was at once handed over to him and displayed by him to the applause of all the spectators, who consisted for the most part of Negroes envious of the happiness of the man who was fortunate enough to possess such a treasure.

Bijou and Télémaque, who had continued meanwhile to go for one another savagely, were eventually separated. Bijou had got off with the loss of a portion of his nose, while Télémaque had lost part of an ear.

It was now the turn of the ponies, and some thirty little animals, all natives of Timor and Pegu, issued from the reserved enclosure with Hindu, Malagasy, or Malay riders on their backs. Their appearance was hailed with loud acclamations, this being a race in which the black population of the Island always shows the greatest interest, since these little animals, being half wild and almost untrained, are so uncontrollable that far more unexpected accidents happen than in the oridnary races. Accordingly, shouts went up from a thousand throats in encouragement of the swarthy jockeys who rode this band of little demons, and who required all the strength and skill they possessed to hold them in and prevent their starting before the signal was given.

Presently, at a sign from the Governor, the start was effected, and they all rushed, or rather flew off, for they much more resembled a flock of birds skimming the ground than a body of quadrupeds touching it with their feet. But hardly had they arrived opposite the *Malartic* memorial than, as usually happens, they began to bolt, as they say in racing phraseology, that is to say, half of them disappeared into the darkness of the woods together with their riders, despite all their efforts to keep them in the course. At the bridge, a third of those who were left had disappeared, so that on nearing the *Dreaper* post you could not count more than seven or eight; while one or two more, having thrown their jockeys, were galloping down the course riderless.

The race was twice round the course, so they flew like a whirlwind past the winning-post without stopping, and disappeared round the corner. Presently you heard loud shouts, then laughter, then nothing more, and every one waited vainly. All the ponies had made off, and not one was left in the course; one and all had vanished, some into the woods of the *Château-d'Eau*, some into the streams in the background, some over the bridge. After waiting for ten minutes, suddenly on the rising slope there appeared, without its rider, an animal which had run through the town, turned by the church, and come back by one of the streets which lead to the Champ-de-Mars, continuing its course at its own sweet will, instinctively, and without any one to

direct it ; while gradually behind it you could see the other
ponies beginning to appear, returning from all directions,
though unfortunately too late. For in a twinkling the first
pony cleared the distance that separated it from the post
passed it by fifty yards, and then stopped of its own accord,
as though it understood perfectly well that it was the winner.

The prize which, as we have said, was a fine gun by
Manton, was handed to the intelligent animal's owner,
a Colonist named M. Saunders.

Meanwhile the other ponies kept coming in from all
directions like pigeons which have been scared by a hawk
and which, having flown off in a flock, return to the dovecot
one by one.

There were seven or eight of them lost altogether and not
recovered for a day or two afterwards.

The next event being the big race, there was now an
interval of half an hour, during which race-cards were
distributed and bets booked.

Among those who betted with most persistence was
Captain Van den Broek who, on leaving his ship, had gone
straight to Viger's, the first goldsmith in the town, an
Auvergnat, and like all his countrymen, renowned for his
scrupulous honesty, where he had parted with 100,000
francs' worth of diamonds in exchange for bank-notes and
gold. Accordingly he was quite ready to face the most
desperate plungers. This he did, putting the whole of his
money, to everybody's great surprise, on a horse called
Antrim, a name entirely unknown in the Island.

There were four horses entered :—

Restoration .	Colonel Dreaper.
Virginie . .	M. Rondeau de Courcy.
Gester . .	M. Henri de Malmédie.
Antrim . .	M. (the name was denoted by two asterisks).

The majority of the wagers were laid on Gester and
Restoration, who at the races in the previous year had
carried off the honours of the day. This year they were
even stronger favourites, ridden as they were by their
owners, both excellent horsemen, while Virginie was running
for the first time.

Notwithstanding this, and in spite of being charitably warned that he was acting as an absolute madman, Captain Van den Broek continued to bet on Antrim, a proceeding which aroused no small curiosity in respect to this unknown horse and his owner.

The horses being ridden by their owners, there was no need to weigh the riders, consequently there was no surprise at not seeing under the tent either Antrim or the gentleman who concealed his identity beneath the hieroglyphics which took the place of his name, and every one expected that he would suddenly appear at the starting-post and take his place in line with his competitors.

In point of fact, when the horses with their riders came out from the enclosure, the person who since the distribution of the race-cards had been the object of public curiosity was seen riding up from the direction of the Malabar encampment. But his appearance, instead of dispelling the uncertainty, served but to increase it; he was dressed in an Egyptian costume, the embroidery of which was visible beneath a hood concealing the half of his face. He rode in the Arab fashion, that is to say with short stirrups, his horse being caparisoned in the manner of the Turks. It was clear to everybody at the first glance that he was a perfect horseman. Antrim too, for no one doubted but that it was the horse entered under this name that had just appeared, Antrim, be it said, seemed to warrant the confidence reposed in him beforehand by Captain Van den Broek, so graceful, supple and so much in harmony with his rider was his appearance.

No one recognized either horse or rider, but, as the entries had been made before the Governor, who must therefore know all about him, the incognito of the new-comer was respected. One person only suspected perhaps the identity of the rider and leaned forward blushing to assure herself of the truth. That person was Sara.

The competitors drew up in a line, numbering, as we have said, four only, since the reputation of Gester and Restoration had discouraged other starters, and every one fancied that the race would resolve itself into a struggle between these two.

As this was only a gentlemen's race the judges had decided that the course should be a run round twice instead of once, so as to prolong the entertainment of the spectators ; each horse therefore had to run about three miles, that is to say a league, which would give a greater chance to such horses as possessed staying power.

The start was made on the dropping of the flag, but in such circumstances it is well known that you cannot determine the actual result by the position of the horses at the early stages. When the first round was half over, Virginie, who, we repeat, was running her maiden race, had gained about thirty yards and Antrim was close at her heels, while Restoration and Gester remained in the rear, being clearly held hard by their riders.

At the hill, that is to say about two-thirds of the circuit, Antrim had gained half a length, while Restoration and Gester had lessened their distance by ten yards ; then they looked like passing, and every one was leaning forward clapping and encouraging the riders, when Sara, either accidentally or on purpose, let fall her bouquet. The unknown horseman saw it, and, without slackening speed, slipped under his horse's belly in the manner of Arab riders picking up the *djerid*, and with wonderful skill picked up the fallen bouquet, bowed to its fair owner, and continued his course, having lost barely ten yards, which he did not appear to trouble himself in the least about regaining.

In the middle of the second round Virginie was overtaken by Restoration, followed by Gester at the distance of a length, while Antrim still kept seven or eight yards behind ; but, as his rider neither pressed him with whip nor spur, it was plain that this slight interval was of no account, and that he would recover the lost ground when he thought it advisable.

At the bridge, Restoration picked up a stone and rolled over with his rider, who, not having lost his stirrups, made an effort to pull him on his legs again. The noble animal struggled, rose, and fell again immediately ; his leg was broken.

The other three continued their course, Gester now leading with Virginie two lengths behind and Antrim at her heels.

But, at the rise, Virginie began to lose ground, while Gester maintained his lead, though Antrim without any effort now began to gain on him. On reaching the *Dreaper* post not more than a length separated Antrim from his rival, and Henri, feeling himself overtaken, began to use his whip. The twenty-five thousand spectators of this fine race applauded loudly, and waved their handkerchiefs to encourage the competitors. Then the unknown horseman bent over Antrim's neck and uttered some words in Arabic, when the intelligent animal, as though he understood what his master was saying, redoubled his speed. Now they were but twenty-five yards from the goal and opposite the first stand, Gester still leading, when the unknown, seeing that there was no time to lose, drove his spurs into his horse's flanks, rose in his stirrups, and, throwing back the hood of his burnouse, shouted to his rival :

" M. Henri de Malmédie, for two insults that you have offered me, I return you but one ; but I hope that it will be an equivalent for both of them."

And raising his arm with these words, Georges, for it was he, struck Henri a violent blow across the face with his whip, which streaked his face with blood.

Then, plunging his spurs into Antrim, he won the race by two lengths ; but, instead of waiting to claim the prize, he continued his course and disappeared, to the profound astonishment of everybody, into the woods surrounding the *Malartic* monument.

Georges was right ; in exchange for two insults received from Henri de Malmédie at an interval of fourteen years he had just repaid one, but it was an insult public, terrible, bloody, one which decided his whole future, since it was not only a challenge to a rival, but a declaration of war against all whites.

Thus Georges found himself, by the irresistible march of events, brought face to face with this prejudice he had come so far overseas to encounter, and the two antagonists were to fight it out in deadly earnest as mortal enemies.

CHAPTER XVIII
LAÏZA

GEORGES was reflecting, in the retirement of the apartment which he had furnished for himself in his father's house at Moka, on the position in which he had just placed himself, when he was told that a Negro wished to see him. He thought very naturally that this was some message from M. Henri de Malmédie, and ordered the bearer to be shown in.

The moment he saw him, however, Georges perceived that he was mistaken ; he had a vague recollection of having met this man somewhere, but where, he could not say.

" Do you not recognize me ? " said the Negro.

" No," answered Georges, " and yet we have met before, have we not ? "

" Twice," replied the Negro.

" Where was that ? "

" The first time at the *Rivière Noire*, when you saved the girl's life ; the second——"

" Yes, of course," interrupted Georges, " I remember ; and the second—— ? "

" The second," interrupted the Negro in his turn, " was when you gave me my liberty. I am called Laïza, and my brother's name is Nazim."

" And what has become of your brother ? "

" Nazim, as a slave, wanted to escape and return to Anjouan : Nazim, now at liberty, thanks to you, has gone away and should be by now at our father's house. I thank you on his behalf."

" And you, though free, have remained behind ? " asked Georges. " That seems strange."

" I will explain that," said the Negro with a smile.

" Do so," answered Georges, who was beginning, in spite of himself, to be interested in this conversation.

" I am a Chief's son," replied the Negro. " I am of mixed Arab and Zanzibar blood, so I was not born to be a slave."

Georges smiled at the Negro's pride, without reflecting that this pride was closely allied to his own, while the Negro went on without seeing or noticing his smile :

" The Chief of Querimbo took me in war and sold me to a
Slave-Captain, who sold me to M. de Malmédie. I offered,
if they would send a slave to Anjouan, to have myself ransomed with twenty pounds of gold dust. They would not
take a slave's word and refused. I insisted for some time
and then—a change occurred in my life, and I no longer
thought of going away."

" Did M. de Malmédie treat you as you deserved to be
treated ? " asked Georges.

" No, it was not that," answered the Negro. " Three
years later, my brother Nazim was captured in his turn and
sold like myself, and luckily, to the same master ; but not
having the same reasons for remaining here as I had, he
wished to escape. You know what followed, since it was
you who rescued him. I loved my brother as my own child,
and you," continued the Negro, crossing his hands over
his breast and bending low, " you I love now as my father.
Well, this is what is going on ; listen, for it interests you
as well as us. There are in this Island eighty-four thousand
coloured men and twenty thousand whites."

" I have counted them already," said Georges with a
smile.

" I suspected as much," answered Laïza. " Out of
these eighty thousand, twenty thousand at least are capable
of bearing arms ; while the whites, including the eight
hundred English soldiers in the garrison, can hardly muster
four thousand men."

" I know that too," said Georges.

" Well then, do you guess ? " asked Laïza.

" I am waiting until you explain."

" We have determined to rid ourselves of the whites.
God knows we have suffered enough to warrant us in
avenging ourselves."

" Well ? " asked Georges.

" Well, we are ready," answered Laïza.

" What is stopping the way, then, and why do you not
avenge yourselves ? "

" We are without a leader, or rather, two have been proposed ; but neither of the two is fitted for such an undertaking."

" Who are they ? "

" One is Antonio the Malay."

Georges allowed a smile of contempt to pass over his lips.

" And the other ? " he asked.

" The other is myself," answered Laïza.

Georges looked hard at the Negro, who exhibited to white men such an unusual example of modesty, to see in what way he was unworthy of the position to which he was summoned.

" The other is yourself ? " replied the young man.

" Yes," answered the Negro ; " but we do not want two leaders for such an enterprise ; we must have only one."

" Ah ! yes," said Georges, understanding, as he thought, that Laïza was ambitious of having the supreme command.

" We want a single, supreme, absolute commander, one whose superiority is beyond question."

" And where are you to find this man ? " asked Georges.

" He is found already," answered Laïza, looking steadily at Georges ; " the only point is, will he accept the position."

" He risks his neck," said Georges.

" And don't we also risk something ? " asked Laïza.

" But what guarantee will you offer him ? "

" The same as he will offer us, an end of persecution and slavery, and a future of vengeance and freedom."

" And what plan have you formed ? "

" To-morrow, after the festival of the Yamsé, when the whites, wearied with the day's amusement, have retired after seeing the burning of the *gouhn*, the Lascars will be left alone on the banks of the *Rivière des Lataniers*. Then will gather from all quarters Africans, Malays, Madagascans, Malabars, Hindus, all in fact who have joined the conspiracy ; once there, they will choose a leader, and that leader will direct them. Well then, say but a word, and that leader will be yourself."

" And who has bidden you make this proposal to me ? " asked Georges.

Laïza gave a scornful smile.

" Nobody," said he.

" The idea, then, is your own ? "

" Yes."

" And who has put it into your head ? "

" You have, yourself."

" How can I have done so ? "

" You can only attain your desire by our aid."

" And who told you that I desired anything ? "

" You desire to wed the Rose of the *Rivière Noire*, and you hate M. Henri de Malmédie. You wish to possess the first, and to have your revenge against the second. We alone can offer you the means of doing both ; for they will not consent to give you the one as your wife, and they will not allow the other to fight a duel with you."

" And who told you that I loved Sara ? "

" I have seen it."

" You are mistaken."

Laïza shook his head sadly.

" The eyes of the head are sometimes deceived," said he ; ." but the eyes of the heart, never."

" You are my rival, perhaps ? " asked Georges with a smile of contempt.

" The only rival is he who has a hope of being loved," said the Negro with a sigh, " and the Rose of the *Rivière Noire* will never love the Lion of Anjouan."

" You are not jealous then ? "

" You saved her life, and her life belongs to you, as is fair ; I have not even had the good fortune to die for her, and yet," added the Negro, looking straight at Georges, " do you think I have not done all I could to win that privilege ? "

" Yes, yes," murmured Georges, " you are a brave man ; but the others, can you reckon upon them ? "

" I can only answer for myself," said Laïza, " and I do so ; whatever can be done with a man who is courageous, loyal, and devoted, that you can do with me."

" You will be the first to obey me ? "

" In everything."

" Even as regards ? . . ."

Georges stopped, and looked at Laïza.

" Even as regards the Rose of the *Rivière Noire*," said the Negro, continuing the young man's thought.

." But why are you thus devoted to me ? "

" The Stag of Anjouan was about to die beneath the blows of the executioners, and you ransomed his life. The Lion of Anjouan was in the toils, and you restored him to liberty. The Lion is not only the strongest, but likewise the most generous of all animals ; and because he is brave and generous," continued the Negro, crossing his arms and raising his head proudly, " therefore Laïza is called the Lion of Anjouan."

" Very well," said Georges, holding out his hand to the Negro, " I ask for one day to make up my mind."

" And what consideration will decide your acceptance or refusal ? "

" I offered M. de Malmédie a very grave insult yesterday in public."

" I know, I was there," said the Negro.

" Well, if M. de Malmédie will fight with me, I have nothing to say."

" And if he declines to fight ? " asked Laïza with a smile.

" In that case I will join you; for, as he is known to be a brave man, who has already fought two duels with Whites, in one of which he killed his opponent, he will have added a third insult to the two which he has already offered me, and then the cup will be full."

" Then you are our leader," said Laïza ; " the White man will not fight with the Mulatto."

Georges frowned, for he entertained the same idea himself. And yet, how could a White man keep the mark of the shame which the Mulatto had imprinted on his face ?

At this moment Télémaque entered with his hands pressed to his ear, of which Bijou, as we have said, had carried off a portion.

" Master," said he, " the Dutch Captain would like to speak to you."

" Captain Van den Broek ? " asked Georges.

" Yes."

" Very well," said Georges. Then, turning to Laïza : " Wait for me here, I will come back to you ; my answer will probably be more speedy than I expected."

Georges left the room where Laïza was, and entered with open arms the one in which the Captain was waiting.

" Well, brother," said the Captain, " you recognized me then ? "

" Yes, Jacques, and I am delighted to embrace you, particularly at this moment."

" You very nearly missed the pleasure of doing so, at any rate on this trip."

" How so ? "

" I ought to have started before now."

" Why ? "

" The Governor looks to me like an old sea-fox."

" Say rather a sea-wolf, a sea-tiger, Jacques ; the Governor is the famous Commodore Murray, formerly Captain of the *Leicester*."

" Of the *Leicester* ! I ought to have suspected it ; then we have an old account to settle, and now I understand it all."

" What has happened then ? "

" This : the Governor came up to me after the races and said in a very gracious manner : ' Captain Van den Broek, you have a very smart schooner.' Nothing wrong, so far ; but he added, ' Might I have the honour of paying her a visit to-morrow ? ' "

" He suspects something."

" Yes, and I who like a fool suspected nothing fell head over heels into the trap, and invited him to lunch on board, which he accepted."

" Well ? "

" Well, on going back to give orders for the aforesaid luncheon, I noticed that they were making signals from the *Montagne de la Découverte* out to sea, and then I began to realize that possibly these signals were being made in honour of me. So I climbed the mountain and examined the horizon with my glass, and within five minutes I sighted a vessel some twenty miles off, which was replying to the signals.

" It was the *Leicester* ? "

" Just so ; they want to blockade me. But, mark you, Jacques was not born yesterday ; the wind is in the south-east, so that no vessel can enter Port Louis except by tacking. Well, for that business, you require at least twelve hours to make the *Ile des Tonneliers* ; meanwhile, I am off, and I am come to find you and take you along with me."

" Me ? What reason have I for going ? "

" Ah ! true, I haven't told you yet. What the deuce made you take it into your head to slash that handsome young man over the face with your whip ? It was not polite."

" Don't you know then who the man was ? "

" Why, yes, for I laid a thousand louis against him. By the way, Antrim is a fine horse and I hope you will give him my compliments."

" Well, don't you remember how this same Henri de Mal-médie, fourteen years ago, on the day of the fight ? . . ."

" What did he do ? "

Georges lifted his hair and showed his brother the scar on his forehead.

" Oh ! yes, of course," cried Jacques. " Shiver my timbers ! yes, you do owe him a grudge ; I had forgotten that little episode. But, so far as I can recollect, that little attention on his part earned him a blow from my fist, which made up for his sword-cut."

" Yes, and I had forgotten that first insult, or rather, I was prepared to forgive him for it, when he offered me a second."

" What was that ? "

" He refused me the hand of his cousin in marriage."

" Oh ! you are delightful, upon my word ! Here are a father and son, who rear an heiress like a quail in a coop, so as to pluck her at their leisure by a rich marriage, and just as she is nicely fatted up, there comes along a poacher who wants to take her for himself. Why, come ! could they do otherwise than refuse her to you ? To say nothing, my dear fellow, of the fact that we are Mulattoes, neither more nor less."

" True, and therefore it is not this refusal which I regarded as an insult ; but, in the course of the discussion, he raised his stick to me."

" Ah ! in that case, he was in the wrong. Then, I suppose, you knocked him on the head ? "

No," said Georges, laughing at the methods of concilia-tion which, in such circumstances, always presented them-selves to his brother's mind ; " no, I demanded satisfaction from him."

" And he refused it ? He is within his rights, for we are Mulattoes. True, we sometimes fight the Whites ; but the Whites do not fight with us."

" And then I promised that I would force him to fight."

" And that is why you struck him across the face with your whip in the middle of the race, *coram populo*, as we used to say at the Collège Napoléon. It was not at all a bad idea ; but the means which you took have not been successful."

" Not successful ! What do you mean ? "

" I mean that, in point of fact, M. de Malmédie's first idea was to fight ; but nobody was willing to act as his second, and his friends declared that such a duel was out of the question."

" Then he will keep the cut of the whip that I gave him ; he is free to do so."

" Yes, but he is keeping something else in store for you."

" What is he keeping for me ? " asked Georges with a frown.

" As the obstinate fellow was still determined to fight spite of all they could say to him, they were obliged, in order to make him give up the duel, to promise him one thing."

" And what have they promised him ? "

" That one of these evenings, when you are at the town, some eight or ten of them will lie in wait for you on the road to Moka, and surprise you at the moment when you least expect it ; that they will then lay you on a ladder and give you five-and-twenty lashes."

" The curs ! but that is the punishment of Negroes ! "

" Well, what are we then, we Mulattoes ? White Negroes, nothing else."

" They promised him that ? " repeated Georges.

" Yes, in so many words."

" You are quite sure ? "

" I was present. They took me for a worthy Dutchman, a pure blood ; they had no suspicions about me."

" Very well ! " said Georges ; " I have made up my mind." .

" You will go with me ? "

" I stay here."

" Listen," said Jacques, laying his hand on Georges' shoulder ; " be persuaded by me, brother ; follow the advice of an old philosopher. Don't stay behind, but come away with me ! "

" Impossible ! it would look as though I were running away. Besides, I love Sara."

" You love Sara ? What does that mean ? "

" It means that I must possess that girl or die."

" Listen, Georges, for my part I do not understand all these refinements. It is true I have never been enamoured, except of my ephemeral mistresses, who are just as good as any others, believe me. And, once you have tried them, mark you, you will be ready to exchange four white girls for a girl of the Comorin Islands, for instance. I have six of them at the present moment, and you can take your choice."

" Much obliged, Jacques. I tell you once more, I cannot leave the Isle of France."

" And I repeat that you are wrong. It is a good opportunity, such as you will not find again. I start to-night at one o'clock, as quietly as I can. Come with me, and to-morrow we shall be twenty-five leagues from here and able to laugh at all the Whites in Mauritius ; not to mention that, if we catch any of them, we can administer to them, by the hands of our sailors, the gratification which they were reserving for you."

" Thank you, brother," repeated Georges ; " it is impossible."

" Very well then ; you are a man, and, when a man says a thing is impossible, it is really and truly impossible. So I must just go away without you."

" Yes, go ; only don't go too far, and you will see something which you don't expect."

" What is that ? an eclipse of the moon ? "

" You will see a volcano blaze forth from the *Passe*

Descorne to the *Morne Brabant*, and from Port Louis to Mahebourg, a volcano as grand as that of the Isle of Bourbon."

" Ah ! that's quite another matter ; you have got some idea of fireworks in your head, apparently. Come, just explain things to me a bit."

" I mean that within eight days these Whites who threaten and despise me, these Whites who would whip me like a runaway Negro, will be at my feet. That's all."

" A little revolt. . . . I understand," said Jacques. ' That might be possible, if there were in the Island but two thousand men like my hundred and fifty Lascars. I say Lascars, from habit ; for, thank God, there isn't one who really belongs to that wretched race : they are all worthy Bretons, brave Americans, true Dutchmen, pure-blooded Spaniards, all that is best in those four nations. But what have you got to sustain the revolt with ? "

" Ten thousand slaves who have had enough of obeying, and think it is now their turn to command."

" Negroes ? Pooh ! " said Jacques, protruding his lower lip in contempt. " Listen, Georges, I know them well, for I sell them. They stand heat well, they live on bananas, they work hard ; in short, they have their qualities, and I do not wish to depreciate my merchandise. But, mark you, they make very poor soldiers. See here, not later than yesterday, at the races, the Governor asked my advice in regard to Negroes."

" In what way ? "

" Yes, he said to me : ' Captain Van den Broek, you have travelled a good deal and seem to me an excellent observer ; now, if you were Governor of some Island, and a revolt of Negroes took place, what should you do ? ' "

" And what did you tell him ? "

" I told him : ' My lord, I should stave in a hundred casks of spirits in the streets through which they would pass, and I should lock my door and go to bed.' "

Georges bit his lip until the blood came.

" Therefore I say again, brother, for the third time, come with me ; it is the best thing you can do."

" And for the third time, brother, I answer, impossible."

" Then there is no use saying any more : embrace me
Georges."

" Good-bye, Jacques ! "

" Good-bye, brother : but, believe me, don't you trust
to Negroes."

" You are going then ? "

" Yes, by Gad, I'm not proud, and I can make a bolt
for blue water, when occasion requires, as well as anybody,
and go as far as ever the *Leicester* likes. Should she invite
me to a game of skittles, she'll soon see whether I decline
the offer ; but, in harbour, under the fire of *Fort Blanc*
and the Labourdonnaie Reboubt, no thank you ! For the
last time then, you refuse ? "

" I refuse."

" Good-bye."

" Good-bye."

The young man exchanged a second embrace. Jacques
then went into his father's room and found him sleeping
peacefully, in complete ignorance of all that had happened.
Meantime Georges passed into the room in which Laïza
was waiting for him.

" Well ? " asked the Negro.

" Well," said Georges ; " you may tell them that they
have a leader."

The Negro crossed his hands on his breast, and, without
asking another question, bowed deeply and went out.

CHAPTER XIX

THE YAMSÉ

THE races, as we have said, were only an episode in
the amusements of the second day. Accordingly, when
they were over at about three in the afternoon, the whole
of the motley multitude that covered the small mountain
made off for the *Plaine Verte*, while the gentlemen and ladies
of fashion who had witnessed the sports, some in carriages,
some on horseback, went home to dinner, and sallied out
again directly the meal was over, in order to be present
at the exercises of the Lascars.

These exercises consist of symbolical gymnastic displays,

including races, dances, and wrestling, accompanied by discordant songs and barbarous music, with which are mingled the shouts of the Negro vendors in the crowd, who do business on their own account or on that of their master, and go about crying, " Bananas ! bananas ! " " Cane ! Cane ! " " Curds ! curds ! fine curdled milk ! " or " Kalu ! fine kalu ! "

These exercises last until about six in the evening, and then begins the " little " procession, so called to distinguish it from the great procession of the next day.

Then the Lascars advance, between two lines of spectators, some half-hidden under a sort of small pointed pagodas, made on the model of the great *gouhn*, and which are called *aïdorés* ; others, armed with sticks and blunt swords ; others, again, half-naked and with torn garments. Then, at a given signal, they all spring into action ; those who carry the *aïdorés* begin to dance round as though on a pivot ; those with the sticks and sabres begin to fight, wheeling round one another, giving and parrying blows with marvellous skill ; while the last beat their breasts and roll on the ground apparently in despair, all crying together or in turns : " Yamsé ! Yamli ! O Hoseïn ! O Ali ! "

While these religious performances are going on, some of their number go about offering boiled rice and aromatic herbs to all comers.

This promenade lasts until midnight ; they then enter the Malabar encampment in the same order in which they had quitted it, not to come out again until the next day at the same hour.

The next day, however, brought a change and enlargement of the scene. After promenading the town in the same way as on the previous evening, the Lascars re-entered the camp at nightfall in order to fetch from it the *gouhn*, the result of the combined work of the two bands.

Covered with the richest papers of the most brilliant and most incongruous hues, illuminated on the inside by large fires, and on the outside by paper lanterns of all colours suspended from every angle and irregular projection, shedding cataracts of changing light over its vast sides, it advanced, borne along by a great number of men. Of these

some were stationed inside, others on the outside, all chant-
ing a monotonous and moonlight dirge ; while in front
of the *gouhn* walked the scouts, balancing at the end of a
rod a dozen feet in length lanterns, torches, suns, and other
fireworks. Upon this, the dance of the *aïdorés* and the
hand-to-hand çombats were resumed with renewed ardour
while the devotees in torn and tattered garments began
once more to smite their breasts, uttering cries of grief
which were taken up by the whole crowd in alternate shouts
of : " Yamsé ! Yamli ! O Hoseïn ! O Ali ! "—shouts
even more prolonged and heart-rending than those uttered
the day before.

The reason of this is that the *gouhn*, which accompanies
them on this occasion, is intended to represent both the
town of Kerbela, near which Hoseïn perished, and the
tomb in which his remains were enclosed ; while in addition,
a naked man, painted to look like a tiger, typifies the miraculous animal who for several days guarded the corpse of
the sacred Imaun. Occasionally he made a rush at the
spectators, uttering a roar as though he would devour
them ; but a man, who walked behind him, representing
his keeper, stopped him by means of a rope ; while a
Mullah who was placed at his side calmed him with mysterious words and magnetic gestures.

For several hours the *gouhn* was carried in procession
through and round the town ; after which its bearers took
the road to the *Rivière des Lataniers*, followed by the entire
population of Port Louis. The festival was drawing to a
close ; the *gouhn* was about to be burned and buried, and
everybody was anxious, after having accompanied it during
its triumph, to accompany it also to its destruction.

When those who carried the immense structure reached
the *Rivière des Lataniers*, they halted on its bank ; then,
as midnight sounded, four men approached with torches
and set fire to each of its four corners. At the same moment
the bearers let the *gouhn* fall into the river.

But as the river is only a mountain torrent and the base
of the *gouhn* was hardly covered by the water, the flames
spread rapidly over all the upper portions, and shot up
like an immense spiral, mounting in wreaths towards the

sky. Then came a strangely weird moment, during which,
by the brightness of this transient though fierce light, you
might see the thirty thousand spectators of all races shouting frantically in all languages, waving their handkerchiefs
and hats, standing in groups, some on the bank itself, the
rest on the surrounding rocks—the latter, in masses darker
in proportion as they receded beneath the shade of the
forest; the former, in an immense circle, seated in their
palanquins or carriages, or mounted on their horses. For a
moment, the water reflected the flames which it was about
to extinguish; for a moment, the whole multitude surged
like a sea; for a moment, the trees threw long shadows
like giants rising from the ground; for a moment, the very
sky was hidden by a red vapour, which made each passing
cloud look like a wave of blood.

But soon the light grew fainter and fainter, and all these
heads became a confused mass; the trees appeared to
recede into the shade; the sky grew pale and gradually
resumed its leaden hue; the heavens were covered with
darker and ever darker clouds. From time to time, some
portion hitherto spared by the fire burst in its turn into
flames, throwing a flickering light upon the crowd and the
surrounding country, and then died out again, rendering
the darkness greater than before. Gradually the whole
framework dissolved into red-hot embers, making the water
in the river hiss. Finally, the last portions that remained
burning were extinguished, and the sky being, as we have
said, overcast with clouds, each one found himself in a
darkness all the more profound as the light that preceded
it had been brilliant.

Then occurred what always happens at the end of public
fêtes, especially after illuminations or fireworks, namely,
an outburst of loud conversation; and every one made
off as fast as possible for the town, talking, laughing, and
joking. The carriages started at a gallop, the Negroes
trotted off with their palanquins; while the pedestrians
in chattering groups followed them as fast as they could.

Whether owing to a more lively curiosity, or from the
habit of dawdling natural to their kind, the Negroes and
men of colour remained to the last; but at length they too

disappeared, some taking the road to the Malabar encampment, others ascending by the bank of the river—the latter
plunging into the forest, the former following the sea-coast.

After a few minutes the place was entirely deserted,
and a quarter of an hour elapsed during which no sound was
to be heard save the murmur of the water rolling between
the rocks, nothing was to be seen, in the bright intervals
between the clouds, save some enormous bats which plunged
heavily down to the river, as if to extinguish with their
flapping wings the few embers that still remained floating
on the surface, and presently rose again and disappeared
into the forest.

Soon, however, a slight noise was heard and two men
could be seen creeping towards the river, moving to meet
one another, and coming, one from the direction of the
Dumas Battery, the other from the *Montagne Longue*.
When only the torrent separated them, they both rose
and exchanged signals ; then one of them clapped his
hands three times, while the other gave three whistles.

Then out of the depths of the woods, from the angles
of the fortifications, from the mangroves that waved on
the margin of the sea, appeared a whole population of Negroes
and Natives, whose presence five minutes earlier it would
have been impossible to suspect. The entire crowd, however, was divided into two quite distinct bands, the one
composed exclusively of Hindus, the other exclusively
of Negroes. The former ranged themselves round one of
the two leaders who had arrived first, a man of olive complexion, who spoke in the Malay dialect.

The Negroes grouped themselves round the other leader,
who was a Negro like themselves, and spoke in turns the
language of Madagascar and of Mozambique.

One of the two leaders walked up and down in the crowd,
chattering, scolding, declaiming, gesticulating, a type of
the low-class ringleader, the vulgar intriguer. This was
Antonio the Malay.

The other, calm, motionless, almost dumb, chary of words,
sober in gesture, seemed to attract attention without seeking
it—true type of the strength which restrains and the genius
which commands.

This was Laïza, the Lion of Anjouan.

These two men were the leaders of the revolt ; the ten thousand half-breeds who surrounded them were the conspirators.

Antonio addressed them first.

"There was once," said he, "an island governed by monkeys, and inhabited by elephants, lions, tigers, panthers, and snakes. The number of those governed was ten times as great as the number of those who governed them ; but the governing class had had the cleverness, cunning baboons that they were, to sow dissension among the governed, so that the elephants lived on terms of hatred with the lions, the tigers with the panthers, and the snakes with all of them. Consequently, when the elephants raised their trunks, the monkeys made the lions, tigers, panthers and snakes march against them ; and, strong as were the elephants, it always ended in their being defeated. If it was the lions who roared, the monkeys made the elephants, the snakes, the tigers and the panthers go against them, so that, courageous as were the lions, it always ended in their being chained up. If it was the tigers who showed their teeth, the monkeys marched the elephants, the lions, the snakes and the panthers against them; and, strong as were the tigers, it always ended in their being caged. If it was the panthers who sprang, the monkeys made the lions, the elephants, the tigers, and the snakes march against them, so that, active as were the panthers, it always ended in their being subdued. Lastly, if it was the snakes who hissed, the monkeys made the elephants, the lions, the tigers, and the panthers march against them, and cunning as were the snakes it always ended in their being reduced to submission. The result was that the governors, with whom this device had a hundred times been successful, laughed in their sleeves every time they heard a revolt mentioned, and at once resorting to their customary tactics, suppressed the rebels. But, one day, it happened that a snake, more sharp than the rest, reflected upon this ; he was a snake who knew his four rules of arithmetic just as well as M. de M——'s cashier knows them. He calculated that the monkeys were relatively to the other animals as one to

8

ten. So he assembled the elephants, the lions, the tigers, the panthers, and the snakes under the pretext of a festival, and said to them :

" ' How many do you number ? '

" The animals counted themselves and answered :

" ' We are eighty thousand.'

" ' Good,' said the snake ; ' now count your masters, and tell me how many they are.'

" The animals counted the monkeys and answered :

" ' Eight thousand.'

" ' Then you are very foolish,' said the snake, ' not to exterminate the monkeys, since you are ten to one.'

" The animals combined and exterminated the monkeys, and became masters of the island, and the best of the fruits, of the fields, and of the houses were theirs ; not to mention that they made the monkeys their slaves, and the she-monkeys their mistresses. . . .

" Have you understood the story ? " said Antonio.

Loud shouts resounded, hurrahs and bravos were heard ; Antonio had produced no less an effect with his fable than the Consul Menenius Agrippa, two thousand two hundred years before, had produced with his.

Laïza waited quietly until the moment of enthusiasm had passed ; then, extending his arms to command silence, he spoke these simple words :

" There was once an island where the slaves desired to be free ; they rose together, and they became free. That island was formerly called San Domingo, it is now called Haiti. . . . Let us do as they did, and we shall be free like them."

Loud shouts again resounded, and hurrahs and bravos were heard for the second time. But it must be confessed that this speech was too simple to move the crowd as Antonio's had done ; Antonio perceived it and conceived a hope.

He made a sign that he wished to speak, and there was silence.

" Yes," he said, " yes, Laïza has spoken the truth ; I have heard tell of a large island away beyond Africa, very far off, where the sun sets, in which all the Negroes are kings. But in my own island, as in Laïza's, in the island of animals as in the island of men, a leader was chosen, but a single one."

" That is so," said Laïza, " and Antonio is right. Power divided is power weakened. I am then of his opinion ; we must have a leader, but one only."

" And who shall this leader be ? " asked Antonio.

" It is for those who are assembled here to decide," answered Laïza.

" The man who is worthy to be our leader," said Antonio, "is he who can pit cunning against cunning, strength against strength, courage against courage."

" That is so," said Laïza.

" The man who is worthy to be our leader," continued Antonio, " is he who has lived with both Blacks and Whites, who is connected by blood with both ; the man, who, though free, will sacrifice his freedom ; the man who, having a cottage and a field, will run the risk of losing them. That is the man who is worthy to be our leader."

" True," said Laïza.

" I know but one man who combines all these qualifications," said Antonio.

" And I also," said Laïza.

" Do you mean yourself ? " asked Antonio.

" No," answered Laïza.

" You agree then that I am the man ? "

" No, it is not you either."

" Who is it then ? " cried Antonio.

" Yes, who is it ? where is he ? Let him come, let him show himself ! " cried the Negroes and the Natives simultaneously.

Laïza clapped his hands three times ; at the same moment the gallop of a horse was heard, and by the first light of the dawning day a horseman was seen issuing from the forest at full speed. Riding into the centre of the crowd, with a simple movement of his hand he pulled up his horse so short that the jerk made the animal fall back on his haunches. Laïza extended his hand with a gesture of supreme dignity towards the horseman.

" There," said he, " is your leader."

" Georges Munier ! " exclaimed ten thousand voices.

"Yes, Georges Munier," said Laïza. "You have asked for a leader who can oppose cunning to cunning, strength to strength, courage to courage; there he is! You have asked for a leader who has lived with Whites and with Blacks, who is connected by blood with both; there he is! . . . You have asked for a leader who was free and would sacrifice his freedom; who had a house and a field, and would risk the loss of both; well, there is this leader! Where will you find another? Where will you find one like him?"

Antonio remained dumbfounded; all eyes were turned towards Georges, and the crowd were talking eagerly.

Georges knew the men with whom he had to do, and knew that he must before everything else appeal to them by his appearance. Accordingly, he was dressed in a magnificent burnouse all covered with gold embroidery; beneath this he wore the tunic of honour given him by Ibrahim Pacha, on which glittered the crosses of the Legion of Honour and of Charles the Third; while Antrim, covered with a splendid crimson saddle-cloth, quivered beneath his master, impatient and full of mettle.

"But," cried Antonio, "who will be responsible to us for him?"

"I will," said Laïza.

"Has he lived with us? Does he know our wants?"

"No, he has not lived with us; but he has lived with the Whites and has studied their sciences; yes, he knows our desires and our wants, for we have but one desire and one want, namely, freedom."

"Let him begin, then, by giving it to his own three hundred slaves."

"That has already been done this morning," said Georges.

"Yes, yes," cried voices in the crowd; "yes, Master Georges has given us our freedom."

"But he is connected with the Whites," said Antonio.

"In the presence of all of you, I declare," answered Georges, "that I broke with them yesterday."

"But he loves a white girl," said Antonio.

"That is an additional triumph for us men of colour," answered Georges, "for the white girl loves me."

" But, if they offer to give her as his wife," replied Antonio, " he will betray us and make his compact with the Whites."

" If they offer her to me, I shall refuse her," answered Georges ; " for I wish to have her of her own accord, and have need of nobody to give her to me."

Antonio wished to raise a fresh objection, but shouts of " Long live Georges ! long live our leader ! " resounded on all sides, and drowned his voice so that he could not make a sound heard.

Georges made a sign that he wished to speak, and every one was silent.

" My friends," said he, " it is day, and, consequently, time for us to break up. Friday is a holiday ; on Friday you shall all be free. On Friday, at eight in the evening, I shall be here at this same spot ; I will put myself at your head, and we will march upon the town."

" Yes, yes," cried all the voices.

" One word more ; should there have been a traitor among us, let us decide that, when his treachery has been proved, any one of us may put him to death that very instant, by whatever death is most convenient, slow or quick, gentle or cruel. Do you agree in advance to his sentence ? For myself ; I am the first to agree."

" Yes, yes ! " cried all the voices ; " if there is a traitor, let him be put to death ; death to the traitor ! "

" Very good. And now, how many are you ? "

" We are ten thousand," said Laïza.

" My three hundred servants are instructed to give each of you four dollars ; for each of you by Friday next must have some weapon. Farewell then, until Friday."

And Georges, waving a salute, departed as he had come, while the three hundred Negroes each opened a bag filled with gold, and gave each man the promised four dollars.

It is true that this princely munificence cost Georges Munier two hundred thousand francs.

But what was such a sum to a man worth millions, and who would have sacrificed his entire fortune to the accomplishment of the project so long determined upon by his will ?

Now, at last, this project was about to be accomplished ; the gauntlet was thrown down.

CHAPTER XX
THE APPOINTMENT

GEORGES returned home in a much calmer frame of mind than might have been thought possible. He was one of those men to whom inaction means death, and who grow greater under the pressure of strife ; he contented himself with making his weapons ready in case of an unforeseen attack, holding in reserve for himself a retreat into the great woods, which he had traversed in his youth, and of which the murmur and vastness, mingling with the murmur and vastness of the sea, had made him the pensive youth we have already seen.

But it was his unhappy father on whom the weight of all these unforeseen events really fell. The desire of his life, for fourteen years, had been to see his children again, and that desire had just been fulfilled. He had seen them both again. But their presence had merely changed the habitual flaccidity of his temper into a constantly recurring uneasiness in regard to them—the one, a slave-captain, perpetually at war with the elements and social laws ; the other, a plotting theorizer, at war with prejudices and men ; both contending with all that is most powerful in the world. Both might at any moment be shattered by the storm ; while he himself, fettered by his habit of passive obedience, saw them both steering for the whirlpool without having the strength to hold them back, and having for his only consolation these words which he repeated incessantly :

" Of one thing, at least, I am sure, and that is, of dying with them."

The interval which must decide the fate of Georges was a short one ; two days only lay between him and the catastrophe which would make of him a second Toussaint-Louverture or a new Pétion. His one regret, during those two days, was his inability to communicate with Sara. It would have been imprudent for him to go into the town to find his usual messenger, Miko-Miko. But, on the other hand, he was reassured by his conviction that Sara was certain of him, as he was of her. There are souls that need but to exchange a glance or a word to understand each other's worth, and who, from that moment, confide in one another with the assurance of conviction. Then he smiled at the thought of this great revenge which he was about to obtain from society, and of this great reparation which fate had in store for him. He would say, when next he saw Sara : " I have not seen you for a week, but that week has been long enough to enable me to change, like a volcano, the face of an island. God desired to annihilate everything by a hurricane, and could not ; while I desired to scatter men, laws and prejudices with a tempest ; and I, more powerful than God, have been successful."

There is a fascinating intoxication in political and social dangers of the kind to which Georges was exposing himself which will produce conspirators and conspiracies till the end of time. The strongest motive power of human actions is, undoubtedly, pride ; and what flatters our pride, sinners as we are, more than the notion of renewing the struggle of Satan against God, or of the Titans against Jove ? In that struggle, as we know, Satan was blasted, and the Titans buried beneath Enceladus. But Enceladus, heaped upon the giants, ever belches forth a fresh mountain ; Satan, though crushed, became the monarch of the infernal regions.

It is true that poor Pierre Munier did not understand such considerations as these.

So, when Georges, after opening his window, had hung his pistols by his pillow and put his sword under his bolster, and gone to sleep as calmly as though he were not sleeping over a powder-magazine, Pierre Munier, arming five or six Negroes in whom he placed confidence, had posted them as sentinels all round the house, and put himself on guard on the road from Moka. In this way a momentary retreat at least was secured for his Georges, and he did not run the risk of a surprise. The night passed without any alarm. It is, moreover, the characteristic of plots hatched among the Negroes that their secret is always scrupulously kept. These poor fellows are not yet sufficiently civilized to enter into calculations of what they may gain by treachery.

The next day passed as the preceding night had done, and the following night as the day; nothing occurred to make Georges think he had been betrayed. Only a few hours now separated him from the accomplishment of his purpose.

At about nine in the morning Laïza arrived. Georges had him admitted to his room. No change had taken place in the general arrangements; but the enthusiasm produced by the generosity of Georges was increasing. At nine in the evening the ten thousand conspirators would be assembled in arms on the banks of the *Rivière des Lataniers*; at ten the conspiracy would break out.

While Georges was questioning Laïza as to the individual disposition of the men, and reckoning up with him the chances of this perilous enterprise, he perceived in the distance his messenger Miko-Miko, who, still carrying on his shoulders his rod and baskets, was walking at his usual pace and approaching the house. His appearance could not possibly have been better timed. Since the day of the races Georges had not even set eyes on Sara.

Self-controlled as was the young man, he could not restrain himself from opening the window and beckoning to Miko-Miko to quicken his pace, which the worthy Chinaman at once did. Laïza wanted to withdraw; but Georges detained him, saying that he had something further to tell him.

In point of fact, as Georges had foreseen, Miko-Miko had not come to Moka on his own initiative; immediately on entering he produced a charming little note, folded in the most aristocratic fashion, that is to say, long and narrow, on which a lady's neat hand had written his Christian name as its sole address. Georges' heart beat violently at the mere sight of the note. He took it from the messenger's hand, and to conceal his emotion—poor philosopher that he was, who dared not show the feelings of a man—went and read it in a corner of the window recess.

The letter turned out to be from Sara, and this is what it said:

" MY FRIEND,—

" Be at Lord Murray's at two o'clock this afternoon, and you will learn what I hardly dare tell you, so happy does it make me. Then, when you leave him, come and see me ; I shall be waiting for you in our summer-house.

" YOUR SARA "

Georges read this letter twice ; he could make nothing of this double appointment. How could Lord Murray tell him anything that would make Sara happy, and how could he, on leaving Lord Murray, that is to say at about three o'clock, in broad daylight, and in sight of everybody, present himself at M. de Malmédie's ?

Miko-Miko was the only person who could explain all this ; accordingly he appealed to the Chinaman and began to question him, but the worthy dealer knew nothing except that Mademoiselle Sara had sent for him by Bijou, whom he had not recognized at first, since, in his struggle with Télémaque, the poor wretch had lost part of a nose flat enough already. He had followed him and found the young lady in the summer-house, where he had been twice already, and there she had written the letter which he had just handed to Georges, and which the intelligent messenger had guessed to be addressed to him. She had then given him a piece of gold, and that was all he knew.

Georges, however, continued to question Miko-Miko, asking him if the girl had written it in his presence ; if she had been alone while writing it ; if her face seemed sad or joyful. The girl had written it in his presence ; no one else was there ; her face denoted entire calmness and complete happiness.

While Georges was proceeding with his inquiry, the gallop of a horse was heard. It brought a messenger in the Governor's livery, who, a moment later, entered the apartment and handed Georges a letter from Lord Murray. This letter was couched in the following terms :

MY DEAR TRAVELLING COMPANION,—

" I have thought much about you since I saw you last, and think I have arranged your little business rather well.

Be good enough to come to me to-day at two o'clock. I shall have, I hope, some good news for you.

"Yours always,

"MURRAY"

These two letters harmonized perfectly with one another. Accordingly, however great the danger for Georges of presenting himself in the town in his present situation, and although prudence whispered to him that to adventure himself at Port Louis, and especially at the Governor's house, was a foolhardy proceeding, he gave ear only to his pride, which told him that it would be almost an act of cowardice to decline to keep these two appointments, given as they were by the only two persons who had responded, the one to his love, the other to his friendship. So, turning to the messenger, he ordered him to present his respects to his lordship and tell him that he would be there at the hour agreed upon.

The messenger went off with this reply.

Then Georges sat down and wrote to Sara. Let us look over his shoulder and read the few lines which he wrote :

"DEAR SARA,—

"In the first place, bless you for your letter ! It is the first I have ever received from you, and short as it is, it tells me all I wanted to know, namely, that you have not forgotten me, that you still love me, and that you are mine, as I am yours. I shall be at Lord Murray's at the hour you name. Shall you be there ? you do not say. Alas ! the only happy news I can expect must come from your mouth alone, since the only happiness in the world to which I aspire is that of being your husband. Hitherto, I have done all I have been able in order to attain it ; all that I shall yet do will have the same aim. Keep brave and true then, Sara, as I shall be brave and true ; for, close to us as happiness seems to you to be, I greatly fear that we have both some trying experiences yet to go through before attaining it.

"No matter, Sara ; my conviction is that nothing in the world can withstand a powerful and unchanging will and a deep and devoted love ; have this love, Sara, and I will have the will.

"YOUR GEORGES"

Having written this letter, Georges gave it to Miko-Miko, who took up his bamboo and his baskets again, and started at his wonted pace for Port Louis, having received, it goes without saying, the fresh payment which his faithful services so well deserved.

Georges was left alone with Laïza, who had heard almost all, and understood everything.

" You are going to the town ? " he asked Georges.

" Yes," replied the latter.

" It is imprudent," replied the Negro.

" I know it, but I must go ; and I should be a coward in my own eyes if I did not go."

" Very well, go then ; but if at ten o'clock you have not arrived at the *Rivière des Lataniers*——"

" It will be because I am a prisoner or dead : in that event, march upon the town and rescue me, or avenge me."

" Very well," said Laïza, " you may count upon us." And these two men who had such a mutual understanding that one word, one gesture, one clasp of the hand sufficed to make them sure of one another, parted without exchanging one further promise or instruction.

It was now ten o'clock, and Georges was informed that his father was asking for him and would breakfast with him. Georges answered by going into the dining-room ; he was as calm as if nothing had happened.

Pierre Munier threw at him a glance in which was depicted all his paternal solicitude ; but was reassured by seeing his son's face just the same as usual and perceiving the same smile upon his lips with which he greeted him daily.

" God be praised, my dear boy ! " said the good man. " When I saw the messengers succeeding each other so rapidly I was afraid they brought bad news, but your air of calmness tells me that I was mistaken."

" You are right, father," answered Georges, " all goes well ; the revolt is still fixed for this evening at the same hour, and these messengers brought me two letters : one from the Governor, giving me an appointment with him to-day at two o'clock ; the other from Sara, who tells me that she loves me."

Pierre Munier remained stunned by surprise.

It was the first time that Georges had spoken to him of the revolt of the blacks and of the Governor's friendship. He had known indirectly of the revolt, and the poor father trembled to the depths of his heart at seeing his dearly-loved child embark on such a road. He stammered some words, but Georges interrupted him.

" Father," said he with a smile, " do you recollect the day when, after having performed prodigies of valour, after having rescued the Volunteers and taken a flag, that flag was seized from you by M. de Malmédie. That day you behaved grandly, nobly, sublimely, in presence of the enemy, as you always will behave, indeed, in presence of danger. That day I swore that some time men and things should be restored to their proper places ; the time has arrived, and I will not shrink from my oath. God shall judge between slaves and masters, between weak and strong, between martyrs and executioners, that is all."

Then, as Pierre Munier, without strength, without power, without resistance to such a will, sank down, as though the weight of the world were pressing him under, Georges ordered Ali to saddle the horses, and, after quietly finishing his breakfast, glancing sadly at his father now and then, rose to go out.

Pierre Munier started and stood up, extending his arms towards his son.

Georges went up to him, took his head between his hands, and, with an expression of filial love to which he had never given way before, drew the venerable head close to him, and imprinted five or six kisses in quick succession upon his grey hair.

" My son, my son ! " cried Pierre Munier.

" Father," said Georges, " you shall have a respected old age, or I shall have a bloody grave. Farewell ! "

Georges hurried from the room, and the old man fell back into his chair with a deep groan.

CHAPTER XXI
THE REFUSAL

AT about two leagues from his father's house Georges overtook Miko-Miko returning to Port Louis; he stopped his horse, motioned to the Chinaman to approach him, spoke a few words in his ear, to which Miko-Miko replied by a sign that he understood, and then continued his journey.

When he reached the foot of the *Montagne de la Découverte*, Georges began to meet people coming from the town; he carefully scrutinized the faces of these passers-by, but he did not observe on the various countenances of those whom chance brought across his path any indication that might lead him to think that the project for the revolt which was going to be put into execution by him that evening had in the slightest degree leaked out. He continued his way, passed the cantonments of the Blacks, and entered the town.

All was quiet there; every one appeared to be occupied with his own personal business, and no general anxiety hovered over the population. The ships were rocking peacefully in the shelter of the harbour. The *Pointe aux Blagueurs* was furnished with its customary loungers; an American vessel, just arrived from Calcutta, was casting anchor in front of the *Chien-de-Plomb*.

The appearance of Georges, however, seemed to create a certain excitement, but it was clear that this was connected with the affair of the races and the unheard-of insult offered by a Mulatto to a White. Several groups evidently dropped, on seeing Georges, the subject of conversation that was occupying them, in order to follow him with their eyes and exchange *sotto voce* some words of astonishment at his audacity in appearing in the town again; but Georges responded to their stares with a look so haughty, and to their whispers with a smile so contemptuous, that they lowered their glances, unable to endure the gleam of galling superiority that flashed from his eyes. Besides, the silver-chased butt ends of a pair of double-barrelled pistols could be seen protruding from each of his holsters.

Georges bestowed his chief attention upon the soldiers and officers whom he met on the road. But both soldiers and officers wore the bored expression of persons who had been transported from one part of the world to another and condemned to exile at a distance of four thousand leagues. Certainly, if any of them had the knowledge that Georges was providing employment for them during the night, they looked, if not glad, at least as if they were not at all concerned.

Georges was reassured by these signs.

He arrived in due course at the gate of Government House, threw his horse's bridle into Ali's hands, ordering him not to leave the place. Then he crossed the court-yard, mounted the steps, and entered the antechamber.

The servants had been given instructions beforehand to admit M. Georges Munier as soon as he presented himself. A footman accordingly preceded the young man, opened the door of the salon and announced his name, and Georges entered.

In this room were Lord Murray, M. de Malmédie, and Sara.

To the great astonishment of Sara, whose eyes had turned to him immediately, the face of Georges expressed a feeling of pain rather than of joy at sight of her; his forehead became slightly wrinkled, his eyebrows contracted, and an almost bitter smile passed over his mouth.

Sara, who had risen quickly, felt her knees give way under her, and sank back slowly into her chair.

M. de Malmédie stood up stiffly, as was his habit, con-tenting himself with a slight inclination of the head : Lord Murray took two steps towards Georges and gave him his hand.

" My young friend," said he, " I rejoice to tell you some news that will, I hope, crown your desires, namely, that M. de Malmédie, being desirous of putting an end to all these distinctions of colour and all these rivalries of caste which for two hundred years have been the bane, not only of the Isle of France, but of the Colonies in general, M. de Malmédie, I say, consents to grant you the hand of his niece, Mademoiselle Sara de Malmédie."

Sara blushed and raised her eyes imperceptibly to Georges,

but the latter contented himself with bowing without making any reply. M. de Malmédie and Lord Murray looked at one another in astonishment.

"My dear M. de Malmédie," said Lord Murray smiling, "I quite see that our incredulous friend does not trust my unsupported word; tell him then that you grant him the request he has made you, and that you wish all recollection of animosity, past and present, to be forgotten between your two families."

"It is true, sir," said M. de Malmédie, evidently imposing a great effort upon himself, "and the Governor has just acquainted you with my sentiments. If you bear any malice on account of a certain incident which occurred at the taking of Port Louis, forget it, as I promise you in my son's name that he will forget the grave insult which you offered him quite lately. As for your union with my niece, his Excellency the Governor has told you that I give my consent to it, and, unless to-day it should be you who decline——"

"Oh, Georges!" cried Sara, carried away by her emotion.

"Do not judge me hastily by my answer, Sara," replied the young man, "for that answer is, I assure you, dictated by an imperious necessity. Sara, since the evening in the summer-house, since the night of the ball, since the day when I saw you for the first time, you have been my wife in the sight of God and man. No other than yourself will ever bear a name which you have not despised in spite of its humbleness; all that I am about to say then is merely a question of form and of time."

Georges turned to the Governor.

"Thank you, my Lord," he continued, "thank you; I acknowledge, in what is happening to-day, the support of your generous philanthropy and of your kind friendship. But, on the day when M. de Malmédie refused me his niece, when M. Henri insulted me for the second time, and I thought it my duty to avenge that refusal and that insult by insulting him publicly and ignominiously, on that day I broke with the Whites, and there is no reconciliation possible between us. M. de Malmédie, influenced by some calculation, some intention which I do not understand, may be ready to meet me half-way, but I will not advance the other half. If Mademoiselle Sara loves me, she is free, is mistress of her hand and her fortune; it is for her to show herself more noble still in my eyes by descending to my level, and not for me to lower myself in her eyes by trying to climb to hers."

"Oh, Monsieur Georges!" cried Sara, "you know quite well——"

"Yes, I know," said Georges, "that you are a noble girl, that you have a devoted heart, a pure soul. I know that you will come to me, Sara, spite of all obstacles, all hindrances, all prejudices. I know that I have only to wait for you and that I shall see you appear one day, and for just this reason, that, the sacrifice being on your side, you have already decided in your generous heart that you will make this sacrifice for me. But for you, M. de Malmédie, for your son M. Henri, who agrees to decline to fight with me on condition that he shall have me whipped by his friends, oh! between us it is war to the death, do you understand? It is a mortal hatred that can only be ended on my part by his death or his humiliation; let your son make his choice then."

"Your Excellency," answered M. de Malmédie with more dignity than might have been expected from him, "you see that I, for my part, have done what I could; I have sacrificed my pride, I have forgotten the old insult as well as the recent one, but I cannot reasonably be expected to do more, and I must abide by the declaration of war which this gentleman has made against me. Only, we shall act on the defensive while awaiting his attack. Now, Mademoiselle," continued M. de Malmédie, turning to Sara, "you are free in regard to your heart, your hand, and your fortune. Act then as you wish; stay with this gentleman, or follow me."

"Uncle," said Sara, "It is my duty to go with you. Farewell, Georges! I do not understand at all what you have done to-day; but I am certain that you have acted as you ought to have acted."

And, bowing with quiet dignity to the Governor, Sara went out with M. de Malmédie.

Lord Murray accompanied them to the door and went out with them, returning a moment afterwards.

His look of inquiry met the steadfast glance of Georges, and a short silence ensued between the two men who, thanks to their lofty nature, understood each other so well.

" So," said the Governor, " you have refused."

" I thought it my duty to act thus, my Lord."

" Forgive me if I appear to question you; but may I know what sentiment has prompted your refusal ? "

" The sentiment of my own dignity."

" That is the only one ? "

" If there be another, my Lord, allow me to keep it a secret."

" Listen, Georges," said the Governor, with a degree of unconstraint which was all the more charming in him, as you felt it to be quite foreign to his cold and placid disposition, " listen ! From the moment when I met you on board the *Leicester* and was able to appreciate the high qualities that distinguish you, my desire was to make you act as a bond which should unite the two opposed castes in this Island. I began by discovering your sentiments, then you made me the confidant of your love, and I agreed to the request which you made to me that I would be your intermediary, your sponsor, your second. For that, Georges," resumed Lord Murray in response to an inclination of the head from Georges, " for that, my young friend, you owe no thanks ; you were yourself anticipating my wishes, you were supporting my scheme of conciliation, you were making the path easy for my political projects. I therefore went with you to M. de Malmédie's and backed up your request with all the authority of my presence and all the weight of my name."

" I know, my Lord, and I thank you. But you saw for yourself that neither the weight of your name, honourable as it is, nor the authority of your presence, flattering as it must have been, were able to spare me a refusal."

" I felt it as much as you did, Georges. I admired your calm behaviour, and I understood from your coolness that you were planning a terrible revenge. That revenge you took publicly, on the day of the races, and on that day it was borne in upon me once more that I must in all probability abandon my schemes of conciliation."

" I had warned you, my Lord, when I left you."

" Yes, I know, but listen to me : I did not regard myself even then as defeated ; yesterday I went to M. de Malmédie, and by dint of prayers and entreaties, by dint of almost abusing the influence which my position gives me, I obtained from the father a promise that he would forget his old hatred against your father ; from the son, that he would forget his recent hatred against you ; and from both, that they would consent to your marriage with Mademoiselle de Malmédie."

" Sara is free, my Lord," interrupted Georges vehemently, " and, thank God, requires the consent of nobody for becoming my wife."

" Yes, I admit it," replied the Governor, " but what a difference, I put it to you, in the eyes of the world, between carrying off a girl clandestinely from her guardian's house, and receiving her publicly from the hands of her family ! Consult your pride, Monsieur Munier, and see if I have not secured for it a supreme satisfaction—a triumph which even your pride did not anticipate."

" It is true," answered Georges. " Unhappily this consent comes too late."

" Too late ! too late for what ? " replied the Governor.

" Excuse me from answering you on that point, my Lord. It is my secret."

" Your secret, poor fellow ! Well, would you like me to tell you this secret which you are unwilling to disclose ? "

Georges looked at the Governor with a smile of incredulity.

" Your secret, indeed ! " continued the Governor, " a well-guarded secret certainly, that is confided to ten thousand persons."

Georges looked again at the Governor, but this time without smiling.

" Listen to me," resumed the Governor, " you wished to ruin yourself, I wanted to save you. I went and found Sara's uncle, I took him apart and said to him : ' You have underrated M. Georges Munier, you have repulsed

him with insolence, you have forced him to break openly
with you, and you were wrong in so doing. For M. Georges
Munier is a distinguished man, of lofty mind and noble
soul ; there was something to be made of such qualifications
as he possesses, and, in proof of this, I tell you that M.
Georges Munier holds all our lives in his hand at the
present moment ; he is the leader of a vast conspiracy ;
at ten o'clock to-morrow evening (it was yesterday that I
was speaking to him) M. Georges Munier will march upon
Port Louis at the head of ten thousand Negroes, and as
we have only eighteen hundred soldiers, we shall all be lost
unless chance should suggest to me some plan for safety,
such as sometimes occurs to men of genius. In short, the
day after to-morrow M. Georges Munier, whom at this
moment you look down upon as descended from a herd of
slaves, will perhaps be our master, and perhaps will choose
to have you in his turn as a slave. Well, sir,' I said to him,
' you can prevent all this, you can save the Colony ; forgive
the past, grant M. Georges your niece's hand which you
refused him, and, if he accepts, if he consents to accept, I
ought to say, for, the parts being changed, the claims may
be changed also, well, then you will have saved not only
your own life, your liberty and your fortune, but also the
lives, liberties, and fortunes of us all.' That is what I
said to him ; and then, at my prayers, my entreaties, nay,
my orders, he consented. But what I had foreseen has
happened ; you had pledged yourself too soon, and you
are not able to withdraw."

Georges had followed the Governor's words with ever-
increasing astonishment, yet with perfect calmness.

"Then you know all, my Lord," he said when the other
had finished.

"I think you must see that I do, and I believe I have
forgotten nothing."

"No," answered Georges, smiling, "no, your spies are
well informed, and I compliment you on the manner in
which your police are organized."

"Well, then," said the Governor, "now that you know
the motive which caused my action, there is still time ;
accept Sara's hand, be reconciled with her family, abandon

your mad scheme, and I will know nothing, I will ignore
everything, forget everything."

" Impossible ! " said Georges.

" Reflect then on the kind of men to whom you have
bound yourself."

" You forget, my Lord, that these men, of whom you
speak with such contempt, are my brothers. They have
recognized me, who am despised by the Whites as their
inferior, as their Chief. You forget that when these men
handed over their lives into my keeping, I consecrated my
life to them."

" You refuse then ? "

" I refuse."

" In spite of my entreaties ? "

" Pardon me, my Lord, but I cannot listen to them."

" In spite of your love for Sara and her love for you ? "

" In spite of everything."

" Reflect once more."

" It is useless, my mind is made up."

" Very good. . . . Now, sir," said Lord **Murray,** " one
final question."

" Put it."

" If I were in your place, and you were in mine, what
would you do ? "

" What do you mean ? "

" Yes ; if I were Georges Munier, leader of a revolt,
and you Lord Murray, Governor of the Isle of France ; if
you had me in your power as I hold you in mine, tell me,
I ask you for the second time, what you would do ? "

" What should I do, my Lord ? I should allow the man
to go out from here who came on your own invitation,
believing he was summoned to an interview, and not being
dragged into an ambuscade. Then, in the evening, if I
had faith in the justice of my cause, I should appeal to
God, that He might decide between us."

" Well, you would be wrong, Georges ; for, the moment
I drew the sword you would be unable to save me. The
moment I had kindled the revolt, I should have to quench
it with my blood. . . . No, Georges, I don't want a man
like yourself to die upon the scaffold, do you understand ?

to die like a vulgar rebel, whose intentions will be calum-
niated, and whose name will be blasted. So, in order to
save you from such a misfortune, to snatch you from your
fate, you are my prisoner, sir ; I arrest you ! "

" My Lord ! " cried Georges, looking round him for some
weapon which he might seize and defend himself with.

" Men," said the Governor, raising his voice, " enter
and seize this man."

Four soldiers, headed by a corporal, entered and surrounded Georges.

" Conduct this gentleman to the Police Station," said
the Governor ; " put him in the room which I made ready
this morning ; and, while keeping a strict guard over him,
take care that neither you nor any one else fail in the respect
which is due to him."

With these words, the Governor saluted Georges, and
Georges quitted the apartment.

CHAPTER XXII

THE REVOLT

ALL that had just taken place had occurred so rapidly.
and in a manner so unforeseen that Georges had had
no time to prepare himself for what had befallen him. But,
thanks to his wonderful power of self-control, he concealed
beneath an impassive and perpetual smile of careless disdain
the various emotions by which he was assailed.

The prisoner and his guards went out by a door at the
back of the house at which the Governor's carriage was
waiting ; and, either by accident or by intention, Miko-Miko
was passing just in front of this door at the very moment
when Georges was getting into the carriage. The young
man and his usual messenger exchanged glances.

Georges was conducted in accordance with the Governor's
orders to the Police Station, a large building the name of
which indicates its use, situated in the *Rue du Gouvernement*,
a little below the Comedy Theatre. Georges was taken to
the room mentioned by the Governor.

This room had evidently been prepared beforehand, as
Lord Murray had said, and it was even clear that there

had been the intention to make it as comfortable as possible. It was neatly furnished and the bed was almost elegant; nothing in the room suggested a prison, except that its windows were barred.

When the door had closed on Georges and the prisoner found himself alone, he went at once to the window, which was about twenty feet from the ground, and looked out on the Hôtel Coignet. One of the windows of the hotel was just opposite the room occupied by Georges, so that the prisoner could see into the lower part of the room, and all the more easily because this window stood open. Georges went back from the window to the door, listened, and heard the guard being mounted in the corridor. Then he went back to the window and opened it. No sentry had been placed in the street, the bars being relied on for preventing the prisoner's escape, and, in point of fact, the bars were so thick as to render such a precaution superfluous. He had therefore no hope of escaping unless he received some help from outside.

But Georges was doubtless expecting this help from outside, for, leaving his window open, he remained with his eyes constantly fixed on the Hôtel Coignet, which, as we have said, rises opposite the Police Station. In point of fact, his hopes were not disappointed; after waiting for an hour he saw Miko-Miko, with his bamboo rod on his shoulder, cross the room opposite to his own, conducted by one of the servants of the house. Georges and he exchanged but one glance; but this look, rapid as it was, restored calmness to Georges' brow.

From that moment Georges appeared almost as much at ease as if he had been in his own room at Moka; from time to time, however, an attentive observer might have noticed that he knit his brows and passed his hand across his forehead. Beneath this apparent calmness a host of reflections were surging in his mind, and, like a rising tide, beating upon his brain with their flux and reflux.

However, the hours passed by without bringing to the prisoner any indication that preparations were being made in the town. Neither roll of drum nor clash of arms was heard. Georges ran to the window two or three times, deceived by a noise resembling the roll of drums; but each time he saw that he was mistaken, and that the sound which he had taken for drums was the noise made by wagons loaded with barrels passing along the streets.

Night was coming on, and Georges, becoming more disturbed and uneasy with its advance, kept going from the door to the window and back again with a feverish movement which he made the less effort to suppress since he was alone; the door remained guarded by the sentinel, while the window remained unguarded except for its bars.

Occasionally Georges placed his hand over his breast, and a slight contraction of his features showed that he was feeling one of those momentary spasms which the bravest of men cannot overcome in critical circumstances. Doubtless he was thinking at such moments of his father, who was ignorant of his peril, and of Sara, who all unknowingly had brought him into this danger. As for the Governor, though Georges maintained against him that cold and concentrated rage which a gambler who has lost feels towards his antagonist, he could not disguise from himself that, on this occasion, he had displayed towards him not only all that gentlemanly conduct which was characteristic of him, but further that he had not arrested him until he had offered him all the means of escape which were in his power. All this, however, had not prevented Georges from being committed on a charge of high treason.

Meanwhile the darkness was increasing. Georges looked at his watch, and saw that it was half-past eight; in an hour and a half the revolt would break out.

Suddenly Georges raised his head and fixed his eyes once more on the Hôtel Coignet, where he had seen a shadow moving in the room opposite his own. The shadowy figure made him a sign; Georges moved from the window, and a parcel was thrown across the street through the bars and fell into the middle of the room.

Georges ran forward and picked up the parcel, which contained a rope and a file; this was the help from outside that Georges was expecting.

Georges held his liberty between his hands; but it was

only in order to encounter the hour of danger that he wished to be at liberty.

He concealed the rope beneath his mattress, and, as it was now quite dark, began to file one of the bars. These bars were sufficiently wide apart from one another to enable him to creep through the opening if one of them were removed.

It was a muffled file, which made scarcely any noise, and, as his supper had been brought to him at seven o'clock, Georges felt almost certain that he would not be disturbed.

However, the work progressed slowly. Nine o'clock, half-past nine, ten, sounded. For some time the prisoner while sawing at the iron bar had thought he saw bright lights shining towards the end of the *Rue du Gouvernement* in the direction of the *Rue de la Comédie* and the harbour. But not a single patrol made its way through the town, not a single belated soldier was going back to barracks. Georges could not understand this indifference on the Governor's part; he knew him too well not to be sure that he had taken all his precautions, and yet, as we have said, the town appeared quite undefended, and as though abandoned to itself.

At ten o'clock, however, he thought he heard sounds gradually increasing in volume proceeding from the direction of the Malabar cantonment, the direction from which, as you will remember, the slaves, after mustering on the banks of the *Rivière des Lataniers*, would arrive. Georges redoubled his efforts; the bar was already completely sawn through at the bottom, and he had just begun upon the top.

The noise continued to increase. There was no room for mistake; it was the sound caused by the mingled voices of several thousands of men. Laïza had kept his word. A smile of joy passed over Georges' lips, a flash of pride lit up his brow; there was to be fighting; not victory, perhaps, but, at least, a struggle. And Georges would be in the thick of it, for the bar now held only by a thread.

So he listened with eager ears and palpitating heart; the sounds came nearer and nearer, while the light which he had already noticed grew brighter. Was there a fire at Port Louis? That could hardly be, for no cry of alarm had been heard.

Georges waited another quarter of an hour, hoping that his anxiety would be relieved by hearing the sound of firing, which would tell him that the work was beginning; but the same strange noise which he had heard previously continued, yet without being intermingled with the noise which he was expecting to hear.

The prisoner then thought that the important thing for him was to make his escape at once. Georges gave the bar a final wrench, and it yielded. He next tied the rope firmly to its support, threw the bar out to serve as a weapon, let himself slide down the rope, reached the ground safely, picked up the bar, and rushed down one of the side streets. The nearer Georges drew to the *Rue de Paris*, which crosses all the northern quarter of the town, the brighter grew the light and the louder the noise; at last he reached the corner of a brilliantly illuminated street, and everything was at once explained to him.

All the streets that led to the Malabar cantonment, and by which the revolted slaves would enter the town, were illuminated as if for a fête, and at different spots in front of the principal houses had been placed casks of arrack, brandy, and rum, with their heads staved in, as if for distribution gratis.

The Negroes had rushed like a torrent upon Port Louis, uttering cries of rage and vengeance. But they arrived to find the streets illuminated, and had seen these tempting barrels. For an instant the orders of Laïza, and the thought that all these barrels might be poisoned, restrained them; but soon their natural craving got the better of their discipline and even of their fears. Some of them fell out of the ranks and began to drink. On hearing their shouts of delight, the other Negroes were unable to keep their ranks, and all this great multitude, sufficient to annihilate Port Louis, was split up and scattered in a moment, crowding round the casks with shouts of joyous infatuation, drinking in handfuls rum, brandy, and arrack, the everlasting poison of the black races, the sight of which no Negro can resist, in exchange for which he sells his children, his father and mother, and often ends by selling himself.

Hence those shouts of strange import which Georges had not been able to explain. The Governor had put into practice the advice given by Jacques himself, and it had turned out only too well. The revolted slaves had entered Port Louis, but their rage had cooled down before they were well across the quarter of the town extending from the *Petite-Montagne* to the *Trou-Fanfaron*, and had expired at a hundred yards from Government House.

At the sight of the strange spectacle which unfolded itself before his eyes, Georges retained no further doubt as to the result of his enterprise, he remembered what Jacques had predicted, and shuddered with anger and shame. These men by whose aid he had reckoned on making a revolution which would overwhelm the Island and avenge two centuries of slavery by an hour of victory and a future of liberty—these men were laughing, singing, dancing, defenceless, intoxicated, staggering; these men three hundred soldiers armed with whips might now drive back to work; and these men numbered ten thousand !

So all this long toil which Georges had imposed upon himself was thrown away ; all this lofty study of his own mind, his own strength, his own worth, was useless ; all this God-given superiority of character, of education at the expense of others, all this was crushed in face of the instincts of a race that preferred brandy to liberty.

Georges realized at once the worthlessness of his ambitions ; his pride had carried him for a moment to the top of a mountain, and had shown him all the kingdoms of the earth at his feet ; then all had disappeared—it was but a dream. And Georges found himself back at the same spot where his delusive pride had seized him.

He grasped his iron bar between his hands ; he felt himself smitten with a fierce longing to hurl himself into the midst of all these wretches and to smash all these besotted heads that had not had the strength to resist the coarse temptation for which he would have to suffer.

Some groups of curious onlookers, no doubt puzzled at this extempore fête which the Governor was giving to the slaves, stood staring at the proceedings with open mouths. Every one asked his neighbour what it all meant, only to find that his neighbour, as ignorant as himself, could not give him the slightest explanation.

Georges rushed from group to group, searching with his eyes these long streets, illuminated and filled with drunken Negroes uttering frantic cries. He was looking amid all this crowd of filthy creatures for a man, the one man on whom he still relied among this general degradation. This man was Laïza.

Suddenly Georges heard a loud noise proceeding from the direction of the Police Station, then a brisk firing began, on the one side with the precision customary to regular troops, on the other with that spasmodic fitfulness which accompanies the firing of volunteers.

So, at last, there was a spot where fighting was taking place.

Georges dashed off in that direction, and in five minutes was in the *Rue du Gouvernement*. He was not mistaken. This small band who were fighting were led by Laïza, who, having learnt that Georges was a prisoner, had gone round the town with four hundred picked men, and had marched on the Police Station to rescue him.

This action had doubtless been foreseen, for, immediately on seeing the little band of revolted slaves appear at the end of the street, an English battalion had moved off to oppose them.

Laïza had hardly hoped to be allowed to rescue Georges without a fight, but he had reckoned on the diversion that would be caused by the rest of the Negroes arriving by the streets adjacent to the Malabar cantonment; unfortunately, as we have seen, this diversion had failed him from the cause which we have related.

Georges took one leap into the midst of the combatants, shouting loudly, "Laïza! Laïza!" He had found one Negro worthy of the name of man; he had found a nature equal to his own.

The two leaders met under fire, and, without seeking

cover, and regardless of the bullets whistling round them,
exchanged a few short hurried words such as a crisis
demands. In an instant Laïza had been told the whole
situation; he shook his head, and merely observed:
. " All is lost." .

Georges wished to give him some hope, urged him to
try some efforts with the drinkers; but Laïza replied,
with a smile of profound contempt:

" Bah! They are on the drink; and, unless the brandy
runs short, there is no hope left!"

But the barrels had been broached in too great quantities
for the brandy to run short.

The struggle was now useless so far as regards the object
with which it had been begun, since Georges, whom Laïza
had come to rescue, was free; it only remained then to
regret the loss of the dozen or so of men who had already
been disabled, and to give the signal for a retreat. But
retreat by the *Rue du Gouvernement* had become an impossibility; for while Laïza's troop faced the English battalion
which had opposed its attempt on the Police Station,
another detachment issued with drums beating from the
powder-magazine, where it had been lying in wait, and
blocked the road by which Laïza with his men had arrived.
They were obliged therefore to make for the streets surrounding the Law Courts and thus regain the neighbourhood of the *Petite-Montagne* and the Malabar cantonments.

Georges and Laïza with their men had scarcely gone
two hundred yards when they found themselves in the
illuminated streets where the barrels were. The scene
was even more disgusting than before; the drunkenness
had made good progress.

Then, at the end of each street, could be seen flashing
through the darkness the bayonets of an English company.
Georges and Laïza looked at one another with a smile
that implied:

" It is not a question here of conquering, but of dying
and dying bravely."

Both, however, wished to make a final effort, and rushed
into the principal street, trying to rally some of the rebels
to their small body. But some of these were hardly in

a condition to listen to the appeals and exhortations of their chiefs, while others ignored them entirely, shouting with drunken voices and dancing with staggering limbs; while the greater number, now in the last stage of intoxication, were rolling in the street, losing more and more every minute the little sense that remained to them. Laïza had snatched up a whip and was belabouring the wretches with all his strength; Georges, leaning on his iron bar, the only weapon which he had touched, stood looking at them motionless and contemptuous, like a statue of Disdain.

After a few minutes, both were convinced that there was nothing to hope for, and that each moment that they stayed there was a year cut off from their life; besides, some men in their own band, led away by force of example, fascinated by the sight of the intoxicating liquor, and made giddy by the alcoholic odour which mounted to their brain, began in their turn to desert them. There was then no time to be lost in leaving the town; indeed it was evident that they had lost too much time already.

Georges and Laïza collected the little band which still remained faithful to them, and which consisted of about three hundred men; then, placing themselves at their head, they marched resolutely towards the end of the street, which, as we have said, was blocked by a wall of soldiers. When within forty yards of the English, they saw their rifles lowered at them, a gleam of flame burst along the whole line and immediately a hail of bullets swept their ranks; ten or twelve men fell, but the two leaders remained unhurt, and the cry of "Forward!" uttered simultaneously by their two powerful voices, resounded through the air.

When they came within twenty yards, the fire of the rear rank followed that of the first, causing still greater havoc among the rebels. Then, almost immediately, the two forces met, and a hand-to-hand combat ensued.

The fray was terrible; all the world knows what English troops are like, and how they die at their posts. But, on the other hand, they had to deal with desperate men, who knew that, if taken prisoners, an ignominious death awaited them, and who, consequently, wished to die as free men.

Georges and Laïza performed miracles of boldness and courage : Laïza, with his rifle, which he had grasped by the muzzle and employed as a flail; Georges, with the bar which he had wrenched from his window and used as all weapons combined. Their men, too, supported them excellently, rushing on the English with bayonet thrusts, while the wounded dragged themselves between the combatants, and, crawling up to the enemy, cut their hamstrings with their knives.

Thus for ten minutes the struggle lasted, furious, desperate, and deadly, no one being able to say which side would gain the advantage. Despair, however, triumphed over discipline ; the English ranks opened like a bursting dam and let through the torrent, which at once overflowed beyond the town.

Georges and Laïza who had headed the attack now remained in the rear to support the retreat. At last, they reached the foot of the *Petite-Montagne*, which was a place too precipitous and too thickly timbered for the English to venture to enter. Accordingly they halted, while the Negroes, on their side, paused to regain their breath. Some twenty blacks rallied round their leaders ; the rest scattered in all directions ; it was no longer a question of fighting, but of seeking safety in the great woods. Georges appointed the district of Moka, in which his father's house was situated, as the general meeting-place for those who wished to rally round him, announcing that he would start in the morning at dawn in order to reach the district of Grand Port, in which, as we have said, were the thickest forests.

Georges was giving his final instructions to the miserable remnants of the force with which he had for an instant hoped to conquer the Island, and the moon, gliding momentarily across the space between two clouds, shed her light upon the group of men whom he commanded, if not with the sword, at least by word and gesture, when suddenly a thicket, distant about forty yards from the fugitives, burst into flame ; the report of a rifle was heard, and Georges fell at Laïza's feet struck by a bullet in his side.

At the same moment a man, whose rapid flight could be detected for a moment in the shadow, sprang from the still smoking thicket into a ravine extending behind him, and, hidden from all eyes, followed it down its length, regaining by a circuitous route the ranks of the English soldiers, who had halted on the banks of the *Ruisseau des Pucelles.*

But, swift as had been the flight of the assassin, Laïza had recognized him, and, before he quite lost consciousness, the wounded man heard these three words muttered, to the accompaniment of a calm but implacable gesture :

" Antonio the Malay ! "

CHAPTER XXIII
A FATHER'S HEART

WHILE the various events which we have just related were taking place at Port Louis Pierre Munier was anxiously awaiting at Moka the dreaded result of the enterprise of which his son had given him a hint.

Accustomed, as we have said, to the everlasting supremacy of the Whites, he had come to regard it not merely as an acquired right, but as a natural superiority. However great the confidence with which his son had inspired him, he could not then believe that these obstacles, which he regarded as insurmountable, would be removed from his path.

From the moment when, as has been described, Georges took leave of him, he had sunk into a profound apathy ; the very excess of the emotions which crowded his heart, and the diversity of the thoughts which clashed in his mind, had thrown him into an apparent state of insensibility almost amounting to imbecility. More than once he very nearly made up his mind to go himself to Port Louis, and see with his own eyes what was going on ; but to go and encounter a certainty required a strength of will which the poor father did not possess ; had it only been a question of preventing a danger, Pierre Munier would have run there.

The day was spent then in an anguish all the more pro-

found because it was confined within his own breast, and
that the man who suffered it did not dare to tell any one,
not even Télémaque, the cause of the dejection about
which the latter questioned him. From time to time he
rose from his arm-chair and went with bowed head to the
open window, looked in the direction of the town as
though he could see, listened as though he could hear;
then, neither seeing nor hearing anything, he sighed and
went back with dumb lips and lack-lustre eyes and sat
down in his chair again.

The dinner hour arrived. Télémaque, who was entrusted
with the ordinary duties of the household, laid the cloth,
set the table, and brought in the dinner; but all these
various occupations were completed, and meanwhile the
man for whom the preparations were being made had
not even raised his eyes. Then, when all was ready,
Télémaque waited for a quarter of an hour, after which,
seeing that his master remained in the same condition of
stupor, he touched him lightly on the shoulder. Pierre
Munier started, and getting up quickly, asked :
" Well, has anything been heard ? "

Télémaque indicated to his master that dinner was
served ; but Pierre Munier smiled sadly, shook his head
and relapsed into his reverie. The Negro perceived that
something unusual was happening, and, without venturing
to ask for an explanation, rolled the whites of his eyes
round, as though to look for some sign that might put
him on the track of this unknown event. Everything
was in its customary place, and all was going on as usual ;
nevertheless it was evident that the expectation of some
great misfortune had come to brood that morning over
the domestic hearth.

The day passed in this manner.

Télémaque, still hoping that hunger would assert its
rights, left the dinner on the table ; but Pierre Munier
was too profoundly absorbed to interest himself in anything except his own thoughts. However, there was a
moment when Télémaque, seeing great drops of perspiration standing on his master's forehead, thought he was
feeling the heat, and offered him a glass of wine and water ;

but Pierre Munier pushed the glass gently aside, saying :—
" You have heard nothing yet ? "

Télémaque shook his head, looked in turns at the floor
and ceiling, as if to ask each of them alternately if they
were any better informed than himself. Then, seeing
that each of them remained dumb, he went out to ask the
Negroes if they possessed any more knowledge than he
did as to the unknown cause of his master's secret uneasiness.

But, to his great astonishment, he found that there
was not a single Negro about the house. He ran at once
to the barn where they were in the habit of assembling
for the *berloque*. The barn was deserted, so he returned
by the huts, but found not a soul in them except the
women and children.

On questioning these he learned that the Negroes, as
soon as the day's work was over, instead of taking their
rest as usual, had armed themselves and gone off in separate
bands, but all making in the direction of the *Rivière des
Lataniers*. On hearing this, he returned to the house.

Aroused by the sound of the opening door, the old man
turned round.

" Well ? " he asked.

Then Télémaque told him of the absence of the Negroes,
and how they had all gone off armed in the same direction.

" Yes, yes ! " said Pierre Munier, " yes, alas ! "

There was then no room for doubt, and this information
concurred in making the poor father believe that the
moment had come when what happened in the Town
would decide his whole fate. I say, *his* fate, for, since
the return of Georges, the old man, seeing his son so handsome and so brave, so confident of himself, so rich in the
experience of the past, so sure of the future, had so identified
his own life with that of his son that he had come to feel
convinced that their existence was inseparable, and that
he should never be able to endure the loss of his son, or
even his absence.

How severely did he reproach himself for having let
Georges go away that morning without questioning him,
without learning to what dangers he was about to expose

9

himself! How did he upbraid himself for not having
insisted on accompanying him!

But the mere idea that his son was about to enter upon
an overt struggle against the Whites had so utterly pros-
trated him that he had felt all his moral force desert him
on the spot. This simple soul was so constituted, as we
have said, that it had no strength except in the presence
of dangers that were physical.

Night, however, had come, and the hours went by without bringing any news, either consoling or the reverse.
Although the darkness which prevailed outside, rendered
even more profound by the light shining in the room,
prevented him from distinguishing any object at the
distance of ten yards, Pierre Munier continued to move,
at intervals almost regular, but gradually diminishing in
length, from his chair to the window and back from the
window to his chair. Télémaque, now extremely uneasy,
had installed himself in the same room; but, devoted as
this faithful servant was, he could not keep awake, and
was sleeping on a chair with his head against the wall,
against which his profile stood out like a drawing in charcoal.

At two in the morning, a watch-dog, which was usually
allowed to run loose about the house during the night,
but which had been left chained up that evening owing
to the general preoccupation, uttered a low and plaintive
howl. Pierre Munier started and got up; but at the
sound of that mournful whine which the superstition of
the Blacks regards as the sure announcement of an approaching misfortune, his strength failed him, and he was obliged
to lean against the table to save himself from falling.
Five minutes later, the dog gave another howl, louder,
more melancholy and more prolonged than the first; then,
after a similar interval, a third, even more funereal and
piteous than the other two.

Pierre Munier, pale and voiceless, the perspiration
standing on his brow, remained with his eyes fixed upon
the door without moving towards it, like a man expecting
some misfortune which he knows will enter that way.

After an instant was heard the tread of a number of
men, and the steps approached the house with slow and

measured pace. They seemed to the poor father like those of men following a funeral procession.

The outer chamber soon seemed to fill with people, but this crowd, whatever it was, maintained silence. Amid the silence, however, the old man heard a groan, and in this groan he seemed to recognize the voice of his son.

"Georges!" he cried. "Georges! in the name of heaven, is it you? Answer, speak, come here!"

"Here I am, father," answered a weak, but calm, voice; "here I am!"

At that instant the door opened and Georges entered, but leaning against the framework of the door, and so pale that Pierre Munier thought for a moment that it was his son's ghost which had appeared in answer to his summons; so that, instead of going towards Georges, the old man stepped backwards.

"In heaven's name," he murmured, "what has happened to you?"

"I am severely wounded, father, but do not be alarmed, the wound is not mortal, for, as you see, I am standing up and walking; but I cannot keep up for long." Then he added under his breath:—

"Help, Laïza, my strength is going!"

And he fell into the Negro's arms. Pierre Munier rushed towards his son, but Georges had already fainted.

With that strength of will which had become the distinctive feature of his character, Georges had determined, weak and almost dying as he was, to let his father see him standing up. And this time his action was not the result of that pride which so often exhibited itself in him, but knowing the deep affection which his father bore for him, he feared lest the shock which he might receive from seeing him lying down might prove fatal to him. Accordingly, in spite of the remonstrances of Laïza, he had quitted the litter on which the Negroes had carried him in relays across the defiles of the *Montagne du Pouce*, and with superhuman courage, and that strength of will which asserted itself even over physical weakness, he had got up, clung to the wall, and, as he had decided what he would do, had appeared to his father standing upright on his feet.

And, as he had foreseen, the shock had in this way proved less violent to the old man.

Nevertheless his iron will now succumbed beneath the pain, and Georges, exhausted by his supreme effort, fell fainting into Laïza's arms.

The father's grief was terrible to witness, even for strong men—a grief tearless and uncomplaining, mute and profoundly mournful. Georges was laid on a sofa. The old man knelt in front of him, passed his arm beneath his son's head, and waited with his eyes fixed on the closed eyes of the other, holding his breath as the other's was suspended, grasping with his other hand the hand of the wounded man, asking no questions, not anxious for details, nor inquiring how the result had come about. He knew everything he cared to know : for there was his son, wounded, bleeding, and unconscious ; what more did he require to learn, and what to him mattered the cause in face of this terrible result ?

Laïza stood erect at a corner of the sideboard, resting on his gun and looking from time to time in the direction of the window to see if it were not yet daylight.

The other Negroes, who had withdrawn respectfully after laying Georges upon the sofa, remained in the next room, occasionally putting their black heads through the doorway, while others were grouped outside in front of the window. Many of them had been wounded more or less dangerously, but no one seemed to think of his own wound.

Every instant their number increased, for all the fugitives, after having first separated in order to avoid pursuit by the English, had regained the dwelling by different roads, just as sheep that have been scattered find their way back one by one to their enclosure. At four in the morning there were about two hundred Negroes round the house.

Meanwhile Georges had recovered consciousness, and had tried to reassure his father by speaking a few words, but in a voice so faint that, though the old man's delight on hearing him speak was great, he signed to him to be silent. He had, however, inquired what was the nature of the wound and what surgeon had dressed it, and Georges, with a smile and a feeble motion of the head, had pointed to Laïza.

It is well known that, in the Colonies, some of the Negroes have the reputation of being skilful in surgery, and that sometimes even the white Colonists send for them in preference to the regular professors of the art. The explanation is quite simple ; these primitive creatures, like our own shepherds who often possess remedies of their own to hold their ground against the cleverest doctors, being continually in the presence of Nature, surprise, as do the animals, some of those secrets which remain hidden from the eyes of other men. Now, Laïza had a reputation throughout the Island as a clever surgeon ; the Negroes attributed his knowledge to the use of certain mystic words and magic enchantments, while the Whites ascribed it to his acquaintance with sundry plants and herbs of which he alone knew the names and properties. Accordingly, Pierre Munier felt more easy when he learned that it was Laïza who had dressed his son's wound. Daybreak was now approaching, and as the time went on, Laïza appeared to grow more and more uneasy. At last he could contain himself no longer, and, under pretence of feeling the sick man's pulse, went over to him and spoke to him in a low voice.

" What are you asking, and what do you want, my friend ? " asked Pierre Munier.

" I shall have to tell you, father, what he wants ; he does not wish me to fall into the hands of the Whites, and he is asking me if I feel strong enough to be carried into the great woods."

" Carried into the great woods ! " cried the old man ; " in your weak condition ! impossible ! "

" There is nothing else, however, to be done, father, unless you prefer to see me arrested under your eyes and———"

" And what ? " asked Pierre Munier anxiously ; " what do they want and what can they do to you ? "

" What do they want, father ? To be avenged on a wretched Mulatto who has had the insolence to stand up against them, and has possibly made them shake in their shoes for an instant. What can they do to me ? Oh ! a mere trifle," added Georges with a smile, " just slice my head off on the *Plaine Verte*."

The old man turned pale, then shuddered from head to foot, and it was evident that a terrible struggle was going on within him. At last he raised his forehead, shook his head, and looking at the wounded man murmured :—

" Take you ! cut off your head ! take my child from me ! kill him ! my Georges ! and all because he is handsomer, braver, and cleverer than they are—Ah ! let them come then ! Let them come ! "

And the old man, with an energy of which, five minutes before, you would have thought him incapable, rushed towards his carbine which was hanging on the wall, and, seizing the weapon that had lain idle for sixteen years, cried out :—

" Yes, yes, let them come and we will see. Ah ! you Whites, you have robbed this poor Mulatto of everything ; you have robbed him of respect, and he said nothing ; you might have taken his life, and he would still have said nothing. But now you want to take his son ; you want to take his child and imprison him, torture him, cut off his head ! Oh ! come, you Whites, and we shall see ! There are fifty years of hatred between us ; come, come, it is time we should settle our accounts."

" Bravo, father, bravo ! " cried Georges, raising himself on his elbow and looking at the old man with a feverish glance ; " bravo ! that's more like your old self."

" Well, yes, to the great woods then," said Pierre, " and we shall see if they dare follow us there. Yes, my son, come ; the great woods are better than the towns. There we are under the eyes of God ; let God look down and judge. And you, children," continued the Mulatto, addressing the Negroes, " have you always found me a good master ? "

" Yes, yes ! " cried all the Negroes with one voice.

" Have you told me a hundred times that you were devoted to me, not as slaves, but as children."

. " Yes, yes ! "

" Well then, now is the time you must prove your devotion."

" Give your orders, master, give your orders," cried all the Negroes.

" Come in, all of you."

The room was filled with Blacks.

" Here," continued the old man, " here is my son, who wished to save you, to set you free, to make men of you, and see his reward. And that is not all, they want to come and take him from me, wounded, bleeding, and in pain. Will you protect him, will you save him ? Will you die for him and with him ? "

" Yes, yes, yes ! " cried all the voices.

" To the great woods then, to the great woods ! " said the old man.

" To the great woods ! " shouted all the Negroes.

Then they brought the litter of branches to the side of the sofa on which Georges was lying, and placed the wounded man upon it, while four Negroes took hold of the four handles. Georges was carried out of the house, accompanied by Laïza, and took the head of the procession ; then followed all the Negroes, while Pierre Munier came out last, leaving the house open, forsaken, and widowed of every human creature.

The procession, which was composed of about two hundred Negroes, followed for some time the road leading from Port Louis to Grand Port ; then, after about half an hour's march, turned to the right, advancing towards the base of the *Piton du Milieu*, in order to reach the source of the *Rivière des Créoles*.

Before disappearing behind the mountain, Pierre Munier, who had continued to act as rearguard, stopped for a moment, climbed a small hill and cast a last look at this fine estate which he was forsaking. He took in at a glance those rich plains of cane, manioc, and maize, those splendid groves of shaddocks, jameroses, and takamakas, that grand horizon of mountains which enclosed his immense property like a gigantic wall. He reflected that it had taken three generations of men, honest like himself, laborious like himself, esteemed like himself, to render this district the paradise of the Island. Then, with a sigh, and brushing away a tear, he turned his eyes away and shook his head, and with a smile upon his lips overtook the litter where his wounded child was waiting for him—the child for whose sake he was giving up all this.

CHAPTER XXIV
THE GREAT WOODS

THE day was breaking as the band of fugitives reached the source of the *Rivière des Créoles* and the rays of the eastern sun lighted up the granite summit of the *Piton du Milieu* ; and this was.the signal for the entire population of the forest to awake also. At each step, the *tanrecs* got up beneath the feet of the Negroes and scuttled off to their holes, the monkeys sprang from bough to bough and scampered out on the tiniest and most flexible branches of the *vacoas*, cypresses, and tamarind trees ; then, hanging down and balancing themselves by their tails, hooked themselves on with wonderful cleverness, after a prodigious jump, to some other tree which afforded them a better shelter. The woodcock got up with a loud whirr, beating the air in his heavy flight, while the grey parrots seemed to jeer at him with their mocking cry, and the cardinal-bird, like a flying flame, flashed by swift as lightning and sparkling like a ruby. In a word, Nature, ever youthful, ever careless, ever fruitful, as is her wont, seemed in her serene tranquillity and her calm happiness ever to mock the troubles and griefs of man.

After marching for three or four hours, the band halted on a plateau at the foot of a nameless mountain, the base of which ran down to the banks of the river. Hunger began to make itself felt, but fortunately, every one had been hunting while on the road ; some with their sticks had knocked over the *tanrecs*, an animal of which the Negroes are very fond ; others had killed monkeys or woodcocks ; lastly, Laïza had wounded a stag, in pursuit of which four men had set out, and which they had brought back at the end of an hour. There were provisions therefore for the whole company.

Laïza profited by this halt to dress Georges' wound ; he had left the litter from time to time to go and pluck some herb or plant, of which he alone knew the properties. On arriving at the resting-place he put together what he had gathered, placed the precious collection which he had just obtained in a hollow of a rock, then with a rounded stone he bruised the simples just as he would have done in a mortar. This operation concluded, he pressed out the juice, dipped a rag in it, and, removing the bandage which he had put on the previous night, placed the newly-soaked compresses upon the two orifices of the wound ; for, by good luck, the bullet had not remained in the wound, but, after entering a little below the lowest left rib, had gone out a little above the hip.

Pierre Munier followed this operation with deep anxiety. The wound was serious, but not mortal ; nay more, it was evident from an examination of the flesh that, supposing no important organ in the interior had been injured, the healing would perhaps be more rapid than it would have been under the hands of one of the town doctors. The poor father none the less went through all the agony which such a sight must needs arouse in him ; while Georges, on the contrary, in spite of the pain which a dressing of this sort was bound to cause him, did not even contract his brow, and restrained even the slightest trembling of the hand which his father held between his own.

The dressing over and the meal finished, they resumed their journey. They were now nearing the great woods, but had still to reach them ; the little band, retarded by the transport of the wounded man, which was rendered still more difficult by the irregularity of the ground, advanced but slowly, and, ever since their departure from the dwelling, had left a track easy to follow.

They marched for about an hour more, following the bank of the *Rivière des Créoles*, then turned to the left, and began to find themselves on the outskirts of the forests, for, up to now, they had only traversed a sort of underwood. As they advanced, mimosas recurring in numerous clusters, and gigantic ferns growing in the space between the trees, rose as high as themselves, while bindweeds of prodigious size, dropping from the top of the takamakas like snakes hanging by their tails, began to indicate that they were entering the region of the great woods.

Soon the forest grew thicker and thicker ; the trunks of the trees were closer together, the ferns were interlaced with one another, the bindweed formed barriers through

which the passage became more and more difficult, especially
for the men who carried the litter. Every moment Georges,
seeing the difficulties which the march presented, made a
movement to get out of the litter ; but, each time, Laïza
forbade him in such a' tone of firmness, while his father
clasped his hands with such a gesture of entreaty, that, in
order not to wound the devotion of the one nor offend the
tenderness of the other, the sick man resumed his place and
let them make fresh attempts, attempts which became
every moment more painful, and which, sometimes,
remained for a long while without result.

However, the difficulties experienced by the fugitives in
penetrating into the interior of these virgin forests formed
almost a guarantee of their security, as these difficulties
would be found even greater by their pursuers, since the
fugitives were Negroes accustomed to such journeys, while
their pursuers were English soldiers accustomed to drill on
the Champ de Mars and the Champ de Lort.

Presently, however, they arrived at a spot so thick, so
full of briars, and of such compact growth, that all attempts
to cross it proved ineffectual. For a long while the little
band went up and down this kind of wall, through which the
axe alone could open a passage ; but this passage, if opened
for the one party, would be equally open for the other, and,
in offering an issue for escape, would afford a means of
pursuit. While searching about, they came upon an
ajoupa, a sort of shed built by hunters as a shelter, and
beneath it the remains of a fire still smouldering ; it was
plain that some runaway Negroes were roaming in the
neighbourhood, and, judging by the freshness of the tracks
they had left, could not be very far away.

Laïza started on their trail. The skill of savages in
following the track of a friend or an enemy across great
solitudes is well known. Laïza, stooping to the ground,
examined every blade of grass bent by the heel, every stone
moved from its bed by the tread of a foot, every branch
diverted from its inclination by the pressure of the passer-
by ; but he arrived at last at a place where all trace was lost.

On one side was a stream which came down from the
mountain and fell into the *Rivière des Créoles* ; on the other,

mass of rocks, stones, and brushwood resembling a wall, t the top of which the forest seemed even thicker than in ther parts, while behind lay the path which Laïza had ust followed. Laïza crossed the stream, and searched in ain on the other side for the track which had led him to he bank. The Negroes, for there were more than one, had herefore gone no further.

Laïza tried next to climb the wall ; in this he was successful, but, on reaching the summit, he saw that it would be mpossible for a band of men, several of whom were wounded, o take such a path ; accordingly, he came down again, nd, being convinced that those whose track he had been ooking for could not be far off, he uttered the various cries by which runaway Negroes are in the habit of recognizing ne another, and then waited.

After a moment, he thought he saw a slight waving of the thickest of the brushwood that covered the boulders forming the wall just described. Anyone else except a man habituated to the mysteries of solitudes would have thought that these branches were being shaken by the wind ; but in that case the waving movement would have been from top to bottom, whereas, on the contrary, this movement seemed to start from the bottom and gradually cease towards the extremities of the branches. This did not escape the notice of Laïza, and he fixed his glance on the thicket. His doubt soon changed into certainty ; through the branches he had perceived a pair of restless eyes which, after roving in every direction, were fixed upon himself ; Laïza then repeated the signal which he had already given, whereupon a man glided like a snake between the loose stones, and Laïza found himself face to face with a runaway Negro.

The two blacks exchanged only a word or two, and then Laïza, returning on the track, rejoined the little band, which now under his guidance took in its turn the same path which he had just taken, and soon reached the spot where he had found the Negro.

They found that an opening, made by moving some of the stones, provided a passage through the wall, and that this passage gave entrance to an immense cave,

The fugitives passed two and two through this narrow passage, so easy to defend. When the last man had passed through, the Negro replaced the stones exactly as they had been before, so that no trace of the passage was left visible ; then he, too, by clinging to the brushwood and projecting edges of the rocks, scaled the wall and disappeared in the forest.• Two hundred men had just been swallowed up into the bowels of the earth, and the most practised eye could not have told the spot at which they had entered.

Whether by one of those chances of Nature often met with, in which the hand of man has done nothing to bring about the effect produced, or, on the other hand, owing to long and foreseeing toil on the part of the runaway Negroes, the top of this mountain, into the side of which the little band had just disappeared, was defended, on one side by a perpendicular rock like a rampart, and, on the other, by that gigantic hedge composed of trunks of trees, bindweed and brake, which had at first stopped the advance of our fugitives. Consequently, the only practicable entrance was the one which has been described, and, as we have said, this entrance was entirely hidden behind the stones that blocked it up and the brushwood that concealed the stones. Thus owing to the care with which it had been hidden from all eyes, the Colonists who, armed on their own account, had hunted runaway Negroes, or the English soldiers, who, acting for the Government, had done the same, had doubtless passed a hundred times without noticing this opening, which was known to the fugitive slaves alone.

But, once on the other side of the hedge or of the cavern, the aspect of the ground changed completely. You were still in the great woods, the lofty forests, the thick cover, but it was at least possible to make your way through them, while in addition there was no lack of the first necessaries of life in these vast solitudes.

A waterfall, that had its source at the summit of the peak, fell majestically from a height of sixty feet, and, after being dashed into spray against the rocks which it wore away by its perpetual fall, flowed for some time in a gentle stream. Then, suddenly plunging into the bowels

of the earth, it reappeared again beyond the enclosed space.
Stags, boars, roe-deer, monkeys, and *tanrecs* abounded ;
and, lastly, in the places where the rays of the sun shone
through the immense vault of foliage, these rays lighted up
shaddocks loaded with their orange globes and *vacoas*
bending under their fruit, the stalks of which are so frail
that the moment the fruit is ripe it falls at the slightest
shake or the softest puff of wind.

So, if only the fugitives were successful in concealing
their retreat, they might hope to live there without wanting
for anything, until Georges should be healed and some plan
for the future determined on, when the unfortunate slaves
who accompanied Georges had decided to follow his fortunes
to the end, whatever line of action he might decide upon.

Wounded, however, as Georges was, he had retained his
usual coolness, and had not examined the retreat to which
he had come for shelter without taking into consideration
all the advantages which the position offered as a means of
defence.

As soon then as he had reached the opposite side of the
cave, he had stopped the litter, and, beckoning Laïza to
his side, had pointed out how, after securing the outer
opening of the passage, they could by means of an entrenchment defend the inner opening, and also mine the cave with
powder, which they had taken the precaution of bringing
from Moka. The plan of this work was at once sketched
out and taken in hand ; for Georges did not disguise from
himself that in all probability he would not be treated as
an ordinary fugitive, and he had sufficient pride to believe
that the Whites would not regard themselves as victors, so
long as they did not hold him bound hand and foot in their
power.

They started at once therefore on the work of defence,
which was superintended passively by Georges and actively
by Pierre Munier.

Meanwhile Laïza was going round the mountain, which,
as we have said, was protected everywhere either by natural
palisades or by precipitous rocks. At one point, however,
these rocks were capable of being scaled with ladders
fifteen feet in length. The road, too, which led to this

natural wall ran along a precipice and would have been
easy to defend but that the band was too few in number
and required to be spread over too many points at once to
allow of any military dispositions being made outside of
what may be called the fortress.

Laïza recognized therefore that it was this spot and the
entrance to the cavern that needed to be guarded more
than all others with the greatest care.

Night was now approaching ; Laïza left ten men to guard
this important post, and returned to give Georges an account
of his examination of the mountain.

He found him in a sort of cabin which had been hastily
constructed with branches. The entrenchment had already
been nearly dug out, and they continued to work hard at
it, in spite of the darkness now rapidly advancing.

Five and twenty men were told off for sentry duty round
the enclosure, the guard to be relieved every two hours ;
Pierre Munier remained at his post in the cavern, and Laïza,
after putting a fresh bandage on the wound, returned to his.

Then every one awaited such fresh developments as the
night would doubtless bring with it.

CHAPTER XXV
JUDGE AND EXECUTIONER

IN point of fact, in a war of surprises like that which was
about to take place between the revolted slaves and their
white enemies, who would not fail to pursue them, the
darkness of night would greatly aid the attack, while adding
elements of terror to the defence.

The night which had just begun was beautiful and
calm ; the moon, however, now in its last quarter, would not
rise until about eleven o'clock.

For men less preoccupied with the dangers they were
exposed to, and especially for men less accustomed to such
sights, the gradual diminution of the daylight, amid these
vast solitudes and the wild region which we have tried to
depict, would have been a magnificent spectacle. The
darkness first invaded the lower regions, rising like a tide
along the trunks of the trees, the sides of the rocks, and

the slopes of the mountain, bringing silence in its train and gradually dispersing the last gleams of day, which fled for refuge to the summit of the peak, where they hung for an instant like the flames of a volcano, then died away in their turn, submerged beneath the sea of darkness.

For eyes, however, accustomed to the night, this darkness is not total; for ears accustomed to solitude, this silence is not absolute. The life of Nature is never quite extinguished; to the sounds of day which are lulled asleep succeed the awaking sounds of night. Amid the loud murmur of the rustling leaves intermingled with the prattling of the streams are heard other noises, caused by the voices or the steps of night—roving animals, sombre voices, stealthy and unexpected steps, which inspire the stoutest hearts with that mysterious emotion reason cannot fight against, since sight cannot reassure it.

None of these confused sounds escaped the trained ear of Laïza; a wild hunter and, consequently, a man of solitude and a traveller in the night, darkness and solitude had little that was mysterious or secret for his eyes or ears. He recognized the nibbling of the *tanrecs* as they gnawed the roots of the trees, the step of the stag making for his accustomed spring, the beating of the wings of the bat in the glades, and two hours passed without any of these sounds disturbing him from his motionless position.

Strangely enough, it was in this part of the mountain, inhabited at that moment by about two hundred men, that the silence was most absolute, and the solitude seemed most complete. The ten Negroes had lain down with their faces to the ground, so that Laïza himself could hardly distinguish them in the darkness, which was rendered still thicker by the shadow of the trees; and though some of them were asleep, you would have said that, even in their sleep, caution made them hold their breath, which could scarcely be heard.

As for Laïza himself, resting upright against an enormous tamarind, whose flexible branches projected, not merely over the path that ran beside the rocks, but even over the precipice which lay beyond the path, he might defy the most trained eye to distinguish his body from the trunk of the huge tree with which, thanks to the night and the colour of his skin, he was completely identified.

Laïza stood thus, silent and motionless, for about an hour, when he heard behind him the noise made by several men walking over ground that is strewn with pebbles and dry branches. These steps, though cautious, seemed to make no effort to conceal themselves ; so he turned without any uneasiness, knowing that it must be a patrol which was advancing towards him. Presently, indeed, his eyes, accustomed to the darkness, distinguished six or eight men advancing, at the head of whom he recognized Pierre Munier by his height and the clothes he wore.

Laïza seemed to detach himself from the tree against which he had been leaning and went up to him.

" Well," said he, " have the men whom you sent to reconnoitre come back ? "

" Yes, and the English are in pursuit of us."

" Where are they ? "

" They were encamped, an hour ago, between the *Piton du Milieu* and the source of the *Rivière des Créoles.*"

" They are on our track ? "

" Yes ; and to-morrow we shall most likely have news of them."

" Sooner than that," answered Laïza.

" Why sooner ? "

" Yes ; if *we* have sent out scouts, *they* will have done the same."

" Well ? "

" Well, there are men prowling about in our neighbourhood."

" How do you know ? have you heard their voices ? have you recognized their step ? "

" No ; but I heard a stag go by, and I knew by the rapidity of his pace that he had been startled from his lair."

" You think then that some prowler is on our track ? "

" I am sure of it. Hush ! "

" What is it ? "

" Listen——"

" Yes, I do hear a sound."

" It is a woodcock flying at two hundred yards from us."

" In which direction ? "

" There ! " said Laïza, extending his hand towards a clump of trees, the tops of which could be seen rising above the ravine.

" And you think it was a man that startled it ? "

" A man or several men," answered Laïza ; " I cannot determine the number."

" That is not what I mean. You think it was frightened by some human being ? "

" Animals recognize instinctively the sounds made by other animals, and are not alarmed by them," answered Laïza.

" So then ? "

" So then they are approaching. There ! do you hear ? " added the Negro, dropping his voice.

" What is it ? " asked the old man, adopting the same precaution.

" The noise of a dry branch which has just cracked beneath the feet of one of them. Hush ! for they are now nearly close enough to us to hear the sound of our voices. Hide behind this tamarind, while I go back to my post."

There was a moment's silence, during which nothing disturbed the quiet of the night, but after a few seconds came the sound of a pebble detached from the ground and rolling over the steep slope of the cliff. Laïza felt Pierre Munier's breath against his cheek. The latter was doubtless going to speak, but the Negro grasped him forcibly by the arm ; the old man understood that silence was imperative, and obeyed.

At the same time the woodcock flew off noisily for the second time, uttering its peculiar cry, and passing over the top of the tamarind, made for the higher regions of the mountain.

The prowler was hardly twenty yards from those whose track he was doubtless searching for. Laïza and Pierre Munier held their breath ; the other Negroes stood as if carved in marble.

At this moment a gleam of silver began to light the summits of the chain of mountains which, through the glades of the forest, could be seen rising against the horizon.

Soon the hollow outline of the waning moon appeared behind the *Morne des Créoles*, and began to move across the sky.

In direct contrast to the darkness, which had mounted upwards, the light came down from above ; but this light penetrated only the open places, leaving the forest, with the exception of a few spots of ground on which the light poured through the chinks of the foliage, in profound obscurity.

At this moment there was a slight disturbance of the branches in a thicket bordering the path and rising above the declivity, of which the rapid slope led, as we have said, to a precipice ; then gradually these branches parted and allowed a man's head to pass through them.

In spite of the darkness, which however at this spot was not so great since it was not overshadowed by any tree, Pierre and Laïza noticed at the same moment the movement imparted to the thicket, for the hand of each sought and grasped the hand of the other simultaneously.

The spy remained for an instant motionless ; then he thrust his head forward once more, examining with eyes and ears the whole of the space disclosed to his gaze, made another forward movement, and then, reassured by the silence which made him think that no one was near, raised himself upon his knees, and listened once more, and still seeing and hearing nothing, finally stood upright altogether.

Laïza then grasped Pierre Munier's hand more firmly to impress on him a greater caution, since, for his own part, he no longer had any doubt but that this man was looking for their track.

And, in point of fact, when the prowler reached the edge of the path, he stooped once more and examined the ground to see if it retained any trace of the tread of a number of men ; then he touched the grass with the palm of his hand to see if it had been crushed ; he touched the stones with the point of his finger to be quite certain they had not been disturbed from their beds ; and finally, as if even the air might have retained some traces of those for whom he was searching, he raised his head and fixed his eyes on the tamarind, against the trunk and beneath the shadow of which Laïza was concealed.

At this instant a moonbeam passed between the tops of two trees and threw its light on the spy's face.

Then, with a movement quick as lightning Laïza disengaged his right hand from Pierre Munier's hand, and, springing with one bound so as to seize at its extremity one of the most flexible branches of the tree which sheltered him, dived with the swiftness of a swooping eagle to the foot of the rock and seized the spy by his girdle; then, giving with his foot an impulse to the branch which now sprang up again, mounted with him as the eagle soars with its prey. Then slipping his hand along the smooth and polished bark of the bough, he fell at the foot of the tree in the midst of his companions, still grasping his prisoner, who, knife in hand, strove vainly to wound his captor, as the snake strives vainly to bite the king of the air which carries him off from the depths of a marsh to his eyrie near the sky.

Then, in spite of the darkness, every one at the first glance recognized the prisoner, who was none other than Antonio the Malay. All this had happened so swiftly and so unexpectedly that Antonio had not uttered a sound.

At last then Laïza held his mortal enemy in his power, and was about to inflict instant punishment on the traitor and assassin.

He was pressing him beneath his knee, looking at him with that terrible smile of the victor by which the vanquished realizes that there is nothing to hope for, when suddenly the distant barking of a dog was heard.

Without loosing the hand with which he grasped his throat, or the hand by which he held his wrist, Laïza raised his head and listened in the direction whence the sound had come.

At this sound Laïza felt Antonio shudder.

" Everything at its proper time," murmured Laïza, as if speaking to himself.

Then, addressing the Negroes who surrounded him :—

" First fasten this fellow to a tree," said he ; " I must speak to M. Munier."

The Negroes seized Antonio by his hands and feet and tied him with bindweed to the trunk of a takamaka. Laïza

made certain that he was tied securely, and then, leading
the old man a few paces away, stretched his hand in the
direction whence he had heard the dog's bark.

"Did you hear that ? " he asked him.

"What ? " asked the old man.

"The bark of a dog."

"No."

"Listen, it's coming nearer."

"Yes, I heard it that time."

"They are hunting us like stags."

"What ! do you think it is we they are pursuing ? "

"What should you think it is then ? "

"Some dog that has escaped, hunting on his own
account."

"Yes, that is possible, after all," murmured Laïza;
"let us listen."

There was a moment's silence, at the end of which more
barking re-echoed through the forest, nearer at hand than
on the previous occasions.

"It is we they are chasing."

"And how do you know that ? "

"That is not the bark of a dog hunting," said Laïza,
"it is the howling of a dog in search of his master. The
devils must have found a dog chained up in some Negro's
hut, and taken him to guide them ; if that Negro is with us,
we are lost."

"It is Fidèle's voice," murmured Pierre Munier with a
start.

"Yes, yes, I recognize it now," said Laïza. "I have
heard it before ; it is the dog that howled last night, when
we brought your son wounded to Moka."

"I quite forgot to bring him when we started ; still, if
it were Fidèle, I think he would be running faster. Listen
how slowly his voice comes nearer ! "

"They are holding him in a leash and following him ; he
has perhaps a whole regiment at his heels. You must not be
angry with the poor beast," added the Anjouan Negro with
a grim smile, "he cannot go any faster. But don't be
uneasy, he will come sure enough."

"Well, what is to be done ? " asked Pierre Munier.

" If you had any vessel waiting for you at Grand Port, I should say that as we are but eight or ten leagues from it, there was still time for us to get there ; but you have no chance of escape in that direction, have you ? "

" None."

" Then we must defend ourselves, and, if possible," added the Negro in a gloomy tone, " die in doing so."

" Come then," said Pierre Munier, regaining all his courage the moment it was a question of fighting. " Come then, for the dog will lead them to the opening of the cavern, and it will take them some time to get in, even when they are there."

" Very well," said Laïza, " away with you then to the entrenchments."

" But why do you not come with me ? "

" I ? Oh ! I must wait here for a few moments longer."

" But you will join us again ? "

" When the first gun is fired, turn round and you will see me at your side."

The old man extended his hand to Laïza, for the common danger had obliterated all difference of rank between them ; then he threw his gun over his shoulder, and, followed by his escort, went off at a rapid pace towards the entrance to the cavern.

Laïza followed him with his eyes until he was quite lost in the darkness ; then, turning to Antonio, whom the Negroes according to his orders had bound to a tree, he said :—

" And now, Antonio, for you and me."

" You and me ? " said Antonio in a trembling voice. " And what does Laïza want with his friend and brother ? "

" I want him to remember what was said on the evening of the Yamsé by the bank of the *Rivière des Lataniers*."

" Many things were said, and my brother Laïza was very eloquent, for everybody followed his advice."

" And among those thing does Antonio remember the sentence pronounced beforehand against traitors ? "

Antonio shuddered from head to foot, and, in spite of the copper tint of his skin, might have been seen to turn pale, had it been daylight.

" My brother appears to have lost his memory," resumed

Laïza in a tone of cutting irony ; " well, I am going to
bring it back to him. It was said that, in case a traitor
should be found among us, any of us might put an end to
him by a death prompt or lingering, gentle or terrible.
Are those the exact words of the oath, and does my brother
remember them ? "

" I remember them," said Antonio in a scarcely articulate
voice.

" Well then, answer the questions I am going to put to
you," said Laïza.

" I do not recognize your right to question me ; you are
not my judge," cried Antonio.

" Then I shall question some one else," replied Laïza.

Then, turning to the Negroes who were lying round him
on the ground :—

" Get up, you others, and answer."

The Negroes obeyed, and some ten or twelve black figures
silently ranged themselves in a semicircle in front of the
tree to which Antonio was tied.

" They are slaves," cried Antonio, " and I ought not to
be judged by slaves ; I am no Negro, I am free. It is for
a court to judge me if I have committed a crime, and not
for you."

" That will do," said Laïza. " We will judge you first,
and then you shall appeal to whom you choose."

Antonio held his tongue, and, in the moment of silence
which followed the injunction Laïza had just given him, the
bark of the dog was heard drawing nearer.

" Since the culprit will not answer," said Laïza to the
Negroes who surrounded Antonio, " you must answer for
him. Who was it that denounced the conspiracy to the
Governor, because some one else and not himself had been
named as leader ? "

" Antonio the Malay," answered all the Negroes in a low
tone, but unanimously.

" It is not true ! " cried Antonio. " It is not true ! I
swear it ! I protest ! "

" Silence ! " said Laïza in the same imperative tone.
Then he resumed :—

" Who was it that, after denouncing the conspiracy to

the Governor, shot at our leader, by the base of the little mountain, and wounded him ? "

" Antonio the Malay," answered all the Negroes.

" Who saw me ? " cried the Malay : " Who dares to say it was I ? Who could distinguish one man from another in the darkness ? "

" Silence ! " said Laïza.

Then, continuing in the same calm tone of inquiry, he said :—

" Lastly, after denouncing the conspiracy to the Governor, and trying to murder our leader, who was it came in the night crawling like a snake round our retreat, to discover some opening by which the English soldiers might enter ? "

" Antonio the Malay," replied the Negroes once more, with the same accent of conviction that had not failed them for an instant.

" I was coming to join my brothers," cried the prisoner ; " I was coming to share their lot, whatever it might be, I swear and protest I was."

" Do you believe what he says ? " asked Laïza.

" No ! no ! no ! " chorused all the voices.

" My kind friends," said Antonio, " listen to me, I entreat you ! "

" Silence ! " said Laïza. Then he continued, with the same accent of solemnity which he had maintained all the time, and which indicated the greatness of the duty which he had imposed upon himself :—

" Antonio is not once, but three times, a traitor ; Antonio then would deserve to die three times, if that were possible. Antonio, prepare to appear before the Great Spirit, for you are about to die ! "

" It is murder ! " cried Antonio, " and you have no right to murder a free man. Besides, the English cannot be far off ; I will appeal to them, I will shout. Help ! help ! They are cutting my throat ! they are——"

Laïza took the Malay by the throat and smothered his cries between his fingers of iron ; then, turning towards the Negroes :—

" Get a rope ready," he said.

On hearing this order, which foreshadowed the fate

awaiting him, Antonio struggled so violently that he broke some of the bonds which held him. But he could not free himself from the most terrible of them all, the hand of Laïza. After some seconds, however, the Negro realized, by the convulsions which he felt running through Antonio's whole frame, that, if he continued to grasp him so tightly, there would soon be no need for a rope. So he relaxed his hold on the throat of the prisoner, who let his head fall on his breast like a man with the death-rattle in his throat.

"I said that I would grant you time to appear before the Great Spirit," said Laïza; "you have ten minutes, prepare yourself."

Antonio tried to pronounce some words, but his voice failed him.

The barking of the dog was heard drawing nearer every moment.

"Where is the rope?" said Laïza.

"Here," answered a Negro, handing Laïza the article which he asked for.

"Good," said he.

And, the office of the Judge having been completed, that of the Executioner began.

Laïza took hold of one of the strongest branches of the tamarind, pulled it towards him and fastened one end of the rope to it, then made a running knot of the other end and passed it over Antonio's head. Next he ordered two Negroes to hold the branch, and, having assured himself that the condemned man, spite of the rupture of two or three of his bands, was still secured tightly, he bade him a second time prepare for death.

The condemned man had now recovered speech; but, instead of using it to implore the mercy of God, he raised his voice to make a last appeal to the pity of men.

"Well, yes, my brothers, yes, my friends," said he, changing his tactics, and trying to obtain by confession what had been refused to his denials, "yes, I am very guilty, I know, and you have the right to treat me as you are doing; but you will pardon your old comrade, will you not? your comrade who used to amuse you in the evenings? poor Antonio, who used to tell you such nice

stories and sang you such rousing songs ! How will you do
without him ? who will amuse and distract you ? who will
make you forget the fatigue of the day's work ? Let me off
my friends ! let poor Antonio off ! I ask you on my knees
for my life ! "

"Think of the Great Spirit," said Laïza ; "for you have
but five minutes to live, Antonio."

"Instead of five minutes, Laïza, kind Laïza," resumed
Antonio in a tone of entreaty, "give me five years, and
during those five years I will be your slave ; I will follow
you, be always at your orders, always ready to obey you,
and, when I fail, or commit the slightest fault, well, then you
shall punish me, and I will bear the lash, the rod, the rope,
without complaint, and say that you are a kind master for
having given me my life. Oh ! Laïza, give me my life,
give me my life ! "

"Listen, Antonio," said Laïza, "do you hear that dog
barking ? "

"Yes ; and you think it was I who advised its being
let loose ? no, you are wrong, I swear it."

"Antonio," said Laïza, "it would not have entered the
head of even a White to employ a dog to hunt down his
own master. This idea was yours, Antonio."

The Malay uttered a deep groan ; then, after an instant,
as though he hoped to melt his foe by dint of humility, he
said :—

"Well, yes, it was mine. The Great Spirit had forsaken
me, the thirst for revenge had made me mad. You must
show pity for a madman, Laïza ; pardon me, in the name
of your brother Nazim."

"And who was it again who betrayed Nazim, when Nazim
wanted to escape ? Ah ! that is a name that you were
very foolish to pronounce, Antonio. The five minutes are
up. Malay, you are going to die."

"Oh ! no, no, no ! not to die ! " said Antonio. "Pardon,
Laïza ! pardon, my friends ! "

But, without listening to the plaints, the entreaties, or
the prayers of the condemned man, Laïza drew his knife
and at a blow cut all the ties which bound Antonio. At
the same instant the two men, at an order from him, let

go the branch, which sprang back, carrying with it the unfortunate Malay.

A shriek, terrible, supreme, a shriek in which seemed to be combined all the strength of despair, resounded and then died away in mournful accents and was lost in the depths of the forest. All was over, and Antonio was nothing but a corpse swinging at the end of the rope above the precipice.

Laïza remained for an instant motionless, watching the movements of the rope as its vibration gradually diminished; then, when it almost described a perpendicular and motionless line against the blue of the sky, he listened once more to the barking of the dog, which was now hardly more than a hundred yards from the cavern. He picked up his gun which he had laid on the ground, and, turning to the other Negroes, said :—

"Come, my friends, we are avenged ; now, we can die."

And, starting off at a rapid pace, he marched at their head towards the entrenchments.

CHAPTER XXVI
NIGGER HUNTING

LAÏZA had not been mistaken, and the dog, in following the track of his master, had led the English straight to the entrance of the cavern. Here he had dashed into the brushwood and had begun to scratch and to bite at the stones. Then the English knew they were at the end of their pursuit.

They immediately sent forward soldiers armed with picks, who fell to work, and in a few minutes effected an opening large enough to admit a man's body. A soldier pushed his body through, in order to look into the opening. Instantly a shot was heard, and the soldier fell, his breast pierced by a bullet ; a second soldier succeeded the first, and fell in the same way ; a third advanced in his turn and shared the same fate.

It was evident from the rebels having themselves given the signal for attack, that they were resolved to make a desperate defence.

The assailants began to go to work more cautiously; sheltering themselves as much as they could, they enlarged the breach so that several men could enter abreast; the drums beat, and the Grenadiers advanced with fixed bayonets.

But the besieged occupied such an advantageous position that in an instant the breach was littered with dead, and the bodies had to be removed to make room for a second assault.

This time the English penetrated to the middle of the cavern, but only to leave a still larger number of dead than at the previous advance; sheltered behind the entrenchment which Georges had ordered to be raised, the Negroes, under the direction of Laïza and Pierre Munier, fired with unerring accuracy.

Meanwhile, Georges, incapacitated by his wound, and lying in his cabin, cursed the inactivity to which he was reduced; the smell of powder which enveloped him, the noise of musketry crackling in his ear, everything, including the successive charges made by the English, aroused in him that ardent fever of battle which makes a man stake his life on the whim of accident. But, in this case, it was much worse, for it was no foreign cause that was being fought out, it was no question of supporting the pleasure of a king, or of a Nation's honour that had to be avenged. No, it was his own personal cause which these men were defending, while he, Georges, the man of stout heart, of adventurous spirit, could do nothing, neither in action, nor even in counsel; and Georges bit the mattress on which he was lying, Georges wept with vexation.

At the second attack, when the English succeeded in reaching the middle of the cavern, they fired, from the point which they had gained, several volleys at the entrenchment, and, as the cabin in which Georges was lying was just behind the entrenchment, two or three bullets whizzed through the branches forming its walls. This sound, which would have alarmed anyone else, consoled and elated Georges, since he reflected that he, too, was in danger, and that if he could not inflict death, he might at least meet it.

The English had for the moment desisted from the attack;

but it was evident that they were preparing for a fresh assault, and you could hear, from the heavy and resounding blows of the pick-axe, that they had not abandoned their project. In point of fact, after a short interval, a portion of the outer wall of the cavern fell in, thereby doubling the size of the opening. Immediately the drums beat again, and, by the light of the moon, the bayonets were seen for the third time gleaming at the entrance to the cavern.

Pierre Munier and Laïza exchanged glances; this time it was evident the struggle would be a terrible one.

" What is your last resource ? " asked Laïza.

" The cavern is mined," said the old man.

" In that case, we have still a chance of safety, but, at the decisive moment, you must do as I tell you, or we are all lost, for it is not possible to retreat with a wounded man."

" Well, I shall kill myself at his side," said the old man.

" It would be better that both of you should escape."

" Together ? "

" Together or separately, it matters little which."

" I shall not leave my son, Laïza, I warn you."

" You will leave him, if it is his only means of safety."

" What do you mean ? "

" I will explain later on."

Then, turning to the Negroes, he explained :—

" Come, children, the supreme moment has arrived. Fire on the redcoats, and don't waste a shot ; in an hour's time powder and ball will be scarce."

Immediately the fusillade broke out. The Negroes as a rule are excellent shots ; they therefore carried out Laïza's injunctions to the letter, and the ranks of the English began to be thinned. But, after each discharge, the ranks closed up again with admirable discipline, and the column, which had been delayed by the first difficulties of the passage, continued to advance up the cave. Not a shot was now fired by the English, who appeared determined this time to carry the entrenchment at the point of the bayonet.

The situation, serious as it was for all, was doubly so for Georges, thanks to the helplessness to which he was condemned. He had at first raised himself on his elbow; then he had got upon his knees, and at last succeeded in struggling to his feet. But, having reached this point, his weakness became so great that the earth seemed to give way beneath him, and he was forced to cling with his hands to the branches which surrounded him. While recognizing the courage of the few devoted men who accompanied his fortunes to the end, he could not refrain from admiring the cool and imperturbable bravery of the English, who continued to march as if on parade, although, at each step they took, they were obliged to close up their ranks. He realized that this time they did not mean to retreat, and that in five minutes' time they would carry the entrenchment, spite of the fire that issued from it. Then, the thought that it was for him, forced as he was to remain an inactive spectator of the combat, that all these men were about to be killed, filled his heart with remorse; he tried to step forward and throw himself between the combatants and put a stop to the slaughter by surrendering himself, since, in all probability, it was against himself alone that they bore ill-will. But he felt unable to traverse a third of the distance that divided him from the English. He wanted to call out to the besieged to cease their fire, to the besiegers to advance no further, and that he would give himself up; but his enfeebled voice was lost in the roar of the fusillade. Besides, at this moment he saw his father stand up, showing half his height above the entrenchment, then advance a few steps towards the English with a branch of fir blazing in his hand, and, amid the fire and smoke, lower this strange torch to the ground. Instantly a train of flame ran along the earth and, burying itself in the soil, disappeared; then, at the same moment, the ground shook, a terrible explosion was heard, a flaming crater opened beneath the feet of the English, the vault of the cavern yawned and sank down, the rocks which lay upon it buried themselves with it, and, amid the cries of the rest of the regiment who were still on the farther side of the opening, the subterranean passage disappeared in a yawning chasm.

"Now," said Laïza, "there is not a moment to lose."

"Give your orders; what must be done?"

" Fly towards Grand Port and try to find refuge on a French ship ; I will look after Georges."

" I will not leave my son, I told you so."

" And I told you that you will leave him ; for, by remaining, you destroy him."

" How is that ? "

" With your dog, which they have still got, they are following you everywhere, driving you into the thickest part of the forest, reaching you in the deepest of caverns, and Georges, wounded as he is, will be soon overtaken. But, on the other hand, if you fly on your own account, they will think that your son is accompanying you ; then it is you they will pursue ; it is you they will be intent upon ; it is you they will perhaps overtake. Meantime I profit by the darkness, and carry Georges, with four devoted men, in another direction ; we shall reach the woods which surround the *Morne du Bambou.* If you find any means of saving us, you will light a fire on the *Ile des Oiseaux* ; then we will go down the *Grande-Rivière* on a raft, and you will come with a boat and take us in at the mouth of the river."

Pierre Munier had listened to all this with eyes fixed, and breathing suspended, pressing Laïza's hands between his own ; then, as he finished, he threw his arms round his neck and cried :—

" Laïza ! Laïza ! yes, yes, I understand ; it is the only way, with all this English pack at my heels. Yes, that is the way, and you will save my Georges."

" I will save him or die with him," said Laïza ; " that is all I can promise."

" And I know that you will keep your promise. Only wait while I go and embrace my son once more, and then I will start."

" No, no," said Laïza ; " if you see him, you will not want to leave him ; if he knows that you are exposing yourself to danger to save his life, he will not allow you to do it. Go then, go ! And follow him, all of you ; four men only come with me, the strongest, most vigorous, and most devoted."

Some dozen men stepped forward, of whom Laïza selected four ; then, as Pierre Munier hesitated to start :—

" The English ! the English ! " he cried to the old man ;
" they will be here in a moment."

" At the mouth of the *Grande-Rivière* then ? " cried
Pierre.

" Yes, if we are not taken or killed."

" Farewell, Georges, farewell ! " cried Pierre Munier.
And, followed by the remaining Negroes, he rushed off in
the direction of the *Montagne des Créoles.*

" Father," cried Georges, " where are you going ? what
are you doing ? why do you not come and die with your
son ? Wait for me, father, here I am."

But Pierre Munier was already far away, and the last
words, especially, were uttered in so feeble a tone that the
old man could not hear them.

Laïza ran to the wounded man, and found him on his
knees.

" Father ! " murmured Georges, and fell back in a faint.

Laïza lost no time ; this fainting fit was almost a stroke
of luck. Doubtless, had Georges been conscious, he would
not have wished to make any further struggle for his life
with those who were pursuing him, and would have looked
upon this solitary flight as a thing to be ashamed of. His
weakness, however, placed him at the mercy of Laïza. The
latter laid him, still unconscious, on the litter ; each of
the Negroes whom he had kept with him took one of its
handles, and, going ahead himself to point out the road,
he made for the direction of the *Trois-Ilots*, whence he hoped,
by following the course of the *Grande-Rivière*, to reach the
Piton du Bambou.

They had not gone a quarter of a league when they
heard the barking of a dog.

At a gesture from Laïza the bearers halted. Georges was
still unconscious, or at least so exhausted that he appeared
to take no notice of what was going on.

What Laïza had foreseen had happened ; the English
had scaled the enclosure, and reckoned on using the dog
in order to overtake the fugitives a second time, as they
had already done once.

There was a moment of painful suspense during which
Laïza listened to the dog's barking ; for some time the

sound remained stationary. The dog had come to the spot where the encounter had taken place ; presently, two or three barks sounded still nearer. The dog was going from the entrenchment where Georges had remained for some time and where his father had gone to visit him. Finally the noise of the barks died away in a southerly direction ; the stratagem of Laïza had been successful ; the hunters were foiled in the scent, and, abandoning the son, were following the father.

The situation was now all the more grave that, during this brief halt, the first gleams of day had appeared, and the mysterious darkness of the forest began to be lighted up. Certainly, had Georges been in his usual health and vigour, the perplexity would have been less, for in that case craft, courage and skill would have been present in equal proportions on both sides, between pursuers and pursued ; but the fact that Georges was wounded made the game unequal, and Laïza did not disguise from himself the fact that the position was most critical.

One apprehension, especially, engaged his thoughts, namely, that in all probability the English might have taken as auxiliaries some slaves trained to the pursuit of runaway Negroes, and have made them some promise, as, for example, of freedom, if Georges should fall into their hands. In that case Laïza would lose part of his advantage as a man intimate with Nature, by being pitted against similar men for whom, like himself, solitude had no secrets and night no mysteries.

He concluded therefore that there was not a moment to lose, and, his uncertainty as to the direction which the pursuers would take being now resolved, he resumed the march, making always towards the East.

The forest had a strange aspect, and all the animals seemed to share in the uneasiness of man. The firing, which had resounded all night long, had awakened the birds in the branches, the boars in their lairs, the deer in their thickets ; everything was on the move, everything in a state of alarm ; you might have thought that all living creatures were seized with a kind of giddiness.

They marched thus for two hours, when it became

necessary to halt. The Negroes had been fighting all night and had eaten nothing since four o'clock the previous evening. Laïza halted under the ruins of a shed which had evidently that very night served as a shelter for runaway Negroes; for, on stirring a heap of ashes, the result apparently of a fairly long stay, they found them still alight.

Three of the Negroes went off to hunt for *tanrecs*. The fourth busied himself in rekindling the hearth, while Laïza searched for herbs to renew the wounded man's bandages.

Strong as Georges was in body and vigorous in mind, his moral forces had been overcome by the material; he was now in a fever of delirium, ignorant of what was going on, unable to help by advice or action those who were trying to save him.

The dressing of the wound, however, appeared to soothe him. As for Laïza, he seemed to triumph over all the physical wants of nature. For sixty hours he had not slept, yet he seemed to need no sleep; for twenty hours he had not tasted food, and yet did not seem to be hungry.

The Negroes came back one after the other with six or eight *tanrecs*, which they hastened to roast before the large fire which their comrade had made; Laïza was rather uneasy about the smoke, but he reflected that they must now have travelled two or three leagues at least from the spot where the fight took place, without leaving any track behind them, and that, even supposing this smoke was observed, it would only be by some outpost sufficiently far off to allow them time to escape before they were overtaken.

When the meal was finished, the Negroes called Laïza, who had remained seated near Georges. Laïza got up, and, on looking at the group, whom he hastily rejoined, noticed that one of the Negroes had received a wound in the thigh which was still bleeding.

This discovery destroyed all his feeling of security; his track would be followed like that of a wounded deer, not, perhaps, because the pursuers suspected the importance of the capture which they might make by following the track, but because the capture of any prisoner, whoever he might be, would be, owing to the information which he would supply, of too great importance for the English not to do all in their power to secure such a capture.

Just as this reflection struck him, and as he was opening his mouth to bid the four Negroes who were squatting round the fire resume their march, a small cluster of trees, thicker than the rest of the forest, and on which his uneasy eyes had rested more than once, burst into flame, a brisk discharge of musketry was heard, and five or six bullets whizzed round him. One of the Negroes fell forward into the fire, the three others jumped up; but, after running five or six yards, a second fell, and then a third about ten yards farther on. The fourth alone escaped safe and sound and disappeared into the woods.

At the sight of the smoke, the sound of the discharge, and the whistling of the bullets, Laïza sprang with one bound to the litter where Georges was lying; and, snatching him up in his arms as if he were a child, dashed off in his turn into the forest, not appearing to slacken his pace in the slightest degree for the burden he was bearing.

Immediately eight or ten of the English soldiers, escorted by five or six Negroes, leaped out of the cluster of trees and started in pursuit of the fugitives, of whom they had recognized Georges to be one, knowing that he was wounded. As Laïza had foreseen, the blood had guided them. They had followed the track, and arrived within half rifle-range of the shed, then had aimed with rested rifles, and, as we have seen, had aimed well, since three out of the four Negroes had been, if not killed, at least disabled.

Now began a desperate chase; for it was evident that, however great the strength and activity of Laïza, he could not succeed in getting out of sight of his pursuers, who must overtake him in the end. Unhappily, he was placed between two dangers almost equally fatal; if he plunged into the thickest of the forest, it might become so dense that it would be almost impossible to proceed farther; if he kept to the more open parts, he would expose himself to the fire of the enemy. However, he preferred the latter alternative.

At the start, and by dint of his rapid dash, Laïza found himself almost beyond range of their rifles, and, had it been only the English with whom he had to deal, he would doubtless have got away. But, though it was perhaps with reluctance that the Negroes joined in the pursuit, still, as they were urged on by the soldiers with their bayonets, they were compelled to go forward, and so run down their human quarry, if not with enthusiasm, at least from motives of fear.

From time to time, when Laïza could be seen through the trees, some shots were fired at him, and the bullets grazed the bark of the trees round him or furrowed the earth at his feet. But, as though he bore an enchanted life, none of these bullets touched him, and his pace was quickened, if one may so say, by reason of the danger which he had just escaped.

At last he arrived at the edge of the glade; a steep and almost unprotected slope, with another thicket of trees at its summit, had to be climbed; but, the summit once reached, Laïza would at least be able to disappear behind some rock, slip down some ravine, and thus baffle the sight of his pursuers. On the other hand, he would remain unprotected and exposed to their fire throughout the whole interval that separated him from the trees.

There was, however, no room for hesitation; to turn to right or left was to lose ground; chance had, so far, favoured the fugitives, the same good luck might still attend them.

Laïza dashed into the glade; the pursuers in their turn, seeing an opportunity of firing in the open, redoubled their speed. Laïza was now about fifty yards ahead.

Then, as though by word of command, each soldier halted, took aim, and fired. Laïza appeared not to be touched, and continued his course. The soldiers had still time to reload their weapons before he disappeared, and hastily slipped the cartridges into the breech of their rifles.

Meanwhile, Laïza was gaining ground rapidly; it was plain that, if he escaped the second discharge as he had done the first, and reached the thicket safe and sound, all the chances would be in his favour. Scarcely twenty-five yards separated him from the edge of the thicket, and, during the brief halt of his pursuers, he had gained a hundred and

fifty yards on them. Suddenly, he disappeared in a bend
of the ground ; but, unfortunately, its windings did not
extend either to right or left. He followed it, however,
as far as he could, in order to baffle his enemies ; but, on
reaching the extremity of the little ravine the shoulder of
which had protected him, he was obliged to climb the slope
once more, and, consequently, to show himself again. At
this moment ten or a dozen shots were fired simultaneously,
and his pursuers seemed to see him stagger. In point of
fact, after taking a few steps, Laïza stopped, staggered
again, fell on one knee, then on both, and laid Georges,
who was still unconscious, on the ground. Then, rising
to his full height, he turned towards the English, extending
both his hands towards them with a final gesture of menace
and fierce malediction, and, drawing his knife from his
girdle, plunged it up to the hilt in his breast.

The soldiers dashed forward, uttering loud shouts of
delight, like hunters at a death-halloo. Laïza remained
standing for a few seconds ; then, suddenly, fell like a tree
torn up by the roots ; the blade of the knife had pierced
his heart.

On reaching the two fugitives, the soldiers found Laïza
dead, and Georges dying. Georges, with a last effort, to
avoid falling alive into the hands of his enemies, had torn
the bandages from his wounds, and the blood was gushing
forth in torrents.

As for Laïza, besides the blow aimed at his heart with
the knife, he had received a bullet in his thigh, and another
which had pierced his breast through and through.

CHAPTER XXVII

THE REHEARSAL

ALL that passed during the two or three days following
the catastrophe which we have just related left but
a vague impression on the mind of Georges. His intellect,
disordered by delirium, retained only dim recollections,
which did not allow him to calculate the flight of time or to
distinguish one event from another. One morning, how-

ever, he woke as from a sleep disturbed by dreadful dreams, and, on opening his eyes, realised that he was in a prison. The Surgeon-Major of the regiment stationed at Port Louis was by his side.

On recalling, however, all that he could remember, Georges succeeded in retracing the events which had happened, but grouped, as it were, in large masses, much as through the fog you get a glimpse of lakes, mountains and forests. Everything came back to him, down to the moment when he was wounded. His arrival at Moka and his departure with his father had not quite escaped his memory, but everything, from the time of his reaching the great woods, was vague and indistinct, like a dream. However, the only indisputable, positive, and fatal certainty was that he was now in the hands of his enemies. Georges was too scornful to put any question, too proud to ask any service, so he could learn nothing of what had happened. His heart was distracted, however, by two terrible anxieties :—

Had his father escaped ?

Did Sara still love him ?

These two thoughts pervaded his whole being; when one of them disappeared, it was to make room for the other ; they were like two ceaseless tides beating in turns upon his heart with their everlasting ebb and flow.

But there were no outward indications of this tempest which was raging in his mind. His face remained pale, cold and unruffled as a marble statue, not only in presence of all who visited the prison, but even in presence of himself.

When the doctor considered the wounded man strong enough to undergo an examination, he informed the authorities, and on the next day the examining Magistrate, accompanied by a clerk, presented himself before Georges. Georges was still unable to leave his bed, but he did the honours of his room nevertheless to the two officials with a patience full of dignity, and, leaning on his elbow, declared that he was ready to answer any questions that might be put to him.

Our readers are too well acquainted with the character of Georges to think that the idea had for a moment occurred to him of denying any of the acts with which he was charged. Not merely did he answer with absolute truth all the questions put to him, but he even promised, not that day, for he felt too weak, but on the morrow, that he would himself dictate to the clerk the whole story of the conspiracy in detail. The offer was too courteous to be declined by the Magistrate. Georges had a two-fold object in making this proposal; first, to hasten the progress of the trial; secondly, to take the whole of the responsibility upon himself.

The two officials presented themselves next day. Georges gave them the account which he had promised; when, however, he was passing over in silence the proposals which had been made to him by Laïza, the Magistrate interrupted him with the remark that he was omitting an extenuating circumstance which, owing to the death of Laïza, could not now be charged against any one.

It was thus that Georges learned the death of Laïza and its accompanying circumstances; for, as we have said, all these events were, so far as he was concerned, shrouded in obscurity.

Not once was his father's name pronounced, either by himself or the others, nor was the name of Sara, for stronger reasons still, as you may suppose, so much as mentioned.

This declaration by Georges rendered any other inquiry superfluous. Georges therefore ceased to receive any visits except from the doctor.

One morning the doctor, on entering the room, found Georges standing up.

" Sir," said he, " I forbade you to get up for some days; you are not sufficiently strong yet."

" That is to say, my dear doctor," answered Georges, " that you do me the injustice of confounding me with the ordinary criminal, who delays the day of trial as long as he possibly can; whereas, I confess it frankly, I am in a hurry to get it over. Now do you think, in all conscience, that it is worth while getting so thoroughly healed, merely in order to die ? For my own part, I think that, provided I have strength enough to mount the scaffold properly, it is all that can be required of me, and all that I can require of God."

"But who tells you that you will be condemned to death?" said the doctor.

"My own conscience, doctor; I have played a game in which my head was at stake. I have lost, and am ready to pay; that is all."

"All the same," said the doctor, "I am of opinion that you need a few days' care still before exposing yourself to the fatigue of a trial and the excitement of being sentenced."

But, that very day, Georges wrote to the examining Magistrate that his wound was completely healed, and that, consequently, he was at the disposal of justice.

Two days afterwards the trial began.

Georges, on appearing before the Judges, looked round him with anxiety and was delighted to see that he was the only person charged.

Then he glanced confidently down the hall; the whole Town was present at the hearing, with the exception of M. de Malmédie, Henri, and Sara.

Some of the spectators appeared to pity the accused man, but the majority of the faces wore an expression of satisfied hatred.

As for Georges, his demeanour was calm and haughty, as ever. He was dressed, as usual, in a black frock-coat and cravat, with white waistcoat and trousers; his double riband was knotted at his button-hole.

An advocate for the defence had been appointed for him, Georges having declined to choose one. His wish was that no attempt even should be made to plead his cause.

What Georges himself said was not a defence, but a history of his whole life. He did not conceal the fact that he had returned to the Isle of France with the intention of overcoming, by all the means in his power, the prejudice oppressing men of colour; only, he did not breathe a word of the causes which had hastened the execution of his protest.

One of the Judges questioned him in regard to M. de Malmédie, but Georges asked to be allowed not to reply.

In spite of the facilities given to the Court by Georges,

the discussion none the less dragged on for three days; even when they have nothing to say, lawyers must always talk.

The Advocate-General spoke for four hours and pulverised Georges.

Georges listened to the whole of this long harangue with the greatest calmness, bowing in token of assent from time to time.

Then, when the speech of the Public Prosecutor was finished, the President asked Georges if he wished to say anything.

" Nothing," answered Georges, "except that the Advocate-General has been very eloquent."

It was now the turn of the Advocate-General to bow, which he did.

The President announced that the discussion was closed, and Georges was taken back to his prison, the sentence having to be pronounced in the absence of the accused and to be communicated to him afterwards.

Georges on entering the prison asked for paper and ink in order to write his will. Sentences inflicted by English law not entailing confiscation, he was able to dispose of his fortune. He left to the doctor who had attended him £3,000 sterling;

To the Governor of the prison, £1,000 sterling;

To each of the turnkeys, one thousand dollars.

This was a fortune to each of the recipients.

To Sara he left a gold ring that had come to him from his mother.

As he was about to sign his name at the foot of the document, the clerk entered. Georges rose, with the pen in his hand, and the clerk read the sentence.

As Georges had always expected, he was condemned to the penalty of death.

When the reading was over Georges bowed, and sitting down again signed his name, without its being possible to notice the slightest difference between the handwriting in the body of the document and that of the signature.

Then he went to a glass, and looked to see if he was at all paler than before. His face was exactly as it had been, pale but calm. He was pleased with himself, and smiled to himself, as he murmured :—

" Well, I thought a man would betray more feeling than that on hearing his death sentence."

The doctor.came to see him, and, from force of habit, asked him how he was feeling.

" Oh! very well, doctor," answered Georges ; " you have made a wonderful cure, and it is annoying that you are not allowed time to complete it."

Then he inquired if the mode of execution had been changed since the occupation of the Island by the British ; and the assurance that it still continued the same greatly pleased Georges, since it was not the ignoble gibbet of London, nor the hideous guillotine of Paris. No, execution at Port Louis had a picturesque and romantic aspect, at the thought of which Georges did not feel degraded. A Negro, acting as executioner, beheaded the condemned man with an axe. It was thus that Charles the First, and Mary Stuart, Cinq-Mars and De Thou had died. The mode of execution enters largely into the question of how death is faced.

Then he passed into a physiological discussion with the doctor on the probability of physical suffering after the head was severed from the body. The doctor maintained that death must be instantaneous, while Georges thought the contrary, and quoted two instances in support of his opinion. Once, in Egypt, he had seen a slave beheaded ; the victim knelt, and the executioner severed his head at a blow, the head rolling seven or eight yards away ; the body immediately rose upon its feet, took two or three aimless steps waving its arms in the air, and then fell, not quite dead, but still in the last throes. On another day, when in the same country, he had been present at a similar execution, and had, in his perpetual desire for investigation, picked up the head at the instant it was separated from the body, and, raising it by the hair to a level with his mouth, had asked in Arabic : " Do you suffer ? " At this question, the victim's eyes had opened, and his lips had moved, trying to frame an answer. Georges therefore felt convinced that life survived for a few moments at least after execution.

The doctor ended by agreeing with his opinion, it being really his own as well; he had thought it, however, his duty to give the condemned man the only consolation that the promise of an easy and gentle death could afford.

The day passed just as the preceding days had done, except that he wrote to his father and brother. For one moment he took up his pen to write to Sara; but, whatever the motive was that restrained him, he stopped, and pushed the paper away, letting his head fall upon his hands. He remained a long time in this position, and any one who had seen him raise his forehead, which he did with the haughty and disdainful movement habitual with him, would hardly have observed that his eyes were slightly red, and that a tear carelessly brushed away trembled at the end of his long dark lashes.

The cause of this was that, since the day when, at the Governor's house, he had refused to marry the beautiful Creole, not only had he not seen her, but had not even heard her name mentioned.

However, he could not believe that she had forgotten him.

Night came; and Georges, going to bed at his usual hour, slept as well as he had done on the previous night. On rising next morning he sent for the Governor of the prison.

" Sir," said he, " I have a favour to ask of you."

" What is it ? " said the Governor.

" I should like to say a few words to the executioner."

" I must have the authority of the Governor of the Island."

" Oh ! " said Georges smiling, " make the request from me ; Lord Murray is a gentleman, and will not deny this favour to an old friend."

The Governor of the prison went out, promising to make the desired application.

As he went out, a priest entered.

Georges held those ideas about religion characteristic of the men of our time, that is to say, while entirely neglecting the outward observances of religion, he was in his inmost heart profoundly impressionable to sacred things. Accordingly, a church, with its "dim religious light," a lonely cemetery, or a passing coffin, produced on his mind a far deeper impression than one of those events which often unhinge the minds of ordinary men.

The priest was one of those venerable old men who do not busy themselves with trying to convince you, but who speak with entire conviction ; one of those men who, reared in the midst of the grand scenes of Nature, have sought and found the Almighty in His works ; in short, one of those serene hearts who draw suffering hearts to themselves, in order to console them by taking a part of the griefs of others upon themselves.

At the first words which they exchanged, they grasped each other's hands.

It was a confidential talk and not a confession which the aged priest came to obtain from the young man ; but haughty in the presence of strength, Georges was humble in the presence of weakness. Georges accused himself of pride ; like Satan, it was his only fault, and, like Satan, this fault had destroyed him.

But yet, at this very hour, it was this pride which sustained him, which made him strong, which made him great.

It is true that what is great with men is not great with God.

Twenty times the name of Sara was on the young man's lips ; but on each occasion he thrust it down to the bottom of his heart,—that gloomy abyss where so many emotions were swallowed up, and whose depths his face concealed, like a coating of ice.

While the priest and the condemned man were talking, the door opened and the Governor of the prison appeared. "The man you asked for is here," he said, " and is waiting until you can receive him." .

Georges turned rather pale, and a slight shudder ran through his body ; his emotion, however, was scarcely perceptible.

"Admit him," he said.

The priest wanted to withdraw, but Georges restrained him.

"No, stay," said he; "what I have to say to this man can be said before you."

Possibly, this proud soul needed, in order to maintain all his strength, to have a witness of what was going to take place.

A Negro of tall stature and herculean proportions was brought in. He was naked, except for his loin cloth, which was of red stuff; his large expressionless eyes denoted the absence of all intelligence. He turned to the Governor who brought him in, and, looking first at the priest and then at Georges, asked :—

"Which of the two is my man ?"

"The young one," answered the Governor of the prison, going out of the cell.

"You are the executioner ?" said Georges, coldly and calmly.

"Yes," answered the Negro.

"Good. Come here, my friend, and answer my questions."

The Negro stepped forward.

"You know that you will execute me to-morrow," said Georges.

"Yes," answered the Negro; "at seven in the morning."

"Ah! seven in the morning; thank you for the information. I had asked to be told the time, but they refused to tell me. However, that is not the question."

The priest felt himself turning faint.

"I have never seen an execution at Port Louis," said Georges; "but as I wish things to go properly, I have sent for you, so that we may have what is called, in theatrical language, a rehearsal together."

The Negro was nonplussed; Georges was obliged to explain to him more clearly what he wanted.

Then the Negro took a stool to represent the block, led Georges to the proper distance from the block at which he ought to kneel, showed him how he should place his head upon it, and promised him that he would sever it at one blow.

The old man tried to rise and go out, not having the strength of nerve to endure this strange ordeal in which the two chief actors preserved an equal impassiveness the one through brutishness of mind, the other by strength of will and courage. But his legs failed him and he sank back in his chair.

The directions for the execution having been given and received, Georges drew a diamond from his finger.

" My friend," said he to the Negro, " as I have no money here, and as I do not wish your time to have been quite wasted, take this ring."

" I am not allowed to take anything from condemned persons," said the Negro ; " but I inherit from them ; leave the ring on your finger, and to-morrow, when you are dead, I will pull it off."

" Very well ! " said Georges.

And without any emotion he replaced the ring on his finger.

The Negro then took his departure ; and Georges turned towards the priest, who was as pale as death.

" My son," said the latter, " I am very happy to have met a spirit like yours. This will be the first time I have ever conducted a condemned man to the scaffold. I was afraid I should give way, but you will support me, will you not ? "

" Make your mind easy, Father," answered Georges.

The priest belonged to a small church situated on the road to the place of execution, in which condemned persons usually stopped to hear a last mass. The church was called St. Sauveur.

The priest in his turn left the condemned cell, promising to return in the evening ; and Georges was left alone.

What then passed within the mind and showed on the countenance of the prisoner, no man knows. It may be, Nature, that pitiless creditor, resumed her rights ; it may be, he turned as weak as he had just been strong ; it may be, when the curtain had once fallen between the public and the actor, all this apparent impassiveness disappeared to give place to a veritable agony. But in all probability it was not so ; for, when the turnkey opened the door to bring Georges his dinner, he found him rolling a cigarette in his hand with as much calmness and tranquillity as a hidalgo on the *Puerta del Sol*, or a fashionable lounger on the *Boulevard de Gand* could have displayed.

Georges dined as usual ; only, he recalled the turnkey

to ask him to have a bath ready for him at six next morning, and to awake him at half-past five.

Often, when reading in history or in the newspaper that such and such a condemned man had been awakened on the morning of his execution, Georges had wondered if this condemned man who had to be awakened had been really asleep. The moment had come for him to satisfy himself by his own experience, and on this question Georges was soon to know what to believe.

At nine, the priest came in again. Georges was lying down reading. The priest asked what was the book in which he was thus seeking a preparation for death, whether it was Plato's *Phædo* or the Bible. Georges held it out to him. It was *Paul and Virginia*.

Strange that, at this terrible moment, it should be this calm and romantic story that the condemned man had chosen !

The priest remained with Georges until eleven. During these two hours Georges did nearly all the talking, explaining to the priest his views of God, and developing his theories on the immortality of the soul. In the ordinary circumstances of life, Georges was eloquent ; during this last evening, he was sublime.

It was the condemned man who instructed, and the priest who listened.

At eleven, Georges reminded the priest that the hour for him to go had arrived, and told him that, in order to keep his full strength for the next morning, he would need to take some repose.

As the old man went out, a violent struggle seemed to be taking place within Georges' heart ; he called the priest back, but as he returned to the room, Georges made an effort over himself.

" Nothing, Father," he said, " nothing."

Georges lied ; once more it was the name of Sara that his mouth strove to utter.

But, yet once more, the old man went out without hearing it uttered.

Next morning when, at half-past five, the turnkey entered his room, he found Georges sleeping soundly.

" It is true then," said Georges on waking, " a condemned man *can* sleep on his last night."

But how long had he lain awake in order to attain this result ? No one knows.

The bath was brought in.

At this moment the doctor entered.

" You see, doctor," said he, " I model myself on antiquity; the Athenians used to take a bath before going to fight."

" How are you ? " asked the doctor, employing one of those commonplace questions which people adopt when they do not know what to say.

" Why, very well, doctor," answered Georges smiling ; " and I begin to believe that I shall not die of my wound."

Then he took his will, duly sealed, and handed it to him.

" Doctor," he added," I have appointed you executor under my will. You will find on this piece of paper three lines that concern you ; I wanted to leave you a souvenir of myself."

The doctor brushed away a tear and stammered some words of thanks.

Georges got into the bath.

" Doctor," he said after an instant, " how many times should the pulse of a calm and healthy man, in the normal condition, beat during a minute ? "

" Why," answered the doctor, " from sixty-four to sixty-six times."

" Feel mine," said Georges ; " I am curious to know what effect the approach of death has upon my blood."

The doctor pulled out his watch, took his wrist, and counted the beats.

" Sixty-eight," he said at the end of a minute.

" Come, come," said Georges, " I am quite satisfied. And you, doctor ? "

" It is miraculous," he answered ; " are you made of iron ? "

Georges smiled proudly.

" Ah ! you Whites," said he, " you are in a hurry to see me die ? I understand it," he added ; " perhaps you needed a lesson in courage. I will give it you."

The turnkey entered to tell the condemned man that it was nearly six o'clock.

"My dear doctor," said Georges, "will you let me come out of the bath ? Don't go away, however, I should like to shake hands with you before leaving the prison."

The doctor withdrew.

Georges, left alone, stepped out of the bath, put on white trousers, polished boots, and a cambric shirt of which he turned down the collar himself ; after which he went to a small glass and arranged his hair, moustache, and beard with as much care as if he had been going to a ball, or perhaps even more. Then he knocked at the door to intimate that he was ready.

The priest entered and looked at Georges. Never had the young man appeared so handsome : his eyes gleamed, his brow was radiant.

"Oh ! my son, my son !" said the priest ; "beware of pride ; pride has destroyed your body, beware lest it destroy your soul also."

"You will pray for me, Father," said Georges, "and God can refuse nothing, I am sure, to the prayers of a holy man like yourself."

Then Georges noticed the executioner, who was standing in the shadow of the doorway.

"Ah ! is it you, my friend ?" said he, "come here !"

The Negro was wrapped in a large cloak beneath which he concealed his axe.

"Your axe cuts well ?" asked Georges.

"Yes," answered the executioner ; "make your mind easy."

"Good !" said the condemned man.

Then he noticed that the Negro was looking at his hand for the diamond which he had promised him the previous evening, and the stone of which was accidentally turned inside.

"Make your mind easy in your turn," said he, turning the stone outwards, "you shall have your ring ; besides, to save you the trouble of taking it, here——" And he gave the ring to the priest, indicating by a sign that it was to go to the executioner.

Next he went to a small desk, opened it and took out the two letters which he had written to his father and his brother ; and handed these likewise to the priest.

Once more he appeared to have something to say to him, for he placed his hand on his shoulder, looking earnestly at him, and moved his lips as if about to speak. But yet again his will proved stronger than his feelings, and the name which struggled to escape his breast died on his lips so softly that no one heard it.

At this moment the clock struck six.

" Come," said Georges.

And he went out from the room, followed by the priest and the executioner.

At the foot of the stairs he met the doctor, who was waiting to bid him a last farewell.

Georges held out his hand, and, leaning towards his ear, said to him :—

" I bequeath my body to you."

And with these words he stepped into the courtyard.

CHAPTER XXVIII

THE CHURCH OF ST. SAUVEUR

THE gate leading to the street was, as may easily be guessed, thronged with spectators. Such sights are rare at Port Louis, and every one wished, if not to witness the actual execution, at least to see the condemned man go by.

The Governor of the prison had asked Georges how he would like to be taken to the scaffold. Georges had answered that he preferred to walk, and had obtained this concession as a final act of kindness on the part of Lord Murray.

Eight mounted Artillerymen waited for him at the gate. In all the streets through which he would have to pass, English soldiers lined the road on each side, to guard the prisoner and keep back the spectators.

On his appearance, a loud clamour arose ; but, contrary to Georges' expectation, the accent of hatred did not predominate in the sounds that greeted his presence.

The cries were of various import, but mostly expressive

of concern and pity, since the sight of a proud and handsome man face to face with death always exercises a powerful fascination.

Georges walked with a firm step, his head erect, his face calm, in spite of the bitter thoughts which were passing through his mind.

He was thinking of Sara,—of Sara, who had made no attempt to see him, who had not written him a line, who had not given him a souvenir,—of Sara, in whom he had trusted, and to whom he owed his final self-deception.

It is true that, possessed of Sara's love, he would have regretted losing his life; but the being forgotten by Sara was the last drop of bitterness in his cup.

And then, side by side with the betrayal of his love came the murmur of his wounded pride.

He had miscarried, then, in everything; his superiority had brought him no profit whatsoever.

The result of this long struggle was the scaffold, to which he was now walking, abandoned by all. When people spoke of him, they would merely say, " The fellow was a crack-brained fool."

As he walked on, continually looking round him, a smile which corresponded well with his thoughts crossed his lips now and then. This smile, outwardly resembling all other smiles, had a bitter source within.

And yet, at every street corner he hoped to see her, he looked for her at every window.

She who had dropped her bouquet in front of him, as he rode in victorious on Antrim, would she not let fall a tear on his path, as he walked defeated to the scaffold ? But nowhere did he see a trace of her.

In this way he walked the whole length of the *Rue de Paris*, then turned to the right towards the church of St. Sauveur.

The church was draped with black as if for a funeral, which, indeed, this might be said to be. For what is a condemned man walking to the scaffold but a living corpse ?

On arriving at the door, Georges gave a start. Beside the good old priest who was waiting beneath the porch was a woman dressed in black, with a black veil.

This woman in widow's weeds, what was she doing there ? for whom was she waiting ?

In spite of himself, Georges doubled his pace ; his eyes were fastened on the woman and he could not remove his gaze from her.

As he set his foot upon the first step of the little church, the woman herself stepped towards him ; Georges cleared the four steps at a bound, raised her veil, uttered a loud cry and fell at her knees.

It was Sara.

Sara extended her hand with a slow and solemn gesture ; a deep silence fell upon the whole crowd.

" Listen," said she, " on the threshold of the church he is entering, on the threshold of the grave he is about to enter, I call upon you all to witness, in the presence of God and man, that I, Sara de Malmédie, come to ask M. Georges Munier if he is willing to take me for his wife."

" Sara," cried Georges, bursting into sobs, " you are the best, the noblest, the most generous of women ! "

Then, rising to his full height, and encircling her with his arm, as though he feared to lose her :—

" Come, my widowed wife," he said.

And he drew her into the church.

If ever victor was proud of his triumph, it was Georges.

In an instant everything was changed for him ; Sara, with one word, had placed him above all those men who smiled as they saw him pass. He was no longer a poor madman, unable to obtain the impossible, and dying with his purposes uneffected ; but a conqueror smitten in the hour of victory, an Epaminondas, plucking the fatal javelin from his breast, but with his last glance seeing the enemy in flight.

So, by sheer force of will, by the sole influence of his personal worth, he, a Mulatto, had made a white girl love him, and, without his making any advance towards her, without his trying to influence her determination by a word, a letter, a sign, this woman had come to wait for him on his way to the scaffold, and in the face of all men, a thing perhaps unprecedented in the Colony, had chosen him as her husband.

Now, he felt that he could die ; that he was rewarded for his long combat. He had fought hand to hand with Prejudice, and Prejudice, while striking Georges a mortal blow, had yet been slain in the struggle.

The brow of Georges was radiant with these thoughts, as he drew Sara into the building : he was no longer a criminal prepared to mount the scaffold, but a martyr ascending to the skies.

Some twenty soldiers lined the aisle of the Church ; four soldiers guarded the chancel. Georges passed between them without seeing them, and knelt with Sara before the altar.

The priest began the nuptial mass, but Georges did not listen to his words ; he held Sara's hand, and occasionally turned to the crowd and cast on them a look of sovereign contempt.

Then he turned back to Sara, who was pale and almost fainting,—Sara, whose hand he felt trembling within his own, and bestowed on her a look full of gratitude and love, as he suppressed a sigh. He was thinking, he who was on the point of death, what a lifetime it would be, spent with such a woman.

It would have been Heaven ! but Heaven is not made for the living.

Meantime the Mass was proceeding, when Georges on turning round saw Miko-Miko, who was doing all that lay in his power, not only by words, but by his gestures, to induce the soldiers who guarded the entrance to the chancel to let him go close to Georges. Devoted as he was to Georges, he wished to see him once more, and to press his hand in gratitude. Georges spoke to the officer in English, and asked that the worthy Chinaman might be allowed to come to him.

There seemed no objection to granting the condemned man this request ; so, at a sign from the officer, the soldiers fell back and Miko-Miko hurried into the chancel.

We have seen how Miko-Miko had vowed gratitude to Georges from the first day that he had seen him. This gratitude had made him seek out the prisoner at the Police Station ; it now came to display itself for the last time at the foot of the scaffold.

Miko-Miko threw himself at his knees, and Georges held out his hand.

Miko-Miko took the hand between his own and pressed his lips to it ; but, at the same time, Georges felt that the Chinaman had slipped a little note between his fingers, and started violently.

The Chinaman, as though he had asked nothing but this last favour, and satisfied with having obtained it, wanted nothing more, disappeared at once, without uttering a single word.

Georges held the note in his hand and frowned. What could be the meaning of this note ? It was, no doubt, of great importance, but Georges did not venture to look at it.

From time to time, seeing Sara so beautiful, so devoted, so detached from all terrestrial love, a grief unspeakable, and such as he had not felt hitherto, seized Georges by the heart and pressed him with an iron grip. In spite of himself, as he thought of the happiness he was losing, he clung to life, and while feeling his soul ready to mount to the skies, felt his heart enchained to earth.

Then he was seized with a terror of dying in despair.

And yet this note which burned in his hand, which he dared not read for fear of its being seen by the soldiers who guarded him, seemed to contain some hope within it, though, in his situation, to hope seemed madness.

He was impatient, however, to read it ; although, thanks to the power of self-control which he always exercised, this impatience was betrayed by no outward sign. Only, his clenched hand crushed the note with such force that his nails penetrated the flesh.

Sara was praying.

They came to the consecration. The priest elevated the Host, the chorister rang his bell, and every one knelt.

Georges took advantage of this moment and, kneeling also, opened his hand.

The note contained but one line.

" We are here—Be ready ! "

The first sentence was in the handwriting of Jacques ; the second in that of Pierre Munier.

At the same moment, and as Georges in his astonishment

raised his head, while all the rest were bowed, and looked round him, the door of the sacristy was flung wide open; eight seamen rushed out and seized the four soldiers in the chancel, presenting a pair of daggers at the breast of each. Jacques and Pierre Munier sprang in, Jacques carrying off Sara in his arms, Pierre dragging Georges by the hand. The husband and wife found themselves in the sacristy; the eight seamen entered after them, using the four English soldiers whom they held in front of them as a shield against the blows of their comrades. Jacques and Pierre closed the door; another door led to the country, and at this door waited two horses ready saddled; they were Antrim and Yambo.

"Mount!" cried Jacques, "mount, both of you, and gallop as hard as you can to the *Baie du Tombeau!*"

"But you and my father!" cried Georges.

"Let them come and take us from my brave seamen," said Jacques, setting Sara in the saddle, while Pierre Munier forced his son to mount.

Then, raising his voice, he shouted:—

"Here, my gallant Lascars! here!"

Instantly a hundred and twenty men armed to the teeth appeared running out from the woods of the *Montagne Longue*.

"Off you go!" said Jacques to Sara, "take him, save him——"

"But you?" said Sara.

"We will follow you; don't be uneasy."

"Georges," said Sara, "in the name of Heaven, come!"

And the girl dashed off at a gallop.

"Father!" cried Georges, "father!"

"I will answer for everything, on my life," said Jacques, striking Antrim with the flat of his sword.

And Antrim went off like the wind, carrying his rider with him, who, in less than ten minutes disappeared with Sara behind the Malabar cantonment, while Pierre Munier, Jacques and his seamen, followed them so quickly that, before the English had recovered from their astonishment, the little band was already on the other side of the *Ruisseau des Pucelles*, that is to say, out of gunshot range.

CHAPTER XXIX

THE *LEICESTER*

TOWARDS five o'clock on the evening of the same day on which the events which we have just related took place, the corvette.*Calypso* was with nearly all sail set hugging the wind, which, as is usual in those latitudes, was from the east.

In addition to her worthy sailors and Master Tête de Fer, the first Lieutenant, with whom our readers are acquainted, if not by sight at least by reputation, her crew had been recruited by three other persons, namely, Pierre Munier, Georges, and Sara.

Pierre Munier was walking backwards and forwards on the quarter-deck with Jacques. Georges and Sara were seated aft side by side. Georges held Sara's hand in his, and was looking at her, while Sara was looking at the sky.

One must have been placed in the terrible situation from which the two lovers had just escaped to be able to analyse the feeling of supreme happiness and boundless joy which they experienced on finding themselves free on that great Ocean which was carrying them far from the land of their birth, it is true, but from a land which, like a cruel step-mother, had not troubled herself about them, except now and again to persecute them.

Nevertheless, a sigh of pain would escape occasionally from the mouth of the one and make the other start. . The heart that has endured long torture does not venture all at once to regain confidence in its happiness.

Still, they were free, with nothing above them but the blue sky, nothing beneath them but the sea, and were flying at their gallant ship's utmost speed from the Isle of France which had almost proved so fatal to them. Pierre and Jacques were chatting, but Georges and Sara did not talk; now and then one would utter the other's name, and that was all.

Pierre Munier stopped occasionally and looked at them with an expression of ineffable delight; the poor old man had suffered so greatly that he knew not how he had the strength to bear his happiness.

Jacques, who was less sentimental, glanced in the same direction, but it was clear that it was not the picture which we have just described that attracted his attention, for his eyes passed over the heads of Georges and Sara, and searched the horizon in the direction of Port Louis.

Jacques was not merely below the level of the general joy, but he even at times became anxious, and passed his hand over his brow as if to dispel a cloud.

As for Tête de Fer, he was sitting talking quietly to the man at the wheel. The worthy Breton would have cracked the head of the first man who showed a moment's hesitation in obeying his orders ; but, apart from this very natural requirement, he was not proud, but was hail-fellow-well-met with every one, and talked with the first that came.

All the rest of the crew had resumed that careless expression which becomes habitual to the countenance of seamen, once the battle or the storm is over ; the men on duty were on deck, the others below.

Pierre Munier, absorbed as he was in the happiness of Georges and Sara, had not failed, however, to notice Jacques' uneasiness. More than once his eyes had followed the direction in which Jacques was gazing, but, seeing nothing but some great masses of clouds in the west, he concluded that it was they that were causing him this anxiety.

"Are we threatened with a storm ?" he asked his son, just as the latter was gazing at the horizon with one of those questioning glances of which we have spoken.

"A storm ?" said Jacques. "Ah! my word! if it were only a matter of a storm, the *Calypso* would care no more than does that gull yonder ; but we are threatened with something more than that."

"What are we threatened with then ?" asked Pierre Munier uneasily. "I thought that, from the moment we set foot on your ship, we were safe."

"Well !" answered Jacques, "it is a fact that we have more chance of escape now than we had twelve hours ago, when we were hidden in the woods of the *Petite-Montagne*, and when Georges was saying his 'Confiteor' in the church of St. Sauveur ; still, without wishing to make you uneasy, father, I cannot say that our heads are yet firmly fixed on our shoulders."

Then he added, without addressing any one in particular :—

" Send a man to the top-gallant yard."

Three sailors at once sprang forward ; one of them reached the place indicated in a few seconds ; the other two came down again.

" And what are you afraid of, Jacques ? " resumed the old man ; " do you think they will attempt to pursue us ? "

" Exactly, father," replied Jacques, " this time you have hit the mark. They have in Port Louis a certain frigate called the *Leicester*, an old acquaintance of mine, and I confess that I fear she will not let us get away like this without proposing a little game of skittles, which we shall be obliged to accept."

" But it seems to me," replied Pierre Munier, " that, in any case, we have at least from twenty-five to thirty miles' start, and that, at the rate we are making, we shall soon be out of sight."

" Heave the log," said Jacques.

Three sailors busied themselves at the same instant with this operation, which Jacques followed with visible interest ; then, when it was finished, he asked :—

" How many knots ? "

" Ten knots, Captain," answered one of the sailors.

" Yes, certainly, that is very good for a corvette keeping close to the wind, and there is, perhaps, in the whole British navy but one frigate that can travel half a knot faster ; unfortunately, that frigate is just the one we shall have to tackle, in case the Governor should take it into his head to pursue us."

" Oh ! if it depends on the Governor, we shall certainly not be pursued," replied Pierre Munier ; " you know that the Governor was your brother's friend."

" Certainly ; but that did not prevent his allowing him to be condemned to death."

" Could he do otherwise without failing in his duty ? "

" This time, father, it is a question of something else
than his duty ; it is his self-respect which is at stake this
time. Yes, no doubt, if the Governor had had the power
to do so, he would have pardoned Georges ; because to
pardon him was to show his own superiority ; but Georges
has escaped from his hands at the moment when he thought
he had got him safe. In these circumstances, then, the
superiority has been on the side of Georges, and the Governor
will take revenge."

" Sail, ho ! " cried the man on the look-out.

" Ah ! " said Jacques, nodding significantly to his father.
" Where away ? " he continued, raising his head.

" Under the wind, coming towards us," answered the
sailor.

" Where is she off ? "

" Off the *Ile des Tonneliers*, or thereabouts."

" Where is she coming from ? "

" Coming out of Port Louis, I should say."

" There we are," murmured Jacques, looking at his
father. " I told you we were not out of their clutches."

" What is it ? " asked Sara.

" Nothing," answered Georges ; " it seems we are pursued, that is all."

" Oh heavens ! " cried Sara, " have you been given back
to me so miraculously only to be taken from me again ?
It cannot be ! "

Jacques meanwhile had taken his telescope and gone into
the main-top.

He gazed for some time with great attention in the direction indicated by the look-out man, then, shutting the tubes
of the telescope together with his hand, came down whistling,
and resumed his place near his father.

" Well ? " asked the old man.

" Well," said Jacques, " I was not mistaken, our good
friends the English are giving chase. Fortunately," he
added, looking at his watch, " in two hours' time it will
be quite dark, and the moon does not rise until two hours
after midnight."

" Then you think we shall succeed in escaping them ? "

" We will do all we can for that end, father, be assured.

Oh! I am not proud, I assure you, I have no liking for adventures in which there is nothing to be gained but hard knocks; and, in this particular instance, be hanged if I abandon my prejudices."

"Why, Jacques," cried Georges, "will you flee before the foe, you, the intrepid and undefeated sea-dog!"

"My dear fellow, I shall always run away from the Devil, when his pockets are empty and his horns two inches longer than my own. If his pockets are full, that is a different matter, and I don't mind running some risk."

"But do you realize that they will say you are afraid?"

"And I shall answer that that is true, by God! Besides, what do we gain by coming to blows with those fellows? If they capture us, our goose is cooked; they will string us up to the yards, every man jack of us. If, on the other hand, we capture them, we shall be obliged to sink them, ship and crew."

"What, sink them?"

"Undoubtedly; what do you want us to do with them? If only they were Niggers, we could sell them, but what is the good of Whites?"

"Oh! Jacques, my good brother, you wouldn't do such a thing as that, would you?"

"Sara, little sister," said Jacques, "we will do what we can; anyhow, when the moment arrives, if it should arrive, we shall put you in a charming little place from which you will not be able to see anything that goes on, and so, as far as you are concerned, it will be as if nothing had happened."

Then, turning in the direction of the ship:—

-"Yes, yes, there she points; you can see the heads of her topsails; do you see, there, father?"

"I see nothing but a white point rocking on a wave, which looks to me just like a gull."

"Well, that is it; your gull is a fine frigate of thirty-six guns. But, you know, the frigate is a bird as well; only, instead of being a swallow, she is an eagle."

"But may it not be some other ship, a merchantman, for instance?"

"A merchantman would not keep close to the wind."

" But we are doing the same."

" Oh ! we ! that is another matter : we were not able to pass Port Louis, for that would have been throwing ourselves into the wolf's jaws, and so we had to keep as near as we could."

" Can you not increase the corvette's rate of speed ? "

" She is carrying every stitch she can at present, father. When we get the wind behind us we will add a few more bits of canvas and make two knots more ; but the frigate will do the same, so it will come to the same thing. The *Leicester* is bound to gain a mile an hour on us ; I know her of old."

" Then she will overtake us to-morrow morning ? "

" Yes, unless we escape her during the night."

" And do you think we shall ? "

" That depends on what sort of a Captain she has got."

" And supposing she does overtake us ? "

" Well, then, father, it will be a matter of boarding, for, you see, an artillery duel is out of the question, so far as we are concerned. In the first place, the *Leicester,* if it be she, and I would wager a hundred Niggers to ten it is, has something like twelve guns more than we. Besides, she has Bourbon, the Isle of France, or Rodrigue to put into for repairs ; whereas we have but sea, space, immensity, for every land is hostile to us. So we want our wings above all things."

" And if it comes to boarding ? "

" Then our chances are improved. In the first place, we possess howitzers, a thing which is not strictly permitted on a man-of-war, but is one of those privileges which we pirates allow ourselves on our own private authority. Next, as the frigate is on a peace establishment, she has probably not more than two hundred and seventy men in her crew, while we have two hundred and sixty, which, you see, especially with fellows like mine, puts things at least on an equality. So make your mind easy, father, and, as the bell is sounding, don't let this prevent us taking our supper."

Indeed, it was now seven in the evening, and the signal for the meal had just been given with its usual punctuality.

Georges gave Sara his arm, Pierre Munier followed them, and all three went down to the Captain's cabin, which had been transformed, in honour of Sara, into a dining-room.

Jacques remained behind for a moment to give some orders to Master Tête de Fer, his Lieutenant.

The interior of the *Calypso* was a curious sight even to a landsman's eye. As a lover adorns his mistress in all possible ways, so Jacques had adorned his corvette with all the embellishments by which a sea nymph can be enriched. The mahogany ladders shone like glass ; the copper fittings, polished three times a day, blazed like gold ; and all the weapons, axes, sabres, and muskets, arranged in fanciful designs round the port-holes through which the guns protruded their iron muzzles, appeared like ornaments arranged by a clever decorator in the studio of some famous painter.

But the Captain's cabin was especially remarkable for its luxury. Master Jacques was, as we have said, a very sensuous young man, and, like people who, when circumstances demand, can make shift with anything, he loved, in ordinary circumstances, to enjoy everything of the very best. Consequently, his cabin, which was intended to serve at once as a drawing-room, a bedroom, and a boudoir, was a model of its kind.

In the first place, on each side, that is to say, both port and starboard, were installed two large divans, under which were hidden with their carriages two pieces of ordnance, which were visible only from outside. One of these two divans served as a bed, the other as a sofa ; the space between the windows was filled with a handsome Venetian mirror in a rococo frame depicting Cupids surrounded with flowers and fruits. Lástly, from the ceiling was suspended a silver lamp, taken no doubt from the altar of some Madonna, the fine ornamentation of which denoted the best period of the Renaissance. The divans and partitions of the walls were covered with a splendid Indian material with red groundwork, on which meandered those beautiful gold flowers, alike on both sides, which seem as though embroidered by fairy needles.

This room had been made over by Jacques for the joint

use of Georges and Sara. However, as the interrupted service at the Church of St. Sauveur did not quite satisfy the girl as to the legality of her marriage, Georges had promptly given her to understand that, if he was admitted to this sanctum during the day, he would find another apartment for the night.

It was in this room, as we have said, that meals were served.

These four persons enjoyed a strange sense of happiness in finding themselves thus united round the same table, after so much apprehension of being separated for ever. They forgot the rest of the world for a time, in thinking only of themselves; forgot the past and the future, in thinking only of the present.

An hour passed like a minute; after which they went up again on deck.

Their first glances were directed astern, looking for the frigate.

There was a moment's silence.

"Why," said Pierre Munier, "the frigate seems to have vanished."

"That is because, the sun being on the horizon, her sails are in shadow," answered Jacques, "but look this way, father."

And the young man pointed with his hand to direct the old man's glance.

"Yes, yes," said Pierre, "now I see her."

"She is even closer than before," said Georges.

"Yes, about a mile or so; here, Georges, if you look you can make out her lower sails; she is not more than fifteen miles from us."

They were at this moment off the channel of the *Cap*, that is to say, they were beginning to leave the Island behind; the sun was setting on the horizon in a bank of clouds, and night was coming on with the rapidity peculiar to tropical latitudes.

Jacques beckoned to Master Tête de Fer, who approached hat in hand.

"Well, Master Tête de Fer," said Jacques, "what are we to think of this vessel?"

" Why, with all due respect, you know more about it than I do, Captain."

" Never mind ! I want your opinion. Is she a merchantman or a man-of-war ? "

" You are joking, Captain," answered Tête de Fer with his hearty laugh ; " you know there isn't, in the whole merchant navy, even in that of the East India Company, a ship that can keep up with us, and this one is overhauling us."

" Ah ! and how much has she gained on us since we first saw her, that is to say, in three hours ? "

" You know quite well, Captain."

" I want your opinion, Master Tête de Fer ; two heads are better than one."

" Why, Captain, she has gained about two miles."

" Very well ; and what ship do you suppose her to be ? "

" You have recognised her, Captain."

" Perhaps ; but I may be mistaken."

" Impossible ! " said Tête de Fer, with another laugh.

" Never mind ! tell me."

" She is the *Leicester*, by God ! "

" And what ship, think you, is it she is after tackling ? "

" Why, the *Calypso*, I fancy ; you know, Captain, she has an old grudge against us for some trifle of a foremast we had the insolence to cut in two."

" Bravo ! Master Tête de Fer ; I knew all you have just told me ; but I am not sorry to see that you agree with me. In five minutes the watch will be changed ; make the men off duty take a rest ; they will want all their strength in twenty hours or so from now."

" Don't you intend to take advantage of the night and alter your course, Captain ? "

" Silence, sir ; we will talk of that later. Away with you to your business, and carry out the orders I have given."

Five minutes later, the watch was relieved, and all the men who were not on duty disappeared below ; at the end of ten minutes they were all asleep or pretending to be asleep.

And yet, among all these men, there was not one who

did not know that the *Calypso* was being chased ; but they knew their Captain and had confidence in him.

Meantime the corvette held on the same course ; but she was now beginning to encounter the swell of the open sea, which could not fail to impede her rate of progress. Sara, Georges, and Pierre Munier went down again into the cabin, leaving Jacques alone on deck.

It was now quite dark, and the frigate had disappeared entirely from view. Half an hour passed, at the end of which Jacques again summoned his Lieutenant, who immediately made his appearance.

" Master Tête de Fer," said Jacques, " where do you suppose we are now ? "

" North of the *Coin-de-Mire*," answered the Lieutenant.

" Exactly ; do you think you could steer the corvette between the *Coin-de-Mire* and the *Ile Plate* without grounding either to right or left ? "

" I could take her through blindfolded, Captain."

" Bravo ! In that case, tell your men to be in readiness, since there is no time to lose."

Each man ran to his post, and there was a moment of silent expectation.

Then, amid the silence, a voice was heard :—

" Ready about ! " cried Jacques.

" Belay there ! Ready about ! " repeated Tête de Fer.

Then the boatswain's pipe was heard.

The corvette paused for an instant, like a horse pulled up short in his gallop. Then she turned slowly, heeling over under the influence of a fresh breeze and a considerable sea.

"Port your helm ! " ordered Jacques.

The steersman obeyed, and the corvette, coming up to the wind, began to forge ahead.

" Keep her away ! " was the next order ; " ease your sheets ! "

These two manœuvres were carried out with the same rapidity and success as the preceding. The corvette fell off ; her after-sails filled, while her fore-sails bellied out rapidly in their turn, and the graceful vessel sprang towards the new point of the compass to which she was directed.

" Master Tête de Fer," said Jacques, after following all the movements of the corvette with the same satisfaction with which a horseman follows the movements of his steed, " you will double the Island, taking advantage of every variation of the breeze, always keeping your luff, and making the best weather you can along the whole belt of rocks from the *Passe des Cornes* to the *Crique de Flac.*"

" Aye, aye! sir," answered the Lieutenant.

" And now, good night," resumed Jacques ; " and call me when the moon rises."

And Jacques, in his turn, turned in with that happy-go-lucky indifference which is one of the privileges of those who are constantly placed 'twixt life and death.

Ten minutes later he was sleeping as soundly as the rawest of the sailors.

CHAPTER XXX

THE FIGHT

MASTER TÊTE DE FER was as good as his word ; he passed successfully the narrows between the *Coin-de-Mire* and the *Ile Plate*, and, after doubling the *Passe des Cornes* and the *Ile d'Ambre*, kept as close as possible to the coast.

Then when, half an hour after midnight, he saw the young moon south of the Island of Rodrigue, he went, according to his instructions, to call the Captain.

Jacques on coming on deck examined all points of the horizon with that rapid glance of investigation which belongs essentially to the mariner ; the wind had freshened and was shifting from east to north-east ; the coast, which looked hazy, lay about nine miles to starboard ; no vessel was in sight either ahead, to port, or astern.

The corvette was off Port Bourbon. Jacques had played the best game that he could have played. If the frigate, which had lost sight of him during the night, had continued her course eastwards, it would be too late for her when day broke to return on her tracks, and he was saved ; if, on the other hand, the Captain of the pursuing vessel had, by some fatal inspiration, guessed his manœuvre and followed him, he still had the chance of escaping observation by hugging the coast and profiting by the indentations of the Island coast line to hide from his enemy.

While Jacques was endeavouring with the aid of a night-glass to pierce the gloomy horizon, he felt a hand on his shoulder and, turning round, saw Georges.

" Ah ! brother, is it you ? " he said, holding out his hand.

" Well," asked Georges, " is there anything fresh ? "

" Nothing at present ; though if the *Leicester* were in our wake, we could not see her at the distance which still separates us. At daybreak we shall know all about it. . . . Halloa ! "

" What is it ? "

" Nothing ; a little veering of the wind, that is all."

" In our favour ? "

" Yes, if the frigate has kept on her course ; if otherwise, this change is as good for her as for us. But in any case, we must make the most of it."

Then, turning to the boatswain, who had taken the place of the Lieutenant, he said :—

" Stand by to hoist the studding-sails."

" Hoist the studding-sails ! " repeated the mate.

Instantly you saw ascending from the deck to the top, and then from top to top-mast, as it were floating clouds which were set outside the other sails. Almost at the same moment you could feel the corvette answer to a more rapid impulsion. Georges mentioned this to his brother.

" Yes, yes," said Jacques, " she is like Antrim, she has a tender mouth, and you do not need to whip her to make her go. It is only a matter of giving her a suitable amount of canvas, and she will make a spanking pace."

" And how many knots an hour are we going at her present pace ? " asked Georges.

" Heave the log ! " cried Jacques.

The order was carried out instantaneously.

" How many knots ? "

" Eleven, Captain."

" That is two knots more than we were making just now.
You cannot ask more from wood, and canvas and iron, and
if we had any other ship at our heels but that demon of a
Leicester, I would lead her as in a leash to the Cape of Good
Hope, and then we would bid her good evening."

Georges made no reply, and the two brothers continued
to pace the deck in silence ; each time, however, that Jacques
returned aft, his eyes seemed striving to pierce the darkness.
At last he stopped and, instead of continuing his promenade,
leaned over the taffrail.

In point of fact, the darkness was beginning to lift,
although the first streaks of day still delayed their appearance, and, in the nascent twilight which began to brighten
like a fog that disperses to give place to a bluish dawn,
Jacques thought he could distinguish, at a distance of about
fifteen miles, the frigate holding the same course as the
corvette.

At the same moment, and as he was extending his hand
to point out to Georges this almost imperceptible dot, the
look-out aloft hailed :—

" A sail astern ! "

" Yes," said Jacques, as though speaking to himself,
" yes, I saw it ; yes, they have followed our track as though
it had remained marked out behind us. Only, instead of
passing between the *Ile Plate* and the *Coin-de-Mire*, they
have passed between the *Ile Plate* and the *Ile Ronde*,
which has lost them two hours. They must have a man
on that ship who knows his business."

" But I don't see anything ! " said Georges.

" Why look, there, there ! " replied Jacques ; " you can
see as far down as her courses, and, when the ship lifts on
the waves, you can see her bows rising like a fish putting
its head out of the water to breathe."

" You are right," said Georges ; " yes, I can see her."

" What can you see, Georges ? " asked a soft voice behind
him.

Georges turned and saw Sara.

" What do I see, Sara ? Why, a splendid sight, namely,
the rising sun. But there is no perfect happiness on earth,
and this spectacle is a little spoiled by the sight of that

vessel, which, as you see, despite my brother's calculations and hopes, has not lost our track."

"Georges," said Sara, "God, who has so wonderfully brought us together so far, will not fail us now, when we have most need of His care, so do not let this sight prevent you from adoring Him in all His works. Look, look, Georges, what a grand sight!"

At the moment, indeed, when day was about to break, you might have thought that the night in her jealousy was trying to increase the darkness. A bluish and transparent light had spread over the sky, growing each instant in extent and brightness; then this light gradually dispersed, passing from a silvery white to a delicate pink, and from a delicate pink to a dark rose. Next, a purple cloud, like vapour illuminated by a volcano, rose on the horizon. This heralded the monarch of the world coming to take possession of his empire, the sun blazing forth as a ruler of the firmament.

It was the first time that Sara had seen such a spectacle, and she stood in an ecstasy of delight, clasping her lover's hand with a love full of faith and religion. Georges, however, who during his long sea voyages had had time to grow accustomed to such sights, directed his first glance towards the object of the general anxiety. The pursuing vessel continued to draw nearer, although she was seen less distinctly, bathed as she was in the flood of light in the eastern sky; while, on the other hand, the corvette must now have been clearly visible to the frigate.

"Come," murmured Jacques, "she has observed us now, for she is setting her studding sails. Georges, my friend," he continued, bending down to whisper to his brother, "you know what women are, and that they sometimes find it hard to make up their minds; you would do well, in my opinion, to give a hint to Sara of what is going to happen."

"What is your brother saying?" asked Sara.

"He doubts your courage," replied Georges, "and I am answering for you."

"You are right, my friend. Besides, when the moment comes, you will tell me what I must do, and I will obey."

"The demon flies as though she had wings!" continued

Jacques. " Dear little sister, do you happen to have heard
the name of the commander of this ship ? "

" I have often seen him at my uncle M. de Malmédie's
house, and I remember his name perfectly ; it is George
Paterson. Still, perhaps he is not in command of the
Leicester at this moment, for I remember hearing some one
say the day before yesterday that he was ill, and, as it was
reported, dangerously so."

" Well, I say that a great injustice will be done to his
Lieutenant if he is not appointed Captain in his place on the
very day that his superior officer dies. Why, it is a pleasure
to have to deal with a fellow like that ; see how his ship
flies ; upon my word, you might call her a race-horse ; if
this goes on, we shall be obliged in five or six hours to have
a brush with her."

" Well, let us have a brush with her then," said Pierre
Munier, who at this moment came up on deck, and whose
eyes, on the approach of danger, gleamed with the ardour
which inflamed his soul in great emergencies.

" Ah ! father, is it you ? " said Jacques. " Delighted to
see you in such good fighting trim, for in a few hours, as I
was telling you, we shall need every man on board."

Sara turned slightly pale, and Georges felt her press his
hand ; he turned to her with a smile.

" Well, Sara," said he, " after having such confidence in
God, will you doubt Him now ? "

" No, Georges, no," replied Sara ; " and when, from the
bottom of the hold I hear the roar of the guns, the whistling
of the bullets, and the cries of the wounded, I shall still
remain, I promise you, full of faith and hope, certain of
seeing my Georges again safe and sound. For something
tells me we have drained the bitter cup of misfortune, and
that, as the darkness has been succeeded by this brilliant
sun, so will our night yield to a bright day."

" Hear, hear ! " cried Jacques, " that's what I call talking
to the purpose. Upon my honour, I don't know how it is
that I don't go about and head off this presumptuous ship ;
that would save us half the trouble and annoyance. What
say you, Georges, would you like to make the attempt ? "

" Willingly," said Georges, " but are you not afraid that

at this distance, should there be any English vessel in Port
Bourbon, she may come out when she hears the cannonade,
and help her comrade ? "

" Upon my word ! you talk as eloquently as St. John of
the Golden Mouth, brother, and we will keep on our course.
Ah ! is it you, Master Tête de Fer ? " continued Jacques,
addressing his Lieutenant, who appeared on deck at that
moment. " You come just in time : here we are, as you
see, off Mt. Brabant ; keep her head west-south-west upon
the mountain. And now we will have our breakfast, a good
precaution to take at any time, but especially so, when you
are not sure of getting any dinner."

And Jacques gave his arm to Sara and led the way below,
followed by Pierre and Georges.

With the object no doubt of distracting his guests, for
the time at least, from the danger that threatened them,
Jacques tried to spin out the meal as long as possible, so
it was nearly two hours before they went up again on deck.

Jacques' first glance was at the *Leicester*, which had plainly
drawn closer, for her battery could now be seen. Yet
Jacques appeared to have expected to find her even closer
still ; for, throwing a glance aloft to make sure that no
change had been made in the sails, he observed :—

" Well, what have you been doing, Master Tête de Fer ?
It seems to me that we are going rather faster than we were
going two hours ago."

" Yes, Captain, yes," answered the Lieutenant, " I should
say it is something like that."

" What have you done to the ship ? "

" Oh ! a mere trifle ; I have shifted some weights and
ordered the men to go forward."

" Yes, yes, you're a good sailor ; and what have you
gained by that ? "

" A knot, Captain, one poor knot, that is all. I have
just hove the log, and we are making twelve knots an hour,
but that won't help us much, and no doubt the enemy has
done the same thing, for he also quickened his pace about a
quarter of an hour ago. Look, Captain, you can see almost
her entire hull. Oh ! we have to deal with some old sea-dog
who will give us, a deal of trouble. It puts me in mind of

the way in which this same *Leicester* chased us when Captain Murray commanded her."

" Ah ! by God ! everything is explained now," exclaimed Jacques ; " a thousand pounds to a hundred, Georges, it is your enraged Governor on board that vessel ; he wants to have his revenge."

" Do you think so ? " cried Georges, rising from the bench on which he was sitting, and grasping his brother's arm, " do you think so ? I declare I should be glad if it were he, for I, too, want to take revenge on my own account."

" It is the Governor in person, I will vouch for it now. There isn't another bloodhound who could have followed our track as he has done. What an honour for a humble Slave-Captain like myself to have dealings with a Commodore of the Royal Navy ! Thank you, Georges ! it is you to whom I am indebted for this good fortune."

And Jacques laughingly extended his hand to his brother.

But with Jacques, in the critical situation in which he would soon find himself, the probability of having to deal with Lord Murray himself was only an additional reason for taking all necessary precautions. Jacques examined the ship's sides ; the hammocks were in the nettings ; he examined the crew ; the crew had already instinctively parted into groups, each man standing near the gun which he was to serve. Everything betokened that he had no need to teach these men anything, and that each man knew as well as he did what was to come next.

At this moment a passing breeze bore the sound of the drum beating on the deck of the enemy.

" Ah ! ah ! " said Jacques, " they can't be accused of being behindhand. Come, my lads, let us follow their example. The sailors of the Royal Navy are good masters and we shall gain by imitating them."

Then, raising his voice, he gave with all the strength of his lungs the order :—

" Clear for action ! "

Instantly the roll of two drums accompanied by the shrill notes of a fife was heard in the battery. Presently the three musicians appeared on deck, emerging from a hatchway, marched round the vessel and went back by the hatchway at the opposite end.

The effect of this sight and of the tuneful concert that followed it was magical.

In an instant, every one was at the post appointed beforehand, armed with the light weapons at his disposal ; the top-men sprang aloft with their carbines ; the musketeers took their station on the deck and gangways ; swivels were got ready, the guns were cast loose, and loaded ; supplies of grenades were placed at every spot from which they might be rained down upon the enemy's deck. Finally the Boat-swain stoppered all the rigging, serpentined the stays of the masts, and saw that the boarding nettings were ready for tricing up, and grappling irons handy.

The activity in the interior of the ship was no less great than on deck. The magazines were opened, the lanterns lighted below, the spare stores prepared ; lastly, the decks were cleared, and two guns run aft as stern chasers.

Then perfect silence ensued. Jacques saw that every-thing was ready, and began his inspection.

Every man was at his post and everything in its place. The inspection, nevertheless, occupied half-an-hour, since Jacques realized that the game he was about to engage in was one of the most serious that he had ever played in his life. During this inspection he examined everything and spoke to each man.

When he returned on deck, the frigate had visibly de-creased the distance between them, and only a mile and a half now separated the two ships.

Another half hour passed, during which certainly not ten words were exchanged on board the corvette ; all the faculties of crew, officers and passengers seemed to be concentrated in their eyes.

Each countenance expressed a feeling in harmony with its owner's character ; that of Jacques, indifference ; of Georges, pride ; of Pierre Munier, paternal solicitude ; of Sara, devotion.

All of a sudden a light puff of smoke appeared on the frigate's side, and the standard of Great Britain rose majestically into the air.

A fight was now inevitable : the corvette could not haul closer to the wind ; and the superiority of the frigate's pace was evident. 'Jacques gave orders to lower the studding-sails, so as not to have any canvas set that would hamper his manœuvres ; then, turning to Sara, he observed :—

" Come, little sister, you see that we are all at our posts, and I think it is time for you to go below to yours."

" Oh ! great heavens ! " cried the girl, " the fight then is inevitable ? "

" In a quarter of an hour," said Jacques, " the conversation will begin, and as, in all probability, it will not be lacking in warmth, it is necessary that those who are not to take part in it should retire."

" Sara," said Georges, " don't forget what you promised me."

" Yes, yes," said the girl, " I am ready to obey. You see, Georges, I am reasonable ; but you——"

" Sara, you will not ask me, I hope, to remain a spectator of what is going to take place, when so many brave men are exposing their lives only for my sake ? "

" Oh ! no," said Sara ; " I only ask you to think of me, and to remember that if you die, it will kill me."

Then she offered her hand to Jacques, held up her face to Pierre Munier, and conducted by Georges, went down the after-companion ladder.

A quarter of an hour later Georges came up again, holding in his hand a boarding-sword and with a brace of pistols in his belt.

Pierre Munier was armed with his embossed carbine, the trusty friend that had always served him so faithfully.

Jacques was at his place on the quarter-deck, holding his speaking trumpet, the token of authority, in his hand, with a boarding-sword and a small iron morion lying at his feet.

The two ships were pursuing the same course, the frigate still pressing the corvette, and already so close that the sailors in the tops could see what was passing on each other's deck.

" Master Tête de Fer," said Jacques, " you possess good

eyes and good judgment, be good enough to go into the mizzen-top and tell me what is going on yonder."

The Lieutenant at once sprang aloft as actively as any common top-man, and in an instant reached the place mentioned.

" Well ? " said the Captain.

" Well, Captain, each man is at his post, the gunners at the batteries, the marines at the gangways, and the Captain on the quarter-deck."

" Are there any troops on board besides the sailors and marines ? "

" I think not, Captain, unless indeed they are concealed in the battery, for I see the same uniform everywhere."

" Good ! In that case the numbers are almost equal, within about fifteen or twenty. That's all I wanted to know. Come down, Master Tête de Fer."

" Wait a moment ! The Englishman is putting his trumpet to his mouth ; if we are quite still, we may hear what he is going to say."

This last opinion was rather in the nature of a conjecture, for, in spite of the silence on deck, no sound reached the corvette ; but the order given by the Captain was none the less clearly explained to the whole crew, for instantly two flashes issued from the bows of the hostile vessel, a report was heard, and two shot ricochetted in the wake of the *Calypso*.

" Good ! " said Jacques ; " they have only got eighteen-pounders like ourselves ; the chances grow more and more equal."

Then, raising his head, he called to the Lieutenant :—

" Come down ; you are no use there now, and I want you here."

Master Tête de Fer obeyed, and was by the Captain's side in a moment. Meanwhile the frigate continued to advance, but without firing any more, having found that she was still out of range.

" Master Tête de Fer," said Jacques, " go down into the battery, and, so long as we are running away from them, use round shot ; but, the moment we come to boarding, use shells, and nothing but shells. You understand ? "

" Aye, aye, sir ! " answered the Lieutenant.

And he went down the after-ladder.

The two ships continued their course for about half-an-hour without any fresh sign of hostility on the part of the frigate, while the corvette, judging it useless to waste her powder and shot, remained insensible to the two challenges from the enemy. But it was evident, from the animation that began to appear on the sailors' faces, and the care with which the Captain measured the distance which still separated the two vessels, that the conversation, as Jacques had said, would not long be confined to a monologue, and that the dialogue was on the point of beginning.

After waiting for another ten minutes which seemed like an age to everybody, the bows of the frigate burst into flame once more, a double report was heard, followed, this time, by the whistling of shot passing through the rigging, cutting a hole in the mizzen topsail and carrying away two or three ropes.

Jacques followed with a rapid glance the effect wrought by these two messengers of destruction ; then, seeing that the damage was only trifling, he cried :—

" Come, my lads, it seems clear that it is we against whom they bear a grudge. Politeness for politeness. Fire ! "

On the instant a double report shook the whole corvette, and Jacques leaned over to watch the effect of his repartee ; one of the two shot had struck full in the bows, while the other had buried itself more astern.

" Well ! " cried Jacques, " what are the rest of you about ?   Give her a broadside ! aim at her masts ; break her legs and clip her wings ; masts and sails are more valuable to her at this moment than lives. Ah ! look ! "

Two balls passed at this moment through the sails and rigging of the corvette, one of which struck the fore yard-arm, and the other carried away the mizzen topmast.

" Fire ! confound you ;   and take example from those fellows. Twenty-five pounds for the first mast of the frigate that falls."

The report followed the order almost immediately, and you could see the passage of the shot through the sails of the enemy.

For nearly a quarter of an hour the firing continued thus on both sides ; the breeze, lulled by the discharges, had almost dropped, and the two ships were moving at scarcely more than four or five knots. The intervening space was so filled with smoke that the gunners fired almost at random ; the frigate, however, still came on, and you could see the tops of her masts rising above the smoke that surrounded her, while the corvette, who had the wind behind her and fired from her stern, was quite clear of this inconvenience.

This was the moment for which Jacques was waiting. He had done all he could to avoid boarding ; but, being forced in pursuit, was about to turn at last upon his pursuer, like a wounded boar. At this moment the frigate was on the starboard side of the corvette, and began to pound her with the forecastle guns, while the corvette replied with her stern guns. Jacques saw the advantage of his position and determined to profit by it.

" All hands on deck for boarding ! " he cried.

The men instantly rushed on deck.

" Stand by to take the mainsail off her ! Man the after port braces and spanker clewlines ! Port your helm ! Port ! Clew up the mainsail and spanker ! "

Scarcely had these successive orders been carried out before the corvette, obeying the simultaneous action of her helm and her after sails, turned rapidly to starboard, having still sufficient way on her to run athwart the frigate's course, and remained stationary, thanks to the precaution the Captain had taken of hauling taut his fore starboard braces. At the same moment the frigate, deprived of her power of manœuvring owing to the damage to her after sheets, and unable to double the corvette with the wind, came on, ploughing through smoke and sea, and willy-nilly ran her bowsprit with a terrific crash into the main-shrouds of the enemy.

At this moment the voice of Jacques rang out for the last time :—

" Fire ! Rake her fore and aft ! Shave them bare as a hulk ! "

Fourteen guns, six of them charged with grape and eight with shell, obey this order, sweeping the deck, on which they cut down thirty or forty men, and bringing the mizzen-mast down. At the same instant a shower of grenades descending from the three tops, scours the forward decks of the frigate, which can only reply to this storm of fire and hail of shot from her fore-top, encumbered as it is by the sail.

At this moment the pirates dash 'forward, rushing headlong and crowding along the yards of the corvette and the bowsprit of the frigate, over the shrouds, the rigging and the ropes. In vain the marines pour upon them a terrible musketry fire; those who fall are succeeded by others; while the very wounded drag themselves along, pushing grenades before them and waving their arms. Georges and Jacques think that victory is already theirs, when at the order of " All boarders on deck! " the English sailors stationed in the battery rush in their turn up the hatchway and gain the upper deck. This reinforcement steadies the marines, who were beginning to fall back. The Commander of the frigate throws himself at their head. Jacques had not been mistaken; it was indeed the old Captain of the *Leicester*, who wanted to take his revenge. Georges Munier and Lord Murray meet face to face, but amid blood and slaughter, sword in hand, as mortal foes.

They both recognize and make for one another, but the confusion is such that they are carried along as if by a whirl-wind. The two brothers hurry against the English ranks, dealing and receiving blows, fighting with coolness and courage; two English sailors raise their axes over the head of Jacques, and both fall, struck by invisible bullets. Pierre Munier is watching over his son, the trusty carbine does its work.

Suddenly a terrible cry, rising above the noise of the grenades, the crackle of the musketry, the cries of the wounded, and the groans of the dying, bursts from the battery, freezing every one with horror.

" Fire! The ship's on fire! " At the same instant a thick smoke issues from the after hatchways and port-holes. One of the shells has exploded in the Captain's cabin, and set the frigate on fire.

At this cry, so terrible, so unexpected, all is hushed for

a moment; then the voice of Jacques is heard, powerful, imperious, supreme :—

"All aboard the *Calypso* !"

Instantly, with the same speed with which they had descended on to the deck of the frigate, the pirates abandon her, hauling themselves one over the other, clinging on to the rigging, jumping from one deck to the other, while Jacques and Georges, with some of the most resolute of the crew, support the retreat.

Then the Governor dashes forward in his turn, pressing hard on the pirates, firing on them at close range, hoping to board the *Calypso* at the same time as her crew. But at this the first arrivals spring into the tops of the corvette, and the shower of grenades and bullets begins once more.

Ropes are thrown to those who still remain on the frigate, and each man seizes hold. Jacques leaps back aboard, Georges remains the last. The Governor makes for him, and Georges waits. Suddenly Georges is seized and lifted in a grasp of iron ; Pierre Munier is watching over his son, and, for the third time that day, saves him from almost certain death.

Then a voice, overpowering all this horrible confusion, roared : "Man the fore port braces ! Hoist the head sails ! Clew up the mainsail and spanker ! Haul in all ropes astern ! Starboard your helm !"

All these manœuvres, ordered in that powerful voice which compels obedience, were executed with such marvellous rapidity that, spite of the impetuosity with which the English rushed in pursuit of the pirates, they were not in time to make the ships fast to one another. The corvette, as though endowed with feeling, seemed to realize the danger she was in, and shook herself free with a vigorous effort, while the frigate, deprived of her mizzen-mast, moved forward slowly, impelled by the sails of her main and fore-mast.

To those on board the *Calypso* terrible scenes were now visible.

In the heat of the contest the first outbreak of fire on board the frigate had been unperceived, so that when the cry of "Fire" was raised, the conflagration had already made such progress that there was no hope of extinguishing it.

It was at this crisis that the force of British discipline compelled admiration. Amid the smoke, growing denser each moment, the Governor taking his place on the port side of the quarter-deck, and lifting his speaking trumpet, which he had kept suspended from his left wrist, shouted :—

" Steady, men, steady ! Trust to me ! "

Every one paused.

" Lower the boats ! " continued the Governor.

In five minutes the jolly boat at the stern, the two quarter boats at the davits, and one of the gigs, were lowered and alongside the frigate.

" The jolly boat and the gigs for the marines ! " sang out the Governor ; " the two quarter boats for the Blue-jackets ? "

Then, as the *Calypso* kept sheering off, she heard no more orders given, but she saw the boats being filled with all those who remained uninjured, while the unhappy men who were wounded, dragging themselves to the gangways, vainly besought their comrades to take them in.

" Lower the two quarter boats ! " cried Jacques in his turn, when he saw that the frigate's boats could not hold the whole crew.

And the two quarter boats were lowered from the davits of the *Calypso* into the water, notwithstanding the strong sea running. Immediately, all who could not find room in the frigate's boats, jumped into the sea and began to swim towards those of the corvette.

The Governor remained on board.

They had tried to persuade him to enter one of the boats, but, unable to save his wounded, he preferred to die with them.

The sea now presented a fearful spectacle.

The frigate's boats were rowing with might and main from the burning vessel ; the sailors who had been left behind were swimming towards the corvette's boats.

Motionless amid a whirlwind of smoke her Commander standing stern and motionless on the quarter-deck, the wounded cumbering her deck, the frigate burned on.

It was a sight so terrible that Georges felt the trembling hand of Sara resting on his shoulder, yet did not turn to look at her.

Having reached a certain distance, the boats were resting on their oars.

This is what now happened :—

The smoke grew thicker and thicker ; then serpents of flame were seen issuing from the hatchways, and crawling along the masts, devouring the sails and rigging ; next the flames burst through the port holes, and the loaded guns went off as the fire reached them. Then a terrible explosion resounded ; the vessel was rent like a crater ; a cloud of flame and smoke rose to the sky ; finally from this cloud, fragments of masts, yards, and rigging were seen to fall into the boiling sea.

This was the last of the *Leicester*.

" And Lord Murray ? " asked the girl.

"If I were not going to live with you, Sara," said Georges, turning to her, " upon my honour, I could have wished to die as he has died ! "